A HIGHER LAW . . .

"Good morning," said a bright firm voice. It wasn't Becky's voice, because she was still submerged in sleep and blankets, her blond head buried in a pillow, but that of the woman who was standing at the foot of his bed. She and the two men with her were all dressed in what looked vaguely like ski jackets. The men stood flanking Scheffler's bed, one on each side.

"Good morning," said the woman again, as if she were now satisfied that he was awake. "We are the police. You may call me Olivia. And you are Thomas Scheffler."

"Police," Scheffler repeated stupidly.

"Not the Chicago police, nor any other police force with which you are familiar. Nevertheless, we are the police. You must answer our questions or we will take you away."

"What do you want?"

"How many trips through the timelock have you made?"

PILGRIM

FRED SABERHAGEN

PILGRIM

Pilgrim has been published previously in parts as *Pyramids* © 1987, and *After the Fact* © 1988, by Fred Saberhagen

A Baen Books Original

Baen Publishing Enterprises
P.O. Box 1403
Riverdale, NY 10471

ISBN: 0-671-87856-5

Cover art by David Mattingly

First printing, December 1997

Distributed by Simon & Schuster
1230 Avenue of the Americas
New York, NY 10020

Printed in the United States of America

PYRAMIDS

ONE

There were too many monsters in the apartment to suit Scheffler. Or in some of the bedrooms anyway, though all were clean and otherwise suitably furnished. Going up and down the hallway, looking for a room to make his own, he found them all dusted and swept and ready for occupation. Even the beds were neatly made. The biggest bedroom was out of the running, of course, being already occupied by the old man's things, obviously the place where he slept when he was home. And it had more than its share of monsters; clearly the old man relished them.

The next room down the hall from the old man's was plenty big enough for Scheffler, and looked quite comfortable except for a set of three monsters, very nearly life-sized, which were enough to put him off. Two of the figures were standing to one side of the old-fashioned brass bed, one on the other. The three statues were of painted wood or stone or plaster; he couldn't immediately be sure of the material just by looking at them. The colors of all three were just as bright as if they had been applied yesterday in Chicago instead of thousands of years ago in ancient Egypt.

From the neck down all three of the standing figures looked human, their brown-skinned bodies wearing heavy jeweled collars and white skirts or loincloths that fell in simple carven folds. From the neck up it was a different

3

matter. One statue had the head of a green crocodile, the second that of a black-feathered hawk, and the third a head unlike any that Scheffler had ever beheld on man or beast before. He couldn't tell if it was meant to represent a ram or a bull or something else altogether. Whatever it was, he didn't relish the thought of waking up in the middle of the night, in an unfamiliar room, surrounded by these three looming shadow-shapes in conference.

He could have moved them out, but it was easier just to pick another room. When you were about to become the sole tenant of an apartment of fifteen rooms, you had a lot of choices. Scheffler moved on to the next bedroom down the hall, found it free of disturbing presence, and dumped his duffel bag and backpack and minor packages on the floor. Peeling off his winter jacket, he threw it atop the pile. This room was a little smaller, but that was all right. As long as he had a bed and a chest of drawers and a bathroom—every bedroom in this place apparently had its own bathroom attached—he didn't need much else in the way of housing. He would do his homework about ten doors away in the study, where as he recalled there was plenty of table space, and about a million books.

From the window of his finally chosen bedroom, twelve stories above Lake Shore Drive, Scheffler could look east as far as the fog-bound horizon of the wintry lake. Sighting at an angle to the north, through a forest of other tall apartment buildings, most of them taller and much newer than the one in which he stood, he was able to catch a glimpse of the lakeside campus of St. Thomas More University. Commuting to class from here was going to be as easy as staying home, or very nearly so. When warm weather came again, sometime in the remote spring, he would retrieve his bicycle from the friend's house where it was stored. He ought to be able to wheel to school in only a few minutes along the path traversing the lakeside park. Meanwhile, even under the worst conditions, he could walk the distance in well under half an hour. When classes resumed after New Year's, Scheffler wasn't going to have to fight the city's surface transportation problems any more. Nor was he going to have to cope any longer with the problems of three roommates in an apartment vastly smaller than this one.

Opening the duffel bag, he started to hang up some clothes in his new closet. Far back in the dim recess there was a bathrobe—or maybe it ought to be called a dressing gown—already hanging, that looked and felt like silk. Maybe it would fit him. Uncle Monty had urged him to make himself at home.

Scheffler unpacked the rest of his modest belongings, throwing some items into the otherwise empty dresser, and establishing himself in his new private bath. All of the plumbing fixtures he'd seen so far in the apartment were modern. Obviously there'd been some remodeling during the past few years.

Having taken possession of a bedroom, Scheffler went back out to the elegantly carpeted hallway, and stood for a few moments looking from left to right and back again, appreciating the quiet. He still had a lot to investigate. This was only the second time he'd been in the apartment, and there was a lot of territory in it that hadn't been covered when his great-uncle had given him the tour on his first visit.

Scheffler turned to his right, and strode along the hallway toward what he had already begun to call, in his own mind, the museum wing.

The apartment occupied the building's entire twelfth floor, and its floor plan was L-shaped. The hallway on this north-south leg of the L, where the bedrooms were, put Scheffler somewhat in mind of a hotel corridor, with rooms opening mostly to his right, and windows, in the alcoves of the wall on his left, looking out over the city. This afternoon the city's atmosphere was dim with post-Christmas, late December murk, and a lot of lights in other buildings had been turned on.

Some of the rooms over on the east-west leg of the L, had good views of the central skyscrapers of the Loop, which were partially visible to the south beyond other buildings of intermediate height; other rooms, on the north side, looked out at more tall apartments, with here and there a glimpse of Lake Michigan.

The front and rear entrances of the apartment building were actually quite close together, near the angle of the L. The normal passenger elevators ascended from the lobby there, and the service elevators from just inside the alley entrance. Here too was the service stair that doubled as interior fire escape. And the largest rooms of the Chapel apartment were near the angle too. Scheffler, passing at this moment through the dining room, impulsively detoured a few steps to see if great-uncle Monty might have left the tall, imposing liquor cabinet unlocked. It turned out that he had, and that the cabinet was well stocked. Not that Scheffler cared all that much about booze, but it was interesting to see that he and the daily housekeeper, Mrs. White, were both apparently considered trustworthy. Attached to the liquor cabinet was a wine rack, holding a score of bottles resting on their sides. Well, maybe Scheffler would try just a sample now and then—Uncle Monty had told him to make himself at home—but there'd be no wild student parties.

Scheffler moved on, running his fingers along the carven backs of five of the twelve near-antique chairs that surrounded the mahogany dining table. There was no dust on any of them. Mrs. White was thorough. He planned to do most of his own eating in the kitchen, where there was a radio, and a table built on a human scale.

From the dining room he progressed into what the old man had called the parlor. This room was a whole apartment in itself, with enough furniture in it for a small house. Still, it wasn't crowded. Here too were a few ancient Egyptian monster statues. An alabaster lampstand, a grandfather clock, and some other furniture that in most houses would have looked very old. Some of the pieces went back decades, maybe even a century, to the era of fringed lampshades and overstuffing. Scheffler had only a vague idea of the dates of different styles of furniture, but in this place a century was only yesterday.

There were some modern items too, but it occurred to Scheffler as he passed through the room this time that he had yet to see a television set anywhere in the apartment. Unless one of those cabinets over there . . . but he'd look into that later. The lack of a TV wasn't going to bother him especially.

Like the monster statues in the bedrooms, the Egyptian artifacts in this part of the house appeared to be undamaged by the ages. In fact they looked quite new. No wonder some of those purchasers, decades ago, had begun to grow suspicious . . . anyway, Scheffler's uncle had told him that none of the stuff displayed so casually in this room was really valuable. There was valuable and valuable, of course. Maybe Uncle Monty scorned these things, but Scheffler didn't think he could afford to buy one if he broke it.

He had left the central area of the apartment behind him now, and was proceeding on down the east-west hallway into the museum wing. From here on, he remembered, things got stranger. Certain objects in these rooms ahead had been puzzling him ever since his first visit, and now he wanted to take a look at them again.

The first door on Scheffler's right in this new hallway was standing open. Inside was the library. When he touched the modern switch just inside the door, indirect fluorescents came on in the book-lined alcoves, where shadowy afternoon had almost become night. Green-shaded work lamps came alive at the two broad tables. For anyone who liked books it was an inviting atmosphere, that of the office or study just waiting for the scholar to come in. All it needed was a fire blazing in the hearth, and there was even an actual fireplace, with some packaged wood beside it. One incongruous element in the library was a tall gun cabinet, containing half a dozen rifles or shotguns, along with a couple of revolvers, obscured behind a glass door thickly reinforced with metal bars. Scheffler tried the door and found it locked. The firearms were held in place by an additional locked rod run through their trigger guards.

There were only a couple of bits of sculpture, in this room—Egyptian again, of course—and these were relatively small and unobtrusive. If he couldn't get his homework done in here, he never would. There was even, Scheffler noticed now, a small electronic typewriter at one of the tables, and a stack of white paper beside it, though no evidence of any work actually in progress.

And, of course, there were the books. Most of the wall space was paneled from floor to ceiling with built-in shelves. Scheffler strolled into the room now and took a volume down at random: *Recherches sur plusiers points de l'astronomie égyptienne*, written by Jean Baptist Biot. Published in Paris, 1823. Old, all right. Next to it was *Längen und Richtungen der vier Grundakten der Grossen Pyramide bei Gise*. By Ludwig Borchardt, Berlin, 1926. Practically new.

Most of the books were in English, and newer than those two. He walked about, continuing his random sampling of the volumes. If this technique was truly giving him a fair representation of the whole, he thought he must be standing in the middle of just about everything that had ever been written on the subject of Egypt, in English or any other language. There was one book at least in what Scheffler thought must be Arabic. No Chinese, as far as he could tell, but he wouldn't have been surprised. Some took in wider subjects, such as the whole Near East and Middle East, and one shelf, holding only very recent books, was devoted to the technical aspects of archaeology in general. He took down a pamphlet only a few months old, that discussed in abstruse high-tech language some current project of probing the pyramids' interiors with cosmic rays.

Then he came to a stop. There, behind glass on a shelf slightly above eye level, were an old wax-cylinder phonograph and a modern tape recorder. Beside the phonograph were a couple of the dark cylinders that were its records. Thanks to memories of his grandmother's attic in Des Moines, Scheffler could identify them for what they were. It was true, of course, that Uncle Monty had been working away at this stuff for half a century or more.

Opening another glass-doored cabinet, Scheffler to satisfy his curiosity pulled out scrolls of thick, unusual, creamy-feeling paper. He undid one scroll and found it covered with what were, for all he could tell, genuine Egyptian hieroglyphics. To his inexpert eye, at least, the small pictographs appeared to have been painted on by hand.

Enough. More than enough. He had been told to make himself at home, but had the feeling now that he was prying into things that he was expected to leave alone.

From the library a wide doorway opened directly into the next room to the west. This was almost as large as the library, and it also was a workroom of sorts. A good share of the floor space was taken up by a central built-in table, about seven feet square and sturdily constructed, as if it were meant to support a model railroad. It held a model, all right, but there were no tracks or trains. Plaster of paris, or some similar substance, had been built and carved into the shape of a four-sided pyramid, occupying almost the entire tabletop, and tipped at the very apex with a dot of what looked like gold. The pale pyramid was readily accessible from all sides, and well lighted from above, once Scheffler had found the proper wall switch.

If you looked closely at the pyramid you could see the dark lines where it must come apart in sections, presumably to allow study of the interior. For about three-fourths of the way up, each sloping side of the pyramid was a series of perhaps a hundred tiny steps; and from each of the four corners of the base a narrow ramp went slanting up across the steps at a gentle grade, to make a right-angled turn at the next corner and go on up again, clinging to the steep sides. The ramps ended at the level where the sides became smooth, about a quarter of the way down from the tiny golden apex.

During his brief tour of the apartment a week ago, Scheffler had naturally noticed this model pyramid and commented on it. His great-uncle Monty had explained how, in the real pyramid, the ramps had been used to haul up the blocks of stone used in construction.

Scheffler had wanted to make some intelligent response. "I seem to remember reading somewhere that there are still different theories on the pyramids. The way they were constructed, I mean."

"There are different theories," Uncle Monty had admitted, in his dry, slightly rasping voice. He had been standing in the doorway, leaning his gaunt body slightly against the jamb. Dapper in a dark suit and flamboyant tie, the old man managed to look considerably younger than his age, which from all that Scheffler had heard had to be somewhere in the late seventies. "There are different theories. But this is how the Great Pyramid at Giza was constructed."

At that point the rasping inflexible voice had paused, and the gray eyes under the bushy gray brows gave Scheffler a hard stare, through fashionable modern steel-rimmed glasses. "Have you taken any courses in astronomy?"

"Astronomy? No, sir. Not at the university, anyway. I did have an astronomy course in high school. Back in Iowa. You mean the pyramids were oriented to the stars somehow?"

"Oh yes. Many of them were. This one certainly was." The old man gestured toward the model, an impatient flick of the wrist. There were gold rings, one with a green jewel, on two of the gnarled but still active fingers. "The Great Pyramid at Giza," he repeated. "Built by the great Pharaoh Khufu to be his eternal tomb and the eternal repository of his treasure." The old eyes and the old voice were for some reason judging that repository, and perhaps the Pharaoh, harshly. "And it served also as the base of departure for his spirit to its place among the stars ... that pyramid was already ancient, of course, when Tutankhamen lived and died, of whom we hear so much. It had been in place for more than a thousand years when Abraham of the Old Testament was born."

"There are three of them there now, aren't there? Three large pyramids, near Cairo?"

"Yes. This was the first, and remains the largest." Suddenly Scheffler's great-uncle had seemed to be trying to make up his mind about something. "Look here, ah, Tom. There's a certain unfairness about what I'm doing, going off like this on short notice, turning over the care of this apartment to you. I want you to know I plan to make it up to you."

"No sir, I don't see it that way at all. Believe me, I'm glad to get a place like this to stay in. And with a place like this, it's natural you'd want a housesitter. It's great for me, handy to school, a good place to study . . ."

The old man sighed; he was reluctantly, or so it seemed, allowing himself to remain persuaded that it was a good idea to leave Scheffler here alone. Never mind that it was his own idea to begin with.

"Mrs. White will handle all the housework," Montgomery Chapel muttered. He had already covered that; he was starting to repeat himself. Perhaps, with age, his mind was wandering a little. Perhaps he was just running through a mental checklist, making sure that he had thought of everything. "What I rely on you to do, is to keep an eye on the place, of course—and deal with all the messages. There's a phone-answering machine—I'll show you presently how that works. In general, I am not anxious for anyone to know where I can be reached, or even that I am traveling."

"I see."

At that point Uncle Monty had gone over to the window and put back a curtain to look out at the falling snow. It was coming down thickly enough to reduce the nearby buildings to gray shadows. "There's one man in particular," he said then, and sighed so deeply that it made him cough. It sounded to Scheffler as if some important information might be going to come out now. "One man in particular I'm not anxious to see. I haven't seen him for a number of years, and his appearance might have changed since then—or it might not have changed very much."

Uncle Monty turned from the window, letting the curtain fall back, and stared at Scheffler. "Looked about thirty years of age when last I saw him. Undoubtedly he's really older. Darker than you. And shorter, average height or less, but he's stronger than he looks. Caucasian blood, mainly, I should say, though there's a suggestion of the Oriental in his appearance. Perhaps a touch of the Negro also."

"What's his name?"

"His real name I don't know. I've heard him called Pilgrim. And Peregrinus, which is the Latin form of the same name." Uncle Monty spelled the variation out. "And once I heard him called just Scar. That was perhaps an abbreviation for something else, because he has no readily visible scars. Of course if he comes while I am gone he might be using some other name entirely. Present himself under some subterfuge. But he has a—how to put it?—a presence about him. I think you'll know him if he shows up."

It was beginning to sound to Scheffler as if his great-uncle's decades of adventure might not be over after all. Maybe his questionable dealings in antiquities weren't concluded either.

Scheffler asked: "What do I do if he does show up?"

"Tell him no more than you can help about where I am. Or about the state of my affairs."

"Right." It was an easy enough promise to make, since Scheffler himself knew next to nothing of those affairs. And up to that time he had known nothing at all of where Uncle Monty was going on this sudden trip. At first Scheffler had thought the trip might well have something to do with the old man's health, but the old man's vigorous appearance argued against that.

"But," Uncle Monty resumed, "if you think that you have seen him, or believe that you have heard from him— you might call the number that I will leave for you, and let me know. There'll be an envelope for you, containing information on how to reach me, on the kitchen counter the morning you move in." He peered at the younger man with what looked to Scheffler like a mixture of cunning and anxiety.

"All right, sir. I can certainly do that. Anything else?"

"I shouldn't like to hear of any wild parties while I am gone." Uncle Monty's eyes didn't exactly twinkle—they glinted. "Though you don't strike me as the type for that. And you are to remain the sole tenant. No one else is to have a key."

"Of course."

"Beyond that—help yourself, to the foodstuffs, and whatever else you may want to use. I expect to be back, as I say, in about four months."

It was at that moment that they heard the outer door open. "That'll be Mrs. White," said the old man, with renewed briskness. "Come along and meet her. I've already told her that my grandnephew is going to be staying here."

They found Mrs. White hanging up her cloth coat just inside the rear door of the apartment, which opened off an alcove of the kitchen. Her galoshes were already sitting, draining the muck of December sidewalks on a small folded rug. Mrs. White was black, and stoutly built. Scheffler would have been hard put to try to guess her age. Her hair contained one dramatic streak of gray, but that looked as if it might have been dyed in.

She acknowledged Scheffler's presence with a bare minimum of words, and looked him over with an air of reserved suspicion. When he made a tentative motion toward shaking hands, she instantly turned away and opened a closet full of household tools.

As Mrs. White started on her day's vacuuming in the bedroom wing, the interrupted tour resumed. The next room down the west hallway after the one holding the pyramid model might have been a small gallery in a museum. It contained more statues and glass cases, and a couple of chairs of carved wood so ancient in appearance that it looked as if it might be worth your life to sit in

one. There were also two mummies. To Scheffler the
lacquered cases and the bandaged figures looked as
genuine as everything else here, as real as anything he
had ever seen in a museum, and in much better condition.
The cases holding the mummies stood open, their lids
beside them, and were at least as finely made as the
antique chairs. Scheffler was on the verge of asking if
the mummies were real, but held back, not wanting to
demonstrate his ignorance.

The glass display cases in the center of the room
contained several model boats, or ships, made of finely
detailed wood and cloth and metal, oars and oarsmen in
place as well as the sails and figures of important
passengers, gloriously decorated. Scheffler paused to look
at them for a while. There was a label that would not
have looked out of place in a museum, though rather
terse: SOLAR BARQUES, FOURTH DYNASTY.

His great-uncle took note of his concentration on the
model boats. The old man said, "Sometimes irreverently
called 'skyboats' by modern students. To bear the soul
on to its final destination."

"Among the stars."

"Yes. In a way. One mustn't expect to find too much
consistency in the next world. Or in this one, for that
matter . . . come along here, there's something I want
to show you."

There was another room after the "Museum Gallery"—
Gallery Two, Scheffler immediately christened it. At the
windowless west end was a large alcove, fenced off by a
formidable steel grillwork that reached from floor to
ceiling. A small closed gate or door in the middle of the
grill made the alcove into a richly furnished jail cell. Richly
furnished indeed, and well lighted. Jewelry reposed on
stands and in niches. More than one of the items looked
like thick and heavy gold.

At the rear of the alcove was a plastered wall, painted in Egyptian figures; and in front of the center of that rear wall there hung a curtain; or maybe, Scheffler thought, it should be called a tapestry, because of the embroidered figures on it. The bottom of the curtain fell a foot or two above the floor of the alcove, and a double step of rough stone blocks led up to the curtain as if it might conceal a doorway.

"The only really valuable things I keep in the apartment," said Uncle Monty, "are in that area behind the grill." He shook the bars gently with an old hand. "Before you leave today, I'll show you where the key to the door is kept. In the remote chance of there being a fire in the building or some such difficulty, then you'd have to be able to get at them."

Responsibilities were mounting. Scheffler wasn't sure at what financial level things became "really valuable" in his uncle's mind. He supposed he ought to make sure, hesitated, then took a stab at it. "Sir? You say the only 'really valuable' things? Then are the other Egyptian things in the apartment all genuine? The statues and furniture and all? It wouldn't be any of my business, except if I'm going to be the caretaker . . ."

Great-uncle Montgomery raised an eyebrow, considering. "You certainly have a right to ask, under the circumstances. I suppose that you've heard, from your mother and others, of the accusations that were made against me, forty years ago and more. How I was supposed to have faked a great many artifacts, and sold them? Well, there was no truth in any of those charges." And the old man looked at him fiercely.

"Yes sir, my mother did say something to me about all that. A long time ago." And she had returned to the subject quite recently, when Scheffler had phoned her to say he'd heard from Uncle Monty. But certainly Scheffler had never heard anyone else talking about it. The old boy was quite wrong if he thought his youthful troubles were still a common topic of discussion decades later.

Uncle Monty pressed on. "You realize, I hope, that nothing of the sort was ever proven, against me or my brother. That no one ever dared to take such accusations to court."

"Yes sir," said Scheffler dutifully. Though 'no one ever dared' was not exactly the way he'd heard the story.

Uncle Monty gestured tersely toward the rear of the protected alcove. "That wall back there is a reproduction of a tomb-wall built in Egypt in the twenty-ninth century BC. The stair-steps and a few of the other stones are original. To move the entire real wall here and install it would have been impossible. With that one exception, everything you see in this apartment is a genuine artifact." He paused, considered, and seemed to decide to stay no more for the moment.

"I see, sir." Although Scheffler wasn't sure he really did. He walked right up to that grillwork, looking through it and resting his hands on one of the horizontal bars.

"Probably the necessity for you to open that grillwork will not arise while I am gone."

"No sir, I didn't mean—"

"However, in case of some emergency . . ." and his uncle beckoned him back into the adjoining room.

Once there, he removed one of the top sections from the model pyramid—it was evidently lighter than it looked—and indicated the chambers revealed inside. "Here—in what some call Campbell's Chamber, after an early nineteenth-century explorer. I'm leaving the key in here." Scheffler saw the key in his great-uncle's hand, and saw it disappear, sliding into a small cavity. There was a faint hard tap as it came to rest. "Not too easy to get at; you might have to tip the whole model on its side, and shake it out, or devise some kind of tool. But it's there. In case of some emergency, as I said."

"Right. In case of fire."

The old man squinted at Scheffler, as if trying to decide what else his young tenant should know. "Exactly," he said at last, somehow managing to convey the idea that fire wasn't really what he'd had in mind, although he'd mentioned it before. Then he turned and moved back into the other room, toward the protected alcove. Scheffler followed.

"Getting that wall built in properly was quite a job," Professor Chapel said. "Many of the bricks and stones, as I say, are genuine. They were brought from Egypt in several shipments. Yes, quite a job to erect it as you see it here. As I say, most of the wall is a modern reproduction, done from photographs. Only the stones of the false door, behind the curtain, and a few of the other parts are original."

"Sir?"

"Yes?"

"Did you say there's a door behind that curtain? A 'false door'?"

"Yes. The door through which the spirit of the tomb's occupant departed for the hereafter. Built right into a wall, as you see. It could not be opened physically."

"Oh. No solar barques this time, hey?"

"Perhaps not . . . as I said before, myths, beliefs, are not required to be consistent." Uncle Monty came closer to smiling than Scheffler had seen him do yet. "Nor, for that matter, is reality. Hm. It took me a long time to discover that."

"Sir?"

"Never mind. The original owner of this tomb was a distant relative of Pharaoh." And the old man was off, delivering a discursive lecture on what he called the Old

Kingdom, of which Scheffler was able to understand very little. The only halfway intelligent comment that he could find to make was that he had seen a room somewhat similar to this one in the Field Museum.

That set off the old man's contempt. Great-uncle Montgomery, dilating on the faults of museums, their greed and general incompetence, grew somewhat breathless. Maybe the Field, or the Oriental Institute, or some of the others, were still nursing hopes that they might come into possession of something of value when he died—well, if so, they'd find out differently.

Scheffler noted silently that the old man did not mention TMU at all—Thomas More University, where he'd been a faculty member in his youth. Evidently, even forty years later they could not possibly harbor even the faintest hope that he would leave them anything at all.

It was only a mild tirade, but still the old man leaned in the doorway wheezing for a few moments after it was over. Maybe his health was shakier than Scheffler had thought at first. Then, with a nod for Scheffler to follow him, he led the way back into the parlor. There, with evident relief, he sank into one of the overstuffed chairs, motioning his grandnephew to take one of the seats opposite him.

It was an impressive room, and evidently his uncle saw him taking note of his surroundings. "I own this apartment, too, of course. Free and clear now. It wasn't a common arrangement back in the Thirties, when this building was put up. Condominiums then were not the popular idea that they later became. But it is mine, and now of course worth a small fortune in itself. Whoever inherits my things will get the apartment too." And he looked at Scheffler earnestly.

Scheffler was vaguely disturbed. Maybe, as he thought about it, even offended. To make matters worse, he also felt, somewhere way down deep, a pang of genuine cupidity. Sure, of course, he would like to be a millionaire. Sure, at this moment he was probably on better terms with the old man than were the one or two other surviving relatives. But at the same time Scheffler wasn't about to start holding his breath until he came into an inheritance. He was doing all right as he was, without a million. He'd be an engineer when he got out of school. And his mother had told him more than one story about this man.

"Look, Uncle Monty, you don't have to pay me anything to do a little house-sitting for you. Like I said, it really helps me out too, and I'm glad to do it. Okay?"

His great-uncle, still wheezing faintly in his chair, had peered at Scheffler narrowly for several seconds, without speaking. Then he had given a slightly crooked smile, as if he were satisfied by what he saw.

Coming back to the apartment a week later, to move in on the scheduled day, Scheffler had found a white envelope waiting for him on the kitchen counter, just as his great-uncle had promised. The envelope was a little bulkier than Scheffler had expected. Inside were ten fifty-dollar bills—"for living expenses," as the note tersely explained. It also gave him a phone number at which his uncle could be reached during the next four months.

The number, starting out 011 20, struck Scheffler as unusual, and he spent a little time with the reference pages of the Chicago phone book. As far as he could tell, his aged and perhaps ailing Uncle Monty had departed for Cairo, Egypt.

TWO

As soon as he had chosen a bedroom for himself, and had taken another brief look at the museum wing, Scheffler started to check out some of the other practical aspects of his new home, beginning with the refrigerator and kitchen cabinets.

The note from Uncle Monty had reiterated that Mrs. White did no cooking and washed no dishes, but otherwise, prospects were bright. The large kitchen contained an upright freezer, the size of a standard refrigerator, well stocked with packages of meat. Scheffler, reading labels, discovered steaks, sausages, lamb and veal. Surely all of this had not been bought just for the house sitter's benefit. The old man might be thin, but he was apparently something of a gourmet. Was it possible that he still entertained heavily? Maybe. That wasn't any of Scheffler's business anyway.

The refrigerator, next to the freezer, was almost empty, but the pantry and the capacious kitchen cabinets held large stores of canned and packaged goods. The gas stove was old, made of black iron, and you needed a match to light it. But it was large and capable-looking. On one of the long counters stood a new microwave oven, with impressive electronic controls. All in all, it appeared to Scheffler that over the next few months he was going to be eating well, and at a minimal cost. He would even be able to put off looking for another part-time job to replace

the one he'd dropped a month ago under the pressure
of schoolwork. He decided to pick out a bottle of wine
some evening soon and drink a toast to Uncle Monty.

Even as well provisioned as he was, there were a couple
of things he wanted to get from the store right away.
Milk and breakfast cereals were regular parts of his diet,
but evidently not essentials to Uncle Monty. Still, Scheffler
was glad he hadn't tried to bring along any of the food
supplies from his old apartment; his former cohabitants
there would be having enough trouble as it was. They
always had plenty of trouble, what with the neighbors,
the landlord, the deadbeat members past and present
of their own group, the noise, the communal puppy—
God, he wondered how he'd been able to stand it as long
as he did. Well, until Uncle Monty had called him out
of the blue one day, he hadn't had a lot of choice. Scheffler
in fact had had to display firmness to keep some of his
roommates in the old place from packing up and moving
along with him. *Fifteen rooms, man, after all. And you're
gonna live there all alone?* But that was one thing his
benefactor had been extremely definite about; no one
else was to move in with him. Scheffler, having come to
know students in his two years at TMU, could quite easily
see his uncle's point of view on this. If one more moved
in there would soon be two more, then five, and maybe
eventually fifteen. Uncle Monty must have known students
too, from his own years at the university, and students'
ways probably hadn't changed all that much over the
decades.

It was dusk and beginning to snow again when Scheffler
returned to his new home from a brief grocery expedition.
He had been able to discover some stores within easy
walking distance, only a couple of blocks west. He looked
into the freezer once more when he got home, and gloated
a little, but he didn't feel like trying to cook anything

tonight. What he really wanted more than anything else at the moment was to talk about his new situation. And, yes, there was a specific listener who came to mind.

When Becky picked up her phone receiver, Scheffler could hear her still talking to someone else in the background. She was a student too, living in another shared apartment.

He waited until he had her undivided attention before he said anything. Then he announced: "Hey, guess who's just installed himself on Lake Shore Drive?"

"Tom! Your uncle really let you take over the place? That's great!"

He read his new phone number to Becky. Looking at the instrument closely, he was struck by how modern the apartment's entire phone system was, just like the lights and the plumbing. Uncle Monty evidently had a keen appreciation of when antiquity was a virtue and when it was not.

Becky was now eager to see the place as soon as possible. Already whoever she had been talking to in her own apartment had effectively ceased to exist for her.

"When can I see it, Tom? It's really just walking distance from my place here, isn't it?"

"Sure, it's walking distance, if you're a fair walker." He repeated the address for her. "It's the oldest-looking building in about two blocks. You can't miss it." She was about to hang up and start out right away when Scheffler had an inspiration and stopped her. "Hey, tell you what, Becky. Why don't you stop at the Chinese place on the way and pick up some food? We can have dinner overlooking the Drive. I'll reimburse you when you get here. Get the kind of stuff you like." He was feeling wealthy.

Only about three quarters of an hour had passed before Becky was standing at his front door, her eyes already wide with the elegance of the lobby downstairs and the small foyer into which she had been deposited by the elevator. Her arms were wrapped around a large brown paper bag from which a couple of white Chinese-restaurant cartons protruded slightly. Scheffler took the bag and Becky came into the apartment, shaking snow from her cap, unzipping her ski jacket. She was on the short side, energetic, with blond hair now flying as she shook her head, and blue eyes now widened even more.

"Wow, what a place! That doorman downstairs gave me a look."

Once inside, and relieved of her winter outer garments, she refused at first to accept his money for the Chinese food.

They had gone Dutch treat before, but this time Scheffler was ready to insist, and thrust cash into her hand. "It was my idea. Anyway, with all the rent I'm saving I'm going to be loaded. There's a lot of stuff in the freezer, too. I just didn't feel like cooking anything tonight."

A couple of minutes later, with the food rewarming in the big gas oven, Becky was commenting on the armored condition of the front door, unusual even for the big city. There were three locks, with bolts like prison bars, that anchored the door at top and bottom, as well as at the side.

"But it doesn't have a chain."

"You don't need any. Closed-circuit TV." Scheffler demonstrated the small screen beside the door. "And this door. It's steel inside the wood," said Scheffler. "Listen." He rapped with a knuckle on the wood-grained surface, which felt like the side of a battleship. "The back door's the same way. Even the windows have grillwork, though I don't see why they need it. Twelve stories up, it'd take a human fly to get in."

"And your uncle still lives here alone?"

"He's my great-uncle, actually. Yeah, my mother says as far as she knows he's been living here alone ever since the place was built. That was around fifty years ago. Maybe he had a lot of guests and parties in his youth."

"Wasn't he ever married?" Becky, still wide-eyed, turned this way and that, admiring things as they strolled back through the dining room and parlor. She paused to touch, with one finger, the statue of a monster.

"Not that I know of. He was engaged once, when he was young, some society girl. She ran off with his brother, and the two of them were never heard of again."

"His own brother, huh? Why didn't he ever move to a smaller place?" Becky had stopped now to admire a different statue. This one had the head of a man.

"Search me. I guess he's been rich all along, or at least ever since he started importing antiques. So he needs room for all this stuff, and he can afford it. I can see why he likes it."

"So can I." She sighed at a tiny chest, dazzling white, sitting on a bookshelf. It looked like it might be solid ivory, and whatever the material, it was all carved from one piece, even the ring-shaped handles. "Tell me again, Tom—oh, it's none of my business."

"What?"

"How'd he happen to pick you for this house sitting job?"

"I'm just about his closest living relative—except for my mother, and they're not exactly on great terms. She'll just barely speak to him in an emergency. That's assuming his brother is really dead, which I guess is a safe assumption after all this time. I forget now what the brother's name was. Anyway I think he was the older, and Uncle Monty's in his mid-seventies now."

"A safe assumption, then."

"Looks that way. Anyhow, Uncle Monty somehow found

out that I was a student here at TMU. And I guess he needed a house-sitter when he decided to go off on a trip. So here I am."

"Lucky you." It sounded like a heart-felt sentiment. "So, where'd he go on his trip?"

"Some mysterious destination. He never really told me." He'd been instructed to say no more than necessary to anyone regarding the old man's affairs; it seemed the least that he could do.

"Oh."

They dined from fine china, arranged on the polished wood of the dining room table so they could overlook the city lights and the dark lake while with silver spoons they scooped beef chow mein and egg foo young from Uncle Monty's oven-proof serving dishes. There was one distant light, a kind of beacon, way out on the winter lake, that Scheffler supposed marked one of the city's water-intake cribs. Nearer, the other apartment buildings and the Drive itself made up a wonderland of changing brightness. Scheffler found some fancy glasses, and picked out a bottle of wine more or less at random. He knew very little about wine, but he didn't suppose there was any vintage intended to go with egg rolls.

They ate, and tried to decide about the wine. They talked a little about the University, at which they shared one class. They exchanged opinions, all of them founded in ignorance, about the various paintings and other collectable objects displayed around the walls of the dining room. It was the longest talk he'd ever had with Becky. He'd been out with her a couple of times, on inexpensive dates, but he hadn't yet made up his mind on what she was like. He wondered, now, if he would have called anyone else tonight if she'd been busy. He suspected he might have waited until she wasn't.

When their meal was finished, they worked together

in a brief but thorough cleanup, getting the dishes into the washer and pondering which of the many settings on its controls would be appropriate. Then with refilled wineglasses they set off on a tour of the apartment, sampling the nighttime views from different windows.

Becky paused for a moment after Scheffler had pointed out the mummy cases to her. They were still halfway across the large room from the mummies. "Tom. You know, I think I can smell the spices? Didn't they use spices? Or something. Almost like incense."

"I bet my uncle never burned incense in his life. He doesn't seem the type." Scheffler moved closer to the cases, sniffing at the air. "There's something, though." It was weird, maybe only suggestion or something, but he thought that he could smell it too. Something, with a suggestion of the unfamiliar, the exotic. "One of the cases isn't too far from the radiator," he offered at last. "Steam heat, and the pipes get hot."

"Tom. After two thousand years?" Then Becky giggled. "Maybe it's his girlfriend and his brother."

"I think it'd be more like three thousand years. Maybe more than that. Anyway, the mummies might be . . ."

"Might be what?"

"Well, my guess is that they could be fakes. It's all public knowledge anyway. Back in my Uncle Monty's youth he and his brother apparently both got themselves into trouble selling forged antiquities."

"Apparently?"

"There's not much doubt that they were. Forged, I mean. A lot of them, anyway." Scheffler sipped his wine. "There was quite a scandal back in the late Forties. His brother had vanished by then, but it looked for a while like Uncle Monty might be taken to court. Anyway that's how I heard the story from my mother. In the end the whole thing was kind of hushed up, because the way things were going it looked like it might reflect on the university, too."

"TMU?"

"Sure. They had a big collection then; I don't know if they still do. And a lot of the important things in their collection were dug up by the Chapel brothers. Or Monty and—Willis, I think that was his name—claimed they'd dug 'em up. Uncle Monty was on their faculty for a couple of years, back in the Thirties. Then was when he and Willis first started traveling to Egypt and importing things. The University of Chicago might have been involved, too, in some way; they were really into Egyptology in a big way then; the Oriental Institute and all that.

"Anyway, in the late Forties and Fifties when the radiocarbon dating methods started to come in, the trouble started. The organic materials, the wood and cloth, in all those well-preserved things that Uncle Monty and his brother had been peddling turned out to be no more than a few hundred years old at the most. Where and how they really got them I don't know. Somewhere in Africa, evidently. Maybe some were genuine and some weren't. I guess forging antiquities has always been a big business."

"But he's still wealthy."

"Oh yeah. Obviously. I guess he had a lot of satisfied customers. And he'd been selling golden artifacts and jewels to private collectors, too. Stuff that was worth a bundle, whether it was antique or not. God knows where he got it all."

Betty was looking around again. "I don't see any gold here in this room. Are these things here—?"

"First he told me everything in the apartment was genuine. Then in the next breath he said the really valuable, quote unquote, stuff was back over there. There's a kind of a special room."

As soon as Scheffler had said it he wished he hadn't. But the words were out. Well, it would hardly be possible to have a visitor here and not show that room off.

"Oh. Can I see?" Becky's big blue eyes were almost prayerful.

"Why not?"

Behind the sturdy steel grillwork, the supposed real treasures waited as before. Becky oohed and ahhed for a minute or two. Then gradually, her gaze became concentrated more and more in one direction. She gave Scheffler to understand that there was one golden necklace in particular, so heavy it was more like a collar, that was almost crying out to be touched.

"Oh, Tom. Do you suppose that I could put it on? Just for a moment?"

He'd seen this coming for several minutes and had been trying to think of what to say when it arrived. "I don't have the key handy. Anyway, I'm not supposed to open the gate."

"But the key's around here somewhere? Please? I'm not going to steal it and run off with it, you know."

"Well."

When Becky saw his genuine reluctance to unlock the grillwork she quit pushing. Cheerfully. There were plenty of other interesting things to look at, outside the cage. Back in the adjoining room, she mentioned something that she'd heard, or read, about how mummies had actually been in oversupply in Egypt, and how in later centuries they had been ground up and shipped to Europe to make medicine.

Scheffler had read something along that line also. "Actually I think it was for aphrodisiacs."

Becky considered that. "You know more on the subject than I thought you would. Are you and your mother your uncle's only relatives?"

"As far as I know."

"So you might be in line to inherit all this stuff. Or will he leave it to a museum somewhere?"

"That's one thing I'd be willing to bet he won't do."

They explored the apartment some more, outside the cage. They looked at some lamps and statues. They became interested in the fireplace in the library, and it turned out to be easy to get a fire going. Scheffler, the expert, found a damper, and pushed it open. Everything necessary was on hand, including packaged piñon logs, some kindling, even long fancy matches. There was no telling where the smoke was going to come out, Scheffler thought, but the chimney was drawing well.

Becky sniffed the air near the hearth. "Smells great."

And it did, more aromatic than the mummies, though almost all the smoke, thank God, was going up the chimney somewhere.

Now Becky turned back to the grillwork and the gold behind it. "Let's turn out the light—I wonder how it looks by firelight alone?"

They were both silent for a while, once the electric lights in the library and both gallery rooms were out. He'd deliberately made the fire small, and the illumination that it gave from two rooms away was weak and unsteady. Under its influence the enigmatic figures on the wall and on the cloth curtain of the false door developed a tendency to sway, and march in place.

"Let's finish off that wine," Becky suggested.

When he came back with the bottle, he stopped in the doorway, where he stood swaying a little like the painted figures on the wall. Becky was still standing where she had been, right in front of the grillwork, but all the clothes she had been wearing were now scattered on the fine carpet. Shoes, socks, red sweater, jeans, a couple of little scraps of finer fabric.

"I know what the trouble was," she said, demurely flicking a glance in Scheffler's direction and away again. "None of those clothes would have gone at all well with real gold. You were quite right not to let me try it on with them." She was posing with her hands behind her, gracefully but almost as if her wrists were tied. The firelight touched her skin and warmed it and went away again.

Scheffler still said nothing. Not watching what he was doing, he groped out with one hand and put the wine down on a table.

"Now," said Becky. She raised her arms and performed a little undulation of her own. "I bet this is what that ancient queen wore the first time she put on that necklace."

He moved away wordlessly to the model of the pyramid, and tried to reach the key. His hands had started shaking, and anyway his hand was too big for Campbell's chamber. But Becky was standing close beside him now, and her hand was just small enough to reach in for the key.

Scheffler's hands were steady enough to fasten the golden collar around her throat.

. . . and, some hours later, while Becky was still asleep, Scheffler slid silently out of his new bed and moved around it in the dark bedroom to crouch down at the other side. With steady fingers he loosened the ancient catch and slid the weighty metal and the jewels away from her perspiring skin.

She did not stir at the parting.

And there, on the bedside table where he'd put it, was the key to the grillwork. He'd even managed to keep track of that.

Walking naked into the darkened grillworked alcove, the necklace in his hands, Scheffler could see, by the last light of the dying fire, one smooth steady reflection as of bright metal, no wider than a pencil line, high up inside what must be the frame of the false door. From this angle he could just see past the curtain's edge, as you never would be able to from outside the grill. There must be something back up in there that shone, that glinted brightly. He'd have to take a look at it again tomorrow. He wanted to know the full extent of what had been entrusted to him.

He put the necklace back into its niche, checked to see that all else was undisturbed, turned and left the alcove, locking the gate silently behind him. Now maybe he'd be able to sleep soundly.

He was halfway back to bed, padding along through the dim kitchen, when the phone rang for the first time since he'd moved into the apartment. He started guiltily. Immediately the half-thought-out idea leapt to mind that his intrusion with the key had set off some kind of an alarm somewhere. Someone was calling to check up.

When he lifted the kitchen receiver from its mounting on the wall, moderately loud noise burst out at him, as if the call were being made, with amplification, from some distant radiophone. "Hello?" Scheffler inquired, frowning.

The voice at the other end was that of a man, and despite the interference it demonstrated presence from the first precise syllable. "Montgomery Chapel, please."

It was a strange hour for anyone to call. "Dr. Chapel isn't in just now, this is his nephew speaking. Can I take a message?"

"Ah. And when will it be possible to talk to Doctor Chapel directly?"

"I don't know. If you'll leave your name, I'll—"

"Ah. Can you then tell me if Dr. Montgomery is now in Egypt? My name is Peregrinus. Has he recently visited

Egypt, or has he discussed with you any travel plans in that direction?"

"My uncle doesn't discuss his travel plans with me." That was well put, Scheffler silently congratulated himself.

"I see." And despite getting no direct answer, the man's voice sounded satisfied, as if its owner had somehow managed to learn what he wanted to know. "Goodbye." The last syllable was as precisely enunciated as the first had been.

The odd noise from the phone faded gradually into an ordinary dial tone, returned in one more burst, and then was gone, nothing at all like the normal termination of a phone call.

Scheffler hung up the receiver. He walked to the east window of the kitchen and stood there frowning out at the sky, in the general direction of Egypt. There was light out there, as if the sun were trying to come up, but as usual in winter it was impossible to see any real horizon across the lake.

had been.

THREE

First dawn, first light.

Across the Nile, the eastern horizon was etching itself
darkly against the great pearl of the slowly warming sky.

Ptah-hotep, Assistant Chief Priest for the Rituals to
Guard the Building of the Tomb, was standing atop the
uncompleted pyramid. His bare feet were planted at the
approximate center of the stone plain, flat and precisely
level, acres in extent, formed by the fiftieth and latest
stratum of construction. His fists were planted on his
hips, his dark eyes raised to the eastern sky as if to confront
a challenger. From this height, two hundred feet and
more above the pyramid's vastly broader base, he beheld
the green valley and the barren desert, both spread out
to receive the dawn.

Hours ago the Moon, pale representation of divine Aah,
had gone down below the western horizon, entering the
underworld domain of great Osiris and of night. Now
only the stars and a few human eyes remained above
the highest completed level of the pyramid to witness
the imminent approach of the Solar Boat, the barque of
the sun-god Ra.

A handful of Ptah-hotep's assistants, who at his direction
had been watching and praying and laboring here since
midnight, were still busy with their sticks and strings and
weights. They were sighting very carefully along the edges
of the last stones put into place yesterday, the start of

the fifty-first level of construction. The target of their careful measurement was the Pole Star, pale and yellow in the Thigh of the Bull, and their goal was to make sure that the pyramid as it rose did not deviate in the slightest from its strict orientation to the four directions of the world. Now the strings in the hands of Ptah-hotep's assistants were being stretched taut, and now Ptah-hotep himself was called to inspect them, and to seal their knots in the lines with clay marked by his seal. The engineers who would shortly be here to direct this day's work had now been provided with a trustworthy standard of true north.

The sealing of the knots had scarcely been finished before another aide of Ptah-hotep, standing many paces away from him at the eastern edge of the plain of stone, called out softly to get his attention. When the Assistant Chief Priest looked that way, the aide raised a hand and gestured downward.

Listening carefully in the morning stillness, Ptah-hotep could hear the faint approaching shuffle of many swiftly moving feet. It would be a party of ten or twelve bearers, transporting some person of importance up one of the ramps. The litter-bearers would be moving at a light trot in the coolness of the morning and they would be preceded by a herald—whose voice now broke the stillness—to cry others out of the way. Not that there was likely to be any other traffic along the ramps now, when the day's actual construction work had yet to get under way.

Ptah-hotep walked at a dignified pace toward the head of the proper ramp, that he might be able to greet the occupant of the litter on his arrival. The priest, having a good idea of who that occupant might be, moved without haste or surprise. Once he had reached the head of the proper ramp he stood with arms folded, waiting patiently.

Now, one by one, even the brightest stars were being

extinguished from the heavens. Most of them were gone
before the herald came trotting into sight, followed closely
by the litter and its jogging bearers. Presently the
conveyance had reached the top, and a voice from inside
ordered the bearers to stop. Then before they had finished
setting the closed chair down, the single occupant sprang
out of it on youthful limbs, and moved quickly toward
his friend Ptah-hotep. The two young men exchanged
first the formal gestures of greeting appropriate to friends
of equal rank, then smiles and a few informal words.

The new arrival was Thothmes, a chief of scribes who
served on the staff of the Chief Builder himself. The
official title of Thothmes' post made it sound obscure,
but it was actually one of considerable importance. He
supervised several underlings who did the actual writing
of most of the Chief Builder's voluminous correspondence.
But in the case of any particular confidential writings
sent from the office of the Chief Builder, it was Thothmes'
own hand that painted the papyrus or incised the clay.
His family was indirectly connected with that of Pharaoh
himself, the Great Khufu, mightiest monarch ever known
in the Two Lands. Khufu had now reigned for almost
eighteen years. Plans for this year's anniversary celebration
were well under way.

The two young officials began their early-morning
conference by casually strolling diagonally across the
artificial plateau toward its northern rim. Given the nature
of their respective offices, it was perfectly consistent with
logic and tradition that they should consult with each
other frequently. Indeed, for more than a year now they
had been meeting every week or so. To a casual observer
it might well have seemed accidental that this talk, like
many of the others, was taking place out of earshot of
any other human.

Today as usual the conservation between Ptah-hotep

and Thothmes got under way with a routine, almost ritualized discussion of the Pharaoh's health.

Thothmes, the shorter and plumper of the two officials, assured his friend that while it was true that Great Khufu had recently suffered from a minor ailment it was of no consequence. Pharaoh had speedily recovered, and was at this very moment busily smiting his enemies on the eastern frontier with even more than his usual enthusiasm.

The Pharaoh's health was a universal topic of conversation; but Thothmes had not ordered out his palanquin so they could discuss it. Nor had he come, really, to discuss the problems of the construction of the pyramid; there was another topic that the two men really wanted to talk about today, one that they touched upon at almost every meeting. But today, as always, it was approached only slowly and indirectly. Sometimes the eyes and ears of the Pharaoh were truly divine in their omnipresence.

When the two friends were standing at the very northern edge of the great plain of stone, many paces from the litter-bearers who had brought Thothmes here, and safely away from all of Ptah-hotep's assistants, the scribe at last felt safe in broaching the real subject of his visit: he had heard nothing about any new impending changes in the plans for construction, at least none that would affect the final positioning of the burial chamber itself, and the layout of the passageways that were to offer the only access to that vault.

"That is good news," Ptah-hotep agreed gravely. Construction of the Horizon of Khufu, the great pyramid that bulked beneath them as they spoke, had been under way for almost eighteen years, since the beginning of the reign; naturally one of the first concerns of any Pharaoh upon ascending to the throne was the design and

construction of his tomb. The concern did not lessen as
the Pharaoh, whoever he might be, grew older. But no
Pharaoh in the past had ever planned his tomb on a scale
anything like this one.

Twice during the past eighteen years, as both men could
well remember, the design of the passages within the
pyramid had been extensively revised, and the location
of the burial chamber had been changed. Each time it
had been necessary for the outside dimensions of the
planned structure to be correspondingly enlarged.

The fact was that both of these men had attained their
positions as replacements for older men, whom the Chief
Builder himself had considered were too closely wedded
to the original plan—too fond of finding reasons why,
even in the fact of Pharaoh's expressed wishes, that plan
should not be changed.

"But the last revision was six years ago. And since then
very much has been accomplished. To revise again at
this stage of the construction . . ." Ptah-hotep left the
sentence incomplete, but his meaning was plain. No
Pharaoh, not even this one, the greatest monarch in living
memory, could count upon an indefinite length of reign.
God and son of a god as any Pharaoh must be, this one
was also an aging man. The outer details of a tomb could
be finished after it was occupied; but here not even the
burial chamber was completed yet. Suppose that, when
Khufu died, his tomb should not be ready to receive his
body? What then? How then, with his mummified body
at risk, could even a Pharaoh hope to attain eternal life?

Thothmes answered obliquely, by relating another story.
Since his last anniversary celebration, Pharaoh Khufu
had crushed yet another set of enemies, settling the double
crown of the Two Lands even more firmly upon his own
head in the process. And despite an occasional minor
illness, Khufu's health was basically good: Pharaoh was

gambling that years of preparation still remained to him.

Both men voiced ritual thanks, praising the gods who were responsible for such good fortune. For this purpose they raised their voices somewhat, that perhaps the litter bearers and the assistant priests might hear, as well as the beneficent gods.

Then Thothmes, speaking more softly again, asked: "And now, my friend, what news can you tell me?"

Alas, there was very little that Ptah-hotep could tell Thothmes that he had not already told him. In the course of his daily work he could observe the actual layout of the constructed passages within the finished portion of the pyramid, as well as the materials used to line and plug the passages, the traps designed to kill or at least discourage thieves. Here on the job site there was as yet no indication that the Chief Builder was intending to change what had already been put in place. And if any plans or orders for a revision in the construction to come had reached the Chief Builder he was so far successfully keeping them to himself. That high lord visited the building site in person almost every day, and on most of his visits talked with the Chief Priest himself or with Ptah-hotep, his chief assistant. The loyalty of the Chief Builder to Pharaoh himself was, so far as Ptah-hotep could see, complete and unquestionable.

Thothmes sighed faintly. "Each man must cope with the gods as best he can, my friend."

Having concluded the most private and essential part of their conversation, the two men now strolled to the eastern edge of the new construction, where a small part of the next tier of huge stone blocks had already been fitted into place—it was along the inner edge of these stones that Ptah-hotep's assistants during the night had stretched one of their sighting lines, which at the first sign of dawn he had been quick to seal with his official seal. Now, exerting themselves in a brief scramble, demonstrating the agility of even sedentary youth, the two friends mounted to the top of the newest stones, reaching the highest possible point of observation. From here they could look out over the greatest possible extent of the Pharaoh's domain, the bottom lands along the river still shadowed by the dying night.

Comparatively near at hand, right on the barren plain within an arrow's flight of the base of the pyramid itself, the work gangs were emerging from their rough barracks into the morning half-light, ragged formations of thousands of men lining up for roll call. Sounds carried faintly to the top of the truncated pyramid hundreds of feet above. Dogs raced barking through the alleys separating the barrack-huts, and the cooks and camp followers were singing, calling back and forth in their perpetual arguments regarding whose duty it would be today to fetch the water. Already a hundred thin plumes of smoke from morning cookfires were going up into the sky, from which even the very last and brightest stars were now steadily being driven by the Barque of Ra. The Boat of Millions of Years was very close to its appearance on the eastern horizon.

In the distance, becoming ever more plainly visible from this height, the Nile flowed beautifully, silver reflecting dawn. To Ptah-hotep the omens of white birds were as always good to see.

Turning restlessly—he had a habit of turning and looking, wanting always to discover something new about the world—Ptah-hotep came to a stop facing straight away from the rising sun. He put out a hand and touched his companion on the arm. "What is that?"

A hand's breadth above the western horizon, a cloud was drifting now. Ptah-hotep had seen clouds in the sky before; on occasion he had seen rain. But never before had he seen any cloud like this one. It was thin as a snake's trail, and as twisted. As they watched, it turned gradually from gray to pink to white in the brightening rays of Ra's onrushing glory.

They gazed in silence at the strange cloud for a long time.

At last Thothmes, oblique once more, said: "There is yet more news about the Pharaoh. Rumors. I did not tell you before because I do not like to repeat every wild story."

"Tell me now."

"The great Pharaoh returned a few days ago from the eastern frontier. Since then he has been hunting out in the western desert, driving his chariot himself, passing close to the Land of the Dead."

"Yes?"

"The story is, that in the course of this hunting expedition, Khufu has had dealings with the gods themselves. That the gods came from the sky, or perhaps from the domains under the Earth, and that they gave to Pharaoh a vast hoard of gold. So much gold that the like of it has never before been seen in one place in the Two Lands."

"They came from the sky? Truly, and dealt with Khufu?"

"It may be that in truth they did."

In the distance the strange cloud paled, dispersing slowly in the clear morning sky.

FOUR

In the morning Becky was rather silent and uncommunicative. Her face looked a little puffy around the eyes, her blond hair disheveled. She was brisk in her movements, though. She even declined to stay for breakfast. Fifteen minutes after her eyes were fully open she was out the door and on her way back to her own apartment. Scheffler had had visions of sharing bacon and eggs and orange juice with her, of looking out at the early morning lake together, of . . . he wasn't sure of what the two of them were good for together, apart from sex. Nor was he sure of the present status of the affair. They hadn't quarreled, no. But Becky hadn't been happy when she left.

He fried and ate his own bacon and eggs, and managed to enjoy them. Today the apartment was his own; Mrs. White wasn't scheduled to come in.

After cleaning up his breakfast dishes, he went back to take another look around inside the enclosure of wealth. The curtain covering the central portion of the rear wall was hung on sliding rings from a dark, inconspicuous metal rod. Scheffler reached up and pulled the curtain to one side—and found himself standing before a door, a very real and modern-looking barrier of dark metal—right in the place where he had been told he would find only a false door, an ancient Egyptian spiritual symbol of some kind.

42

Or had he completely misheard or misunderstood what his great-uncle had said to him? Scheffler didn't think so.

This real, metallic door had nothing at all ancient or Egyptian-looking about it. Rather its smooth surface and sturdy frame suggested something on the order of a bank vault. Except that this door had no sign of a lock, only a simple handle that made it look as if it would be easy to open. An elevator, perhaps? Whatever it was, it was recessed about a foot into the stonework of the ancient-looking wall, and raised high enough above floor level to put it at the top of the two simple stone steps.

Scheffler was still standing there looking at the mysterious door when the telephone rang. He moved to answer it on the nearest extension, which happened to be in the library, where now the ashes in the hearth were cold and dead.

He picked up the receiver fully expecting to hear some kind of unhappy words from Becky. Not that he knew what she was unhappy about, but women were—

"Hello?"

"Hello. Tom?"

"Yes sir." Scheffler had no doubt at all about the voice. Uncle Monty. It sounded clear enough to be a local call.

His distant great-uncle asked him: "Have you encountered any problems yet?"

Scheffler's eyes swung back to the other room, the grillwork and the mystery beyond. He hesitated momentarily. "No sir, not really." He didn't want to explain that he'd already opened the grillwork; Uncle Monty might not be willing to classify his nephew's reason for doing so as a true emergency. "There was one phone call for you—the man you mentioned to me. He did identify himself as Peregrinus."

That provoked immediate excitement at the other end

of the line, signified by dry coughing. "What did you tell him?"

"Nothing. Just that you weren't available, that he could leave a message if he wanted, and I'd see that you got it. But he wasn't interested in leaving a message."

"Did he say he'd call back? Or what?"

"He didn't say. I haven't heard from him again."

"Well." Great-uncle Montgomery sighed. "You probably will. But that brings me back to my object in calling you. There's an alarm system I forgot to mention to you, connected to the place in the apartment where the most valuable items are—you follow me?"

"Yes sir."

"It's nothing to be concerned about, really, but I would appreciate it if you'd reset a certain control for me."

"I see, sir." Was it possible that Uncle Monty already knew he'd trespassed in the sanctuary? Were there perhaps hidden cameras somewhere in the apartment? Electronic sensors, transmitting warnings all the way to Egypt? But that seemed crazy.

His great-uncle's voice went calmly on. "You'll recall I showed you where I keep the key for the grillwork door."

"Yes sir."

"There's no hurry. But when you have time, get the key, please. In the rear of the false door—you remember?— you'll find some controls. One is marked with a little white label, days and months and so on. I'm sure you'll find it self-explanatory. Just reset it to the current date. Is that clear?" It was a courteous question, not a demand.

In the rear of the false door. That didn't really make sense—did it? Not in view of the actual door that Scheffler could see at this moment from two rooms away. But he still didn't want to admit how far his explorations had already gone. So he hesitated, until the moment for confessing the truth had passed.

"Yes sir. I'll do that. Sounds easy. I suppose if there's any difficulty I can call you back." That would be the way to play it, he congratulated himself silently. Call the old man back in a few minutes, and announce that the discovery of the real door had just been made. Good thinking, Scheffler.

"Yes, certainly," said the voice on the telephone. "Call me back if any problems should come up. But I don't anticipate you'll have any difficulties. I'll be talking to you again in a little while."

"Yes sir."

And Uncle Monty had hung up, before Scheffler could decide whether to add anything else. As if, Scheffler thought, to forestall any last-minute questions. He stood there for a few moments looking at the phone in his hand. Then he replaced it in its cradle and went back into Gallery Two.

As soon as he pushed gently on the handle of the dark metal door, it opened for him, sliding smoothly sideways into the wall of ancient brick.

For the moment Scheffler forgot all about looking for the labeled control he was supposed to find. He was gazing into a room that was about the same size as the closet in his bedroom, maybe eight feet deep, seven high, and six feet wide. The walls were of some dark material that looked to Scheffler more like painted wood or plastic than metal. Scattered over all the walls of the chamber from floor to ceiling were small, dim lights. Indicators, perhaps, though they also provided faint illumination. Some of the lights were of an almost ultraviolet blue. Some of them were orange like fireplace embers, some were plain red and some were white. Standing in the doorway of this closet made Scheffler feel as if he were on the point of climbing inside some kind of three-dimensional instrument panel. What a control center, was his first thought. What an alarm system Uncle Monty must have.

But no, this was too much. All of this had to add up to more than an alarm, however complex. Moving into the room, he looked around. None of the myriad lights were labeled, at least not in any way intelligible to Scheffler. Some of their glassy surfaces were shaped in ways that suggested they might be symbols, but certainly they were no letters or numbers or mathematical signs that he could remember seeing before.

The carpet in here was another oddity, being of a totally different color and quality than anywhere else in the apartment. This was almost black. The texture was coarse, almost like that of artificial turf—

The door of the little cell was sliding closed behind Scheffler, moving in such smooth silence that it was almost completely closed before he started to react. And before he could reach the door and stop it, the little box of the room was completely sealed around him.

The tiny lights on the dark walls provided only a minimum of illumination. There was a swaying beneath Scheffler's feet, a momentary sensation of falling, and now he was sure that this had to be an elevator, some damned private, secret conveyance, and it was rushing downward.

The motion was not a continuous free fall, but it was uncomfortably close to that. Scheffler grabbed for the small glassy projections of the lights on the wall, trying to maintain his balance in the shifting semi-weightlessness. He could see no controls, nothing that the old man had talked about. Damn Uncle Monty, anyway! What did this have to do with an alarm system? And how was he supposed to be accountable for the apartment and its treasures when he hadn't been told about this?

Built in along each long side of the elevator, Scheffler

now noticed, was a low, narrow projection like a couch or a bunk, just about long enough for a man to lie down on. He didn't want to lie down but it would be good to have something he could hang on to. And on the bunks he could now make out what looked like safety belts. Choosing a moment when the gravity felt comparatively reliable, he lunged for one of the couches and held on.

The inward senses of his body assured him that the elevator was still going down. But now that Scheffler had had a moment or two in which to think about it, the existence of an elevator here didn't make any sense at all. It didn't even seem that there ought to be space for it within the architecture of the apartment building. And where was it going to come out?

But here it was, obviously, and he was in it, and it was still taking him down. How long ought it to take for an elevator to descend twelve stories, when it was almost falling freely? Not this long. By this time he ought to be on ground level, either wrecked or landed safely. The thing looked ultramodern, but the ride suggested that something was badly in need of repair. At least fresh air was circulating nicely in the car.

Jerk and stop, jerk and stop. Repeatedly Scheffler's weight dropped away and then returned to him. And what kind of elevator was it that needed couches aboard, equipped with safety straps? Fantastic ideas were elbowing their way forward. He was being kidnapped. Or transported to the secret underground pleasure palace shared by the millionaires of Lake Shore Drive. Or else this was someone's idea of a joke . . . it was hard to picture Uncle Monty relishing a joke.

Fall, and stop, and fall again.

Grimly Scheffler held onto his safety belt. How long *could* it possibly take to get down a mere twelve stories? How many basement levels could there be? Maybe the elevator, unused for years, was hopelessly broken, and simply jiggling him up and down. The trouble was that he never felt beneath him the extra pressure from the floor that would indicate an upward acceleration. Or else the thing was booby-trapped somehow, and anyone who got into it without knowing the secret code was in for—

At last, a real stop. The floor felt steady once again. Stability persisted, going on for long seconds until he began to trust it. This impression of cessation, of finality, was reinforced by the cessation of a sound that Scheffler had not really heard until it stopped. It had been an almost subliminal hum, something like a cooling fan, something like a quiet engine, but not really quite like either. The ensuing silence was intense. Living in Chicago, you could go for weeks and months without really being out of the sound of traffic. But he had achieved that now. Even in his hunting forays as a youngster he had never experienced such an intense silence.

Slowly, but with increasing confidence as stability endured, Scheffler arose from his couch. Now he noticed that, as if to confirm the fact that a definite change of state had taken place, the pattern of lights around the door had altered. He thought that must mean something. A pattern so complex ought to have some meaning beyond mere decoration.

And what was there to do next, except to try the door? The weighty panel slid open for Scheffler at his first touch upon the inside handle. Outside was chiefly darkness, with only the indirect dim glow emanating from within the elevator itself to reveal what appeared to be the opening of a narrow, rocky tunnel. The air wafting in from the tunnel was almost uncomfortably warm, and laden with faint, exotic odors, as if it might be coming from the boiler rooms, the furnace rooms, of a dozen strange apartment buildings. But there was no light out there at all. And the aromas coming in grew stranger, blending into the oddest, outdoor, watery, fishy, mudbank kind of smell. Not strong, no, but strange indeed.

All that Scheffler could really see out there was dark rock, making up an uneven floor, two crude walls without much space between them, a crumbling overhead. The overhead portion appeared to come to an end after a few yards. All of it was very dark and very rough-looking, as if only the crudest essential tunnel had been hacked out here below the city—somewhere far below.

He wasn't about to go exploring down that tunnel without a light. He did venture to step outside the elevator, and examine the wall beside the door for any kind of switches. There wasn't even a button for the elevator itself.

As soon as Scheffler re-entered the car, the door closed behind him. Good enough. Everything must be automatic. He would ride back up to the apartment, get Uncle Monty on the phone regardless of what time it might be now in Cairo, and ask him some questions. His list of questions was getting longer by the minute.

One difficulty with this plan manifested itself at once. There were no obvious controls inside, either. As soon as the door was securely closed, the floor of the elevator again sank weightlessly beneath Scheffler's feet. The sensation of falling, or nearly falling, assured him that once more he was going down. Almost floating, thrashing the air with his arms and clawing at the carpet with his feet—when they were able to find purchase—he struggled back to his couch. Once more he anchored himself there by gripping one of the safety straps. If it was lunacy to have an elevator that carried people down to a dark tunnel under the city, what was it when the machine next carried them down farther, to who knew what? This berserk elevator was running away with him . . .

Perhaps five minutes passed on this leg of his journey before the motion stopped. Again the cessation of the faint whispering sound was accompanied by renewed stability of the floor, all confirmed by a new pattern of the lights.

Once more Scheffler disengaged himself from his supportive couch and stepped over to the door, this time moving on knees that felt a little weak. He drew in a deep breath before he pushed the inside handle.

Letting out his breath, he stepped out of the car and was back in the apartment, standing just in front of what he had once been told was a false door. Outside the windows of the museum room, the morning for a change was turning bright and sunny.

The door of the elevator—or whatever it was—was once more closing itself behind him. Thoughtfully, Scheffler let it close, then pulled the tapestry curtain back into place. It wouldn't do for Mrs. White to notice that anything behind the grillwork had been moved or changed. Or Becky, for that matter. Or anyone else.

Moving mechanically, Scheffler locked up the grillwork door again, and put the key back inside the model pyramid where Uncle Monty had kept it. He had no fear that Becky was going to come in and rip off anything. She might be a schemer, but she had other plans than that.

Next he went out into the hallway, where he squinted out of windows and paced off distances. The crude measurement confirmed his earlier idea—there simply wasn't space enough inside the building for the elevator to be where it was—where he had just seen it. Where he had just entered it and ridden up and down. Or ridden somewhere.

Uncle Monty, Uncle Monty. You have some heavy explaining to do. But how could anyone explain this?

The vague fear generated in Scheffler by the strange

experience was turning into anger. He was supposed to be responsible for the contents of this damned apartment, and how could he—but that was only the start of the problem.

A dawning suspicion that his great-uncle had set him up for something—something unpleasant at best. Thinking back over what he knew of the old man's reputation, Scheffler did not find it reassuring.

He could call his mother in Iowa, who after all had known her uncle for a long time, and ask her—but what could he ask her, really? She'd probably already told her son all that she really knew about the old man. After all, she hadn't seen or talked to him in decades. If Scheffler tried to explain what was happening now, she'd think that he'd gone crazy. For which her son could hardly blame her.

His thoughts kept coming back to that damned elevator. He still called it that, in his own mind, because he couldn't think of what else to call it. Whatever it was, it represented a way out of the apartment that he hadn't been told about, and presumably a way in as well. Right into the treasure trove.

He had to go back and unlock the grillwork again and take another look at the elevator door, because the more he thought about it the less he could believe that it was really there. But the door was there, all right. And when Scheffler touched the handle, it slid open obediently to show him the dark-walled little car with all the lights.

Again he closed everything up, and started walking around through the other rooms of the apartment, trying to think. Call Uncle Monty back, sure. Wake him up and demand some answers. But think a little first.

He visited all the rooms of the apartment in sequence, but looking at furniture and painted monsters didn't help. What had just happened wasn't a story you could take to the police. There was no crime involved, as far as he could see. And how would it sound when he tried to tell it? "You see, my great-uncle has this peculiar elevator built into the apartment building where he lives. You get into it, and it takes you down to a coal mine somewhere . . ."

No, it wasn't a story he could take to anyone else. Not yet anyway. Not until he knew more. Maybe there was some reasonable, logical explanation. Maybe Uncle Monty really meant well by his nephew after all.

Having achieved nothing during his interval for thought, Scheffler went to the phone in the kitchen and tried calling his great-uncle, dialing direct to Cairo. There was a minimum of noise on the line, and presently an unfamiliar man's voice, that said something in a foreign language. It switched to accented English as soon as Scheffler started speaking.

"Is Doctor Chapel there? This is his nephew, calling from Chicago."

"Dr. Chapel mumble mumble unintelligible," the voice at the other end responded. "I can take a message."

"Tell him his nephew called." Scheffler found himself shouting as if that were likely to help. "From Chicago. Ask him to call me back."

He repeated that several times, with variations, getting in return more vague reassurances, mumbles and electrical interference. He could only hope the word would be passed on.

And then he went and got out his books and tried to do some schoolwork. It was hopeless.

Another twenty-four hours passed with no return call. In the course of that time Mrs. White came, worked silently and went away again, and Scheffler went out to the grocery store and back once more, and spent some hours going through the motions of studying. Not knowing in what he was about to become involved, or how deeply, he refrained from calling Becky, though there were hours when that was difficult.

December thirtieth. The next-to-the-last day of the old year.

Eventually, the only course of action that Scheffler could settle on was that he had to go back and take another look at that subterranean tunnel, this time of course carrying a light. Maybe this time some obvious explanation would suggest itself.

That evening, just before he'd made his decision, the phone rang for the third time since he'd moved into the apartment. He picked up the receiver with a barrage of questions ready, expecting Uncle Monty's voice. But this time it was Becky.

She was in a pensive mood but not antagonistic, ready to discuss what their relationship had meant to each of them so far, and what its prospects might be for the future. From the way she sounded, uncertain and possibly regretful, Scheffler gathered that the prospects were not that good.

"I don't know, Tom. It's not you, I mean not anything about you. It's me. I mean, I'm just trying to think some things through in my own mind."

"Me too."

"The other night was fine, don't get me wrong. Once we got into bed it was beautiful. But—I really acted like a whore, didn't I?"

"No. No."

"Yes I did. I mean, just to get my way, just to get to wear that gold. I mean that must be the way that my behavior looks to you."

"No. I mean, no, I don't think of you that way. Not at all." The truth was he didn't really know how he did think of her. Except that if it hadn't been for the damned mysterious elevator, or whatever the hell it was, he'd probably be busy this minute trying to talk her into coming back to warm his bed again. He mumbled a few more words, making his best attempt at being reassuring. He tried to give the impression that he was busy with deep thoughts.

"I understand." Becky's voice was sweetness itself. "I've been thinking too, Tom. Thinking a lot."

Not about the same things, I'll bet. For a moment Scheffler wasn't sure that he'd kept himself from saying that aloud.

"Tom, I want you to respect me as a person."

"I do. I said I did." He realized suddenly that she must be waiting for him to invite her back. He forgot about his reasons for not doing so. "When are you coming over again?"

"I don't know. Not tonight."

They talked a little longer, inconclusively he thought, except for agreeing that both of them were going to think some more.

When he had hung up the phone, Scheffler sat there for a long time with his hand still on it, trying to make up his mind whether or not to try once more to call his Uncle Monty. The first effort along that line hadn't done him much good. And he doubted that Uncle Monty would tell him the truth anyway.

He thought back to the tour of the apartment that his uncle had given him—how carefully the old man had called his attention not only to the treasure but to the existence of a door behind the curtain. Pointing out the steps. Returning to the subject of the wall and how much trouble it had been to build. And almost harping on the existence of the key. And then the phone call, prodding Scheffler, actually instructing him to go back to the mysterious door, just in case he hadn't already done so out of curiosity or greed.

Somehow Scheffler got through the rest of the day, though he could neither study nor do much of anything else. Several times he walked into Gallery Two and looked through the grillwork. But he let it stay locked.

Next day, New Year's Eve, Mrs. White was due again. Scheffler arose fairly early, and breakfasted, and got out some books to try to convince himself that he was studying.

He started trying to make conversation with Mrs. White when she came in, right on schedule. But she had little to say on any subject, and absolutely refused to be drawn into any discussion of the antiquities, or of any of Dr. Chapel's affairs. Except, when Scheffler asked her pointblank if she ever cleaned inside the grillwork alcove, she admitted that she did not, and in fact had no idea how to open it.

"The Professor, he do all that in there himself. I cleans the rest of the place, that's all, Mistah Scheffler. Now excuse me, please, I got my work to do." And she turned busily away.

Scheffler reflected that Uncle Monty had probably spent decades inculcating that attitude in Mrs. White. He probably paid her well also. Scheffler could testify that the old man could be generous when it suited him.

Late that afternoon, when Mrs. White was safely gone, Scheffler, his anger growing again, went back into the elevator to risk another ride and have another look around. He was going to have to do something about the situation, but he was afraid that whatever he tried to do was going to leave him looking like an idiot.

This time he brought along a flashlight that he'd discovered sitting on his uncle's dresser. Perhaps the batteries were a little weak, but they'd do for a start.

The elevator once more began to move as soon as its door had closed him inside. He was treated to a journey very much like his previous one, and deposited in what might have been the same place.

Might have been. It was a rocky tunnel, or at least a crevice, but he couldn't be sure it was the same one at all, because now it was bathed in daylight. Not that he could see anything of the sky; the long overhang of rock just outside the elevator prevented that. But some twenty yards or so in front of him along the angled passage, the high walls of grayish rock were bathed in what certainly looked like direct sunlight. And the temperature had become truly ferocious. The moment Scheffler opened the elevator door, heat like the breath of a furnace struck him in the face.

By daylight the scene outside the elevator door appeared about a thousand times more improbable than it had by night. The two walls of the passage were, on the average, no more than about a yard apart. The narrow floor between them, a surface almost too uneven to be called a floor at all, was more of the same rock. The overhead brow of rock, extending out several yards from where Scheffler stood inside the elevator, trailed small roots and little clods of earth here and there from cracks in its underside.

Scheffler dropped his useless flashlight on one of the couches, and with grim determination stepped out of the doorway. Moving with the necessary slow care on the tricky footing, he made his way far enough down the passage to be able to see the sky. Yes, there was indeed an unclouded sky above. He was still standing in the shade, but he could feel the heat from that sky, and from all the rocks around him.

The faintest of sounds was audible behind him. Wheeling, he saw that the elevator door was closing, already almost closed. Scrambling recklessly on slanted rock, he sprang toward that door. Too late to catch it before it closed, he threw himself against the outer handle.

The door slid open for him at once.

Scheffler let the door close again, slowly, against the gentle pressure of his hands. Then he opened it again, satisfying himself that it was not going to lock him out. But so far it had always opened for him, hadn't it? In the end Scheffler decided fatalistically that it was going to be all right.

Turning his back on the elevator, he got down to the business of exploration, which presented difficulties from the start. Here near the elevator door the rock walls of the fissure were almost twenty feet high, and dangerously smooth. Scheffler wasn't at all sure that he would be able to climb either of them, or between them, without a fall. He began to move along the fissure, looking for an easier way up.

At the first sharp bend of the passage, only a few dark yards along, he turned to look back. Already the dark gray surface of the elevator door was practically invisible within its shadowed recess.

And when he looked up it was obvious from this point that there was no fifteen-story apartment building towering above the elevator. Only the thick brow of rock, and then the empty sky. The final proof that he was now in a different world did not really come as a surprise. Scheffler had already begun adjusting to that fact, though he had not really begun to deal with it consciously.

He turned and moved again along the fissure. It changed direction every few yards, so that he was never able to see very far ahead. But before he had gone this way for more than fifty yards, the end of the fissure had come into sight. It opened at a slight elevation, looking out across a desert wasteland. About a mile away, at the bottom of a long gentle slope, there coursed an enormous river, both banks lined with greenery.

Near the open mouth of the fissure the slope of its walls diminished, and simultaneously their height decreased. Here it was easy enough to scramble out. Scheffler got his head above the walls and was able to look about him freely.

He had emerged now into the open heat and glare of that high sun. But at first Scheffler hardly noticed the sun at all.

He should have been warned by the disappearance of the apartment building. But the scene before him was beyond any preparatory adjustment that he might have been able to make.

The sun was high in that cloudless hearth of sky—never mind that it had been late afternoon when he left Chicago. To Scheffler's right, and again to his left, the broad river wound gently to the far horizon. From his slight elevation in the flat land he could see how the wide bands of greenery following both banks were patterned everywhere with irrigated fields. Away from the river, the world was almost entirely dry wasteland, marked here and there by low plateaus. Scheffler was standing on one of these plateaus, which was streaked by dry rocky fissures like the one he had just climbed out of. In the direction opposite the river, the horizon was brought a little closer by low, barren hills.

On the river's near bank, about a mile from where Scheffler was standing, gray-brown buildings clustered. It was an extensive cluster. Squinting into shimmering heat, he could not tell if those distant walls were inhabited, or only ruins. At this distance he could see no signs of life among them.

From close beside the group of buildings, whatever they might be, a canal, both banks lined with tall palms, had been dug in the general direction of Scheffler's vantage point. This waterway, following the low ground as much as possible, passed the barren rock where he was standing at a distance of about a hundred yards.

From that point the canal went on in a straight line toward the high ground about a mile in the other direction. It appeared to stop just before it got there, in a last cluster of palm trees at the foot of a low, rounded hill of solid rock.

Looming gigantically atop that high ground was the original of Uncle Monty's model pyramid, the whole unmistakable geometric mass of it wavering in the heat. Just as in the model, the construction ramps on this full-sized pyramid went up three-fourths of the way to the top. And above the level where the ramps terminated, the slanting sides were finished as smoothly as those of any building in Chicago. The apex was marked by a visible speck of gold.

Scheffler, oblivious to the sun, stared open-mouthed at the pyramid for some time. Eventually he turned again, continuing to scan the circle of the horizon in hopes of coming upon something that made sense. His gaze returned to the river. White birds flew between him and that distant bordering of greenery, and for a moment he could see their wings distinctly outlined against black mud. And now he thought that the palms along the canal were dancing. The glare of the sun, almost directly overhead, seemed to reverberate within his brain.

Without realizing that he had made a conscious decision to retreat, Scheffler found himself crouching and sliding back into the fissure in the rock. Sharp gray rock tore at the heel of his left hand as he braced himself coming down, but he was hardly aware of the damage. Once at the bottom of the fissure, down between the rough rock walls, he began to retrace his steps toward the elevator.

The conveyance was still there, waiting for him. The door opened for him at once. Scheffler went in, pondering the fact that he had just been given a look at the Great Pyramid. Apparently the monument hadn't even been finished yet, although near the top a good share of the highly polished sheathing was already in place, making the surfaces near the top shine like the snowcap on a mountain . . .

Scheffler hadn't been able to see any of the workers, of course. The pyramid had been too far away. Nor had he seen any other people, anywhere. Maybe they all took a siesta in the middle of the day. With heat like that you couldn't blame them. But the pyramid was there. The same basic, four-sided shape as the model. What else could it be? There had been the same construction ramps that Uncle Monty had discussed, angling upward along those mountainous sides . . .

Dimly Scheffler became aware that he had hurt his hand. It wasn't much. It wasn't anything.

The motion of the elevator stilled, the ghostly sounds of its passage quieted. He got up from the couch and went to open the door.

Outside, in the darkening space of Gallery Two with its grillwork gate, he stared at the gems of Uncle Monty's great collection. Scheffler looked at the things now as if he had never seen any of them until this moment.

Then he made his way slowly through the apartment to his bathroom, where he carefully washed his injured hand. He stared at the almost infinitesimal particles of grit, of gray stone, as they were dislodged from the inconsequential wound to go swirling down the drain. To him they looked more marvelous than moon rock.

In his uncle's bathroom Scheffler found a package of Band-Aids, and applied one to his hand. Then he went walking through the other rooms of the apartment, staring at a hundred artifacts. They all looked different to him now than they had an hour ago.

Then, moving mechanically, he went into the kitchen and made himself some coffee.

And then, slowly, tentatively at first, Scheffler began to think.

It had become quite dark in the kitchen before he noticed that the message light on the phone-answering machine was blinking at him.

It was Becky's recorded voice that greeted him when he flipped the switch. He needed human company. He scarcely hesitated before beginning to dial her number.

FIVE

More than a year had passed since Ptah-hotep and Thothmes, along with most of the other subjects of Pharaoh Khufu, had observed a strange, small cloud drifting in the western sky at dawn and pondered its meaning.

During that year Ptah-hotep had been promoted, and was now Chief Priest for the Rituals to Guard the Building of the Tomb. Unlike his predecessor in that august office, whose laziness had eventually been his downfall, Ptah-hotep continued as an active observer of the day-to-day progress of the construction project. Now, at midday, he was standing atop the fifty-fifth and currently highest tier of the great pyramid, looking down into a square pit that gaped at the approximate center of the structure.

The pit in its unfinished state was about fifteen paces long by ten paces wide, and half as deep as it was wide. It had not been dug into the solid stone, but created by allowing the layers of construction to rise around it. According to the plan of construction, last modified seven years ago and still being followed by the Chief Builder, this cavity would one day serve as the final resting place of Pharaoh, whose stone sarcophagus was already in place at its bottom. The granite sarcophagus, too big to fit through the narrow interior passageway through which the funeral procession would one day drag the coffin, had been hauled up a ramp on a sledge, just as all the building blocks were hauled. Then as soon as the floor of the pit was finished the hollow stone receptacle had been carefully maneuvered into its planned position, and left there as the tiers of stonework rose around it.

Besides the sarcophagus, the cavity already contained a number of loose granite slabs, each of carefully measured size. These slabs, like the sarcophagus, were too large to have been brought in later, through the one planned narrow passageway that would remain when the pyramid was finished. Some of these slabs were intended to provide the finished lining of red granite for the chamber holding the sarcophagus, while others were designed to be used as plugs, blocking the last means of access to the chamber after the king had died and his mummy had reached its final resting place.

Today the scribe Thothmes was once more visiting his friend Ptah-hotep. Thothmes still held the same post that he had held a year before, and he was evidently prospering in office, for he looked a little plumper now than he had at that early morning meeting a year ago.

Surrounded by the fire of the noonday sun, the two men sat together, taking advantage of the shade of a canopy of fine cloth held over them by Nubian slaves. They sat almost immobile in the midday heat, while round them by the thousands Pharaoh's loyal subjects thronged and chanted, coming and going in an apparent melee that was actually closely controlled by the shouts of overseers. The great plan went forward, as it had year after year, decade after decade. Gangs of men labored, according to its dictates, at dragging, shaping, hoisting, hammering and mortaring into place the day's quota of enormous and finely finished building stones.

Inside the deep stone pit which yawned at the feet of the two officials, a swarm of some of the more skillful artisans, nagged by a few overseers who seldom shouted,

were laboring under the shade of a larger canopy. Their
job consisted of the final fitting and finishing of the granite
slabs that were to serve as lining for the inner walls of
the tomb chamber, and of the slabs that were to serve
as traps and plugs. The aesthetic qualities of the latter
were not of much concern, but still they had to be precisely
measured and precisely cut and smoothed, so that their
position when they had been set in place might be exact,
and their final motion sure when it was triggered.

"The Pharaoh plans well," Ptah-hotep observed. Since
he had joined his friend atop the pyramid today, other
ears had been continually within range of their
conversation, which therefore had tended toward
platitudes. They had been unable to exchange but little
information about those aspects of the design before
them that continued to be of deepest interest to them
both.

"No mere man can fathom the plans of the god-king,
our Pharaoh," Thothmes said to his friend now.

Ptah-hotep looked at the other carefully. In past years
it had been possible now and then to see a twinkle in
the eye of Thothmes; but today Ptah-hotep could detect
no trace of mockery on the face that had just delivered
that solemn utterance. Moving daily in exalted circles,
at the side of the Chief Builder himself, evidently trained
a man to the finest self-control in every detail of behavior.

And just now, by a sudden and unpredictable chance,
there came a moment in which no one was near enough
to overhear and understand them—aides, overseers, and
laborers were all at a safe distance. And Ptah-hotep had
long ago made sure that his pair of Nubian shade-holders
did not know the Egyptian tongue—nor, being tongueless
themselves and naturally illiterate, were they well able
to communicate anything that they might learn. Thothmes
seized this opportunity to add, in the same tone: "Yet

again the Pharaoh has changed his mind about the final arrangements for the protection of his tomb."

"Ah," said Ptah-hotep, in something like a sigh. It was a bit of news that he and his fellow plotters had been anticipating and worrying about for years. Such repeated changes in a tomb's design were unprecedented—of course the whole scale of the project was unprecedented also. Yet, Pharaoh being Pharaoh, the news was not entirely unexpected by Ptah-hotep.

Construction was now, of course, much farther along on the overall structure than it had been years ago when the previous changes of plan regarding the interior had been announced.

Ptah-hotep said: "I am certain that Khufu has in mind what happened to the tomb of his father. Snefru had not been for two years in the realm of the blessed before his burial place was despoiled by skillful robbers." Both men had been much too young to have taken part in that robbery, almost a score of years in the past, but both remembered hearing the rumors of it shortly after it occurred. It had been accomplished by the same secret group, at once the cult of Set and a band of thieves, to which they themselves had belonged for years.

And now again the moment had passed in which unguarded speech was possible. Aides to both men were again hovering near them.

Ptah-hotep leaned a little closer to the pit. He was keeping an eye, as was his duty, upon the current progress of the work. Below him a foreman paced and shouted, and a dozen diorite hammer-stones rose and fell, smoothing a piece of granite toward perfection. A few paces away along the bottom of the pit, at the site of a projected anteroom to the burial chamber proper, some of the massive granite slugs were already being levered and wedged into the places where they were to remain poised until just after the burial of Pharaoh. Then, from those cunningly contrived niches, those tons of rock would slide down to seal forever the Ascending Passage, the last human access to this inner portion of the completed tomb.

"And all this work presently being completed below us?" the youthful Chief Priest asked, when the next moment came in which he might speak freely.

"All of it is to remain in place," Thothmes replied in a low voice. "And the overall size of the pyramid will remain what is called for in the present plan. The new plan— involves certain additions later in the construction."

That cried out for explanation. But once more untrusted ears were coming near. It was obvious that any detailed discussion on this sensitive subject was going to have to wait till later.

An exchange of information with Thothmes was not the only clandestine bit of business that Ptah-hotep was trying to accomplish today. He was attempting also to arrange secretly for the leader of one particular work-gang, a man named Sihathor, to be able to observe these inner arrangements of the pit. To this end Ptah-hotep had been instructed, by his superior in the secret cult of Set, to keep an eye out for a man who wore a red fillet with white tassels round his head.

As usual, one gang after another was appearing in rapid succession atop the pyramid, each group of eighteen or twenty men dragging into sight a sledge supporting a mass of several tons of stone. Turning his gaze casually to keep the three ascending ramps under his surveillance, the Chief Priest was managing to eye the leader of every gang alertly. But so far no red fillet with white tassels had appeared. Headgear of any kind was uncommon among the laborers. Usually the gang leaders, like the men they directed, wore nothing but a twist of cloth about the loins.

Neither Thothmes nor Ptah-hotep were clothed much more heavily than that, though their short white skirts were of fine linen, and each wore tokens of his office. Thothmes now raised a hand, toying with a gold boss on his jeweled collar of rank.

Ptah-hotep fidgeted inwardly. Doubtless, the priest supposed, Sihathor's gang was still in the process of hauling their first sledge of the day up here from the terminus of the canal. As soon as Sihathor did appear, Ptah-hotep meant to accomplish his secret purpose by calling the man here to this shaded place of observation, and asking him about some supposed irregularities in the stone-hauling quotas as reported by other gangs. Other gang leaders, chosen at random, had been interrogated earlier in the day. It was going to look as if Ptah-hotep were merely too lazy to leave his patch of shade. The eyes of Pharaoh might be anywhere.

Sihathor, and some at least of the gang of men whose labor he now directed, were natives of one particular village about two days' journey up the Nile. Traditionally the men of that village were excellent stoneworkers. Another tradition shared by many of them, requiring many of the same skills, just as ancient but less talked about, was that of tomb-robbing.

Ptah-hotep and Thothmes had reverted again to innocuous conversation, and were still engaged in it when a man wearing a red fillet with white tassels at last appeared. Sihathor was pulling his own share of the weight, as many of the gang leaders did, on one of the ropes attached to the sledge. He also was leading his men in chanting as they struggled to deliver their rock. Ptah-hotep had already managed to turn the conversation back to the subject of daily quotas and the honesty of their reporting. It ought to be easy to check up on, but clever, indolent men might find some

way to cheat their Pharaoh out of the work they owed
him.

Now, as if suddenly remembering the survey he had
begun earlier in the day, Ptah-hotep called to one of his
aides who was passing and ordered him to bring the leader
of the most recently arrived workgang to his side.

In obedience to the aides of the Chief Priest, Sihathor,
a gnarled and wiry man of middle age, was soon standing
before the two officials in an attitude of humble
submission. From this position his downcast eyes were
able to see plainly everything that the senior plotters
wished him to see: the broad outline as well as many
details of the construction down in the pit.

It was at this potentially awkward moment that Sebek,
another of Ptah-hotep's aides, the newly appointed
Assistant Chief Priest, chose to reappear earlier than
expected from an errand. He was on the scene in time
to witness the questioning. Ptah-hotep did not fail to note
this fact. He suspected his new assistant Sebek of being
one of the eyes of Pharaoh. As if to confirm his suspicions,
this official then favored Thothmes and Ptah-hotep with
a long, suspicious glance. Both were aware of this
inspection, and felt it inwardly, though neither gave any
outward sign of having noticed it.

Sihathor took his apparently slow-witted time about
answering three or four routine questions, the same
queries Ptah-hotep had put to the other gang leaders
earlier in the day. Then he was dismissed, as they had
been.

Next, Sebek, who had been hovering closer than Ptah-
hotep liked, was dispatched again upon some logical
errand, and the two friends were able to resume a
relatively private conversation.

Thothmes, who was intrigued with the details of the
actual construction and ever eager to get a close took at

them, inspected with great interest the positioning of
the granite slabs below. Without looking up from them
he asked in a whisper: "What do you suppose your assistant
thought of it all?"

Ptah-hotep shrugged fatalistically. It was too late now
to worry about that. "Time and the gods will tell."

"And our cult-brother the stonemason?"

"My soul is not that of a stonemason; I do not know.
We have done our part in giving him the chance. And
presumably he has done his, seeing and remembering
the things that we were able to put before his eyes."

"Of course, my friend." Thothmes stretched his arms
and returned to a safer subject. "And what will be the
fate of the last legitimate workers in the tomb, after the
burial? Those who are to trigger the fall of the stone
plugs, and thereby close the last means of access? I have
often wondered about that. See the way those plugs are
situated? To the eye of a scribe, at least, it would appear
that the only way to release them will be from inside
the tomb."

Ptah-hotep held his reply until another chance for free
speech arrived. "That I suppose can hardly matter if there
is going to be a new plan anyway."

"I do not know details of the new plan yet. But I wonder
how the plugs were to be released, or the men to escape,
according to the plan that is in concrete form below us."

Ptah-hotep made a gesture confessing his own
ignorance. "I do not know. I see no method by which
those workers might escape. But not all the design has
yet taken form here, and it is unthinkable that they should
be allowed to remain sealed inside, and thus share for
eternity this monument, the Horizon of Khufu himself.
In the final plan some means of egress must be provided
to allow them to get out alive."

"Great is the wisdom of Pharaoh."

"Great beyond imagining. But in this matter he has yet to make his wisdom clear to us."

Ptah-hotep the Chief Priest looked around him. The chanting of the workmen was louder than usual but none of the aides were near. Now it was again likely, but this time by no means certain, that he and Thothmes could no longer be overheard. He could not quite make up his mind whether it would be too dangerous now to press Thothmes for more details on the revised plans of construction. His curiosity was so great that he could hardly restrain himself from doing so, and yet he managed to maintain restraint a little longer.

Ptah-hotep summoned one of his personal servants a little closer, and ordered cool beer to be brought for himself and the Scribe. Outside their small island of shade, the naked bodies of the workers passed back and forth continually, either straining at stones or shuffling into position to strain at stones again. Stone and sledge grated upon stone; the noise of the artisans' hammers in the pit reverberated through the heat, and the sound of the workers' chanting droned on and on into the ears, filling the skull until it was no longer heard. Such noise could be of use, though, to help keep unwanted ears from hearing other things.

The two men exchanged fragments and morsels of relatively innocent information, reviewing the latest gossip each of them had heard. The rumors of several years ago persisted, concerning the Pharaoh's encounter with the sky gods in the Western Lands. Such durability in a rumor was often an indication that it contained some truth. Often, but by no means always.

The size of the golden treasure in the story had now become more definite. Even two such officials of the Court were awed by the amount, even when they discounted it by half, as the treasure in all stories must surely be discounted. The feelings of these particular officials were intensified by the fact that it was the robbery of this very treasure that they had long been engaged in plotting. For what else would any Pharaoh do with his greatest treasure, except to bury it with him in his tomb, and thus keep it with him for eternity?

"I have heard it, friend Ptah-hotep, from the mouth of the overseer of the Treasure himself—there are always wild rumors, of course, but this one I have heard from the man himself—"

"Yes?" Ptah-hotep prodded, when the nearest man who could understand them was again safely out of earshot.

"I have heard that the smiths and other metal-workers, using their fine balances, have discovered, to their awe, that this gold from the sky is even heavier than ordinary gold."

The Chief Priest did not know what to say. But he did not want his friend to think him dumbfounded, so he replied: "Perhaps something of the kind was only to be expected, given the origin of the metal."

"Perhaps."

Presently the Scribe spoke again. "It was found in pieces of a peculiar shape, or at least it was in such pieces when the smiths were given it to work on. And there were pieces of another metal found with the gold. An unknown material, dark and lustrous, which has proven impossible to work with because of its hardness, and because of a tendency of the pieces to return to their original shapes, even when deformed by great heat and force. And I understand that some of the smiths who tried to work with the strange metal sickened and died soon afterward, despite all that the priests and physicians could do for them."

"And have you seen any of these arrivals for yourself?"

"No. No, I have not been able to see anything of the sort. The Palace is full of secrecy, as always."

Ptah-hotep was silent. It had occurred to him, just in the last few moments, that possibly this whole story about gold from the sky, strange metal from the gods, was nothing more than an attempt to frighten away potential tomb-robbers. What, after all, had he or Thothmes really seen of any such divine intervention? Only one peculiar cloud.

The Pharaoh certainly partook of divinity, and his will was not to be thwarted lightly. But tomb-robbing was among certain people an ancient and honorable profession. To some it was even a form of worship; and Ptah-hotep had observed with his own eyes that those who were engaged in that worship and that profession often led long and prosperous lives.

Khufu might be of truly divine cunning. But his was not the only divine power. Thieves, of whatever rank and station in life, had their god too, and around the neck of the Chief Priest there hung his hidden amulet of Set.

Ptah-hotep prayed.

SIX

Late on the first morning of the new year in Chicago, some hours after his first look at the Great Pyramid, Scheffler at last had his chance for breakfast with Becky. He had returned her phone call on New Year's Eve and had invited her over, and again she had slept with him. This time neither of them had mentioned or even looked at the cage of golden treasures. They had dined on Scheffler's cooking, toasted each other with champagne at midnight, listened to the radio, and talked of a number of things. They had spent the first hours of the New Year in bed. Scheffler had said nothing at all to Becky about his adventure in the elevator.

After her late breakfast Becky went back to her own apartment, this time in a better mood. Scheffler didn't understand the change, but he was grateful for it.

He cleaned up the dishes. There would be no interference from Mrs. White today, a holiday. He plunged into Uncle Monty's library, looking for helpful information.

Quickly he realized that if the thousand books held anything that would be useful to him, he had no idea how to get at it. None of the titles he looked at said anything about magic elevators.

Settling on the antique record player as the oddest thing in sight, he got it out of its cabinet and considered trying to play one of the ancient wax cylinders on it. The old records were all tagged with homemade labels, lettered

73

in fading ink with cryptic titles, such as *SIHATHOR ON STONEWORK, March 1937.*

Struck by an idea—it seemed a sane and logical one for once—Scheffler compared the wax recordings with the cassettes stored in a box beside the small modern recorder. The cassettes too were labeled, and many of the titles were the same. Maybe the old man had simply re-recorded them for convenience.

THOTHMES READING STELE, 9/37, was not the most promising title Scheffler could imagine, but neither were any of the others. He put the tape on the machine anyway. It was noisy, poor quality audio, doubtless, as he had suspected, a re-recording of one of the wax cylinders. At the start a man's voice, recognizable as Uncle Monty's, recited: "This was recorded during the second year after our first contact. My date of home departure for this one is September 8, 1937. Return same date."

Following the introduction another man's voice, unknown to Scheffler, performed a lengthy, halting recitation in a language Scheffler did not think he had ever heard before. He supposed it might be Arabic. Or, for all he knew, it might be the tongue spoken by the builders of the Great Pyramid. One was about as useful to him as the other.

If this example was typical, all that the recordings seemed likely to prove was that Uncle Monty had been studying languages as well as archaeology. And it would take days to listen to them all.

Scheffler turned the machine off, giving up on the recordings, at least for the time being.

He got to his feet and moved around the library again. So far he had been examining things that were in view. A man with secrets would probably keep them hidden. Near the fireplace a low, sliding door built into the wall suggested the presence behind it of a closet or cubbyhole designed to bold firewood; but the door, Scheffler discovered, had been lightly nailed shut. He'd already noticed there were some tools, in a small closet near the kitchen.

With the nails pried loose he swung the door open and found himself looking into a deep, low closet, almost filled with an assortment of things, everything but wood. Most conspicuous was a modern outboard motor, of modest size and lightweight construction. It was obviously brand new, still tagged with some of the manufacturer's paperwork which confirmed it as a very recent model. Behind the motor, and further concealed under a pile of miscellaneous junk, were several opened boxes of dynamite—modern also, if the red plasticized shells of the sticks were any indication—along with a battery-powered detonator, some wire, and a small box of blasting caps.

Scheffler put the objects back. He nailed up the door again, and sat in a chair to think.

If he'd come across this treasure trove before he'd found the elevator, he'd have been certain that his uncle was crazy, just flat-out crazy, plotting bank robbery or terrorism. But the elevator, and what it led to, made the whole world crazy. With the Nile so handy, an outboard was probably perfectly relevant.

And with a Pharaoh's tomb, and doubtless a lot of smaller ones around, so was dynamite.

Around the middle of the day Scheffler felt he had to get out of the apartment for a while. The need to outfit himself for his next expedition to the land of the pyramid— he had no doubt that he would have to go at least once more—provided a reason, or at least an excuse. He had five days before school started again, and he had to get this settled. In a few minutes he was walking out of the apartment building, braving a fall of freezing rain.

Walking west, toward a street where he knew there were a couple of surplus stores, Scheffler blinked into the rain. Between Becky and his other distractions he hadn't managed to get a whole lot of sleep during the preceding night.

There had been moments during that night when he had thought wistfully of locking up the grillwork door again, losing the key, and trying his best to forget about the whole thing. But it wasn't the kind of thing that you could very well forget.

When he had seen a little more of pyramid-land for himself, Scheffler decided, it would probably be a good idea after all to call up his mother in Iowa, and probe her for some more information—any scrap might help— about her uncle's past. He'd talked to her at Christmas, of course, and they'd discussed his house-sitting job. His mother had agreed he ought to take it even if it kept him from visiting home over the holidays. But if he talked to her in the mood he was in now, she would know that something was seriously wrong.

Squinting into the frozen mush hurled at him from the skies, Scheffler felt a soreness across the bridge of his nose, and wondered if his brief exposure in pyramid-land might have started to give him a sunburn. Certainly the first essential for his explorer's outfit was going to have to be some kind of broad-brimmed hat. If no appropriate hat turned up in the surplus stores he was about to visit, he would try ransacking some of the remoter closets and cabinets in the apartment—such poking around as he'd done already suggested that there might be rich resources. And a really thorough search, for information as well as useful items, would be a good idea anyway.

What did he need for exploring besides a hat? There were shoes to be considered. A pair of high, ankle-protecting gyms ought to be just what that rocky desert called for, and Scheffler already owned a pair of those.

The neighborhood changed fast in this part of the city when you walked west. He hadn't been squinting into the sleet for very long before he reached the street where the surplus stores flourished. Entering the one he thought might offer him the best selection, Scheffler picked up a plastic basket just inside the door, and started shopping.

Here was a very cheap plastic canteen, which he at once dropped into his basket. But then on second thought he put the plastic bottle back and selected instead a couple of metal ones that came with cloth covers, and a webbed belt to hang them on. Two canteens were not going to be too many for a man walking around in that dry heat for any length of time; and that, Scheffler expected, was just what he was going to have to do.

He'd have to wear a long-sleeved shirt; but no problem, he had some of those. He rubbed his nose gently and grinned. Becky hadn't mentioned it; maybe she thought he'd been to a tanning parlor. He could see himself going back to school after New Year's with a good case of sunburn, and his friends asking him where he'd gone skiing. And here they'd all been thinking he was about to apply for food stamps.

He moved along the aisle. Now hunting knives appeared before him, a cheap-looking selection carefully locked up inside a sturdy case. The grillwork protector on the case was not nearly as strong as some he'd seen. Fortunately he already had a good knife—somewhere. He'd had it since his fifteenth birthday, as he recalled, at a time in his life when he'd been very enthusiastic about hunting squirrels and rabbits. God, that seemed like twenty years ago, though it was only five.

Trouble was he was pretty sure that his hunting knife wasn't in Chicago. Back home in Iowa seemed more likely.

Well, with his extra expense money he could certainly buy one if he had to. But first he'd see if he could find one when he went through the apartment. A good knife would be expensive.

Scheffler turned a corner in the store. Down here in the next aisle were camouflage pants. But Scheffler already had some old khakis, that he thought were even more likely to blend invisibly into that desert background. Ought he, when he went back to look at the pyramid, try to hide and sneak and keep himself from being seen? Hell, yes, he supposed so. Who would he be hiding from, ancient Egyptians? He shook his head; he must be crazy. But then he ran a finger over the gritty reality of the small Band-aid on his hand. He wasn't imagining that. And that pyramid he'd seen hadn't put itself together. That was another thing he could be sure of.

Here were some compasses. A good idea, also cheap. He picked one up and dropped it into his basket. And waterproof matches. Matches were like a knife, something that you always took along when you didn't know where you were going. You never knew when they might be needed.

Halfway along the next aisle, Scheffler came upon some first aid kits. He looked at them without enthusiasm. He'd formed the opinion that most of the medical kits sold in stores were inadequate in one way or another, a ploy to get rid of assorted cheap supplies of doubtful utility that weren't selling very well on their own. He'd do better to make up a kit of his own, from materials in the apartment. Maybe he should have started his outfitting there, and only gone to the stores for what he failed to find in the closets. Well, he had wanted to get out of the apartment, and here he was, so he'd seen what he could find.

There was a snakebite kit, cheap. Scheffler passed it

by, then came back and dropped it into his shopping basket.

Backpacks. The one he used for school was small, but he thought it would be okay. He wasn't intending any extended camping trip.

Here was another locked display case, this one containing the binoculars. Sure. Great. But now that he thought about it he seemed to remember, on a high shelf inside the case of rifles in the apartment, a couple of pairs of binoculars in leather cases. The gun case was locked up, but given the circumstances he intended to find a way to get it open.

Another thing he meant to take along to pyramid-land on his next trip was a notebook and some pencils—no problem there.

And how about a camera? Scheffler had started thinking now. His brain seemed to be working a little better away from the apartment. He knew that Becky had a Polaroid, and he supposed she'd let him borrow it. The trouble, of course, was that she would be curious. Maybe he'd be able to come up with some kind of a story to satisfy her. Probably he wouldn't, though. He'd never been very good at lying.

Gazing around the store and its wild assortment of junk and valuables, Scheffler briefly pondered the possibility of bringing a video camera along. He decided that the possibility was not a strong one. He didn't know offhand where he might borrow such a machine, and certainly he wasn't going to lay out the cash to buy one. A Polaroid, just possibly. All right, yes. He still had almost all of Uncle Monty's five hundred. He'd stop at another store on the way home and buy himself a camera.

And when he went to look at the pyramid again he ought to bring along some food. Yes, he would a few supplies into his pack before he left. Candy bars, trail mix, that kind of thing. Again, he wasn't planning an overnighter. But you never knew.

Walking back to the apartment from his shopping trip, squinting his eyes into the freezing rain again—whichever way you walked it seemed to catch you right in the face— Scheffler kept wondering if Mrs. White might, after all, know something about the elevator. It just didn't seem reasonable to him that she could have cleaned the rest of the apartment for decades and not have at least some suspicions regarding the supposed false door.

Whether or not that monstrous, incredible mass of stone up on the hill was the original Great Pyramid of Giza, it was still there when Scheffler went back again to take a look at it through heat and sunlight. Still there, in the broad daylight of what was either midmorning or midafternoon, though it had been dusk in Illinois when he pulled the tapestry-curtain back into place and closed himself into the elevator once more.

Standing in the savage sun-glare on the lip of the rocky fissure, he pulled the cheap compass out of his shirt pocket and established to his own satisfaction that here it was midafternoon and not midmorning. For this purpose he was going to be daring and assume that, whatever else might happen to the world, the sun still came up in the east.

So the river was east of him, and the pyramid about the same distance to his west and a little south. Last night Scheffler had done a little reading on the geography of Giza, the district of the Pyramids just east of modern Cairo, and he had to admit that the situation he was looking at here seemed to correspond exactly. Everything he could see indicated to him that he was standing on the west bank of the Nile.

The hardest part of that to deal with was that if Khufu, or Cheops as the Greeks came to call him, was still building his great tomb, the year ought to be somewhere near three thousand BC.

Whatever, and whenever, here he was.

Scheffler drew a deep breath, then almost matter-of-factly put the compass away again and got his borrowed binoculars out of their leather case hanging around his neck. As it turned out he hadn't had to break into Uncle Monty's gun cabinet to get at the glasses; the back of one of the drawers in the old man's dresser had given up a set of keys, one of which fit.

With the glasses raised to his eyes, under the broad brim of his new Aussie hat, Scheffler stood in one place for what felt to him like a long time, looking things over in detail.

He started with the pyramid itself. Now he could see many details of the stonework, and of the construction of the ramps that lined its sides. The stone was pale and new-looking, and glared at him. The heat-shimmer continued to make observation difficult, but he thought that with the binoculars he would have been able to see people moving about on the pyramid if anyone were there. It was hard to be sure, though, because there was nothing on the monument or near it to give him a good grasp of its scale.

At last he looked away from the pyramid, and swept the landscape around him with the lenses. No one in sight at all. Had he caught everyone at siesta time again?

Turning around, Scheffler aimed the glasses downhill at the city—or ruin, or whatever it was—where the canal split off from the river. The distance was about the same as that of the pyramid, and this view was equally quivery and unrewarding. The whole world looked dead with heat. But as soon as he looked away from buildings, and began to examine the cultivated land that lay in green strips along both sides of the river, he started to find nonhuman life in plenty. There were many irrigated fields in sight, and in some of those fields Scheffler could observe four-footed animals, evidently some kind of cattle, moving about and grazing. But there was still not a human worker to be seen.

Birds, as before, wheeled in the sky, and skimmed the brown surface of the distant river. At one place close to the near bank Scheffler spotted a log-like object that appeared to be drifting upstream. But if it was a boat, no one was in it.

Along the more distant reaches of riverbank, where the land appeared to be flatter and less rocky, the binoculars could resolve the irrigated fields into neat rectangles and lozenges, separated by mud walls and punctuated with clusters of huts. But even in the villages no one was moving.

He tried the nearby canal, but the binoculars could not penetrate the palm trees and other growth that covered the banks. Presently he put the glasses back into their case that still hung around his neck, and started to walk down the rocky slope toward the canal.

He had not gone more than a few yards when he came upon a collection of artifacts. There was quite an armful of stuff, including pottery, jewelry, textiles and carvings of white and black stone. All of it had been left, jumbled together, in a bushel-sized depression in the rock. Down in the hole the objects would be almost impossible to see from any distance, but otherwise no trouble had been taken to conceal them. They were simply there. As if, perhaps, they were waiting to be collected.

Scheffler left the things where they were and walked on. Sand crunched under the soles of his high-topped gym shoes, and heat radiated at him from all directions.

He made his way cautiously in under the palm trees on the near bank of the canal.

It was indeed a narrow waterway, no more than eight or ten yards wide, and here where the canal was deeply dug the earthen banks of it were high. A footpath followed closely along the top of each bank. The waterway itself, as far as Scheffler could see along its length in either direction, was almost clogged with stalled sailboats and narrow barges or rafts. Some of the boats appeared to be made of nothing but bundles of reeds, but still each of the vessels lined up along the near bank carried at least one massive squared-off block of stone. Each pale stone block had at least one of its surfaces highly polished, almost enough to mirror the sun. In contrast the boats along the far bank were all unloaded, and riding much higher in the water. Loaded or unloaded, none of the vessels were manned, or tied up. All appeared to be drifting freely in the muddy, practically currentless water. One or two of the loaded craft had sunk; one of these remained partially above the surface of the shallow water, and moss was growing on its stone cargo.

As far as be could see, none of the boats were equipped with outboard motors. Here and there a sail hung in rags.

The trail running under Scheffler's feet, right along the top of the bank, had been trodden deeply by many feet. But a long time had passed since there was heavy traffic, and now it was becoming overgrown by grass.

After a minute of looking to right and left, up and down the canal, and still failing to discover any sign of human life, he turned and followed the trail in the direction of the pyramid. He did not forget to memorize some minor landmarks first, so he would know where to leave the waterway again on his way back.

Before he had walked for many yards along the path he was startled by a sudden scurrying movement ahead of him. An object his eyes had told him was a log had abruptly grown short legs and a long tail, and was in motion. With a chill down his spine Scheffler recognized the crocodile for what it was before it splashed into the water.

After a thoughtful pause, in which he tried and failed to follow the creature's progress among the drifting and sunken boats, he continued on his way. Belatedly it now occurred to Scheffler that his Uncle Monty's gun cabinet might represent something more than an extravagant hobby of the old man's youth.

Birds rose crying from the trees ahead of Scheffler as he moved along, to settle down again as soon as he had passed. After the incident of the crocodile they made him start. A fish—or something—splashed nearby in the water. If there were any human beings ahead of Scheffler on this path, these sounds might warn them of his approach. But his boyhood experience with squirrels and crows and rabbits suggested that the birds here, at least, were behaving as if they had not been disturbed by people for many hours, perhaps for days.

Scheffler moved on. At least here in the shade of the palm trees he was spared the very worst of the heat. The path along the far side of the canal was totally empty. Both paths looked as if at one time armies had marched on them and worn them into the banks; perhaps men had walked on them, towing the boats along.

On beginning his walk Scheffler had estimated that the pyramid was approximately a mile away. As he moved along he began to revise this distance upward. The structure grew and grew, becoming more unbelievable as he approached it, and it was obvious that he still had a considerable way to go. How high was it from base to peak? Twenty stories? Thirty? More? He had read some numbers concerning the Great Pyramid in the book last night but he couldn't recall them now. Certainly the monument he was approaching was massive beyond any building that Scheffler had ever seen before.

The skyscrapers of Chicago, or any other city, would be mere splinters of stone and steel if they were set down beside it, though a few of them would be taller. The base of the pyramid must occupy acres and acres of ground space. And the really unbelievable part was that every block of that tremendous mass had been quarried by hand, then brought to the construction on these boats, dragged and lifted into place with human sweat and muscle . . .

But where was the army of workers now? It was time, thought Scheffler, for him to take that question seriously. Maybe he ought to cut short his exploration efforts until he had it figured out. The appearance of the boats, and the fact that some of them had sunk, suggested that the project had been abandoned. The job of putting up the pyramid certainly wasn't finished, though the bulk of the structure had been completed. The ramps for the construction were still in place along the massive sides. And these stones in the boats looked like components of the outer casing, of which only a small portion had actually been installed.

Presently Scheffler reached the end of the canal. It was a large circular pool with no other outlet, occupied by more boats and rafts, some of them loaded, some not, all deserted. Again a few had been dragged to the shallow bottom by their loads. Here, at a broad dock, began a double roadway, leading overland to the pyramid. The trail of stone blocks continued along one of the roads, leaving the rafts and the brown-sailed riverboats behind, and advancing from here on by means of a line of wooden sledges. Loadbearing sledges were on the roadway to Scheffler's right, while the empty ones had been coming back along the left. The sledges, loaded and unloaded alike, were as motionless and deserted by their owners as the boats. All was silence and stillness in the heat. Sand had drifted over some of the wooden runners.

The pyramid, built on slightly higher ground, was now so close ahead that Scheffler had to tilt his head back to get a good look at it. He moved on toward it, along the road that bore the blocks.

Reluctantly, but feeling a compulsion to do so, Scheffler left the shade of the canal-side palms and trudged on up the barren hillside, squinting into unrelenting heat.

When he had reached the top of the first rise he was able to see the remainder of the roads that stretched between him and the pyramid. They were occupied by hundreds more of the sledges. After passing through an area of barrack-like huts, the roads blurred into a great terminal area of ground rendered flat and barren by the traffic of construction, that appeared to surround the base of the pyramid. From each corner of the base that he could see, a ramp went up, bearing stones and sledges with it.

Scheffler stopped beside the nearest sledge to examine it more closely. Two ropes of strange-looking fiber had been attached at the front end. The ropes were lying loosely on the ground, as if the men who must have been pulling on them had simply dropped them and walked away. It must have been men who had hauled the stones, for these were not harnesses for animals. These were simply ropes, long ropes, made to be gripped and pulled by many hands. Scheffler paused to pick up one of the lines. It felt rough and strange. The unfamiliar fiber, whatever it was, was uneven in thickness, not put together by a machine. In contrast the sides and edges of the stones themselves appeared incredibly smooth and straight.

And there were the two ruts, slick-surfaced, in each roadway, made by the runners of the sledges, or perhaps made for them. The ruts looked as if someone had worked on them to make them smooth.

Belatedly Scheffler recalled the Polaroid slung at his side. He stopped now and got the camera out of its case and used it, several times. He was unfamiliar with it and worked slowly, but to good effect. He caught the pyramid itself, still in the middle distance, and took a couple of good shots of the blocks of polished stone on their sledges in the foreground. He decided that he would pause on his way back and get some pictures of the canal. What he'd do with the photos when he got them home he didn't know yet. But it seemed to him there ought to be something that could be done. Eventually someone was going to have to know about all this.

The sun, he thought, was already noticeably lower in the sky than it had been on his arrival. He was approaching the pyramid from an angle that would soon allow him to take advantage of its slowly lengthening shadow. All right, he would go on, for a little while longer anyway. But he mustn't fail, no matter what, to get back to his elevator before dark. Once night fell it would be all too easy to miss the way. He could imagine falling into that canal, or stepping on a crocodile invisible in darkness.

Scheffler moved on, setting a fairly good pace but stopping at short intervals to look around, and pausing frequently to sip from one of his canteens. It was a good thing he'd brought two—already he'd gone through almost a quart of water, he realized. Coming into this heat directly from winter was just too much.

Now he began to notice that here and there along the trail were pottery jugs, some smashed, many still intact. Most of them were large vessels, twenty-gallon size or bigger. Probably they were meant to be carried by two men, because each pot was complete with its own long shoulder-pole and sling. Scheffler paused to move one of the intact big jugs with his foot. No water left in it now. How long would water take to evaporate in this dry heat?

Shadow was darkening the pyramid on its north and east faces—the great building seemed to be aligned precisely with the compass, just as Uncle Monty had said— and the shade was stretching out with tantalizing slowness to meet Scheffler as he advanced. Everything else around him was jumping and quivering in the energy of this desert furnace. He tried the binoculars again, but now the more he looked through them the less he saw. The heat appeared to be increasing—if it weren't for his hat and his long sleeves, he thought, he'd be dead by now, fried to a crisp. Next time he'd bring the other pair of glasses— those, as he recalled, were only seven-power. Maybe less magnification would be better in this shimmering glare.

The watch he wore on his left wrist, showing just slightly beyond the end of his long shirtsleeve, looked strange and out of place. He'd forgotten again to look at it when he arrived, so it wasn't going to help him any. Next time maybe he'd just leave it home.

Scheffler was beginning to be frightened. He was suffering from the heat. And at the same time he realized that in a strange and almost unfamiliar way he was enjoying himself.

At last he stepped into the shadow of the pyramid, and stopped to wipe his forehead. Shade helped enormously against the heat.

Now, just ahead of him, between him and the base itself, stretched the rows of mudbrick huts. Their gray walls were indistinguishable one from another, and their roofs were of reed bundles or dried palm leaves. These shacks, as he passed among them, looked just as unpopulated as the rest of the surrounding world.

Then he was startled again, as a dog, a little gray-brown mutt without a collar, ran out from somewhere and barked at him. It came within a few yards of Scheffler, then circled away. It looked scrawny and sounded vicious, and its eyes were those of a wild animal. Scheffler, who generally liked dogs and did well managing them, called to the beast but it would not come to him.

Eventually the dog got tired of making noise and disappeared. Scheffler pushed on toward the pyramid, pausing several times to look in the doorless openings of the nearest huts. The shadowed interiors contained a few more pottery jars, and rags of cloth, scattered about or hanging on simple racks. He thought that he could detect, very faint, the musty smell of crowded humanity, blended with odors of smoke and spice, hanging in the air inside the huts. But no fires had burned for some time in the small hearths, and no one was there.

As Scheffler gained yet higher ground, and was able to see over most of the huts, he came in sight of stone buildings in the middle distance. These were much larger and more substantial than the huts, though insignificant in comparison with the pyramid itself. They stood within a stone's throw of its northern flank. Again Scheffler paused to look, but no one moved among those buildings either.

There were no other pyramids anywhere in sight. Khufu's was the first to be built here, Uncle Monty had said.

And now, at last, Scheffler had reached the base of the artificial mountain itself.

Scheffler put out a hand and touched its stones, still hot from the day's sun. Then he moved through shadow along the east face of the pyramid's base, until he reached and turned the northern corner. The north side was still tenuously in shade. Almost in the center of the north side and about forty feet above the ground—still quite near the bottom—was a small dark gap that undeniably looked like an entrance. *The* entrance. It was certainly the only one in sight. He couldn't remember if the model back in the apartment had more than one.

He climbed to the mouth of the dark, open hole, scrambling up the giants' stair of beautifully fitted limestone blocks, each tier four feet high or higher. When Scheffler reached the entrance, he found it was too small for him to walk into it erect. He felt reluctant to go into it at all. The passage was filled with darkness and went down and into the pyramid at an angle of thirty degrees or so.

Scheffler had his flashlight in his backpack. But he didn't feel like trapping himself or confining himself inside a cave. First he wanted to see more of this world.

He walked along the same tier of stones until he reached the ramp that went up from the northeast corner, and then stood looking up the long gentle slope of the ramp, no more than ten degrees or so, he estimated. The narrow roadway—it was hardly wider than one of the sledges that it carried—extended for about seven hundred feet, climbing diagonally across the giants' stairway of stone blocks, before reaching its first sharp corner. The ramp was built of much less carefully finished stone in smaller blocks, topped with mud bricks and surfaced with clay. The dried crust of its upper surface had, like the roads below, been smoothed and slicked into two almost glossy ruts, spaced to accommodate sledge runners. At several places along the ramp, groups of the loaded sledges were now jammed together. It looked as if some had slid down into others, like motor-vehicles on an icy hill. But here all the drivers had simply walked away.

Between the ruts the clay crust of the ramp was rough

and hard, offering a good grip to climbing feet. Scheffler went on up. All along the way there continued to be pottery fragments, as of broken water jars. And here and there, as on the road and pathway below, some of the jars had fallen without breaking. Or they might have been set down carefully, intact, in that last moment before the work force vanished.

An interesting question: how, why, to where in this desert, would an army of men vanish and not take their supply of water with them? It would only make sense, perhaps, if they were going to the canal, then to the river. But in that case you would think they'd at least take their boats along.

Scheffler, trudging slowly upward, climbing the Great Pyramid, began to realize that if he stayed on the ramp he'd have to walk about a mile to get to the top. Besides, that roundabout route would bring him back into the sun, whereas if he stayed on the northern and eastern faces of the pyramid he could continue in the shade. So when he was about halfway along the northern face, he deserted the ramp and began to climb the great stair made by the side of the pyramid itself. Still each tier of blocks was something like four feet high. It wasn't easy going, but Scheffler was in good shape and he kept at it, with an occasional pause to rest and look about and sip at a canteen. One of his canteens was completely emptied by this time, and he'd made a good start on the second.

When he came to the next leg of the ramp, running diagonally athwart his path, he used the hunting knife he'd borrowed from Uncle Monty to dig small grips and toeholds into the clay portions of the construction, and so went on up.

The climb between ramps was harder than he'd expected, and for a time he went back to trudging along a ramp again, coming out into the sun when he'd turned

a corner, but forging ahead anyway. By now he'd totally
lost any sense of how long he'd been here. Even the heat
could almost be forgotten, as the world below him spread
out farther and farther with his ascent.

Sometimes he stopped and looked around. There was
never anyone to see.

Anxiously he kept an eye on the sun, not wanting to
be caught here after dark. The sun was getting lower.
But he couldn't bring himself to turn back yet. He went
on up.

Working his way around another cluster of stalled
sledges, he came upon a discarded leather sandal, plainly
made and sadly worn. He picked up and turned over in
his hands the morsel of blackened, hardened hide. The
thong that had once attached it to a human foot was
broken. The outline still to be seen on the inner surface
of the sole showed that the wearer's foot had been
considerably smaller than Scheffler's; in fact it was hardly
within what he would have considered the adult range
of size.

He tossed the relic behind him on the ramp. Then,
after a moment's thought, he turned around and retrieved
it, stuffing it into one of the side pockets of his pack.
What he still wanted was evidence, evidence of the reality
of this place to take back with him, even though he wasn't
sure what he was going to do with the evidence when
he got it home. Maybe he just wanted to be able to look
at it in Chicago.

He snapped another Polaroid, catching the shadow of
the pyramid falling across some of the workers' shacks
below.

Then he once more moved on, and up, through the
enveloping silence and the heat.

The triangle of the east face was narrowing noticeably
around him now; the pointed summit was much closer

than it had been. At the very apex, the topmost stone, smooth and sharply pointed, glinted as if its surface were pure gold. The upper few yards of the pyramid, already sheathed in the smooth casing-stones, were pale and smooth and gleaming. The ramps stopped at the lower edge of the finished portion. Evidently the plan was to remove the ramps from the top down, as the last stage of the building progressed downward.

Scheffler paused to try the binoculars once more. From this height, which he estimated at forty or fifty stories above the river and its valley, he could look over the stone walls of the settlement on the near bank, and see down into its empty streets. In one place there, color and movement caught his eye. He looked for a full minute before he was convinced that it was only a couple of bright banners, stirring in a faint breeze.

He could still see no one in the city. Or anywhere else. No one at all.

He let the binoculars hang on their sling around his neck, and wiped his forehead. He looked down.

He froze.

There was a cigarette butt, a genuine, filterless cigarette butt, flattened as if by a careful shoe, on the rock right at his feet.

Scheffler looked up, and around. He could feel this almost-pristine world trying to turn into a giant movie set before his eyes. As if there were, or could be, anyone in the world who was able to build a movie set like this.

He wiped his forehead. The heat was getting to him. He decided not to go on all the way to the top today. Time and water were running out on him. Stooping, he picked up the butt, and buttoned it carefully into his shirt pocket.

Enough for today. He would have to call it enough,

unless he was prepared to spend the night. He wanted to get home and think.

He was halfway down the enormous slope again, moving faster on the descent, when the voice from below, hailing him, broke jarringly into his thoughts.

"Hallooo!" It was a high voice, thin and piercing. It had to be that of a woman or a girl.

Scheffler looked down, to see a tiny helmeted figure in khaki, waving its arms at him. Mechanically he returned the wave. Why not? It was certainly too late now to avoid being seen.

"Yoouuu! Come down here!"

He couldn't tell if the words that the thin, imperious voice was shouting at him constituted a warning, or an order, or something in between. Anyway, he had no intention of doing anything else but going down.

Changing the angle of his descent, he went down the giant shadowed stair at a good pace, one short jump after another. Meanwhile the tiny figure below, evidently eager to meet Scheffler at close quarters, began to struggle its way up. The advantage of speed being naturally with the descending party, the two of them were fairly close to the ground when they met.

It was indeed a young woman who had hailed him. She was wearing somewhat more formal exploration garb than Scheffler's, but it was worn and dusty. She was about his own age, he thought. Her face, despite the lightweight pith helmet that shaded it pretty effectively, was burned and cracked around the lips. Eyes of a startling shade of blue looked out from that band of shade. Her hair, black or dark brown, had been tied up under the helmet, but it was coming loose, and Scheffler could see how sand and dust had been ingrained in every strand. She was wearing a light khaki jacket with long sleeves to protect her arms, and the kind of riding pants—jodphurs, he seemed to remember they were called—that puffed out at the thighs. Battered and dusty leather boots enclosed slim ankles. A large canteen hung from her webbed belt at one hip, and a large pistol holster held a large revolver at the other.

She stood with her arms folded, waiting suspiciously until he was only four tiers above her. Then she demanded: "Who're you?" And, in almost the same breath: "Where's Monty?"

Scheffler came to a stop three tiers above her, gasping in the heat. "He's, uh, he couldn't come. He asked me to kind of look after things for him."

"Damnation." She tapped a couple of times, impatiently, with the toe of one boot on the stone. "You're one of his students from the University, I assume." At close range and low volume the young woman's voice was still high, but it was well-controlled now and not unpleasant. It carried to Scheffler's ears a trace of some indefinable accent, possibly some variety of British. Australian, maybe? He was no expert on accents. Perhaps she was, after all, a few years older.

"That's right. A student. Tom Scheffler." He intended to let the lady retain as many of her assumptions as possible.

By now her eyes had fastened on the camera case hanging around Scheffler's neck, and her indignation was rising. "What's that? A camera? Damn it, did Doctor Chapel tell you to come here and take pictures?"

"Uh, yes. But I haven't taken any yet."

"You'd better not. God. Pictures. I'll have to talk to him, I don't know what he's thinking of." The young woman, tilting her head back to look up at him, and squinting even in the shade, took off her pith helmet long enough to struggle briefly with her long, damp hair. She really was uncommonly good-looking, Scheffler thought.

She asked him, sharply: "And why couldn't the good Doctor Montgomery make it here today?"

"Well. He didn't really tell me why." Scheffler realized that he probably sounded like a hopeless idiot. Not that he minded, as long as he could learn something.

Her blue eyes glared at him. "And I suppose he's promised you a share."

Ready to be agreeable, Scheffler nodded.

The young woman's wrath was slowly building; though, as Scheffler observed gratefully, it did not appear to be aimed so much at him as at the absent Monty. She said: "Well, you're in it now, and there's nothing to be done about it. That's that. Your share will have to come out of his, not ours. And for God's sake don't take any pictures."

"Okay."

"And what were you climbing way up there for? The view? We don't have time for that kind of stuff just now."

"Okay."

"You can carry back an armload of artifacts, we've left some near the timelock. And we've got an inventory of that batch." The last sentence seemed to be intended as a warning.

Scheffler nodded. "I saw them there in a kind of pothole when I came—"

"And for God's sake, next time come armed. We even heard lions last night. It won't be long before they're bold enough to come right up here to the pyramid. And did Monty tell you about the water?"

"I . . . no."

"You can drink from the river, or the canal, if necessary, as long as you're returning within a couple of hours— because, you see, the lock itself will take care of any bacteria you might pick up. If you're staying here longer than a few hours, I wouldn't chance it."

"Uh, no, of course not."

Once more she looked at him suspiciously. "You're keeping quiet about this." It was more a statement than a question. "I assume that Monty made it very clear to you what'll happen if you don't."

"Sure. I'm keeping quiet."

"Well. All right, get to work, then. We do need the help. Take back that stuff we left in the pothole, and get rid of that camera. Stop, wait a minute. Is Monty coming through tomorrow? He's not sick or anything, is he?"

"Doctor Chapel looked fine when I saw him. As far as I know he's all right."

"I see you're carrying his binoculars."

"He loaned them to me."

"All right, then, get on with it." She waved her hand in dismissal. "We'll have more stuff for you by tomorrow morning."

Scheffler nodded, and made his way past her down the great stair of the unfinished pyramid. He moved along about as quickly as was feasible in the heat, heading for the elevator—he would have to start thinking of it as the timelock now.

Halfway to the canal he looked back once. The nameless young woman was still watching him.

He hastened on his way, listening for lions.

EIGHT

The great Pharaoh—unchallenged Lord of the Two Lands, beloved of Osiris and Ra, Isis and Horus, peer of a multitude of lesser gods than those—was dead. Khufu's unexpected passing, after an illness of only a few days, had taken his entire kingdom by surprise. Caught unprepared were priests and generals, nobility and peasants—all of the circles of intrigue within the Palace, as well as all of Pharaoh's worshippers and friends, within the Palace and without.

And all of Pharaoh's secret enemies.

Since that shocking day when Great Khufu had breathed his last, Aah the moongod had twice passed through his cycle of unceasing change. The final steps of the embalming process had been finished only three days ago, and only today had the Pharaoh's funeral procession completed its slow and majestic progress from one temple to another, in the vicinity of Memphis and the Palace. Only today had those last rites reached their culmination with the entombment of the Pharaoh's mummy, along with the bulk of his personal treasure.

His stupendous tomb, the pyramid upon which a generation of his people had spent long seasons of their labor, was still not entirely finished, but on the day after Khufu's death the Chief Builder had pronounced it ready to receive and to protect the Pharaoh's body.

✧   ✧   ✧

"Perhaps," said Ptah-hotep to his friend Thothmes, "we built too quickly and too well."

It was late in the afternoon on the day of Pharaoh's burial, and the two men were sitting together on a small terrace on one of the higher roof-levels of the Palace. It was a secluded place and free of eavesdroppers.

The inhabitants of the Palace had been especially affected by the prolonged rituals of mourning. Even now those ceremonies had not quite ended. As Ptah-hotep and Thothmes talked, they could hear the endless wailing of the women in a distant courtyard. And in a closer courtyard, almost directly below them, the two men could see the slow steps of the dancers beginning the celebration of the Feast of Eternity.

"Whether we built too well or not," said Thothmes, "we were certainly promoted at the wrong time." With the notable exception of the Chief Builder himself, none of the officials who had supervised the construction of the passages inside the lower and middle levels of the pyramid had been allowed to remain in the same jobs while the upper third of the structure was completed. Shortly after that day some years ago when Ptah-hotep had arranged for Sihathor to see into the pyramid's heart, both Ptah-hotep and Thothmes had been given positions in the Palace. Nominally both changes had been promotions; but from that day to this, neither man had been able to learn anything more regarding any final changes that Pharaoh might have decreed in the design for his tomb.

"Tomorrow the funeral singers will be silent in the Palace," said Ptah-hotep. "And the dancers will be still at last." Despite the fact that his secret plans of many years were not about to be brought to fruition, he felt an emptiness. Khufu's reign had endured for twenty-three years, and Ptah-hotep, like many another subject, could remember no other Pharaoh.

"And tomorrow the preparations for the new Pharaoh's coronation will begin," Thothmes offered. "Already everyone's thoughts have turned to that."

"That is all to the good if we are going to act this very night," Ptah-hotep said.

Thothmes signed agreement.

From their high vantage point the two friends could see the mourning city of Memphis spread out below them, and part of the broad river. They could also see, at least two miles away, the almost-finished pyramid. From where they stood the great mass of stone lay partially in shadow, and faintly blue with distance. Ptah-hotep was thinking that there was no telling how long it might take Sihathor and his expert crew to break their way through all those granite plugs and deadfalls, or alternately tunnel around them through the softer limestone. Of course the job would be—or ought to be—enormously simplified by the secret information Sihathor had already been given. But at best forcing an entry would be far from easy—and it would be complicated by alterations in the design made during the last few years. Certainly to reach the burial chamber would take many days and many nights for even the most skillful and industrious grave robbers.

"Our rendezvous with the stonemason is set for midnight?" Thothmes asked softly.

"Yes. If you and I depart by boat from the Palace docks at sunset, we should have ample time to reach the place."

"I foresee no problem. No one now attends the docks." From where the two men sat they could observe the deserted piers lining the canal. A multitude of small boats, all sizes and all shapes, were waiting to be used.

The news of the Pharaoh's death had spread rapidly to the ends of his kingdom, and for the past two months all but the most necessary work had come to a halt across the land. Artisans, priests and laborers of every kind had turned away as much as possible from their usual tasks, and for two months many of them had been working to their capacity in preparation for the greatest funeral procession in history.

Even the last phase of construction on the Horizon of Khufu had been halted temporarily, two months ago. The finishing touches could be given the pyramid, the remainder of its outer sheathing of finely polished stones set into place, the great construction ramps torn down and the rubble from them cleared away, just as well after the funeral as before. As a consequence, Thothmes and Ptah-hotep, as well as the officials who now directly supervised the construction, had been able to take time out from their administrative jobs for an extended period of official mourning.

All of the commanders of the military units detailed to take the first shift as guardians of Khufu's tomb had already been subverted; by the leaders of the robbers' cult of Set. The cult already claimed a few of those officers as members. The others, long impoverished on soldiers' pay, when made aware of golden opportunity, had agreed to keep their men at a convenient distance.

As for Dedefre, the Pharaoh to be, it was whispered within the Palace that he would not be greatly saddened to know that his father would be unable to keep all his treasure with him for eternity.

"It is time," said Ptah-hotep to Thothmes softly. "Let us go down to the docks and select a boat."

Like almost all the other subjects of Pharaoh Khufu, Sihathor the stonemason, the son of an ancient and respected line of quarry workers, masons and tomb-robbers, had piously observed an extended period of ritual lamentation. But that was over now. Like many another busy workman across the land, the stonemason had shortened his formal mourning because of practical considerations. Two days ago Sihathor, accompanied by half a dozen carefully chosen assistants, and well equipped with tools and supplies, had started downriver from his home village.

Now, shortly before sunset on the day of Khufu's burial, Sihathor was docking his boat at a deserted landing on the west bank of the Nile, close to the land of the dead that sprawled across the desert west of Memphis and the Palace.

Whenever the expert robber undertook an expedition to this great burial ground, he began by transporting himself and his working family downstream. Sailing his borrowed fisherman's boat back upstream when the job was over occupied him for a few more days, depending on the wind. He and his crew of helpers always engaged in some actual fishing enroute, which not only provided them with some fish but helped to allay suspicion.

Of his two professions, the secret one was by far the more profitable. For that reason, as well as for secrecy, the forty-year-old patriarch Sihathor much preferred to use family members, both male and female, as his helpers. Every one of the six assistants disembarking with him this evening was related to him by blood or marriage. There were three men, two of them his sons and one his son-in-law, two young women, daughter and daughter-in-law respectively; and one half-grown boy, Sihathor's youngest son. The two young couples had left their own small children in their home village, in the capable care of their grandmother, Sihathor's good wife.

The day was waning fast as the family of Sihathor tied

up their boat and left it behind them. But night had not
yet come; the sun still glowed above the western land of
graves and death as they lifted their burdens of tools
and provisions and made their way along a path that
threaded its way between irrigated fields toward the
nearby desert. Around them was heat, silence and stillness,
all field workers having been excused from labor on this
day of Pharaoh's burial.

Thus far the way was familiar to Sihathor, and to several
of his helpers who had come with him on previous
expeditions. The patriarch and leader of the band of
robbers advanced alertly, moving in advance of the others.
Secret messages had reached him at his village, assuring
him that tonight he would find no soldiers in his way.
Yet sometimes he had received misleading messages from
the cult-leaders. Soldiers who were thought to be safely
bribed did not always stay that way. And it had been said
for a long time that the Chief Builder, and certain of
the high-ranking priests of the sun-god Ra, had committed
themselves with the most fanatical vows to the protection
of Khufu's mummy.

There had been no devotees of Set among the officials
at the pyramid during Sihathor's last tour of duty there
as a conscript laborer, almost a year ago. No one in
authority had been there to put the final secrets of the
tomb's construction before his eyes, and he had been
unable to get near those secrets on his own.

Since that one day years before, when he had been allowed
one glimpse into the pyramid's unfinished heart, the
stoneworker's thoughts had often returned to it. In his
memory he had gone over and over the arrangements of
traps and blocks and barriers. The design might well have
been changed since then, of course—there had been rumors
that Pharaoh, however decisive on other matters, had been
chronically unable to make up his mind on this one.

But as yet Sihathor had said nothing to anyone, not even his family, about these matters. None of the helpers with him tonight were aware of the true goal of this expedition. None of them, not even his wife at home, dreamt that he had been chosen to lead the actual entry into the tomb of Pharaoh himself, or that the operation might begin tonight. He had instead told his helpers that their objective was a much more modest tomb. Not until the last moment, if everything went well, would he reveal even to his own sons the true objective of this journey.

Having progressed less than a thousand paces inland from the bank of the Nile, Sihathor and his followers came to the abrupt boundary of cultivated land. The path went on visibly for a few score paces into desert soil, before fading with the hardness of the ground.

Now, a few hundred paces farther in the same direction, and the sand grew softer underfoot; and they were moving on a circuitous route through the City of the Dead, the vast burial ground within a mile or two of Memphis, and of the pyramid.

As they passed among the first graves, Sihathor and his co-workers were carrying with them a good supply of food, mostly figs, dried fish, and bread, enough to sustain them for some days inside the pyramid. No one had expressed surprise at the amount of the provisions; he wondered if any of the young people were wondering about it silently. It would be necessary to emerge at night for water. The young men were also carrying, in slings of papyrus and cord, their heavy dolerite hammers, egg-shaped rocks bigger than fists but smaller than human heads, and harder even than granite. They carried the pounders in the businesslike fashion of workers going to a quarry.

As he walked, Sihathor could hear behind him the quietly eager voices of the young people, speculating softly on the probable amount of loot they might obtain tonight. He smiled faintly to himself, thinking of their awe and delight when at last they learned the truth.

Sihathor's secret appointment with the two officials was not scheduled until midnight. That was hours away, too long to simply wait in idleness. If conditions and omens continued to appear favorable, he meant to improve the intervening hours by opening—partly for practice, partly for the almost certain profit—a much more modest tomb than that of Pharaoh. As for the pyramid itself, well, despite his eagerness Sihathor still had some doubts. He would be certain that the job was actually his only when he was actually at work inside one of those dark passageways.

Besides, though the loot extracted from Pharaoh's tomb would undoubtedly be fabulous, almost all of it would certainly go to the leaders of the cult of Set. Not that Sihathor was about to cross those leaders openly, but still he felt some resentment. Like the other powerful people of the world, they tended always to demand too much from the poor. Sihathor still considered himself a poor and humble man, though in fact, after a long and successful career, he possessed hidden wealth enough to rival the lesser nobility. As his secret career prospered, Sihathor and his wife had continued to live simply in a mudbrick hut but little bigger than those of the other inhabitants of his village. Two of his children, older than any of those with him on this expedition, were already living in Memphis, making their way in the world with social advantage, thanks to favors purchased by their humble father's hidden wealth.

Many years ago Sihathor had established a working relationship with the lord of the villa to which his village was nominally attached. This arrangement allowed Sihathor's periodic absences from his home village and his ordinary work there to go unquestioned by any authority. Sometimes the lord of the villa fenced his stolen jewelry and other valuables for him. On other occasions the grave robber had himself paddled his borrowed fishing boat along the waterfront of Memphis to sell his treasures. A man who knew where to seek buyers could manage in this way to reap much greater profits, though Sihathor always took care to reserve some item of particular value for his lord on his return to his village. That was of course in addition to the share that inevitably had to be set aside for the priests of Set.

Now Dhu-hotep, the older of the two sons of Sihathor who had come with him, asked his father to which part of the vast, sprawling cemetery they were headed.

"You will see presently." The fact was that Sihathor, as he continued to move in the general direction of his rendezvous, did not know specifically what small tomb he would shortly attempt to rob. He would not know until it materialized before his experienced eyes out of the heat-shimmer of late afternoon. There appeared to be no need to wait for darkness; the City of the Dead looked as deserted by the living as it could be.

Presently a tomb of suitable appearance came into Sihathor's sight. When this happened, the stoneworker blessed Set for guiding him to the proper place. Then he walked around the low, broad structure, considering it with professional attention.

The tomb was large enough to be that of some wealthy person, a little bigger than any peasant's house. But the portion above ground was so low that a man could easily see over its flat stone roof. Fresh stone chips and other signs of construction indicated that this was a recent interment, and therefore it was not very likely to have been robbed already. Reading the inscription on a stele, Sihathor saw that the burial had been that of the wife of some comparatively minor Palace official.

Now Sihathor moved closer, eyeing the details of the stonework professionally in the last rays of the sun. This was only a simple mastaba-tomb, presenting no real tricks or problems. But still, to get at the valuables that were certain to be inside was going to require some heavy stone-breaking.

Only now did Sihathor signal to his family that they had reached their destination.

Before settling down to work, even before prayers, he first established a lookout—that, in the active service of Set, always came first. Then he gathered the rest of his people together and led them in a few prayers to Set, a type of devotion to which all of them were accustomed.

The members of his family responded fervently. These were young people who realized and appreciated both the great opportunities and the dangers of their position.

Just as their prayers were finished, the moment of sunset came.

The lookout—Sihathor's daughter-in-law, named Sepet—had been stationed atop the tomb. At the moment when the sun sank below the horizon, she gave a sharp outcry.

Speaking together, her father-in-law and her husband demanded to know what was the matter.

"What have you seen?"

But only reluctantly did the young woman try to explain. "I was looking toward the sunset, and I saw . . ."

"What?"

"I saw the Barque of Ra."

The others members of her family stared at her in bewilderment.

Sepet gestured helplessly. "I do not mean simply the sun. I saw . . . the Boat. With oars, and sails like glorious clouds. And Ra himself, Ra-Harakhty, standing in the middle, with his countenance like flame."

There were no clouds, glorious or otherwise, to be seen in the western sky.

Still, though they all doubted, no one really scoffed at the vision. Some thought that it represented an omen unfavorable to any important undertaking, and advised immediate retreat.

But Sihathor, knowing much more was at stake tonight than this small tomb, refused to be easily discouraged. He sent two people to scout the cemetery in all directions, to make as sure as possible that they were not going to be disturbed. Then Sihathor selected the spot on the stone wall of the tomb where he judged it would be easiest to force an entry. In a new tomb like this one the surface of the stone had not yet had time to discolor, and this made the job of selection somewhat harder; discolored stone sometimes revealed its flaws, places where it could more easily be broken.

Then he motioned to his aides to get to work.

Sihathor's eldest son and son-in-law, each holding a hammerstone in an easy two-handed grip, now lifted their implements of dolerite, and one after the other let them fall. With two hammers rising and falling steadily on the same spot, pulverized limestone began to trickle rapidly from the point of impact, and flakes of the same material flew thick and fast. The workmen were young and energetic, and it was possible to watch the hole in the tomb's flank deepen, moment by moment. If it had been a granite block here, such as they were certainly going to find in Pharaoh's tomb, Sihathor thought, progress would have been considerably slower. Added to that when they reached the pyramid would be the difficulties of working inside a cramped and almost airless passage. But somehow they would find a way; the power of Set would not desert them.

Tonight the men did not sing as they worked, as they

ordinarily would have done—during a normal job of mere stonework.

The women, not needed for any heavy tasks as yet, spread out to keep watch, each of them at a small distance in a different direction. Meanwhile Sihathor himself, aided by his youngest son, whose name was Temu, saw to the creation of a small fire. The fire had to be located in exactly the right place, and shielded by cloth screens, so that it would remain almost invisible at a distance while providing just enough light for the men with hammers to see what they were doing. As usual on his tomb-robbing expeditions, the robber had brought fire with him on the boat all the way from home, a smoldering punk of oily wood, hidden and protected in several layers of dampened skins.

As the younger members of his family labored and stood guard, the thoughts of Sihathor began to wander. Naturally enough they moved ahead to the time when he would have the honor of leading the way into the tomb of Pharaoh. Some, at least, of the masters of his cult would be there when the time came to enter the burial chamber. Already Sihathor was honored by being trusted by the mighty; Ptah-hotep himself, who had been Chief Priest for the construction of the tomb, whose name Sihathor knew but would never speak if he could help it, had spoken directly to the humble villager, who afterward had been summoned to take part in the greatest robbery ever planned or executed since the beginning of the world. The mighty men who were in charge of the enterprise knew many things that he, a poor peasant and stonecutter, would never know; yet, Sihathor told himself frequently, when it came to dealing with the rocks, the walls and doors and traps, he was the one man in all the land of Khem they called upon for help.

Dutifully Sihathor took time out from his musings to supervise the work. Then, as everything remained so quiet, he gave in to the soft pleas of Temu his youngest son, and allowed the lad to take a turn at pounding on the rock. The hole had already grown deep enough to allow only one hammerer to reach the bottom; after considering the advantages and disadvantages, Sihathor ordered that the hole be slightly widened. The work went on at high speed, the workers relieving one another frequently.

Listening to the quick hypnotic thud of the stone hammers, Sihathor went back to meditating about one of his favorite subjects, Pharaoh's gold. Or dreaming about it, rather . . .

When he looked up, it was with deep awareness that something was subtly off-key, although the thud of hammers went on as before, and the cemetery seemed as dark and quiet as ever.

But something was wrong. Sihathor's experienced instincts could not be mistaken in such a matter, though none of the lookouts had noticed anything as yet.

An owl, disturbed somewhere nearby in the cemetery, flew overhead in absolute silence.

Sihathor's shout of warning sounded only moments before torch bearing soldier-guardians of the necropolis came leaping upon his family out of the night.

Casting tools and provisions aside in a mad scramble, Sihathor and his people took to their heels. Even as they fled creeping soldiers without torches rose up to seize them, shouting to try to immobilize them with terror.

Sand flew from beneath Sihathor's pounding feet. Small tombs and large loomed out of the darkness and fell behind him as he ran.

Somehow, to his own astonishment, he avoided capture. After brief moments the shouts of the soldiers fell behind with the torchlight. Another pair of pounding feet gained on him. As they drew near he turned in fear to recognize the small form of his youngest son.

Presently Sihathor slowed his pace, then stopped. Drawing Temu with him behind a tomb, he settled in to regain his breath, to watch and wait. It was amazing. For the time being at least, the cemetery was quiet and dark again.

Soon another dim lone form appeared—not a soldier, or a ghost, but Sihathor's son-in-law. The three conferred in whispers, then started stealthily for their boat. It was a standing arrangement that survivors of a raid should meet there if possible.

Two others were already at the boat when they arrived; everyone but Sepet had managed to get away. The family looked at one another, half-frightened by such good fortune, and muttered prayers to Set.

Exchanging stories, they learned that each of them had had a hairsbreadth escape from capture. Soldiers who had had them surrounded, almost caught, had vanished in the winking of an eye, their weapons and torches with them.

Huddled together around the beached boat, Sihathor's family heard the voice of a young woman calling to them through the night. Hesitantly they answered the call. In a few moments Sepet joined them. She was walking strangely, and when she drew near they saw that her arms were tied together behind her back.

Her tale of escape was stranger even than the others. She had been caught and bound by the soldiers. Then to her vast surprise she had suddenly found herself alone again; the soldiers had all abruptly vanished. After a while she had struggled to her feet and made her way, arms still bound behind her, to the boat.

For a long time after Sepet's story no one said anything.

Now, it seemed, the world was again as it had always been, the night was just another night, with the stars stable in their places above. The Nile flowed as always, and the night-birds cried and hooted. But the lights of the pursuing soldiers had vanished as completely as if the marsh had swallowed them.

Sihathor, after asking the opinions of each member of his family, praying to Set, and taking thought, decided that they had been saved by some beneficent power; the best thing he could do would be to try to keep his rendezvous with the high officials in the neighborhood of the pyramid. If they encountered soldiers again, well, he could revert to his identity as poor fisherman and small trader, whose boat had been capsized by a hippopotamus. It was not an unlikely accident to meet with in the Nile, not even here near the metropolis of Memphis.

Once more he and his family set out on foot, heading inland from the boat. But now, feeling it necessary to detour widely from his previous route, Sihathor soon came into unfamiliar territory. The pyramid of course was visible even in the dark, but Sihathor was no longer confident of being able to reach the place of rendezvous. It was beside a canal, but he knew that more than one canal traversed the area, and all of those waterways were unfamiliar to him.

Not being able to find the two officials disturbed him, but not as much as the strange occurrences of the night. Yes, something very strange indeed was happening in the land tonight. Eventually he decided that the best thing to do was to lie low and wait for morning. No one could really blame him for failing to keep a rendezvous in an area where patrols of soldiers were searching actively.

Besides, all the rock-breaking implements, along with their means of making fire and most of their supplies, had been abandoned near the little tomb, and were probably lost for good.

After making their way back somewhat closer to the river and the marshes, the better to support their story of an upset boat, the family settled in as best they could to wait for dawn, taking turns at sleeping uneasily and standing watch.

They were now quite close to the great pyramid.

NINE

Scheffler was straining every muscle to run, trying his
damnedest to propel his body straight up the gigantic
stair-steps formed by the unfinished side of the Great
Pyramid. But something was going wrong with his legs
right from the start, and by the time he had taken the
first couple of steps he was almost paralyzed, reduced
to trying to crawl with painful slowness.

The dark-haired woman peering down at Scheffler from
behind the golden triangle at the top of the pyramid
had her pistol drawn and she was about to shoot him.
Her blue eyes were deadly. But he had to keep on going
up the great steps anyway, because below him there were
crocodiles, and they were coming up. He could see the
yellow eyes of the crocs and their great white teeth. Even
with their stumpy legs they were climbing much faster
than he could move. Scheffler let out a choked cry as
one of the animals turned into a lion and bounded closer,
and he whimpered as the lion sank its claws into his
back.

And now a real, full-voiced cry burst out of Scheffler's
throat, and with it he was jolted into wakefulness. Someone
had actually been shaking him awake, strange fingers
poking at his back.

"Good morning," said a voice. It was a bright, firm voice
and very real. It wasn't Becky's voice, because she was
still submerged in sleep and blankets, her blond head

half buried in a pillow. The hand that had been shaking Scheffler was a man's, but the voice belonged to the woman who was standing at the foot of his bed. She and the two men with her were all dressed in what looked vaguely like ski jackets, wearing winter caps upon their heads, appropriate to the season. The men stood flanking Scheffler's bed, one on each side.

Good morning, the woman had said. It might indeed be morning technically, but the bedroom was still as dark as night. Barely enough light was coming in from the streets and buildings outside to let Scheffler see some features of his visitors' faces. He looked at them all and swallowed and lay still.

"Good morning," said the woman again, as if she were now satisfied that he was awake. She was dark, and looked quite young in the semi-darkness, and her voice was pleasantly nondescript. "We are the police. You may call me Olivia. And you are Thomas Scheffler."

"Police," Scheffler repeated stupidly.

"Not the Chicago police. Nor do we represent any other political entity with which you are familiar. But nevertheless we are police. I could show you our documents of identification, but I'm afraid you'd find them meaningless."

The speaker, like her companions, was tall and well-proportioned, and when she moved her head enough of her face became visible to suggest that she might be attractive, not that, just now, he cared. She was standing with her hands folded in front of her as if ready for prayer or meditation.

Scheffler sat up in bed. He rubbed his face with his hands. Somehow he was not really surprised by this intrusion. Not that he had been expecting it, exactly, but he had been expecting something, some kind of an intervention. Or at least part of him had been hoping for one. In fact, under his shock he could already feel an undercurrent of something like relief.

"What do you want?" he asked, and looked sideways again at Becky, who still had not stirred.

"Your companion is going to sleep through our interview," said the woman who had called herself Olivia. "I think we have no business with her. But we have with you."

"Oh." He looked at Becky again, then back to his interrogator. "What business?"

"We want you to answer some questions for us. We are police, as I have said, and we have evidence that a long series of crimes have been committed within our jurisdiction. So far I have no reason to think that you are guilty. But you certainly have information bearing on these crimes, and on the guilty parties."

So far the two men were only standing by, watching and listening in silence. Scheffler looked at Becky yet again. No movement there. He said: "I'd like to get up and put on my pants."

"Go ahead," cheerfully allowed Olivia. She made a gracious gesture.

The man standing at the right side of the bed moved courteously aside. Scheffler got up and pulled on the pants he'd left on the bedside chair, and then pulled his borrowed silk dressing gown over that. Being at least half dressed made him feel a little braver. He faced Olivia and squared his shoulders. "What right do you people have to come in here and ask me questions?"

"I have explained who we are. I must warn you that you are now temporarily under our jurisdiction. If you refuse to answer questions here, you will be taken elsewhere for questioning."

"That's kidnapping."

"In your legal system, yes. But our legal system will supersede yours whenever the two come into conflict." Olivia obviously had her answers ready, as if she had expected they might be needed. She sounded supremely confident, and still patient. The two men were waiting patiently too, watching Scheffler steadily. They were both built as big as he was, though one was a little shorter. The taller one had his arms folded, the other his hands, in ski gloves, hanging loose.

"If you're working under a legal system," Scheffler asked them, "then don't I have the right to counsel? Legal advice?"

Olivia continued to do the talking for her side. "If and when you are arrested, you will be provided the kind of counsel that I think you mean. But I don't think matters are going to come to that. I think you have become innocently involved."

One of the men said, in a voice so deep it was surprising: "If it's advice you want, the best advice anyone can give you right now is to co-operate with us."

Scheffler looked the three intruders over again, taking them in one after another. All three of them looked back with calm professional readiness. Becky slept on, breathing peacefully.

He sighed. "All right. What questions do you have?"

The woman turned her head and said something to one of the men in a language that Scheffler could not understand. The man turned and left the room.

She smiled at Scheffler then. "How many trips through the timelock have you made?"

He tried to remember. Then suddenly something about the whole business struck him as very funny. Maybe it was his visitors' matter-of-fact approach; or his own calmness, almost relief, in the face of their questioning; or Becky's continuing to sleep. Whatever it was, Scheffler began to laugh. He bent over, and straightened up again, and wiped his eyes on the sleeve of his robe. It took him a little while to regain full control.

Apparently this reaction too was not unexpected; his interrogator still waited patiently.

"You know," Scheffler told her at last, "at first I thought it was an elevator."

Olivia allowed herself to share, to the extent of a brief smile, in his amusement. "Logical and natural under the circumstances," she reassured him. "How many trips?"

Scheffler thought back. "There were three, altogether. The first was very brief."

"And where did you go each time?"

Somehow it had never occurred to Scheffler until this moment that there might have been more than one possible destination. "Each time to the same place—in ancient Egypt. The Great Pyramid was under construction there—I could see it as soon as I climbed out of a hole in the rocks—so it could hardly have been anywhere else."

Olivia nodded, without comment. The man who had left the room now returned, carrying a small statuette, one of the items that Scheffler had brought back from his last trip, and left on a table in the library. The man who brought in the object now said something to the woman in their own language, and tossed his find on the foot of the bed.

She pulled a small device out from somewhere and touched it to the statuette; then she turned back to Scheffler. "How much gold did you bring back from there altogether? You won't incriminate yourself by answering but it's very important that I know."

"Gold? None. On the first two trips I brought nothing. Your man there has obviously found the collection of things I did bring back, on the third trip. That's all. Oh, except for one worn-out sandal in my backpack. I just picked that up as a sort of souvenir. Oh, and a cigarette butt."

"Cigarette butt? Why did you bother with that?"

"I don't know. It seemed incongruous, lying where it was. It seemed like evidence or something."

Olivia only looked at him. "Anything else?"

"No. As for the valuables—well, I didn't consider that I was stealing." That sounded foolish when he heard himself say it; still, it was true.

"Perhaps someone gave them to you to bring back here," Olivia suggested. When he hesitated over his answer, she added: "Let me assure you that we know about the two twentieth-century people who are still there. Even they may not be in serious legal trouble yet—but if I'm going to help them I have to know as much as possible about them. The truth of what they have been doing."

"I don't know what they've been doing. I saw only one of them, a young woman. Yes, she told me to bring the stuff, and I went along with what she said. I don't even know her name. I saw her only once, and that was brief. But I'll tell you what I can."

"Very good." His interrogator rewarded him with a broader smile. "You say that you've made three trips. Describe them all to me, in some detail please."

Scheffler did. The words flowed swiftly once he got started, and his sense of relief established itself more firmly.

Olivia took it all in. No one was making notes, but maybe, Scheffler supposed, they were somehow recording what he said.

When he paused, after completing his recital of the third trip, she nodded as if satisfied. "And now, tell me about your uncle—no, he's your great-uncle, isn't he?— Montgomery Chapel. When did you last see him?"

Scheffler told it all, as well as he could remember it, beginning with the first invitation from Uncle Monty to come to the apartment. If he had been willing to lie to keep Uncle Monty out of trouble, he wouldn't have had any idea what sort of lie would be helpful. Right now, based on actual experience, he didn't feel like sticking his neck out for Uncle Monty. He would prefer to trust Olivia. So far these self-proclaimed police seemed like decent and reasonable people and it was a relief to be able to tell his story to someone.

The patient questioning went on. The men, as if to make sure they got their turns in, each spoke up a couple of times, asking Scheffler in the same calm manner about some details of his story. From the overall course of the questioning, Scheffler got the idea that these people were more interested in Uncle Monty than in anything else—except, perhaps, in gold. They kept coming back to gold, but he thought they believed him when he kept insisting that he'd never taken any.

They were all four of them still standing in the bedroom. He might have to answer questions, but he'd be damned if he was going to invite these intruders to sit down.

"Anyone else involved?" Olivia asked him casually.

"In getting stuff from ancient Egypt? Not that I know of." Now Scheffler was beginning to feel tired. He wanted to sit down, and the bed was available, but Becky, snoring faintly, was still in it and he feared to wake her up. Also he feared that sitting would put him at some kind of psychological disadvantage.

"What about a man named Pilgrim? Or possibly Peregrinus?"

"Ah, him. Well, I don't know what he's involved in, but I've had a couple of phone calls from him since I moved in here. I think one of his messages is still recorded on the phone."

"What did he want?"

"To know how he could reach my uncle. I told him I didn't know."

Olivia said nothing to that. If the message was still on

the phone, Scheffler decided, she and her men had probably already examined it.

Instead she said: "Tell me if you've ever seen this man," and brought a flat little item out of a pocket of her ski jacket. Scheffler, ready to be shown a photo, found himself looking at a wonder. He would have had to describe it as a holograph, but it was fancier than anything he'd ever seen along that line before. A complete molded image of a man's head, glowing in full color, sprang up from a small flat disk when Olivia held it in her palm. She rotated the bust this way and that, and when Scheffler stared at it without recognition she did something that called up changes in the hair, the beard, and the coloring of the image.

"No, I've never seen him, anywhere, anytime, that I can recall. But then I never saw the man who phoned."

They asked Scheffler to show them the photos he had taken on his last trip to the land of the pyramid. He got them out of his dresser drawer, and Olivia looked them over. Then without apology she put them into a pocket of her jacket. "I don't suppose you made any copies of these? The process used by your camera is not one that routinely makes multiple copies, is it?"

"No. To both questions."

Abruptly, somehow surprisingly, Scheffler's visitors were ready to leave. Olivia told him: "We're taking along these things that you did bring back at the request of the young lady. And we're taking the sandal too. You will perhaps understand if I do not give you a receipt?"

He shrugged. He drew a deep breath. He felt relieved. "I think I can understand that," he said.

The lady said: "As for the other ancient items in this apartment, they have been here for decades, and to remove them now would probably be more disruptive than to leave them. Thank you for your cooperation, Tom.

We're leaving now, and the chances are that you won't see us again—but it's not impossible that you will. I or one of my associates here might be back to see you within a few days. Because your formal testimony may be wanted, regarding the activities of Dr. Pilgrim and others."

"I suppose you can come and drag me away, if you want me. But there won't be much I can say."

"Don't let it worry you. We'll see to it that interference with your normal life is held to a minimum. I doubt that you'll even miss a day of school." Olivia's smile was half wintry and half motherly. Suddenly it occurred to Scheffler for the first time to wonder how old she was. Her face was unlined, that was all that he could say. He had seen enough of it now to be sure of its attractiveness.

She went on: "The young lady there should wake up normally in an hour or so. We have no business with her. Meanwhile, if you keep your nose clean—is that the proper figure of speech?—you're out of it. In the clear. Home free. Understand?"

"I understand."

"Probably I don't need to tell you to stay out of the timelock from now on."

"No, you don't."

"But I'm telling you anyway, officially. Stay away from that device altogether. Don't even touch the curtain. You can't realize how lucky you were that none of the control settings were changed—what might have happened to you when you used it. What might have happened to a portion of your city here. In a few days, you can go back to where the door of the timelock is now, and that door will be gone—understand? There will be nothing there but the normal wall of this apartment building. But for a few days stay clear entirely."

"I'll stay away from it."

"See that you do. And don't worry about anything else.

If you should want to try to call your great-uncle and tell him about this visit of ours, go ahead. But you'll be wasting your time and we'll arrest him anyway. If, as is likely, he never returns here from his current trip to the Middle East, well, feel free to report him missing as soon as you think proper. I don't suppose you'll miss him unduly."

Scheffler said nothing.

"You can even tell people about us if you like. But if you tell anyone I expect they'll think you're crazy."

Scheffler nodded. He had already come to that conclusion.

"Don't worry about anything else. We'll take care of it."

Olivia's smile brightened minimally. The three intruders filed out of his bedroom, taking the statuette with them. A minute later, he thought he heard a door close—somewhere. Becky stirred, and turned over, and mumbled something. But she was still asleep.

When Scheffler went to look, both the front and back doors of the apartment were closed and locked, just as he had left them when he and Becky went to bed.

He walked over to Gallery Two. Peering in through the grillwork, he could see that the curtain was hanging in place, and all the treasures that were supposed to be in the protected area were still there. He felt a certain perverse temptation to open up the grill and take one more look at the false door, but the urge was very weak and easy to resist. He was safely out of it all now, and well out of it. And if Uncle Monty wasn't coming back, so what? Under the circumstances, considering the risks in which his uncle had placed him, Scheffler didn't consider that he owed the old man a thing.

All the same, he experienced an unexpected but definite twinge of regret. In a few days he would go back to school and finish learning to be an engineer. No matter where he spent the rest of his life, nothing like a timelock was ever going to happen to him again.

For a long time, for almost an hour, Scheffler roamed the apartment, shuffling along on weary legs. He felt exhausted but at the same time too keyed up to try to go back to sleep. He kept wishing Becky would wake up, and at the same time he was glad she didn't. There was nothing credible that he could tell her, very little indication that they'd had any visitors tonight. But he was not at all tempted to believe he'd dreamed the visitors. All the things he'd carried back with him from pyramid-land were gone, including his photographs, and his ancient sandal. That was the only change.

Maybe they'd left him his cigarette butt. Yes, it was still there, buttoned into his shirt pocket. Big deal.

He went to the liquor cabinet, and opened a bottle of aged whisky that bore a name he assumed must be one of the most respected in the business—he didn't know that much about the subject—and poured himself a good, stiff drink. Scheffler seldom touched the hard stuff, but under the circumstances it seemed the only appropriate action he could take.

Then he went back to bed and without undressing again lay down beside Becky, the remains of his drink within reach. He wondered if he was ever going to be able to sleep again.

Scheffler's second unexpected waking of the night was considerably more violent than the first. Becky screamed, as both of them were tipped out of the heavy bed onto the floor. Scheffler rolled over to stare up into a gray dawn light. Strange, ominous-looking weapons like crystalline rods were aimed at them, gripped in the hands of two things whose size and generally grotesque appearance reminded him of Uncle Monty's statues.

Two monster-headed creatures, clothed in strange fabric and helmeted in opaque glass, were standing one on either side of the bed, just where Olivia's escort had been an hour or so ago. They were not statues, nor did they look at all ancient or Egyptian. The darkness that might have softened their shapes vanished when someone hit the wall switch and all the lights in the room came on.

The figures who were aiming what he assumed were peculiar weapons at Scheffler looked monstrous indeed, but one visitor, standing at the foot of the bed, was certainly a human being. And Scheffler had seen his face before.

The man bowed slightly, smiling down at the two people who were huddled on the floor. His very precise voice was alarmingly familiar. "We have spoken on the phone, Scheffler. My name is Pilgrim."

TEN

The man's dark eyes were hypnotic, holding an intensity of life that no holograph could have conveyed. The face was, in its own way, handsome. And the precise voice was the same one that had spoken to Scheffler on the phone, though now it sounded much wearier.

"Scheffler? No need to be terrified of me. Not just yet anyway. We have plenty of time for that. Get up. Get dressed. You and the young lady both. Desert outfits for both of you, please. Please don't be terrified, not now, we're in a hurry. The industrious Olivia must have told you some unkind things about me. I'll have to speak to her about that." Pilgrim's accent was slight but very distinctive. Scheffler, if pressed to come up with a definition, could only have called it suave.

Certainly Pilgrim's were the features that Olivia had shown him in the holograph, though now the man's gaunt face was rimmed with a beard, short and patchy and unkempt, as if he simply had not had the chance to shave for many days. His age, Scheffler thought, might have been somewhere between thirty and forty. Physically he was rather small, not nearly as big as Scheffler had somehow expected despite Uncle Monty's description. But in spite of the lack of size the impression of magnetic force was there.

Scheffler, still clad in the dressing gown over his jeans, got slowly to his feet. Becky, clad in nothing at all except

127

the sheet that she was clutching around her, sat on the floor and whimpered.

Pilgrim smiled at her in a not-unkindly and yet impatient manner. In his precise actor's voice he said: "You must get up and dress, my dear. For the desert."

"For the desert," she repeated, nodding as if to show that she was willing to be obedient. Then she added helplessly: "I don't know what you mean."

Scheffler shook his head when Pilgrim looked at him. "She doesn't have any desert outfit," Scheffler said. "She doesn't know anything about it."

"Well, I suppose that's possible. But if not she will soon learn. My dear, if you would prefer to do your dressing in the closet—well, obviously you would prefer that—take whatever garments you have and put them on in there—you do have *some* clothing at hand, I take it? Of course you do. Scheffler, be a good fellow and go with her. And be quick about it, both of you. Clothed or unclothed, we are all about to depart on a journey."

Scheffler helped Becky to her feet. Then he led her, still wrapped in her bedsheet, across the room. On the way they both grabbed up garments from a chair and from the floor. She went on into the closet and began putting things on, while he stood in the closet doorway, trying to shield her from view as much as possible as he completed his own dressing. Pilgrim's eyes, red-veined and weary though they were, had followed Becky appreciatively as she crossed the room.

"What are they going to do to us?" she whimpered to Scheffler as she tugged up her jeans. It was as if she thought the intruders couldn't hear her as long as he was standing in their way. He mumbled something as he struggled to get a shoe on while standing up. He supposed it wasn't a very encouraging reply but it was the best that he could do.

Fully dressed, he felt more angry than afraid. Being dragged out of bed by strangers twice in one night was just too damn much. But when Scheffler turned around, meaning to confront this new invader boldly, he found himself again facing one of the short but monstrous figures that he had seen when the lights first came on. In the interval between then and now his mind had suppressed the nature of those shapes, but now here was one of them again, not a hallucination, not some result of interrupted dreams and blurry eyes and glaring light, but real.

No more than five feet tall, the thing stood in the doorway to the hall. Still pointing a slender crystalline rod with attachments, that had to be a weapon. The threat was implicit in the thing's attitude. In a moment its fellow, similarly armed, had reappeared in the dark hallway behind it.

Scheffler came to a halt, unable to say anything, staring at the two misshapen helmets, glassy but opaque, and the two unearthly bodies in strange, tight suits. Both of the small beings had moved completely back into the bedroom now, and they continued to point their rods at him.

Pilgrim was watching him intently. "They're not going to eat you, my lad. They are members of my crew, as impeccably human as you yourself, though Earth has never been their home."

"Your crew."

"Yes."

"Where are you from?"

"Long ago and far away. They need a bit of help in breathing when they come here, that's all. Hence the helmets. We all need a bit of help from time to time, don't we? I'm going to need some help from you. And you and the young woman are going to need my help for a while now, just to stay alive."

And now Scheffler noticed for the first time that Pilgrim

himself was injured. The smaller man was keeping his left hand in the side pocket of his trousers. And at the wrist of that arm, under the sleeve of Pilgrim's upper garment, Scheffler could see what looked like the end of some kind of cast or splint. The jacket whose sleeve concealed most of the cast somewhat resembled the upper garments that the police had worn.

Becky, peering past Scheffler, got a good look at what had just come in from the hall. She reacted with a gasp and clutched him by the arm. Scheffler could discern on the two odd creatures—or at least on their garments, for none of their skin was showing—some of the same signs of wear and tear that Pilgrim displayed. The two silent beings, though of approximately human shape, were too thin and angular to be men, women, or children born of Earth. The joints of their limbs, being slightly displaced by terrestrial standards, provided even more convincing evidence of their alien origins. So did the configuration of the glassy helmets, implying the shape of the heads inside. Their hands were covered in mitten-like gloves that hid all details of form.

Pilgrim was growing impatient with his victims. "Are you dressed yet, wench? Come come. Step out here boldly, I don't bite. Nothing worse than a little adventure lies ahead for you, and you will emerge from it intact if I have my way, and I generally do."

Scheffler turned his head to Becky. "Better do what the man says," he urged apologetically. He was thinking that if Pilgrim intended rape or murder, he wouldn't have ordered her to get dressed.

Whatever Becky might be thinking, she didn't have much choice, and followed Scheffler out of the closet. Pilgrim waved a hand, in what looked like a consciously theatrical gesture, to signal his captives to follow him out of the bedroom.

Escorted by silent monsters, two men and a woman traversed the dimly lighted rooms and hallways of the apartment until they came to Gallery Two. The grillwork door was already standing open, though Scheffler could see no sign that it had been forced. The lock must have been cheated somehow, or simply opened with a key. Not Scheffler's key; he could still feel that in his pants pocket, where he had put it yesterday before Becky arrived. It wasn't exactly that he hadn't trusted her, but . . .

The cloth curtain decorated with Egyptian figures, that Olivia had warned him never to touch again, had already been pulled aside. The dark doorway to the elevator stood open. Becky was staring at all this in total incomprehension.

Pilgrim paused for a moment in the sanctuary, pointing to one after another of the gold artifacts in their niches. He said something to his companions, speaking in the most alien-sounding tongue that Scheffler had ever heard from human lips. One of the diminutive monsters answered, a startling buzzing speech that did not sound as if it could be produced by human lips at all.

Evidently Pilgrim did not particularly like the answer he had been given, but it was not unexpected. Now with a grimace he had turned back to his captives, and was gesturing them forward, into the open door of the elevator.

Scheffler moved forward obediently and then stopped on the threshold. There were two figures already inside the little dark-walled room, one of them lying bound on one of the couches. A hand pushed Scheffler roughly in, and now he could see that it was Olivia who lay on the couch. The policewoman's face was pale and drawn and her eyes were closed. A third monster, helmeted and armed like the two who had come to Scheffler's bedroom, its knees and elbows bent at somewhat inhuman angles, was crouching beside her as guardian.

Becky was shoved in beside Scheffler, and then both

of them were pushed toward the rear of the car. Becky's
face was controlled, and she had stopped whimpering,
but she clung to Scheffler's arm with the grip of a drowning
woman. Pilgrim and his cohort crowded in after them.
Looking back, Scheffler could see how the last creature
left outside closed and locked the grillwork door and
pulled the curtain shut before entering. Then the door
of the elevator slid closed.

Pilgrim observed Scheffler's stare at Olivia. "I suppose,
Scheffler," the cultured voice inquired, "you were warned
to have no dealings with me? Told that I was the most
savage criminal in the Galaxy? Inevitably to be arrested
within the next ten minutes?"

"I don't think so. I don't remember."

"It doesn't matter what you were told." Pilgrim made
a dismissive gesture with his good hand. Then he leaned
back against the elevator wall, rubbing his eyes tiredly.
"But you see the police didn't have quite the success in
arresting me that they anticipated. Well, it's not the first
time."

Olivia had opened her eyes and was gazing stonily up
at them all. She said nothing, and Scheffler wasn't sure
that she was fully conscious.

Now Pilgrim had turned to face the dark wall, and the
fingers of his uninjured hand moved over the illuminated
projections beside the door. The pattern of the little lights
across the wall was changing under his touch. Over his
shoulder he said: "Please make no attempt to change
any of these. I want to be able to return you to your
apartment, Scheffler, when the time comes. If you and—
what is your fair companion's name?"

"Becky." She spoke up for herself, in a voice that
surprised Scheffler with its firmness. "Rebecca Haggerty."

Their kidnapper gave her another appreciative glance.
Then he finished with whatever he was doing to the wall,

stabbing at it with his fingers like a pianist, and faced them again. "Rebecca Haggerty and Thomas Scheffler, I mean neither of you any harm. If possible I will see to it that you are restored to your normal world, once I have got my hands on what I want. If, that is, you still prefer your normal world—it does have its disadvantages, you know?" Pilgrim's was a mild, inquiring, schoolteacher's gaze. And even as he asked the question the time-elevator began to move, gravity weakening and coming back in spurts beneath the passengers' feet.

"That's what we'd prefer, yes," said Scheffler. Becky clutched at him again and he patted her hand in reassurance. This was really the smoothest ride that Scheffler had taken yet in this device. The gravity was remaining almost constant. No doubt Pilgrim had made just the right adjustments.

The little man shrugged elegantly. "Ah well. It is not impossible that you will change your minds. But as you wish. The more willingly you both cooperate with me while we are traveling companions, the more likely you are to have your choice at the end of the journey."

"Co-operate in what?"

"In whatever may come along. The little day-to-day things that add up to make life worth living."

"Okay. Whatever you say. Is she badly hurt?" With a nod Scheffler indicated Olivia, who still seemed to be having trouble getting her eyes to focus on anything.

"I'm afraid she may be." Pilgrim sounded genuinely—though not intensely—regretful. "We fought a skirmish since she saw you last. Neither of us, as you see, emerged unscathed." He moved his injured arm a trifle, gently, without taking the hand out of the pocket. "But really I have no more wish to hurt her than to harm you. Possibly she will survive to try to arrest me once again."

Becky asked, in a lost voice: "Where are we going?"

Obviously she was still unable to make any sense at all out of the elevator and its unique ride.

Pilgrim came close to twinkling at her. "Scheffler can explain that to you. Not very thoroughly or accurately I suppose, but well enough to serve the immediate purpose. It's a place he has already visited. Or if words fail him you can see for yourself since we shall soon be there." The little man smiled at Scheffler. "When we arrive, he will indicate to me how far the gold-hunting has progressed up to now. How much of the Pharaoh's treasure, if any, remains unplundered."

"I didn't see any gold when I was there," Scheffler protested. "I didn't hunt for any."

"Oh, did you not?" Momentarily Pilgrim's gaze was a dark implacable force that probed him coldly. "Perhaps not. If that is true, then I suspect that even by the standards of your own world you have been badly cheated. Cheated by your two friends who are still at work there now, and by your own great-uncle. But don't let that depress you; your respected great-uncle Montgomery Chapel seems to have cheated almost everyone who ever tried to deal with him. Including me." Gradually Pilgrim's face had assumed a wry expression, as if to indicate that he was able to accept the situation as a joke. And then, as if in afterthought: "I mean to talk with him about that."

Scheffler wondered if the man before him was insane. He felt no hope of being able to predict what he'd do next.

The time-conveyance bounced a little more. Becky moaned and muttered, but it was a minor disturbance by the standards of Scheffler's first three trips. Everyone inside the car held on in one way or another, grabbing a strap or at least bracing a hand against the wall. Becky continued to grip Scheffler by the arm. And at least one of the rod-weapons stayed pointed at Scheffler all through the bouncing ride. He was by far the biggest being in the group, but right now it didn't seem that size and strength were going to do him any good.

The vehicle stopped. He estimated that the ride had lasted no more than two minutes.

The door opened, on what was becoming a familiar sight to Scheffler, the entrance to the fissure in Egyptian rock. This time it was not full daylight outside, but not full night either. The mildness of the heat that washed into the car suggested to Scheffler that they had arrived near dawn rather than dusk. Becky sniffed the air, and her confusion reached new heights. She stared at him, seeking enlightenment.

Pilgrim was first out of the timelock, looking around him warily. Now at last he had drawn a weapon of his own, which appeared to be a shorter version of the rod-devices still brandished by his three unearthly followers. After looking around, Pilgrim motioned for the others to follow him.

Olivia, on being released from the couch, said very little but demonstrated a willingness to cooperate under duress. She was able to stand and walk with only a minimum of help. Becky moved spontaneously to the other woman's side and helped her to stay on her feet.

When everyone was out of the car, standing almost in single file in the confined space of the fissure, and the door had closed behind them, Pilgrim faced Scheffler.

"I want you to tell me what arrangement you have made for meeting the other two twentieth-century people who are still working here."

"I don't have any arrangements at all with those people. I don't know anything about them. Except I talked to one of them for a couple of minutes. Ask Olivia." Then, seeing how the policewoman swayed on her feet, Scheffler was sorry he had brought her into it. In a burst of something like bravado he added: "We could try standing here and waving our arms. Maybe they'll see us."

Pilgrim did not react to the comment. He did turn to Olivia, as if wondering whether he ought to ask her as suggested.

But at this point Olivia spoke up unexpectedly, addressing herself to Becky and Scheffler.

"I warn you, you must do nothing to help this man. Nothing more than you are absolutely forced to do."

One of the small unearthly things raised its weapon, aimed at her. Pilgrim gestured it away. "No. Let her say all that she feels compelled to say. Let her say it now, and we can perhaps get on with business."

Olivia had winced away from the weapon when it moved in her direction. Now she caught her breath and went on, speaking to Becky and Scheffler.

"More is at stake here than you can realize. In the name of the Authority, I . . ." The futility of that appeal, incomprehensible to her hearers, evidently struck her. For a moment she was silent, then blurted out: "This man is guilty of what you would call genocide."

"A lie," said Pilgrim calmly. His urbane manner was unshaken. "An absolute lie."

Scheffler said nothing. Looking at Olivia, who now slumped in exhaustion, leaning heavily on Becky's supporting arm, he was quite willing to believe what she had told him.

Their kidnapper asked the policewoman, with seeming courtesy: "Are you quite finished?"

Olivia said nothing. She licked dry lips, stared at nothing, and continued to lean on Becky.

"Then let us be on our way. Follow me, all of you." Pilgrim gestured minimally and began to lead the way along the fissure.

When they reached the end of the rocky passageway

there was still light enough in the sky to give them a good look at the pyramid. Becky gasped audibly.

Pilgrim paused there, gazing at the monument back-lighted against the sunrise, ignoring the rest of his party for the brief time it took them to catch up with him.

In a few moments captors and captives were more or less gathered together at the end of the fissure. Pilgrim surveyed them briefly and gave the signal to advance again. They were in the process of climbing over the low rocks at the end of the fissure, and had just about got all their heads out above the level of the rocky hill, when a voice challenged them out of the gathering night.

Scheffler ducked at once, getting his head back down between the walls, and pulling Becky down beside him. Olivia, dependent upon Becky for support, slumped into a gradual fall. One of the monsters was crouching slightly, in a good position to keep an eye on all the prisoners. The glassy helmet gleamed faintly in the light, and Scheffler wondered what shape and color of eyes might be inside it.

Meanwhile Pilgrim and his two other crew members were calling and buzzing their own challenges back into the night.

Pilgrim's voice, surprisingly loud, roared out: "Who is it, then?"

After a pause of a few seconds, the distant voice replied: "Willis Chapel." A pause. "Is that Pilgrim?"

"Yes." The tension in the air relaxed. It was quite obvious that the two sides recognized each other.

Or at least they thought they did. Scheffler wasn't sure. That challenging bellow out of the dusk hadn't sounded to him like the voice of any eighty-year-old man.

ELEVEN

The day of Pharaoh's burial was over, the fires of sunset already beginning to fade from sky and river, when Ptah-hotep and Thothmes descended to the Palace docks. The two officials needed only a moment to select one of the numerous boats that waited almost motionless in the still water at dockside. Their choice was one of the smaller craft that might have been able to carry six people at the most. Still it was larger than they needed; there would be no servants to do the rowing for them on this trip. Taking up paddle and pole, they launched themselves out into the broad canal that would carry them to the Nile.

Thothmes, standing amidships, poled the boat forward, while Ptah-hotep, sitting in the stern armed with a paddle, did what he could to help. Their maneuvers with these rivermen's tools were at first a trifle awkward. But both men had some boating experience, gained on sporting expeditions into the marshes, and they experienced little real difficulty.

When they steered out of the canal and into the river itself, the lightly loaded craft rode skittishly in the swift current that caught them up and swept them toward their destination. If all went as well as they hoped tonight, Ptah-hotep and Thothmes would probably hire boatmen tomorrow for the return trip upstream. But to be able to avoid the eyes and ears of the rivermen on this crucial trip downstream was worth a little trouble.

Around them, the vast river ran dark and nearly silent through the deepening night. The flotilla of vessels of all types that had dotted the Nile's broad surface during the funeral procession of the Pharaoh Khufu had now dispersed.

Almost directly ahead of their small craft, some distance inland from the western bank, the Horizon of Khufu reared its dark looming triangle against the sky. Today, somewhere near the center of that towering mass of stone, the final sealing of the inner chambers and passageways had been carried out by fiercely loyal retainers of the dead king. Whatever last tricks the Pharaoh and his Chief Builder had had in mind to foil robbery had now been played.

Swiftly the current bore the small craft along. The torchlights of the Palace were already far behind when Thothmes paused, standing balanced like an acrobat with his pole; the water had become too deep for him to reach the bottom with it anyway. He said softly: "Is that a boat upstream from us? Following us?"

Ptah-hotep, the better to listen, ceased to paddle, letting the boat drift freely. Looking upstream, into the south, he was able to see very little except the deepening night itself. When he held his breath he could hear nightbirds, insects, the tiny lap of waves along the wooden sides of their small boat, the almost inaudible murmuring of the night breeze crossing the immense river. There was no chanting of boatmen to be heard, no sound of oars or paddles.

"I can see nothing out of the ordinary," he whispered. "I hear nothing. Do you see a boat following?"

Thothmes was silent. He sat down carefully, still looking upstream and balancing his pole. At last he shrugged.

A moment later, Ptah-hotep started paddling again. It was necessary to guide their progress now; mere drifting would not bring them to the inlet of the canal they wanted. The sound made by the faint trickle of the water from the paddle with each stroke was very faint.

Daylight had entirely fled from the sky long before Ptah-hotep and Thothmes were able to steer their small craft from the swift river into another almost stagnant canal, this one leading straight toward the pyramid. The waning moon had not yet risen; yet the officials, Ptah-hotep in particular, were so familiar with the way that the starlight was sufficient to let them find the canal and guide their boat into it. This palm-lined waterway had been dug decades ago, to carry to the pyramid's construction the stones that came by boat from distant quarries.

Now their course lay down the middle of the narrow canal, between the idle lines of the construction boats that were still waiting where they had been stopped at the announcement of Pharaoh's death. Most of the boats on the right bank were heavily laden with stones for the outer sheathing of the pyramid, and most of the boats on the left were empty. All were awaiting the resumption of normal daytime labor that would take place within a day or two, after the formal coronation of Dedefre.

Many times had Ptah-hotep, in his capacity as guide and observer of the daytime work, passed in a small boat through this canal. Now even in the moonless darkness there was small chance of his missing the spot where he wanted to put ashore. At a little distance from this point, the mason and skilled robber Sihathor should be waiting for them, to receive the final confirmation that he and his workers could begin their labors this very night.

Now, taking the pole from Thothmes, and pushing hard with it against the shallow bottom, the former Chief Priest guided their vessel in toward the right-hand bank.

Thothmes behind him had picked up the paddle and now plied it quietly.

As soon as the prow of their craft had grounded, Ptah-hotep stepped ashore. He tied the boat up to a handy stake, though the chance that it might drift away in this virtually motionless water seemed very small. Caution, particularly in all matters having to do with the business of the cult of Set, was a long-ingrained habit. Thothmes watched him but said nothing.

Now the two men crept silently inland toward the appointed place of rendezvous. This was a small but distinctive outcropping of rock, so close to the canal that it was surrounded by palm trees. Under the palms, with most of the starlight shaded out, a deeper darkness reigned.

Thothmes and Ptah-hotep groped about, doing their best to make a minimum of noise, finding only rocks and treetrunks. They took turns whistling and calling softly. But Sihathor was not here. That was not really surprising, they decided, looking at the stars. Certainly they had arrived too early; it was not yet midnight.

The two men settled in to wait, sitting on the large rock, beginning to judge time's passage by the slow turn of the familiar stars. Meanwhile they talked, and remarked on certain odd signs that seemed to be taking place to mark the death of Pharaoh. Several people in the Palace had reported seeing odd things among the stars last night. There were always a few such reports, of course, when many people watched the skies; but it appeared that the frequency of these signs might be increasing.

The friends fingered their amulets, and prayed to Set for the success of their enterprise. Time passed, as time will.

"It is midnight now," Thothmes said at last. "And the stonemason is not here yet."

Ptah-hotep arose from the flat rock and walked out from under the vague shadow of the palms, to get a better look at the constellations, the better to judge the time.

Looking up at the night sky, he frowned.

"What is it?" his companion asked. His eyes, accustomed to the darkness now, had read that frown even by starlight.

"I thought that I saw something," Ptah-hotep declared reluctantly. "Moving among the stars."

"Something? What?"

"I do not know. It came and went too swiftly. Like a fish—no, more like a ripple in the water of the Nile."

"That was the comparison used by some of the people in the Palace this morning, describing to me the start of their own visions." Thothmes, moving uneasily, got to his feet and joined his friend under the unshaded sky. But now there was nothing out of the ordinary to be seen.

Nothing else unusual occurred for some time. It was well past midnight when they reluctantly gave up on Sihathor and made their way back to their borrowed boat.

In whispered conference the two officials now wondered if Sihathor might have failed to receive the message telling him to meet them. Another possibility was that he had misinterpreted his orders and gone straight to the pyramid. Of course, he might also have been delayed or even arrested on his way. But other cultists had assured Ptah-hotep and Thothmes that the officers detailed to guard Khufu's tomb, and the nearby cemetery, had eagerly accepted their bribes and removed themselves and their men from the immediate area.

Untying their boat, Ptah-hotep and Thothmes pushed off again and once more paddled toward the looming shape of Khufu's pyramid, sharp-angled, black, and enigmatic against the stars.

"Wait! Hold!" Ptah-hotep's whisper was low but piercing. Then he pointed silently, letting the boat drift with the force of his last paddle-stroke. Far behind them, almost as far back as where the straight canal joined the river, the lights of several torches gleamed. Light sparked a coppery gleam from weapons.

"Soldiers!" Thothmes whispered.

"It may be only that some patrols have been sent out for the sake of appearances. Back there, they are still well distant from the area they have been bribed to avoid."

"It may be so," allowed Thothmes. His tone carried more than a little doubt. Other possibilities, that neither man felt like mentioning aloud, were that there had been treachery at high levels within the cult—or that the Chief Builder, or some other enemy of Set, had fathomed the cultists' plot and sprung a trap.

Just as suddenly as the frightening distant torches had come into sight, they disappeared again. The abruptness of the disappearance was disconcerting.

"Did you see that? They're moving quickly, away from the canal. But which way are they moving? If they come this way we should be able to see them."

"Let them come," said Ptah-hotep, "We are still officials of the Horizon of Khufu. We have every right to be here, at any hour we choose."

"But they will be suspicious. And what about our stonemason? And his crew, he must have brought helpers with him."

"They must fend for themselves. I expect that they are all crafty peasants, capable of doing so, should the soldiers happen to come across them." Ptah-hotep took up his paddle again and used it softly.

For the distance of a spearcast the two friends made progress without incident in their small boat. Then Thothmes clutched Ptah-hotep by the arm, violently, and pointed. A giant face, many times human size but blue and dim almost to invisibility, appeared to be looking out at them from the left bank of the canal. The countenance was indistinct, and the features of it irregular, but it appeared to be alive. Those vast eyes rolled up toward the stars as the small boat drifted past. It looked to Ptah-hotep like the face of a god, some god whose name and attributes he might once have heard but could not now remember.

The face faded out of sight even as they gaped at it. Then something, another vague apparition, that might have had the shape of a bird or of a boat, went streaking across the sky. It was come and gone again before they could be sure that it was really there.

Shivering, the two men cast down their pole and paddle and sat close together in their boat. Thothmes, his teeth chattering, pronounced: "W-we have reached the Underworld."

"No!"

"We have fallen into the Underworld, I tell you!"

Ptah-hotep again expressed a violent dissent. "This is not the Underworld! This is nothing like it!"

"Oh, and have you visited the Tuat before? We have been cursed by Pharaoh, and by Ra, and by Osiris for our plotting." Thothmes was almost sobbing in his despair.

"We have not." Ptah-hotep steeled his nerve. "Rather the power of Set is being demonstrated. The power that will enable us to rob the tomb as we had planned. We are going on."

Thothmes, saying nothing except to mutter prayers and incantations, slumped into the bottom of the boat, covering his face with his fingers. He was abandoning his fate into the hands of Ptah-hotep and of the gods.

Ptah-hotep understood this. He set his jaw and paddled. When he had reached the turning basin, he docked the boat and stepped ashore and tied their vessel up again. Thothmes, who by now was somewhat recovered, followed him ashore fatalistically. They made their way on foot toward the base of the pyramid, where now new signs of strange activity became visible. A faint, eerie light was washing over the great mass of Khufu's tomb, coming from some object in the northeastern sky. It combined with the light of the newly risen moon to produce a pale, ghostly effect.

The source of the strange illumination was visible, and drawing closer.

It resembled a giant, translucent bird, and it was coming silently down out of the starry sky and settling, gliding toward the ground with its immense triangular wings stiffly outspread. The apparition landed very near the pyramid. Its light dimmed almost to nothing.

"A god! Or the vessel of a god."

"Or of gods. Of course. But which?"

Quivering with fear, but excited as well with hopeful anticipation, Thothmes and Ptah-hotep advanced step by step.

As they drew nearer, the two officials could see the shimmering, ghostly, gigantic winged shape more clearly. It looked less birdlike now, much less alive, as it sat waiting on the sand—for what?

"It is the barque of dead Pharaoh," Thothmes whispered.

"No, surely. It must be that of Ra himself."

"But what does its presence here, now, mean?"

By now the moon was clear of the horizon, and by moonlight the vessel—if such it really was—looked both like metal and like crystal. It changed shape slightly as the two men watched it, but otherwise remained virtually motionless. Details of its configuration altered from one moment to the next, but always the outline of it was there, as insubstantial as a cloud of wind-blown sand, and yet as constant as the rocks. It was an enormous thing, dwarfed

of course by the pyramid above and behind it, but certainly
far bigger than any real boat that Ptah-hotep had ever
seen, or any of the wooden Barques of Khufu that had
been buried in their several pits around the pyramid.

"I wonder," he muttered at last. "Though it flew it cannot
be a bird or a bat. Nor is it really of the proper shape to
be a boat."

"Do you now intend to dispute with the gods as to what
shape their boats must be? Let us be gone."

"No. No, we have been summoned here to see this. Is
not the night sky under the control of Set?" Ptah-hotep
knew he must sound confident. But he was not sure that
he was right. He only knew that he could not turn his
back without investigating the marvel before him.

Suspended between advance and retreat, the two
conspirators remained at the distance of a long arrow-
flight from the winged thing, huddled among the sand
and rocks.

"Are we then to stay here through the night?"

"Why not? The night sky belongs to Set. And we are
officials concerned with the safety of Khufu's tomb. We
have the right to be here."

It was not soldiers that Thothmes had been concerned
about, not any longer. But he made no further protest
now.

The remaining hours of the night passed slowly. Only
with the near approach of Ra to the horizon in the east
did Ptah-hotep and Thothmes dare to approach again
the strange gigantic vessel resting on the sand.

They were halfway there when Ptah-hotep clutched
his companion by the arm. From around one end of the
strange ship, as if it might have emerged on the far side,
a figure moved. It looked quite human.

"It is a god!"

"It may well be. What did you expect?" Although, Ptah-hotep told himself, it looked very much like a man. Soon it was followed by another like it. And then a third.

The next thing that happened was even more astonishing; Thothmes and Ptah-hotep beheld a small group of people who appeared to be nothing more than simple Egyptian peasants, coming out of the desert near the gigantic craft. In a matter of moments the humble newcomers were mingling with the deities on what appeared to be terms of familiarity.

Thothmes was almost outraged; in a way embarrassed, and certainly emboldened. "If peasants can approach the gods so casually, and talk to them, then we must also. It is our duty to go forward, my friend."

Ptah-hotep, staring at the distant group, jumped to his feet suddenly. "Is that the stonemason I see? The man we were to meet? If he can stand there talking to these gods, then all is well!"

The two officials stood erect and marched forward. Only when it was too late to turn back did they realize that there were also other gods on the scene, these smaller than grown men, swathed in strange clothing, with glassy heads, and obviously inhuman in their shape. But misshapenness in such beings was really no surprise.

The middle-sized one of the man-shaped gods at last caught sight of the two officials of Pharaoh where they were hiding, and beckoned vigorously for them to approach. But when the god spoke, its language was incomprehensible: "Willis! Look here! We've got a couple of important gentlemen come to talk things over!"

"Important?"

"Wearing a sizable fortune in pectoral collars. Look at them!"

Montgomery Chapel, exulting aloud to his elder brother,

approached the two elegantly dressed but obviously frightened Egyptians and tried to start to talk to them.

Sihathor and his family had managed to get but little sleep. Toward morning the patriarch himself had deliberately stretched out in the sand for a nap—if the gods wanted him they would come and get him, and he was not going to stay awake indefinitely for anyone else.

There had been moments during the night in which even Sihathor himself had been about two-thirds convinced that he and all his family were dead. Still, Osiris, Lord of Eternity and Weigher of Hearts, had never appeared, and the stonemason had taken that as reassurance that he could not yet have truly entered the Underworld.

Exposed under the cold stars tonight there might well be ten thousand unguarded tombs, ready to be robbed. But for the time being thoughts of robbery had been put aside.

One of the young people in his family had argued that this was a punishment, from those gods who did not like tomb-robbing.

Sihathor put down that notion haughtily. His clandestine profession was an ancient one, honorable in its way even if its practitioners were forced to be secretive. Did not Set, like other gods, deserve honor and worship?

Even as they were considering that point, his youngest son and his daughter set up a clamor, announcing that they had observed several additional strange signs in the heavens. Sihathor listened to the details, but he was no wiser when he had heard them.

Another one of the young people, argumentative and pessimistic, put forward another explanation. They were indeed all dead, but had been eaten by crocodiles, or killed in some other way that resulted in the destruction of their bodies. Therefore, instead of appearing immediately before the Weigher of Hearts, they must make their way through this peculiar world.

"That is ridiculous!" But Sihathor was not quite as certain of any of his answers as he made himself sound. It was the business of a leader to appear to be certain, no matter what.

In the darkness just before dawn, when all of them had awakened, Sihathor and his family witnessed a very strange sight indeed, the descent of a great spiritual boat or bird out of the heavens.

Creeping closer to the pyramid, they saw the strange visitor land and remain motionless upon the sand. Perhaps it was the solar Barque of Ra himself—though that could hardly be, for now the sun was coming as usual over the horizon to the east, reflecting glory in the Nile.

Two of the three strange, man-like gods from the Barque were making unmistakable signs for the stonemason and his family to approach.

When they knelt before the first man-god, he indicated with gestures that they should get to their feet. With smiles he and his fellow indicated that they were pleased with Sihathor and his family.

Then the three gods drew apart, and conversed for a long time among themselves.

Sihathor's people took advantage of this interlude to resume their own debate. One suggestion raised by a member of the party was that all these were only indications of the turmoil afflicting the whole universe as a result of the death of Pharaoh.

Others of the group continued to argue among themselves as to whether, in the face of such marvels, they should even consider going on with the robbery of Pharaoh's tomb.

❖   ❖   ❖

Pilgrim stood beside his ship, telling Monty and Willis that he would have to leave almost immediately. He had already set up the timelock and demonstrated its operation.

The agreement among the three of them was quickly solemnized. And then, almost at once, Pilgrim and his ship and crew were gone.

Young Montgomery Chapel, his eyes ecstatic, looked at his brother. "Easy as falling off a log, Will."

"You're right." Willis shook his head dazedly and looked about him. "This is incredible," he said, not for the first time. "Are we sure that timelock thing is going to work?"

"We saw it work, didn't we? I know, I know. I don't suppose we're sure of any of it. But I'll take it, as opposed to being an assistant instructor at fifteen hundred a year. It's a damned great shock, but it's the real thing, all right. What kind of world this fellow is from, and what he'll do when he has his hands on the gold, is more than I can say. But when a chance like this presents itself we've got to take it."

"Of course. Only . . ."

"Only nothing. Of course there may be risks."

"Such as what?"

Montgomery sobered. "Well. I don't say we shouldn't keep our eyes open. What do we know about this man? I mean besides the fact that he has the power to do incredible things—such as bringing us here—and that he was apparently telling us the truth when he said he came from a different world. We've agreed we don't even know his real name."

Willis nodded. "It strikes me that all the indications are he's hiding out, on the run, from something or someone. I think the signs are pretty conclusive along that line. If we help him—" The elder Chapel shrugged. "We might be making some enemies who are equally powerful, or perhaps more so."

"That's what I'm getting at, yes."

"Did you ever ask him if he's on the run?"

"Did you? Not quite the kind of question I'd like to pop to that fellow. Anyway, what good would it have done? Would he have told the truth?"

That really didn't seem likely.

But the Chapel brothers couldn't spend much time thinking about the risks. Not now. Because now, waiting for them a few yards away, stood the Great Pyramid.

All theirs.

TWELVE

All his life, first in the old world ruled by Pharaoh, and then during the two years he had lived in this new world in which gods walked the earth, Sihathor had been a light sleeper. He was a naturally early riser, too—except when circumstances required him to work late at night. Therefore it was not surprising that strange voices coming shortly before dawn, even distant voices, should awaken him now.

He had been dreaming of his old life, in the years before the never-to-be-forgotten day of Pharaoh Khufu's funeral. In those years the land of Khem had been filled with people, and gods had neither walked the land routinely, nor drawn their signs and wonders through the sky. In his dream Sihathor had been able to return for a time to his old house, in his old village, where his wife of more than twenty years had been sleeping as always at his side.

Now, awakening from dreams, he found himself in his new, uncertain life again. He was lying in the mudbrick hut of modest size which he had built with his own hands, close under the walls of Khufu's funerary temple. In that temple two years ago a few of the visiting gods and two high officials of the Court had taken up their residence. Once it would have been blasphemous for anyone, even high officials, to live in a temple, or for peasants to build a hut against a temple wall. But a new world, as these

152

descended gods were fond of explaining, was bound to
be governed by new rules.

The woman now stirring toward wakefulness at
Sihathor's side was much younger than the wife of his
youth. This one, who had wandered here alone from her
own depopulated village far downstream, had already
borne Sihathor a child; but still he would have given much
of his accumulated wealth to have his true wife back.

But no one wanted his wealth, for that or any other
purpose. Of what use was it to have treasure in this
transformed world?

Still the stonemason considered himself far more
fortunate than most. Most of his family, at least, had
survived the coming of the gods to earth. Life went on,
and a man had to cope with it as best he could.

Stirred by curiosity about the unfamiliar voices that
were still drifting across the wasteland, Sihathor got to
his feet, stooping to keep his head below the low reed-
bundle roof, and moved to the doorway where he could
stand upright.

He could tell from the appearance of the sky that Ra
in his eternal progress was now traversing the last hour
of the night, only minutes below the eastern horizon.
In the same direction were the marshes, and the small,
new fields in which most of the handful of workers toiled
daily. And just south of the temple, as always, towered
the mighty and overshadowing tomb of Pharaoh Khufu.
But this morning something new was happening. The
unfamiliar voices that had awakened Sihathor were
approaching the pyramid and temple from the west and
north, the direction of the path leading to the Gate to
Heaven, that the gods called their timelock.

For the past two years and more, ever since the
marvelous day and evening of Pharaoh's burial, Sihathor
and his extended family had been working here, near

Pharaoh's temple and pyramid, serving the gods who had come in human shape. Sihathor himself had grown to be almost on familiar terms with these particular gods. That he had never been able to identify them with any members of the known pantheon was no great concern to him. The deities named and enumerated ran into hundreds if not thousands. He had never tried to count them. Only a few priests could hope to know them at all.

Moving forward a little now, out of the doorway of the hut, he caught sight of the file of beings who were approaching along the path. Among the newcomers Sihathor recognized the god called Pilgrim—he had not visited here for two years, nor had the small, deformed ones who served him. And three of the arriving party, two women and a man, were beings Sihathor had never seen before. Those three appeared to be under guard, but he presumed that they too were divinities of some kind.

That there should be conflict among the gods was no great surprise to Sihathor. It was certainly not unheard of for the deities in songs and stories to quarrel violently among themselves. He drew himself up—these visiting gods did not particularly enjoy obeisance—and waited standing outside his hut, as ready as he could be for whatever the world might bring him next.

Scheffler and Becky Haggerty, one of the small aliens following close behind them, walked in the pre-dawn darkness across rock and sand. During the moments when they did not have to concentrate to find their footing, they could look up at what Scheffler realized must be the night sky of ancient Egypt.

The other two aliens, escorting Olivia between them, were ahead of Becky and Scheffler. And up in the very front of the small procession walked Pilgrim and the man who had identified himself as Willis Chapel. Willis—if this youthful man could really, possibly, be Montgomery Chapel's older brother—was moving like one who knew the landscape well. He stayed away from the canal, taking a more direct route across the sandy waste toward the pyramid. Walking beside him, Pilgrim had pulled out a flashlight, and those two at least were having no trouble finding their footing. They were talking together, but Scheffler could not hear what they were saying.

But already it was becoming easier for everyone to walk. Once they had gone beyond the area of hard rock that surrounded the fissure, a small trail became apparent in the gradually perceptible daylight.

"Where are we?" Becky whispered. At the moment she sounded more enthralled than terrified.

"Ancient Egypt."

"That's not funny, Tom."

"I know that. I know that very well. Look at that thing ahead of us."

Becky looked at the pyramid, and moaned, and mumbled something to herself.

And Scheffler, with an outdoorsman's compulsion to orient himself, looked up into the sky from which the fainter stars had already faded. He was suddenly more shaken even than Becky. He could not find Polaris, or the Big Dipper and its pointers that ought to have guided him to the pole star.

The stars were wrong. And that, more than anything else that had happened to him yet, made the strangeness of it all sink in.

Unbelieving, he tried to read the sky again. Hopeless. It was not that there were clouds. Rarely if ever before in his life had he seen such a clear sky, or so many stars, flung prodigally from one horizon to the other. The Milky

Way was staggering, or it had been a few minutes ago before the dawn began to wipe it out. But of the few constellations he knew, there was not one that he could recognize.

And now even the brighter stars in the east were starting to disappear.

Their steady, trudging pace was bringing the Great Pyramid closer. And with it came a surprise that distracted Scheffler from the sky. This time he was approaching the pyramid from the northwest, a different direction than on his solo trip. The trail Pilgrim and Willis were following led around the pyramid to the middle-sized low building Scheffler had glimpsed on his earlier trip, that huddled within a hundred paces of the pyramid's northwestern corner. He supposed it must be a temple of some kind.

As the small group, with Pilgrim and Willis in the lead, drew near the building, people were gathering tentatively in front of it to meet them, coming out of huts built inconspicuously against the temple's flank. These were Egyptian people, Scheffler thought. Builders of the pyramid? There were ten or twelve of them, dark of hair and skin, mostly young adults. A few of both sexes were entirely naked, and none was wearing more than a loincloth in the endless warmth. One teen-aged mother nursed an infant. Some of the people were coming out of the huts with primitive stick-handled tools in hand, as if they were about ready to go out to the fields.

Pilgrim, as he approached this assembly, waved to one of its members, a wiry man of middle age, in the manner of a man greeting an old friend. In return the man bowed and smiled and spoke to Pilgrim in accented English. Still more people, and a few more, as if someone were calling them to see the visitors, were coming out of the huts, until Scheffler thought there might be twenty altogether. Probably he would have seen them during his explorations if he'd gotten to this side of the pyramid at ground level.

Pilgrim had halted his group now, captors and prisoners mingling irregularly. Here were two more Egyptian men, coming down an open stairway from the temple's roof, wearing wigs, fine short linen skirts and jeweled pectoral collars. Willis introduced them to his fellow Americans as Thothmes and Ptah-hotep. The pair bowed, deeply and gracefully, and offered greetings in strangely accented English. Scheffler gathered from something they said to Pilgrim that they had just concluded their daily morning ritual greeting to Ra and his royal barque.

Pilgrim looked uncomfortable with people bowing to him. "I had thought you might have trained them out of that," he said to Willis. "You've had two years."

Willis shrugged. "It's not that easy. They seem to prefer to do us honor. Can't see that it does any harm." Eyeing the three newcomers from Chicago uncertainly, he explained: "There were only a small handful of natives here at the start, less than a dozen. But over the past two years others have been drifting in from up and down the Nile.

"Now I suppose there are between twenty-five and thirty, counting the newest generation. Nicky's been running a regular child care clinic."

"Where's everyone else?" Scheffler asked. "The rest of the population?"

Willis looked at him. "I'd say they've evacuated this entire area," he replied at last. Scheffler couldn't tell if Willis thought there was more to it than that or not.

Scheffler met Olivia's eyes, and thought that he could

read a bleak helpless warning in them. He knew what genocide meant, even if Willis had never heard the word before.

In this case it could mean that Pilgrim, in gaining or defending his access to this time and place, had somehow wiped out almost the whole native population.

"Tom Scheffler," Scheffler said, sticking out his hand. "And you're Willis Chapel? Doctor Montgomery's older brother?"

"That's right," said the young man casually. Willis was certainly under thirty, about as tall as Scheffler if not as strongly built. "And you must be one of his students. Nicky was saying something about having met you." Willis shook hands firmly. "Are you having some kind of trouble with Pilgrim?"

Pilgrim was approaching. When he spoke he sounded affable. "Look, Scheffler, we don't want to spend our lives pointing weapons at you. If I tell my people to relax their vigilance, you won't do anything stupid, will you? Like trying to use the timelock? One of my people is going to be keeping an eye on it. If I can't count on your reasonable cooperation, the next best alternative is to lock you away somewhere. I don't want to think about the other alternatives beyond that. Will you at least agree to a temporary truce, until we can discuss making it permanent?"

Willis was frowning, listening to this. Scheffler looked at the helpless Olivia, and at Becky, who looked back at him appealingly. "All right," he said.

"A wise decision." Pilgrim signed to his diminutive crew members to put their weapons away. Then one of them beckoned to the newly paroled prisoners, and Scheffler and Becky and Olivia followed him—or her—or it—into the temple. Pilgrim, following, was saying something about assigning them living quarters. But inside the temple the wiry, middle-aged Egyptian, Sihathor, took over as their guide.

Sihathor, in loincloth and red headband, stopped in front of Scheffler and bowed again. "You are the Lord——?"

"I'm not the lord anything. My name is Scheffler, Tom Scheffler."

"Scheff-ler. Very good, sir." Sihathor had something of the manner of a servant in an old movie. "And this lady?"

"Her name is Olivia. She's not well. She's been hurt."

Sihathor turned and called out something in a different language. Presently two of the Egyptian women came in to see what they could do for Olivia.

Then Sihathor turned back to the other new arrivals. "And this lady?"

"My name is Becky Haggerty."

"Lady Beck-y . . . ?"

"Not lady anything." She turned impatiently away from the dark patient face. "Tom, what is all this? For the last time, what's really going on here? Or am I just going crazy?"

"If you're crazy I am too. I wasn't kidding when I told you this was ancient Egypt. Get that through your head to begin with. That thing just outside is really the Great Pyramid. I ought to know, I've climbed it most of the way to the top."

Sihathor, smiling, was moving right along with the program to orient his honored guests. Conducting Scheffler, Becky and Olivia down a high-walled corridor, he pointed out to them a wide choice of quarters. Olivia appeared too dazed right now to take much interest. The rooms were many, the ceilings high in all of them, the stone walls all open at the top.

❖   ❖   ❖

Just as the guided tour returned to the common room where it had started, some food arrived, carried on a large wooden tray by an Egyptian waitress who was wearing nothing at all but a transparent cotton miniskirt. The girl wasn't bad looking, either, until she smiled and showed the sad state of her teeth. The newcomers sat down in silence and began to eat.

There were small, flat cakes of some kind, and several varieties of fruit, all delicious though Scheffler could not identify any of them. The drink offered in earthenware cups had a flat, vaguely beery taste. Sihathor, smiling, assured them that it was really beer. Scheffler opted for the alternate beverage, water from a five-gallon jerry can. Olivia was again fully awake. She had some trouble moving her arms and swallowing, but with a little help she could manage.

They had not been at breakfast long before Pilgrim joined them, announcing that Willis was being unavoidably delayed with some new work. Then their kidnapper made a surprising announcement. "Scheffler, I would like to send you back to the apartment of your worthy relative— you are not yet being released, let me hasten to add. It will be only a foraging expedition, from which I shall expect you to return. When we came through just now I was in too much of a hurry. Time for all the works and hands of days, that lift and drop a question on your plate. That's T. S. Eliot. Your language has found some worthy poets."

Scheffler no longer felt capable of much surprise. "Go on."

"It appears that we—all of us—are going to be working here for some time, and—"

"All of us?" Becky sounded surprised.

"Indeed. And we are going to need more supplies.

Fortunately the supply of safe drinking water already accumulated here by the Brothers Chapel should be adequate. But we shall need certain items such as food, tools, clothing, and sleeping bags. Two-way radios would be a great convenience. And weapons. I wish to speak to you particularly, Scheffler, about weapons."

Scheffler asked: "What do you mean by 'for some time'?"

"I have in mind a matter of only days. Probably no more than that at either end of the timelock. But however long it takes. You see, there is gold here, somewhere, gold that I must have." He paused with a sigh. "You think you understand that, but you do not.

"My crew and I have homeworlds of our own. Whether you believe me or not, our goal is the same as yours—to go home, there to be left in peace. Olivia's basic goal is to prevent our doing so."

"Not true." The policewoman's voice was weak, but she used it unhesitatingly. "It is not the law I serve that keeps you from going home. The laws of nature do that."

"Oh? Then, by your law, my crew and I are free to take the gamble?"

She appealed with her gaze to Scheffler and Becky. "He means to gamble with far more than his own life and the lives of his crew. Other lives and even other worlds are at stake." She faced back to Pilgrim. "You know what your insane attempt would do to space and to time. You know, but you don't care what happens to other worlds and other people. That is why we are determined to stop you."

"In practical terms it seems to amount to the same thing. We are to be arrested and detained for trial. Well, we respectfully decline to submit to your beneficent laws."

Again she looked at Scheffler and Becky. "For him to force his way back to the world he wants to reach is impossible."

Scheffler asked: "Then why not let him try?" He felt unreasonably rewarded when Pilgrim shot him an appreciative glance.

"Because the kind of effort he is determined to make involves illegal activities on his part. Activities that pose a great danger to a vast number of innocent people. It would take too long to explain it all."

"Nevertheless we continue to make that effort." Pilgrim sighed profoundly. "We are going to try."

He pushed aside the remains of the modest portion of food that he had taken. "A little background, for the benefit of Miss Haggerty and Mr. Scheffler. Somewhere around five thousand of your years before your time, my crew and I found ourselves in the world that would one day become yours, in a time and place that you would describe as ancient Egypt. Dear Olivia's minions—efficient as always—were there, too, and we fought one of our many inconclusive skirmishes.

"My ship was somewhat damaged—never mind the details, but certain components essential to its proper functioning were lost. The most critical parts happened to be made of gold." Pilgrim sighed again. "Not ordinary gold. A very special kind. Gold of atomic mass two-oh-three, stabilized to suppress the normal radioactivity of that isotope—I know that I am talking nonsense by the standards of your twentieth century science, but you can take my word for it. Or not, just as you choose. The fact remains that I must regain that gold, the same gold that I lost, if my crew and I are ever going to get home."

"So," said Scheffler, "it must be around here somewhere, and we're all drafted to help you dig for it."

"How quickly you grasp the essential point. Now, about sending you, Mr. Scheffler, back to the apartment. Miss Dietrich—Nicky—will go with you to help gather supplies.

She has also, I believe, a certain personal reason for
wanting to make the trip."

"Why can't I go back too?" Becky demanded.

Pilgrim glanced at her, but did not bother to answer
that directly. "Scheffler, I must be sure that I can trust
you before I send you back. There is now a temporary
truce between us—can it be made permanent? Will you
bring firearms and ammunition here, and not attempt
to fire them at me when you arrive? Do you now have a
realistic grasp of the situation?"

Scheffler looked at Olivia, who shook her head. "I think
you must do as he says," she told him weakly, reluctantly.
"Not only because he threatens you. Even his ship in its
present location is a danger to innocent people. It should
be moved. Right now that is more important even than
arresting him. Or killing him." She coughed.

"Thank you," said Pilgrim, and got to his feet. Taking
a last mouthful of melon, he said through it: "I leave
you three to your discussions. Other matters are going
to occupy me for most of the day. Sleep, for one thing."
In a moment he was gone.

Scheffler asked Olivia: "What's going to happen to us?"

"I think it unlikely that Pilgrim will harm you unless
you actively oppose him. I can advise nothing better than
cooperation now. It is best you help him get his gold,
get his ship moving again. He will be stopped somewhere
else."

"I haven't noticed any good chances for stopping him
yet."

She smiled wanly. "Nor have I. But be patient. You
are good people, I think, both of you. You won't be blamed.
Now I'm going to try to sleep."

Scheffler and Becky, free to move around in the temple
and its vicinity, had a chance to talk things over between

themselves. Right now the scene was peaceful. Egyptian children, feeding geese in an enclosure just outside the temple, smiled at them. He tried to explain how he had stumbled into all of this and inadvertently dragged her with him. He didn't have much success explaining.

For most of the day Nicky had been too busy to see much of the newcomers. For the past two months, ever since Monty had gotten her involved in this, she had spent increasing amounts of time trying to teach the Egyptians the rudiments of sanitation. Sometimes she was hopeful about the results—no longer did she see the children's faces covered with black flies, and none of the infants was really sick.

Today, when at last she had time to take a good look at the new arrivals, she wondered aloud who they were. She recognized Scheffler, of course, from their earlier encounter.

"He said he was a student," she remarked to Willis, who agreed in his calm way that Scheffler had confirmed that.

And Nicky wondered aloud at the strange clothing worn by Scheffler's young blond companion. What were students up to these days? Of course it was always something new and crazy.

"It looks like she put on some of her brother's clothes to go adventuring," Nicky remarked. That sweatshirt, she thought, was too small to be Scheffler's. And with its incomprehensible faded mottoes, it was strange even for a collegiate brother.

Willis could tell her very little more about the three people who had arrived under guard, but who now seemed to be working willingly with Pilgrim. "He's evidently picked them up somewhere to help out. But the older woman seems to be ill."

"Well, this is really his project, I suppose," Nicky allowed uncomfortably. "He ought to be in charge."

Then Willis changed the subject. "I hear you're going back to the apartment for supplies. Are you going to talk to Monty this time?"

"I'm going to try."

"You were going to tell him four days ago when he was here, and you didn't."

"Will, I'm the one who has to talk to Monty. Really, it's nothing directly to do with you."

"You know how I've come to feel about you, Nicky."

"I know." She didn't sound at all happy about it.

Meanwhile, Pilgrim and Scheffler were talking again. Scheffler asked him: "What are those . . . people, on your crew? Or should I call them something besides people? What are they?"

Pilgrim was not inclined to be understanding. "I have told you that they are as impeccably human as you are yourself. By any civilized definition."

"All right, that's what I was trying to find out. What are they called?"

"In your language, the closest one can come is something like *Asirgarh*."

"What about your language?"

Pilgrim made some kind of liquid sound. "Would you like me to repeat that?"

"All right. Whatever. Your crew. I guess I'll call them that. I can't tell one of them from another."

The small man flicked him an unreadable glance. His attitude seemed to say that Scheffler could call anyone anything he liked.

And then, shortly before Scheffler's departure with Nicky, Pilgrim took him aside again. "I want to make sure that you understand certain facts—if for example you were to tell the Chicago authorities, or try to tell them, exactly what is going on here—what do you suppose would be the result?"

"They wouldn't believe me."

"True. Oh, very true. But not the answer I was hoping would spring first to your mind. What if by some ghastly mischance they did believe you? Suppose you were to concoct some half-credible story of a ring of criminals engaged in smuggling artifacts? Of kidnapping and violence? For a young man of even minimal imagination it should not be difficult to bring those police to the apartment. What would happen when they rode the elevator? Have you thought of that?"

"You've still got Becky here."

"Ah. That was the reply that Miss Haggerty and I were both hoping to hear from your manly lips. We rejoice. Still, with a little effort, a man in your position might convince himself that she still needed rescuing—and even manage to imagine a daring scheme to rescue her."

"All right, suppose something like that were to cross my mind. No doubt you've got an answer for it."

"You will be further tempted by the presence of weapons in the apartment. I would like to make certain that I can trust you to bring back some of those weapons too. Not only we but the Egyptians here now stand in some danger of wild beasts."

"I suppose you'll have a good answer for me too, if I show up with a loaded rifle and point it at you."

"It is always a pleasure to deal with someone of your intelligence." And Pilgrim smiled.

There were at least two ways, thought Scheffler, a statement like that could be taken. Damn it, he couldn't decide if he should be planning to call Pilgrim's bluff or not. He imagined himself jumping the little man and getting the grip that would be needed to break his neck. Despite the disparity in size and weight, he wasn't at all sure whose neck would get broken.

Genocide. Something had caused the disappearance of almost an entire population. Maybe everyone in the vicinity of the pyramid and Memphis had been affected. Maybe everyone in Egypt. Maybe everyone.

His kidnapper was talking again: "Scheffler, I very much need your voluntary cooperation, as I have said. That will greatly speed the conclusion of my business, in your world and this one, and allow me to take my departure from both of them as quickly as I can."

Seeing that Scheffler was hesitating, the little man pressed on: "Never mind what I implied just now about threatening Becky. I withdraw all threats."

"Then she can come back with me?"

"No. Will you take my word for it that your Chicago authorities will not be able to prevent my doing what I wish, here and in Chicago as well? Have you heard what Olivia my enemy advises you?"

"Several times. But a few hours ago she warned us not to help you. She said—"

"I know what I said to you then." Olivia made a sound that was part sigh and part gasp of pain. "I was wrong."

Scheffler turned to her, nodded his head toward Pilgrim. "Is he crazy?"

"He is not what you mean by crazy, no. Once he was a great man . . . there is a word, I think, in one of your languages—hubris."

Pilgrim, listening, smiled in acceptance of the compliment.

"He's responsible for what's happened to the population here. Yet now you're saying that we should do what he wants."

"Your refusal will not stop him. It will only prolong the situation here, make it more dangerous . . . yes, I can only advise that now to help him will be best for everyone. So he can move his ship." She sounded half-dazed, a little incoherent.

Darkness had already fallen before Pilgrim was finally ready to send them on their way. Then Scheffler and Nicky walked with him to the timelock. He set the controls, and leaned toward the passengers, waiting until he had their full attention before he spoke.

"Change none of these settings." His voice and face were totally, grimly serious. "Else huge mice will emerge from the wainscotting, and eat you up."

He slid the door shut to close them in.

THIRTEEN

Nicky was carrying their shopping list, tucked into a pocket of her jacket. The list had been made out chiefly at Pilgrim's direction, but everyone had been free to nominate items for inclusion. Scheffler had seen the list briefly—it included not only weapons, but sleeping bags, all kinds of food and tools, as well as the dynamite and the outboard motor from the hidden cache in the apartment. Pilgrim must have assumed that those items had been restocked.

There was another request, not written down. At the last moment before they left the temple, Becky, suddenly sounding more like a tourist than a kidnap victim, had given Scheffler a key to her own apartment, and instructed him to go there and get some of her things. Her roommates, she thought, would not be back yet from their holidays. Pilgrim had thought it over and nodded his approval to the plan.

"I guess Monty's been busy," Nicky frowned. She had extracted the list from her pocket now, and was looking at it, meanwhile bracing her free hand against the wall as the elevator bobbed them up and down. "He's got one outboard motor in Egypt already; I wonder why he needs another?"

"The one you've been using there might be a little old."

"Old? I don't think so. It's a nineteen thirty-five model." Nicky's opinion of Scheffler's wit was not getting any

169

higher. "And why does he want 'two-way radios'? None of us are radio operators. And where would we set them up?"

Scheffler drew a deep breath. "Ah, excuse me, but—your name is Nicole—?"

"Nicole Dietrich. Monty and I are—were engaged to be married. Call me Nicky, we're all informal under these conditions. Is Monty in the apartment now?"

"He wasn't there when we left." Scheffler didn't want to stare at her, so, with a sudden effort, he stared instead at the light-speckled black wall in front of him. He'd had a lot of other things to think about, and it had just dawned on him in the last few moments that Nicole Dietrich never doubted that she was going back to the nineteen-thirties.

Was it possible that she was right? Scheffler didn't think so. They had to arrive at the nineteen-eighties version of Uncle Monty's apartment if they were going to pick up two-way radios there, and a modern outboard motor.

He cleared his throat and asked his companion: "What do you think of Pilgrim?"

Now it was her turn to stare with puzzled blue eyes at Scheffler, probably wondering just what his own connection with Pilgrim was. "A very clever man," she said at last. "Something of a bully, from what I've seen. I can't say I'm crazy about him. Why?"

Scheffler let out a puff of breath. "I can't say I'm crazy about him either. I can't figure him out. But now I seem to be working for him, although I've been told that he's a criminal."

"What he may be in his own world, I don't care," Nicky said firmly. "As long as he doesn't get us into serious trouble in ours." Still she appeared to be mostly absorbed in her own problems. "Do you know why Monty hasn't come through the timelock in the last four or five days?"

Scheffler hesitated. It was certain, then, that Pilgrim

hadn't told her, probably hadn't told Willis either. "Monty doesn't tell me why he does things," he said at last. *Jesus*, he was thinking. *What's going to happen when she gets there?*

She looked down at herself and frowned. "I've spent the last four days working in that hellhole, and I'm ready for a shower. While I'm cleaning up you can begin getting together some of the things on the list. What's the matter, what are you staring at?"

Scheffler blinked. "Sorry," he said. He had been gaping at her despite his resolve not to do so. She probably thought he was envisioning her in the shower. That would be fun ordinarily, but this time he had been thinking of what was going to hit her in the next few minutes. He ought to warn her somehow, but he couldn't think of what to say.

He said: "You don't—"

"I don't what?"

"Nothing. It can wait." Under her superior stare, Scheffler sighed, and shut up. He was sure Pilgrim was enjoying his little joke.

The journey this time was a short one, and before Scheffler had thought of any way to phrase a warning they had arrived. Maybe, he thought again, he was mistaken about what was going to happen.

When the door of the elevator opened, they were looking at the familiar reverse side of the curtain in a darkened Gallery Two. At this point, Scheffler supposed, there was probably no way to tell in which of several decades they had arrived. He stood back, watching as Nicky got out first.

She had no hesitation in striding out and boldly pushing the curtain aside. But a moment later she had run into the locked grillwork and recoiled in surprise.

"Monty's had this installed, then," she said, more to

herself than to Scheffler. Those startling blue eyes flicked
directly at him and away again. "He kept talking about
getting something like this put in, but . . ."

Darkness filled the apartment, except for the erratic
wash of lights that came in around and through the
draperies and blinds from distant traffic and from other
buildings. Scheffler by this time was at Nicky's side,
unlocking the grillwork gate with the key he had carried
in his pocket. There was no trouble in reaching around
from inside to get at the keyhole. "I think Monty had it
installed some time ago," he said, standing back to let
her go out first.

Nicky, if she heard that remark at all, must have decided
to ignore it as gross stupidity; the grillwork hadn't been
there four days ago. She was already striding past Scheffler
out of Gallery Two and down the hallway. Fifty years
ago, he supposed, one of the bedrooms here in this grand
bachelor apartment must have been hers, at least
unofficially, and he supposed that she was headed for
that room now. She hadn't bothered yet to turn on any
lights.

He stayed right on her dusty boot heels all the way
down the dim hallway to the kitchen, where she detoured.
After four days in ancient Egypt a good cold drink of
water evidently took precedence even over a shower, a
choice that in the light of his own experience he found
understandable.

Nicky pulled off her pith helmet and tossed it aside.
She strode across the kitchen, which like the rest of the
apartment was half-illuminated from outside by the lights
of distant vehicles and buildings. Approaching the sink
she reached for a glass from the drainboard—then stopped
abruptly. Scheffler, behind her, could tell from the angle
of her head that she was staring at the sink; the counter,
the nineteen-eighties faucets.

Reaching to the wall beside him, he switched on the kitchen lights. A certain suspicion was beginning to bother him—he kept remembering the way Pilgrim had smiled, seeing the two of them off—and the first thing he was anxious to get a look at was the wall clock. It read six forty-five, a reasonable time for darkness on a winter evening. And then, to allay his suspicions further, he turned to the wall calendar that hung beside the telephone. With relief Scheffler saw that it was the same calendar he remembered—doubtless it had been contributed by Mrs. White, for on its upper leaf, the reverse side of last month's dates, were displayed a religious picture and a message from a South Side funeral home. It was turned to the same month, January, as when Scheffler had seen it last, and—he made sure—the year was the same also.

But neither clock nor calendar could give him any reassurance about the exact date. The kitchen didn't look as if Mrs. White had cleaned it since his departure, and that helped a little.

Scheffler thought for a moment, then went to the refrigerator and opened it. The milk and cottage cheese he'd left were still there, the contents of the containers at the same levels as he remembered them. When he opened them and sniffed they still smelled fresh. He might have been gone an entire day, he told himself, relaxing inwardly. Conceivably two days. No more than that.

Nicky had turned away from the sink, to stare at him while he went through his routine at the refrigerator.

"What is this?" she demanded, in a suddenly suspicious voice. "Everything here's changed." Her voice dropped off, losing confidence, over the last three words, as if an inkling of the truth had hit her suddenly.

Scheffler did his best to break it gently. "You've been saying that you left this apartment four days ago. But at this end the time scale has been a little different—"

Evidently she hadn't yet made up her mind that his replies might be worth listening to; she didn't wait for him to finish this one. "What has he done to this place? All of this—"

She broke off. Her eyes had become locked on Scheffler's again, and what she saw there, largely pity, must have hit her hard. For the first time since Scheffler had met her she looked vulnerable. She turned away from him, only to be confronted by the nineteen-eighties model freezer and refrigerator, at which she stared in shock.

Direct action seemed to be called for. No use fumbling around trying to break it gently now. Wordlessly Scheffler moved to the kitchen wall beside the nineteen-eighties phone. He took down the calendar from the wall and held it up in front of Nicky's eyes.

Nicky looked from Scheffler's face to the page and its terrible numbers, and back to his face again. From deep in her throat there came the kind of small sound that a lost child might have made. Then she backed up until she was stopped by the Formica counter beside the sink. She leaned with her hands against the counter behind her, and stared at Scheffler again. Now her gaze was urgent, pleading, as if there were nowhere else she could turn for help.

"This is what year it is," said Scheffler softly and patiently. Then he tossed the calendar aside. During the elevator ride and just afterward he had been starting to look forward to this moment, in a way. But now he was not enjoying it at all. "At this end, you've been gone about half a century."

Nicole was silent for a long time, trying to come to grips with that. He could see her fighting down incipient panic. Then absently she turned back to the sink, and filled her glass. At last she got the long drink of cold water for which she'd hurried to the kitchen. Then she had half a glass more, taking her time about it.

"Fifty years," she said at last, her back still to Scheffler, and put the glass down hard beside the sink.

Then she moved toward the window as if she wanted to look out. Scheffler, wanting to be helpful, went to raise the shade, but she waved him back.

"I see, now," Nicky said, not bothering with trying to see out through the window. "I see now. Let me think for a minute. The settings on the timelock must have been changed the last time Monty used it. When he came back here . . . four days ago." She looked up at Scheffler sharply. "If the settings could be readjusted again, would that give us, Willis and me, some chance of getting back—?"

He was standing with arms folded, leaning back against the kitchen counter, shaking his head gently. "You're asking the wrong man, lady. This timelock thing is all as new to me as it is to you. Maybe even a little newer. But I suspect it's not just as simple as getting into that car and pushing a button or two for where you want to go. The paradoxes and so on that Pilgrim talks about. And I definitely wouldn't try changing any of the settings unless I knew what I was doing. I've figured out that much. Even if Pilgrim hadn't warned us not to do it. Mice in the wainscotting." Scheffler remembered the Monty Python bit with sheep hiding in the walls, but of course Nicky wouldn't. "I wouldn't put it past him," he muttered to himself.

"No. I wouldn't try it either. That's why Pilgrim was so ready to trust me to come back," Nicole meditated, with bitter anger growing. "He knew that this would happen." Then she looked at Scheffler sharply. "Who are you, really?"

"Just what I said, a student at the university. Also a somewhat distant relative of Will and Monty. When I was a little kid my mother used to tell me about how you and Will had double-crossed great-uncle Monty and run off together."

He had thought she might react to that, but evidently she was still numb from the first jolt. "My parents—" she said, and didn't finish.

"Fifty years," Scheffler reminded her gently.

"Fifty years." Nicky shook her head as if to clear it, and was silent again. Then her practicality started to return. "Anyway, I assume that even in the nineteen-eighties gold is still gold. If we can keep our deal with Pilgrim going, we can still sell gold. Right?"

"I think what we ought to shoot for is just getting everyone out of this in one piece. And I don't think Olivia's people will be that easy to get clear of. You haven't seen any of them except her?"

"No."

"But she has given her blessing to what we're doing now. And you're right about the gold. Three hundred and something dollars an ounce, the last I heard. If I remember right."

"And even if Pilgrim does get away with all the gold, there's still a market for Egyptian antiquities, I presume? My God, no one else in this time has opened a timelock to the past, have they?"

"No. No one in the world I know about. And sure, there's still a market for the ancient stuff too." He hadn't thought he would ever be able to feel sorry for his great-uncle, after the man had used him as a guinea pig and practically arranged to have him kidnapped. But looking at Nicky he came close. He thought he could be sorry for any man who lost her. God, but she was beautiful, even now, grimy and worn out with exhaustion. And right now she was shocked, and desperate, and therefore, Scheffler would be willing to bet, more than a little dangerous.

Scheffler added: "I'd estimate it's a much bigger market than the one you knew. But you're going to need help, before you just run out and start trying to sell things. Guidance. Until you know this world, someone's going to have to guide you through it."

"I'm sure," she said, reappraising him, "you will be very helpful." Then she turned away, speaking over her shoulder: "I'm going to find my old room, and take a shower, according to plan—is there anyone else in the apartment?"

"There shouldn't be. Unless some more of Olivia's police have come in through the window or however they do it. Or Pilgrim and Uncle Monty have more enemies that we don't know about."

"Olivia. She's police, then?"

"From Pilgrim's world, wherever that is, and trying to arrest him. She and her friends were here once before. I didn't get the impression that any of them are the kind of people who just give up."

Nicky's shoulders slumped a little. "Serious crime is something we didn't bargain for when we got into this. Or at least I didn't."

"Maybe you didn't. Maybe Willis didn't either, for all I know. Monty seems not to have had much trouble making the adjustment."

"Are you sure Olivia's really some kind of police?"

"About as sure as I can be of anything in this mess. Why?"

"But still you say she told you to co-operate with Pilgrim—"

"That's right."

Nicky heaved an exhausted sigh. "Then why shouldn't we? I doubt if her people are about to pounce on us. We'll get the food and other things and take them back, and worry about the rest of it later."

She stood for a long moment with her face buried in her hands, as if she hoped to get some rest that way. Then she straightened her neck with a toss of grimy hair. "But there's no tearing hurry. If it's been, my God, fifty years, my own clothes are obviously all gone—is there anyone currently living here whose clothes I could borrow?"

"Afraid not. If I take time to go over to Becky's apartment . . . but she's much shorter than you, nothing would fit. There's an automatic washing machine here, and a dryer, if you want to run some laundry. I'll show you how they work. I can also loan you a robe."

"I don't suppose they'll iron things, will they? Your laundry machines?"

Presently Nicky had vanished into a bedroom. She was quick and decisive about choosing one, confirming Scheffler's earlier guess about her having had a room here. It was across the hall from Scheffler's. Through the closed door he could hear the water in that private bath start running.

He went into the bedroom that had become his own, and looked at his face in the mirror there, and wondered who he really was and what he ought to be trying to do next.

Looking at himself, and taking a cautious sniff or two, he decided that a shower and change of his own might be the best practical way to start.

Her water was still running when he came out of his room, freshly washed and clothed, and he set about getting some food ready for immediate consumption. If he had understood Pilgrim's final instructions correctly, he and Nicky would be able to stay here for several hours and still be gone no longer than an hour at the other end.

When Nicky emerged, swathed in a robe and towels, he demonstrated the latest in washer and dryer technology.

While the machine was running she joined him at the kitchen table.

While they shared roast beef sandwiches she began to ask Scheffler questions about the Eighties, starting with what was visible to her at the moment, the food, the containers it came in, modern freezing and microwave thawing. She accepted in an abstracted way the evidences of wealth and plenty in the apartment; probably, he thought, she took that for granted anywhere in the twentieth century, having never known any other kind of life except when she went camping. But part of her mind was obviously elsewhere. Doubtless it was back in the ancient land with Willis.

While Nicky was finishing her milk and sandwiches Scheffler went to the room where the gun rack was and started to look over the possibilities. He was accustomed to shooting a .22, preferably scope-sighted. With that kind of rifle he had once been able to knock the heads off squirrels with fair consistency at a range of up to fifty yards or so. Of course now that lions and crocs were going to be the targets, it was obvious that something bigger in the way of bullets was required. That was no problem here. Whoever had stocked the gun rack seemed to have had his very needs in mind.

Nicky joined him presently. She was still in her borrowed robe, walking barefoot and chewing on a last morsel of bagel, with her dark hair trying to escape from under a towel. She asked: "What about those funny-looking weapons that Pilgrim and his creatures are carrying? Do you know how they work?"

"No, but I respect 'em. Whatever they are they're from a different world than the nineteen eighties. And Pilgrim seems to think we're likely to need some of these."

The rifles in Uncle Monty's fancy wooden cabinet were a far cry from the .22's Scheffler remembered from his

teenaged hunting years. These were beautiful and
obviously expensive things, with oiled stocks of exotic-
looking woods and what looked like hand-tooling on the
breeches and barrels. They were well cared for too. But
to Scheffler weapons like these were somewhat unfamiliar.
At first glance he mistook the first one he picked up for
a shotgun—it was a double-barreled piece with a bore
diameter of about half an inch, and broke open at the
center for loading. Not until Scheffler had broken the
action open did he realize that he was holding a rifle.
Good God, what did they shoot with a thing like this,
elephants?

While he went rummaging among the firearms, Nicky
dug into drawers in the bottom of the gunrack, with the
air of someone who already knew what ought to be there.
Her slender sunburnt hands came out of a drawer with
cartridges. The brassy shapes looked huge to Scheffler,
who was used to small game and target shooting. These
came packed in small, old wooden boxes that looked like
items from an antique shop.

"Here. Tom." He thought it was the first time that she
had used his name. "Weatherby .460, I think that's what
you need for the rifle you're holding. If you want
something even bigger, there's a Nitro Express. I think
that runs .577. Supposed to be able to knock down an
elephant. I've never tried it myself. I only weigh a hundred
and fifteen, and I've seen how it kicked Will when he
fired it. He'd heard that the hippos in Egypt might be
dangerous, but so far we've only seen them at a distance."

"Lions, I suppose?"

"Haven't seen one myself. But you can hear them,
especially at night."

Whatever the effective range of this ammunition, or
the intended targets, there were no scope sights on these
rifles. Maybe it wasn't considered sporting to shoot a lion

or a crocodile or an elephant—until the critter charged you. Scheffler could go along with that. Live and let live was fine with him. And anyway there was no guarantee that after forty or fifty years the cartridges were going to fire. Of course his uncle had obtained a fresh supply of dynamite; maybe he'd updated the ammunition too. With a brass cartridge Scheffler found it harder to tell.

He and Nicky did what they could to scrounge up other items on the general shopping list. Digging into the hiding place where the dynamite had been concealed fifty years ago, they got out the modern replacement stores that Scheffler had already discovered. There were the blasting caps and electrical detonator, as well as the potent sticks coated in red plastic.

When a gentle chime from the laundry room announced that Nicky's clothes were dry she took them into her room to dress. Scheffler meanwhile looked into the freezer for frozen meat, and began to gather other supplies. Someone had ordered toilet paper, and he rummaged in several bathrooms to collect enough. There were other items on the list. He began to haul things down the hallway to Gallery Two.

At the last moment Scheffler thought of trying to do something else in secrecy from Nicky. Now was his chance to come up with a masterstroke of cleverness, if he had one in him. While she was dressing he considered going into the kitchen and quickly leaving a message on the phone-answering machine. He could record something there that would reveal the secret of the hidden "elevator," then unplug the machine. Mrs. White in her determination to have things in proper order would certainly plug it in when she next entered the apartment. Was that next entry scheduled to take place on the following morning? He couldn't remember.

The end of the cord would be left lying right on the

kitchen counter, and there was no way Mrs. White could fail to see it. She might ignore it though. Meanwhile the others, whatever electronic juggling they might manage, would hardly be able to get at the message to erase it unless they were to return to the apartment.

Some story about a ring of smugglers and illegal excavators, that would be it. That, if Scheffler and Becky were to disappear, would provoke an investigation that none of the other parties would be anxious to have. Especially if old Montgomery Chapel were to vanish from the face of the earth at about the same time.

Scheffler considered it all carefully. He thought about Pilgrim, and Becky, and Olivia. He didn't do it.

Nicky came out of her room, fully dressed again, wearing the clothes she had arrived in, clean now, but badly wrinkled. While she was gone the pile of supplies in front of the grillwork door had grown substantially, and Scheffler was getting down toward the bottom of the list.

"I'm going to take the time," Scheffler announced, "to run over to Becky's apartment and get the stuff she asked for. I don't know if any of her roommates are there or not—she thought they were probably all still home for the holidays. Want to come along and see a little of the new world?"

Nicky looked doubtful. Before she could reply, there was the sound of a key entering a lock from the front door of the apartment. There was no time to use the closed-circuit TV to see who was trying to get in. No chains on that door, of course. Just those beautiful locks, that someone with the right key could always open from the outside.

"Who—?"

"Mrs. White. The housekeeper. She's the only one who has a key. Unless—" With frantic motions Scheffler sent

Nicky into the adjoining room. He put down the rifle he was holding and faced the doorway expectantly.

The door opened. It was his great-uncle Montgomery who walked in.

The old man, dressed as nattily as ever, in fur cap and fur-collared coat, stopped in his tracks at the sight of his sunburnt grandnephew. The look on Uncle Monty's face was not exactly surprise; it was as if he had been expecting to find drastic changes of some kind.

"What's happened—?" he started to ask.

At that moment Nicky stepped in from the next room. The light Winchester was still in her hands, though not aimed anywhere in particular.

Monty turned. He gaped at her. Then a small object dropped from his right hand to thud gently on the carpet— it was a pistol. Then his eyes rolled up and he collapsed to the floor.

Scheffler sprang forward. His first move was to close and lock the front door of the apartment, which his great-uncle had left open behind him. Then he bent over the crumpled figure on the carpet, making sure that the old man was still breathing. Then he picked up the pistol— a small revolver—and after a moment's thought dropped it into his own pocket.

Nicky pressed forward, staring at the fallen man. "What happened? Who in the hell is that?"

Scheffler sat back on his heels. Somehow angered by her attitude, he said: "This is the man you were going to marry."

He hadn't meant it to come out quite so much like an accusation, but his own nerves were nearly shot. Nicky turned pale and knelt down too beside the victim. The whole time-displacement business, Scheffler supposed, hadn't really been real to her until that moment.

But Nicole recovered quickly. After a moment she said,

"I'll get some water." She sprang up briskly to her feet, then turned back for a moment in hesitation. "Maybe brandy would be better."

"It's in the dining room," Scheffler called after her.

By the time she came back with two glasses, brandy in one and water in the other, the old man was sitting up, trying to push free of his grandnephew's supporting arm. Monty looked at her with exhausted eyes, to which intelligence was now returning, like a curse.

Once more Nicky knelt lithely down beside Montgomery Chapel, looking back at him with fascination. In a moment she said softly, "Monty, you damned old—Monty, what's happened, what've you done?"

Montgomery Chapel stared at her. He took another sip of brandy and water before he would trust himself to speak. But it appeared to Scheffler that his mind was working all the time. At last he said, "I have grown old, my dear, over the course of fifty years. I wonder if you will be able to accomplish as much as that."

"Now what are we going to do with him?" She had turned back to Scheffler, and now she spoke angrily, in shock, as if the old man couldn't hear her. "What can we do now? Can we just leave him here?"

"I don't think," said Scheffler, "that Pilgrim would want us to leave him here."

"To begin with," said Uncle Monty, making a sudden effort to take charge, "you must tell me what has happened."

"Pilgrim's back," said Nicky, turning back to her fiancé as if reluctantly compelled. "The man you told me about."

Uncle Monty, unsurprised, nodded feebly. "I feared as much. Where is he now?"

"At the other end of the timelock, in the usual place. He has a woman with him—a prisoner—" Nicky stopped.

"Who?"

"She says her name's Olivia, and she represents herself as being a police agent," said Scheffler. "Not from this century. Maybe not from this planet, I don't know."

"Ah." Uncle Monty ruminated on that point too. But it seemed that the existence of Olivia did not take him by surprise. "I expected something like that, too. What else?"

"What else?" Scheffler could hear his own voice cracking awkwardly with strain. "What else? That ought to be enough. We're going to have to take you back there with us."

"Oh, I insist upon it." The old man fought his way up into a sitting position. "For fifty years I have been waiting for the lock to open so I could make that journey once again. Nothing is going to keep me from it now."

Montgomery Chapel was on his feet again, standing alone in his bedroom with the door closed while he changed into desert clothing. The garments all fit well enough, being almost new. He'd had them for a few years though he'd seldom worn them. They were part of his continuing policy of readiness.

Having gained a few minutes alone with the door closed was something of an accomplishment. Scheffler was naturally suspicious of him, and had looked ready to drag his great-uncle forcibly into the timelock if he had argued about going.

Montgomery had to smile at himself in the mirror when he thought of that; he was as well prepared as a man his age could be to go to ancient Egypt. For decades, ever since he'd adjusted the controls of the timelock and shut it down, he'd been aware that almost certainly it would open again one day. And he'd thought that this month, of this year, was one of the most likely times for that to happen. Pilgrim had evidently made the same calculation.

Of course the plan of shutting down the timelock hadn't worked out just the way Montgomery had hoped. Far from it . . .

Buttoning up his khaki shirt, Montgomery looked closely at himself in the bedroom mirror. Old man, are you really ready to go adventuring again? But the question was only rhetorical. The answer was, yes, he was ready, readier than he had ever been. Of course the body at his present age couldn't do nearly as much as it had once been able to accomplish. But the mind—the all-important mind—was quite as capable as ever. And the mind had been granted fifty years of study in which to prepare for this enterprise.

There came a knock on Montgomery Chapel's bedroom door. It caught him at an awkward moment, just when Pilgrim was intruding again into his thoughts, and the sound chilled Montgomery Chapel like the knocking in *Macbeth*.

But this time it was only young Scheffler at his door, coming suspiciously to check up on what the old man was doing. And then to complain in injured tones about all the difficulties he'd had to go through: being menaced by strange dwarfish aliens, and then kidnapped. Why hadn't this great-uncle warned him such things were likely to happen in this apartment? And, worst of all, they hadn't happened only to Scheffler, but to some innocent and unsuspecting friend of Scheffler's too.

Montgomery was calm and soothing. In response to his questions it turned out that Scheffler's friend was a young woman, who had been sleeping here last night, and was now apparently being held hostage by Pilgrim at the other end of the time-connection.

Thinking it was time he put the youngster on the defensive, Montgomery demanded: "Did Pilgrim hurt you? Either of you?"

"No. It's just that he forced us to go along with him."

That was about what Montgomery would have expected; but he said, "Then I would suggest you count yourselves fortunate. You don't realize, perhaps, just how fortunate. Tell me the details."

As Montgomery pieced the story together, Scheffler and the young woman had been surprised by Pilgrim and several of the *Asirgarh*. (At that Montgomery sighed, privately. He had only glimpsed those creatures briefly, fifty years ago, and he had been hoping that they wouldn't come back.)

Then the two captives had been taken through the timelock—apparently the first trip for the girl but not for Scheffler—and shortly thereafter Scheffler had been persuaded to cooperate actively with his captor. Pilgrim had trusted him enough to send him back to collect arms and other supplies.

"All that Becky and I want is to get out of this!" the young man concluded earnestly.

Nicky had come into the room behind Scheffler as he spoke, and she had been listening to the explanation as if at least part of it might be news to her also. She was still looking at Montgomery in a puzzled and thoughtful way, which under the circumstances was hardly surprising.

When Montgomery had heard the story through, he faced the two young people with his best air of kindly authority. "I never expected that it would come to this, my boy. Nicky, my dear, I'm sorry. Very sorry indeed not to have spent the last half-century with you."

Young Thomas Scheffler looked at him in frank disbelief. "You didn't expect anything like this?"

"No, of course I didn't. Do you think I would have left you alone here if I had anticipated any such intrusions?"

"Yes. I think you set me up for this."

Montgomery, looking wounded, shook his head.

"You set me up to fool around with your timelock. So if anything happened to the first person to use it again after fifty years, it'd happen while you were safely far away."

Montgomery did his best to look sadly bewildered. After a moment he sighed, and said: "I suppose that it must appear that way to you." Then he stop fiddling around with his spare clothing on the bed and faced his grand-nephew squarely. "Look here. Some explanations are obviously in order. Nicky's heard them before, but you haven't. I—along with my brother Willis—first became involved with Pilgrim half a century ago. So I know something of what I'm talking about when I tell you what he's like."

"I'd like to hear."

"Of course. Well, to make a long story short, my brother and I were both young scholars then, intensely interested in the East. And one day this man—approached us.

"We didn't know what to make of him at first. He told us that his name was Peregrinus—later he used Pilgrim. Of course we understood that those names were aliases. He was obviously wealthy and knowledgeable, but some of the things he said made us suspect that he was mad . . . until he demonstrated certain powers that convinced us he was not mad at all. He showed us his spaceship. He took us in it to ancient Egypt. I can tell you that now, without fear you'll think that I'm a lunatic.

"At that point we had to believe his claims that he could make us immensely wealthy.

"So—rightly or wrongly—Willis and I struck a deal with him. He provided—from where I don't know—the money for me to buy this apartment, in this building, which was then under construction. He said there were several reasons this site would make a convenient location for the timelock, and he saw to it—somehow—that the timelock was installed and functioning. Once Will and I went through it with him—well, you've done that now yourself. Perhaps you can begin to understand what it meant to two young archaeologists in the Thirties. If you can understand that, you can understand much that followed.

"And there were also the implied threats, quite subtle

at first, of what was likely to happen to us if we didn't do exactly as he wished. By then we had some understanding of his power. Also we had begun—too late—to have new doubts and fears. We undertook to work for him in ancient Egypt while he was gone. There were circumstances, he said, that would keep him from staying to do the work himself.

"Willis and I didn't know it, but the police—Olivia's police—were already after Pilgrim at that time. He told us nothing about any of that—his fugitive, criminal status in his own society—until he had to. Somehow he managed to elude his pursuers, to fence them out from this entire region of spacetime—I suppose from the whole Earth, during most of the twentieth century. The only problem from his point of view was that, in order to fence them out, he had to fence himself out of the region as well. For a time.

"Now. This is the part that Nicky hasn't heard yet." Montgomery's throat felt dry, and he stepped into his bathroom for a glass of water. The explanation was going well, he thought, perhaps because much of it was the truth.

He came back into the bedroom and faced his audience again. "Another problem developed later—fifty years ago for me, Nicky, four days ago for you. The timelock stalled. For some reason it ceased to function properly. We had come to believe that it was perfect, I suppose. It seems simple enough in operation, but obviously it is based on a science far beyond anything born of the twentieth century.

"Pilgrim and the *Asirgarh* had departed by then. I was stuck here when the malfunction happened, and Will and Nicky were trapped in ancient Egypt—it appears now they didn't realize that they were trapped, if only for four days."

"No, we didn't." Nicky had paled slightly under her tan.

"The world of course believed that they had betrayed me and run off together . . . there was no other explanation I could offer for their absence."

Nicky, standing in the doorway, appeared to be moved by that. Montgomery could only try to imagine what the treacherous, faithless bitch was feeling at the moment.

Montgomery could see from the changed expression on the young man's face that at least a seed of doubt regarding his great-uncle's guilt had now been planted in his mind. Well, that would have to do for now. Later, whatever else might happen, he would have to cultivate that doubt.

The real challenge, of course, was going to come when he faced Pilgrim.

Not that he had quite disposed of Scheffler yet; here came another question.

"One more thing, sir."

"What's that?"

"The people. There in Egypt. I'd like to know what happened to them all."

"Ah. I take it that by 'all' you mean the bulk of the native population?" Montgomery put on a grim face; this was going well. "There are, or were, a few survivors."

"That's right, a few. A handful of Egyptians living with your brother and the others by the pyramid. What happened to all the rest? I got the feeling no one there wanted to give me a straight answer about that."

"Ah." Montgomery hesitated, deliberately. "I suppose Pilgrim is the only one who could really do so—if he would."

"How's that?"

Montgomery proceeded as if reluctantly. "My idea is that . . . something happened there, when the timelock was established. Perhaps having too many people around, in the way, would simply have been inconvenient for Pilgrim." Montgomery paused again, looking at his grandnephew. "At first he told us, Willis and me, that most of the populace had probably taken fright and run away when they saw his ship. Later—I began to have doubts about that explanation. But by then of course the crime—if indeed there was a crime of the kind you fear— had already been committed. There was nothing for Willis and myself to do but make the best of the situation. Try to help the surviving Egyptians in every way we could. Which we have done."

"Wow," said the young man, soberly.

"Perhaps you are beginning to see what I mean, about Pilgrim. He may have conducted himself like a perfect gentleman, so far, with you and the young lady who was with you here—"

" 'Perfect gentleman' would be stretching it some."

"Now, if I might continue dressing alone?"

Nicky and Scheffler went out into the hallway, talking seriously.

Montgomery could have finished his hasty physical preparations in their presence, but he needed to reorganize his thoughts as well. Young Scheffler's survival had not really surprised him. No, he had allowed for the possibility that the young man might be able to make it to Egypt and back through the timelock without destroying himself and perhaps some sizable portion of Chicago.

No, what had really stunned Montgomery was Nicky's return, not only still alive but as young and beautiful as ever. *That* was a vision he had never expected to be confronted with again in a million years. In that first moment today, when he'd seen her with a rifle, he had been sure she knew what he'd done and meant to shoot him.

He wondered if her youthful presence was going to turn out to be more than he could bear. All the gods, ancient and modern, knew it was going to take him time to come to grips with it. And now that the passage to the past had reopened, and events were starting to move rapidly again, he was not likely to be allowed enough time to think or even to pull himself together.

Well, perhaps that was just as well under the circumstances.

He was dressed and packed now, ready to go or very nearly. He rejoined the two young people in the kitchen, where they were pulling a few choice items out of the freezer to take along.

It suddenly occurred to Montgomery, looking sidelong at how they worked together, the youthful Nicky and his relative, to wonder if these two were now lovers. Had Willis already been jilted too?

As they began loading their cargo—two-way radios, outboard motor, dynamite, rifles, a jumble of odd containers—into the time vehicle, young Thomas Scheffler made it clear that he was not yet through being suspicious. "Have you actually been in Egypt?" he demanded of his great-uncle.

Montgomery Chapel raised a haughty eyebrow. "What do you mean?"

"I mean twentieth-century Egypt. Within the past few days. That was a Cairo phone number you left for me. But you said you were going to be gone four months."

"My boy, what difference does any of that make? I went looking for help, information, and I didn't find it. I'll provide you with a complete itinerary of my trip if you want one. But where I was last week is hardly relevant to the problems we are facing now."

Scheffler still was not satisfied. "And what was that one call all about? You haven't explained that yet. Sending

me in there to look at the false door—that is one of the
realest doors I have ever seen in my life. And what was
all that crap about how I should make an adjustment on
your alarm system?"

"It was done out of a concern," Montgomery pronounced
in a nobly injured tone, "for your welfare. You haven't
lived with that device as long as I have." He had spent
some time in thinking up that answer, just in case it should
be needed.

The immediate effect was confusion, as Montgomery
had hoped. "Let's get on with it," the impatient youth
muttered, tightlipped. "Maybe you can show me what
you mean when we get into the damned thing."

Montgomery nodded grimly, and began to survey the
food supplies that still remained to be loaded. He had
more answers ready if there should be more questions,
as seemed likely. More answers to provide more confusion,
that was all the young idiot deserved. No, think logically,
think accurately. The boy wasn't an idiot. He'd survived
both the timelock and an encounter with Pilgrim, in good
shape. But good answers were something Montgomery
owed to no one.

For decades he had made plans for his return to ancient
Egypt. But now he was having trouble concentrating on
the plans he'd made. Many of them had suddenly been
rendered irrelevant anyway. Nicky, Nicky, Nicky! She was
unchanged, absolutely. Not that her presence matched,
quite exactly, the fifty-year-old image in his memory; but
he was sure that it was his memory that had devolved.
Even her clothing, he thought, was the same in which
he'd seen her last, on that never-to-be-forgotten day of
half a century ago. The day he'd smiled at her and Willis
for what he'd thought would be the last time, and closed
himself into the timelock, and done the best he could to
take his vengeance.

Then today, instantly, in the first moment when he saw her standing beside Scheffler, Montgomery had understood immediately what must have happened, even though the possibility of such a twist of fate had never occurred to him before. The shock of recognition, and the fear of her rifle, had made him faint. For a moment, as Montgomery's consciousness faded, he had feared that he was dying without being shot. But he had survived that shock and now he could assume that he was going to live a while. The doctors always told him that he had a strong heart for a man his age.

But the implications of Nicky's survival were gradually becoming clearer to him now. And they were enough to cause another kind of shock, more subtle and more long-lasting.

His first and most obvious question had already been answered. Willis had survived too. Only four days for him; why not?

Next question: Did Nicole and Willis yet realize what he had attempted to do to them? That after watching Pilgrim set the controls a number of times, he'd gambled on being able to close them off from their own world for fifty years? Judging by Nicky's behavior today, it would seem they had never guessed anything of the kind; and for that Montgomery could be thankful.

For most of his life he'd been assuming that the faithless bitch and her lover were dead, had died within a matter of days after he'd shut down the timelock on them and marooned them in that hellish environment. The stockpile of clean drinking water could not have lasted much longer than that. When a month had passed in Chicago after he'd cut them off he had been certain that his revenge was complete. To Montgomery it had seemed unquestionable that once they were denied the prophylactic powers of the timelock, infection of some kind must have killed them even if the heat and wild beasts had not.

Even supposing Nicky to somehow have survived the initial dangers, filtering and boiling river water and finding safe food, she must have withered rapidly into old age, her beauty dried and baked and starved away, within a year or two of being marooned in that environment.

She and her lover, he imagined, could hardly have found each other still appealing after the first days. Montgomery had long relished the mental picture of them as shriveling near-skeletons, clawing the thickening blood out of each other's veins in the last extremity of thirst, fighting feebly over the last drops of clean water in the last canteen.

But no. The dream, so satisfyingly enjoyed for decades, had been a dream and nothing more. Nothing like it had ever happened. It turned out now that his hideous revenge had been only a glorious daydream. Far from being crushed by the masterstroke of his retaliation, his intended victims had not even realized that they had been found out. In the four days of their isolation they had probably not even tried to use the timelock. For them it had been four days without Monty, four days in which to grapple and pant at will, never dreaming that he had discovered their betrayal.

That at least was good.

Because now, his revenge would have to be accomplished all over again.

Fifty years later, having finished his personal preparations, getting ready to leave through the timelock once more, he exchanged a few more words with Nicky. Her manner toward him was hesitant and odd, but he supposed that under the circumstances it could scarcely be otherwise. Montgomery heard enough from her to convince him completely that neither she nor Willis understood what he had meant to do to them. They had no idea that he'd seen them in the grass at the edge of the marsh, going native together in the heat.

Nicky said to him, "There was something I was going to tell you."

"What was it?"

She hesitated, appearing to struggle with herself. At last she said, "It doesn't matter now."

Doesn't matter now, hey? Of course not. I am an old man now, and what could such things as love and betrayal matter to the old? What feelings do they have?

Montgomery asked her for more details about Willis, trying to put the questions with just the appropriate amount of concern. Willis, as he had feared was in good health.

By this time they had everything they were going to bring with them loaded into the timelock. It made a great pile, just about leaving room for three people to get in with it. Montgomery did not forget to close both grill and curtain after him. Mrs. White, he was confident, would confine her activities to cleaning, and mind her own business if she noticed anything odd in the apartment. He had trained and rewarded her for decades to that end.

Montgomery Chapel hadn't been inside the timelock now for fifty years. And it was smaller, more ordinary-looking, somehow, than he had remembered it . . . entering the little black-walled car again brought memories flooding back, their details sharp and sudden. As if more memories were what he needed now.

Scheffler, as well as Nicky, appeared to accept the ride as a matter of routine, almost as if the time machine were an auto or a streetcar. How many times had Scheffler ridden it already? But that was probably immaterial now.

Sitting on one of the remembered black couches, Montgomery closed his eyes against the little, winking

lights, gripping the safety belt and letting his head sag
against the wall.

The sharpest memory of all was only a few hours old.
The look on Nicky's face, at that moment when she had
recognized him, behind this ruined mask of age that he
was forced to wear. That look was one memory, among
others, that Montgomery Chapel knew he was going to
carry to his grave.

Was it possible he still desired her, wanted her, after
all that had gone by?

And now the bitter horror of a new realization was
growing in Montgomery Chapel: the horror of the fact
that, as matters stood right now, Nicky still had her life
ahead of her. And Willis had his too. Decades of youthful
vigor for both of them to look forward to—perhaps
together.

Was it too late now for an old man to have the last
laugh on them, and Pilgrim too? Perhaps, after all, it
was not too late. There might still be a chance for
Montgomery Chapel to wipe the youthful arrogance from
her lying, treacherous face, and replace it with other
things. Beginning, of course, with fear.

Then, of course, there was the matter of the gold.

The treasures of the buried Pharaoh, beside which all
the wealth that he and Willis had brought back from Egypt
in two years shrank to insignificance. For half a century
that Pharaonic gold had never been far from Montgomery
Chapel's thoughts. He would have to rank it even ahead
of revenge.

Or would he?

His own thoughts, now that the time for action was
upon him again, were strange to him. To his surprise he
could not be sure that revenge was not the most important
thing again.

If it was not so already, it might be when he had seen

her once more with Willis. He was going to see the pair of them together again now. That might be enough to tip the balance.

He had expected to have a free hand back there, once the fifty-year interdiction he had imposed upon the timelock was over, and his idiot grandnephew had been allowed to try it out, just in case—no. He had to stop thinking of young Scheffler as an idiot. Underestimating others was certain to lead to trouble.

. . . he had dreamt so often of going back to Pharaonic Egypt. There his first joy would be to discover the bones of his faithless lover and his treacherous brother. Perhaps even their whole carcasses, mummified by the exquisite dry heat. Sometimes the dream-search in which Montgomery sought their desiccated bodies was prolonged through whole days of delicious anticipation. In other versions of the dream he came upon their bodies almost as soon as he stepped out of the lock, found them where they had died watching for the door to open, praying in vain for him to temper the justice of his judgment. Wherever they were, the attitudes of their remains would present, somehow, some evidence of the final despair and agony that must have overwhelmed them.

All dreams, of course. All nonsense. Instead of that, he was now confronted by both the living bitch and the breathing, traitorous brother. The pair of them not only living but triumphantly young, unaware that he had ever tried to strike at them, to make them pay . . .

He would have to stop this. It was necessary that he control his thoughts. There was no use in dwelling on the fact that his revenge had failed. No use at all. He was going to need his brain to deal with urgent problems.

Their vehicle ceased to move, bringing their passage through spacetime to a soft and easy halt. Scheffler, who had apparently spent the interval lost in thought, was

still silent now, though he looked as if he might burst
out with more questions at any moment.

Now, at the journey's end, when the young man pushed
the door of the timelock open, Montgomery was eager
to step out. Even revenge and treasure could be
momentarily forgotten. He was suddenly, youthfully
impatient to see it all again. As if returning to this ageless
land might, somehow, restore his own youth . . .

Sunlight and heat burst in on them when the door slid
open. And the smells—how could he ever have forgotten
them? And this, the true and changeless Egypt, unlike
any other landscape of his youth to which an old man
might return, was all unaltered. Naturally. Here in the
time of the Pharaohs only four days had passed.

Scheffler, looking every bit the young adventurer at
home in a strange land, stepped out of the timelock boldly,
first grabbing up a weighty bag of cargo with one strong
hand, carrying his rifle in the other like an experienced
hunter. Nicky, hauling somewhat smaller baggage in each
hand, followed with her light Winchester slung over her
back.

Montgomery, doing his part, picked up the small pack
of his own things and stepped out. As for firearms, he
must leave those to others, at least for now.

Willis, unchanged by fifty years, was on hand and waiting
for them, near the mouth of the fissure. Perhaps he had
been worried about Nicky, perhaps he had come to help
with the baggage they were scheduled to bring back.
Pilgrim, of course, would not have told Willis what to
expect when he saw his brother again. Pilgrim cared for
nothing except his gold.

"Nicky. I was getting worried," said tall Will, taller than
ever now in Montgomery's eyes, and came toward her
and appeared about to kiss her, with almost the casual
attitude of an old husband. Only at the last moment before

he touched her did the presence of his unrecognizable brother strike him. He turned, gesturing. "Where's Monty? Who's this?"

No one answered Willis immediately. He didn't repeat the question, but rather fell silent. He looked a little apprehensive, as if he might be about to guess the truth.

Montgomery said; "You ought to know me, Will. If you don't you'll learn to know me again."

At first even the sound of his voice wasn't enough to make it real to Will. Staring at Montgomery, he blurted: "Good god, you sound like—no. But you *look* like my grandfather. But that's impossible, he's—"

Nicky, unwilling to endure this mental fumbling any longer than necessary, had to intervene. "It's Monty. Can't you see?"

After that Willis said nothing for a long time, but only looked at him. Meanwhile Willis's face went through a whole repertoire of responses.

At last, even now not really understanding, he said, "Monty? What the hell happened?"

Montgomery said, "I got old. It will happen to you too, you poor fool. If you live long enough."

And then Montgomery raised his head, and for the moment forgot even about his brother and the whore. Because Pilgrim was approaching, along the faint path from the direction of the pyramid.

The slight, dark figure striding jauntily toward them looked much the same as it had fifty years ago, and so did the face, except for the unshaven cheeks—how much time had Pilgrim lived through, subjectively, since their last meeting? And where? Montgomery knew enough by now to realize that he would probably never have the answers to those questions.

Pilgrim, recognizing him instantly, spread his arms as if in welcome. "Monty! Dear Monty. It's been a long time, hasn't it? I don't suppose you'd believe me if I said you are looking well—never mind. There are matters on which I wish to speak to you." Despite his decades of preparing himself mentally, knowing that this moment would almost certainly arrive one day, Montgomery had to swallow, and for a moment he had difficulty in speaking. Then he said, easily enough he thought, "I'm ready to talk with you anytime. I've held to our bargain."

"Have you now? It is a relief to hear it. I had supposed it might have been you who maladjusted my machine. Fortunately no serious inconvenience has resulted. I have been concerned lest you be suffering unnecessary pangs of guilt . . . but that can wait. How goes the hunt for gold?"

Montgomery looked at Willis. Willis said, "Nothing new in the last four days—Monty."

Montgomery said to Pilgrim, "Actually, as I suppose Will has told you, we've been putting off looking for your special gold. There were plenty of other things for us to do. From the drift of your conversation before you left, we didn't suppose that you'd be back so quickly—here, in this local time."

Pilgrim ignored the answer, and began to check over the supplies that had just arrived.

At first, confronting his brother and then Pilgrim, Montgomery had scarcely noticed the unforgettable heat of Egypt. But now it assaulted him as of old, demanding that he acknowledge its sovereignty. The sun fell like a weapon on his pith helmet and his khaki-covered back. In his recent years in Chicago he'd been working on plans for a wearable body-cooler, a refrigerated wristband powered by light batteries. But satisfactory technology to perfect the device had been lacking.

Now everyone had picked up a share of the supplies. Nicky was moving away from him through the sand and the heat, and Monty went trudging after her with only his own light baggage in hand. Heat and weakness assailed him. He knew that he was already tottering, before they had walked halfway to the pyramid. He felt himself suddenly an insane, ridiculous figure. Nicky. He no longer knew whether he still loved or hated the slender body that moved ahead of him, just that he wanted to bring it within his reach. His aged mouth worked, trying to form words.

Treacherous footing—or something else—betrayed Montgomery and he fell down; he'd been too many years on sidewalks. But no damage done. When someone's youthful hand reached out to help him up again, he forced himself to thank them, smiling cheerfully and convincingly. He struggled on.

FIFTEEN

That night when it came time to sleep Scheffler shared one of the temple's stonewalled, unfurnished rooms with Becky. But he quickly discovered that they were not going to share a sleeping bag. There were plenty of unused rooms available in the temple, more even than in Montgomery Chapel's apartment, and after he was rebuffed he offered to go and find a room of his own. But that wasn't satisfactory either; Becky didn't want to be left alone and unprotected, and she insisted it would be his fault if anything happened to her.

Feeling responsible, he stayed.

Their cheerless, doorless bedchamber was a high, comparatively cool vault with a floor of granite. Its limestone walls, like those of the rest of the temple, were solid and windowless for the first twelve feet or so above the ground; above that height the walls were mostly open to the air except for pillars, carved into the shape of petals and flowers, supporting more slabs of stone that formed the roof.

Willis and Nicky, before retiring themselves, had kindly assured the newly arrived couple that the really poisonous snakes were not too common here so close to the pyramid. The continuous turmoil of construction, going on for decades, must have driven every kind of bird and beast away from the area, but it was now more than two years since construction had ceased, and the wildlife was coming back. For the last month or so, Willis said, he had been routinely barricading the open doorways of the temple every night with little fires. Some of the Egyptians—whose own huts were largely protected by flimsy screens and magic spells—had voluntarily started taking turns on watch, keeping up the fires.

When Scheffler, having already resigned himself to separate sleeping bags, tried to kiss Becky goodnight, she pushed him away again. "How can you think of that under these conditions?"

He thought he could think of it almost anytime and he wasn't really sure which of the current conditions turned her off. He couldn't see her face; he had already switched out their small electric lantern, one of several he and Nicky had hauled back here from Chicago. Faint traces of indirect light from someone else's lantern came down the pale stone corridor and in through the open doorway of their room. Meanwhile the massed stars looked in through the broad open windows under the high roof.

Scheffler said: "I don't think anyone's going to intrude on our privacy. If Pilgrim were after your body he'd have made a move by now."

Becky said nothing. She rolled over, turning her back on Scheffler.

"Has he?" Scheffler pursued.

"No." It sounded like a grudging admission.

"As for his crew members in their glassy little helmets, I really doubt they're interested."

But Becky wasn't interested in talking about them. "Just don't. Not now."

"All right. Good night, then." He pulled his shoes off and then stretched himself out, clothed, atop his sleeping bag. It was still much too warm to think of getting under any kind of cover.

She didn't answer.

"Becky?"

"What?" She kept her back turned to him.

"I'm sorry I didn't have a chance to get to your apartment and pick up your other clothes and things. When Uncle Monty showed up we thought we'd better head back here right away." He paused. "And I'm sorry I got you into this."

"I am too."

And that appeared to be that for conversation. At bottom Scheffler really didn't consider himself all that guilty. But he didn't argue. After all, he supposed that some small measure of responsibility for Becky's kidnapping was his. But minute by minute he was feeling that responsibility less and less.

Insects that had started to seek out the electric lantern's light when it was on had vanished when he turned it off. The night was dark and quiet, but Scheffler stayed awake. The hardness of the stone beneath his sleeping bag was all too evident. He tried first lying on his belly, then on his back. Sleep would not come, whatever position he adopted.

He didn't think it was Becky's anger and rejection that were keeping him awake; he supposed it would have been worse if she had been sweet and not blamed him at all.

But he was too keyed up to sleep. The world around him had a seductiveness, an attractiveness of its own. *Ancient Egypt*, he kept repeating silently to himself, in mindless incantation. This place, where I am, is really *ancient Egypt*.

Something howled outside the temple, somewhere not far away. It didn't sound like one of the grubby dogs, of which he had seen several before nightfall. He had the heavy Winchester standing in the nearest corner of the room, if he should need it.

Pilgrim was trusting him with it. That was something

to think about. Pilgrim the purported mass murderer.

After a time Scheffler was certain from the sound of Becky's breathing that she slept. He sat up and put on his shoes again, then walked quietly out into the corridor, leaving the rifle where it was. He wasn't especially worried about leaving her alone. She had refused his somewhat tentative offer of a firearm, complaining, as if it too were his fault, that she didn't know how to use guns anyway.

He remembered a stairway nearby here, leading up toward the sky. Enough starlight was coming in from the high openings along the top of the corridor to let him find the stairs and mount them. The stone steps conveyed him through another doorless opening, to the roof. There Scheffler stood on flat slabs of stone, under those mysterious stars, beside the ominous and almost overhanging bulk of the great pyramid. He drew a deep breath of the cooling night and listened to more animal sounds. He was reminded of the presence of the marshes and the river not far away.

Now, with a moment to relax and think, and the black bulk of the pyramid to guide him, Scheffler could be sure that he had his directions straight; he knew where north ought to be. But it was still impossible to find Polaris. Nor was there any constellation he could recognize as the Big Dipper.

How far above the horizon ought the Pole Star to be here? He tried to estimate the latitude of Egypt. He wasn't in the southern hemisphere, surely. No, North Africa wasn't that far south of Europe.

The temple was a sprawling building with a big roof, and Scheffler had been standing on that roof for several minutes before he realized that he was not alone. It was the glow of a cigarette, as someone drew on it, that told him. His eyes were well used to the dark by now, and when he had moved a few steps closer to the other silent person there was enough light in that glow to let him recognize Nicky's face.

She had just been sitting there in silence and darkness. Watching him, evidently. There was no sign of anyone else with her.

"Hello," he said.

"Hello yourself." It came out as a sigh, weary but not unfriendly.

Scheffler looked up at the sky again, and gestured helplessly with both hands. "I don't know what to say about it."

"It'll do that to you. Day or night." Nicky drew on her cigarette again, then offered him one. "Even if they're fifty years old, they're pretty good."

"Thanks anyway. I don't use 'em."

"Oh? I suppose nobody in the Eighties smokes any longer. I hope I'll still be able to drink."

He walked closer to her and sat down, on roofstone that was still almost hot from the day's sun. "I was looking for Polaris," he announced, gesturing vaguely into the sky.

She turned on her seat, searched momentarily, then pointed with a slender arm, somewhat lower in the northern sky than Scheffler had ever seen Polaris. One star was bright and yellow. "The Pole Star is up there, but it isn't Polaris. It's what we in the early twentieth century would call Alpha Draconis. Precession of the equinoxes, you know."

"Oh. Yeah." Vaguely he remembered something about that.

"And you can't really recognize the Dragon—that's Draco—or the Dipper either. Five thousand years will do that to most constellations, they tell me. But I suppose you know a lot more about astronomy than I do."

It didn't sound as if she really supposed anything of

the sort. "I don't know as much as I should," Scheffler admitted.

"Monty and I were both interested at one point." She sighed again. "He taught me most of what I know about it."

"How long have you been here, Nicky? In Egypt, I mean."

"A couple of months, off and on. It seems longer. As soon as Monty and I got engaged he let me in on the secret." She was silent for a few moments. "I thought he was crazy at first. I never imagined anything like this— of course."

"In the nineteen-eighties we'd say 'it blew my mind.' "

They talked. Scheffler didn't want to come right out and ask, but he was wondering what it had been about Monty that had first attracted her. All he could think of was that young Monty must have been someone entirely different from old Monty.

Nicky blew invisible smoke at the stars. "When I saw that old man crumpling to the carpet today . . ."

"That must have been a rough moment."

"I've had rougher. Never a stranger moment, though, than when I realized who he was . . . and then realizing that now I might never have to tell him that it was all off between us. That maybe that problem at least had taken care of itself."

"So, it's been you and Willis for a while?"

The orange spark between her fingers marked out a sharp gesture. "It's never been me and Willis. He's— declared his intentions, as I believe they used to say in the old days. But that's all. I was never interested."

"Oh," said Scheffler, feeling a certain illogical relief. Then he asked: "Do you have any idea what's happened to all the people?"

"The natives? Monty and Will have always told me that

most of them must have been driven off when Pilgrim's spaceship arrived. After seeing all the rest of this I could believe he has a spaceship. I got the feeling they weren't really worried about it, so I didn't worry. Why do you ask?"

"I'm getting worried about it. Did Pilgrim ever say anything on the subject?"

Nicole drew on her cigarette. "I never laid eyes on Pilgrim until today, when he showed up with you and Becky. I could tell Will and Monty were afraid of him, the way they talked about him. Now I can see why."

"Is Will sleeping now?"

"Probably. He was snoring when I went past his door. His room's just down the hall from mine. Why?"

"I'd like to have a better talk with him sometime. But let him sleep. What about Monty?"

"He's in another room. I wasn't going to look in on him."

The two of them talked on the high roof, while the stars pivoted slowly on Alpha Draconis. Neither of them noticed a passing ripple among the stars.

"What do you know about Pilgrim?" Nicky asked. "Is he from—some other planet?"

"Maybe. He didn't really say. Some place at least as unlikely as this one, I bet."

When Nicky announced that she was tired, Scheffler walked her back to her room. Sure enough, the heavy masculine snores were coming from another dark doorway down the corridor from the one into which she disappeared. That was good.

Then he went back to the room where he had left his sleeping bag. There was a painting over the lintel that helped him identify the room in the unfamiliar corridor. Just inside the doorway he paused; beyond the high windows the moon had risen, and he could see that Becky was gone. Her sleeping bag and her shoes were still here.

Wait a minute, he cautioned himself, before you start running around in a panic. She's probably just gone to the john. There were latrines, rather like stone outhouses, built into the temple on its eastern side.

Turning back into the darker corridor, he listened. Then he heard the two soft voices at no great distance in the night, and recognized one of them as hers. He couldn't be sure yet about the other, but it certainly didn't sound as if she was in any trouble. None that she was anxious to get out of, anyway.

He suspected that a large part of his guilt, in Becky's eyes, was for not telling her days ago that he had access to all these marvels of gold and treasures. And he suspected he might have been forgiven that omission by now, except that he no longer controlled the access to the gold and marvels.

Scheffler lay down on his own sleeping bag. This time he fell asleep at once.

When he awakened, to morning sunlight falling in through the high windows onto yellow stone, he lay for a time almost peacefully, trying to decide if the carved heads of the columns holding up the roof were supposed to represent papyrus stalks or lotus blossoms, or what exactly. Becky still had not returned, not even to collect her shoes. But he wasn't especially perturbed about her absence. Scheffler lay listening to birdcalls, and marking the progress of the sun across the finely pitted surface of the wall.

Then he heard Becky's voice, somewhere outside. He couldn't distinguish the words, but she sounded cheerful enough. Then Pilgrim's voice, this time loud enough to be easily recognizable, said something. Then she laughed.

❖   ❖   ❖

On his way back from his morning trip to the latrine, Scheffler stopped in the corridor beside an open window-space that had been made low enough to afford a good view of the outside. It was a spot well-chosen for a window, and he stood there for a minute or two, taking in the morning beauty of the Nile and the lush growth that clung so narrowly along its banks.

Presently he saw Becky again. She was coming around the side of the temple alone, now wearing some spectacular jewelry, as well as her jeans from nineteen-eighties Chicago. Her Chicago sweatshirt was gone, and she had improvised a halter top from a scarf of white linen to take its place. She gave Scheffler a challenging look in passing, and then marched on without speaking.

When Scheffler rejoined the others that morning, in the large temple chamber that served as a common room, he found that Sihathor and the other Egyptians had again risen early. He saw Ptah-hotep and Thothmes coming down an outside stairway from the temple roof. Some of their compatriots were already at work cooking and housekeeping, while others had gone to work their modest fields along the edge of the marsh. Sihathor pointed out the place, and explained that there it was easy to get water to the crops.

Scheffler, watching the surviving Egyptians and speaking to one or two of them, got the impression that they were generally content with their lives.

"Where are the rest of your people, Sihathor?"

"Gone. All gone from the earth." The man sounded resigned, if not unconcerned.

"Whose fault is that?"

"Fault?"

"Has someone done wrong to you? Who did it?"

"I am not a god, only a poor man. It is not for me to say who has done wrong."

And the man went on with what he was doing, taking an inventory of the food supply, making hieroglyphic notes with a ballpoint pen on a small notepad of twentieth-century paper.

Scheffler went out of his way to speak to the next Egyptian he encountered, the tall, unusually good-looking girl who had served breakfast. Her name was Nekhem, and she had a story to tell—how, on the night following Pharaoh's burial, she had suddenly found herself alone in the royal palace. All of the other inhabitants—nobles, courtiers, priests and servants alike—had utterly disappeared. It had taken Nekhem days to discover the small band of survivors living in the vicinity of the pyramid.

"You mean the other people in the Palace went away in boats? Or how?"

"Not boats. Not go away. Just gone."

And Scheffler could find out nothing more from Nekhem than that.

Counting heads, including those of small working figures in the distance, Scheffler confirmed that there were now around twenty-five Egyptians living in the temple vicinity and serving the intruders who were willing to play the role of gods. If that many people had found their way here in two years, how many might still be living in the entire country? It didn't seem likely to Scheffler that there would be more than a few hundred.

Soon he encountered Becky again. By now she had gone further in her adoption of native dress. The semi-transparent linen sheath she had put on looked great, even if it was rather long, but she wouldn't be able to do much work in it.

Becky was not completely unwilling to talk to him when she saw that he was neither enraged nor devastated by her defection. And she was ready to defend their kidnapper, saying what had happened to the natives might not be Pilgrim's fault after all.

Olivia, Scheffler supposed, was most likely to know the truth. He found her sleeping, looking more or less comfortable if pale. At least she gave no sign of being in great pain. Scheffler supposed that her captor probably wouldn't want her to regain her health too rapidly.

Pilgrim, coming in while Scheffler was still there, said: "I have done all that I can for her, until I can summon my ship. And I dare not do that until I have at least some of the gold I need to restore its functions. To get here my ship will use practically all of its stored energy." The cast had now been removed from Pilgrim's arm, and he had discarded his ski jacket and shaved. The arm appeared to be functional, but he still had his gaunt, strained look.

Sihathor and his people, enjoying some of the gods' canned food that they had learned to like, talked now about the aged Monty; when first they recognized him as the young man they had known come back, they had interpreted his changed condition as the result of divinity's curse.

"Only riding the Barque of Ra through the Underworld might help him now."

Willis had just been told by Nicky that the world to which he had expected to return was barred to him forever.

He wouldn't take her word for it; maybe the girl had got it wrong somehow. Hurrying to Pilgrim, Will asked questions. The answers were not to his liking. "You're the one who's always saying there's always a way! Now you tell me there's no way for me to get back where I belong!"

"I have made a determination to return to my home. You are free to make a similar determination if you choose."

"You mean it's possible after all? But how will that help me? If you refuse to help?"

Pilgrim was silent.

"You mean that first we have to find your gold. All right. Will you help us to get home then?"

Pilgrim was unperturbed. "I mean nothing but what I have said." And that was all the satisfaction Will could get from him.

It still had not occurred to Will to blame his brother for his and Nicky's fate.

Nicky herself was not that much concerned about blaming anyone. In a way she was already looking forward to the nineteen-eighties, a time she suspected might be as exotic as the one she stood in now.

Later in the morning Pilgrim ordered most of the available people to come with him to the pyramid. They were going to get down to serious work.

SIXTEEN

Approaching the pyramid, Pilgrim sent Sihathor and a crew of Egyptians ahead into the entrance, assigning them to some task inside. Scheffler didn't catch what it was. Monty announced his eagerness to go with them, and Pilgrim raised no objections.

Then, to Scheffler's surprise, the little man led the rest of his workers on a climb up one of the construction ramps.

"Where are we going?"

"Up to the very top, bold youth. The capstone, I am informed, may well be solid gold. It would be very convenient to discover that the late Khufu had concentrated my fortune for me there."

They climbed, Pilgrim taking the lead and setting a deadly pace. Scheffler, remembering his days on the high school track team, kept up with him for a while, and then allowed himself to fall back among the *Asirgarh*. Despite their short legs they were doing better than anyone else.

The nature of Scheffler's companions limited conversation during the climb, though one of the creatures returned his nod of greeting. Always the capstone beckoned, in the form of a distant golden twinkle. He thanked God for his wide-brimmed hat and his full canteen.

The ramp angled its way up, and then up some more. Presently they had surpassed the height attained by Scheffler on his first solo effort.

At last Pilgrim's tireless figure came to a halt, at the level where the ramp ended, some forty yards or so below the top. From here the only way to climb farther lay over a fifty-degree slope of smooth, bright limestone. It would be tricky climbing on the glossy polished surface. Scheffler supposed that an agile human with good sticky shoes might make it, but for the *Asirgarh* it proved to be no trick at all. One of them went up quickly and with obvious confidence, reaching the golden capstone in moments.

The capstone was a miniature pyramid, about four feet from top to base, about the same height as one of the ordinary building stones. Its entire surface if not its volume was what looked like solid gold. The *Asirgarh* who had climbed to it needed only a moment to scrape samples from the gold. Then he—or she—was sliding down to stand on the top of the ramp beside Pilgrim, who quickly dropped the gathered shavings into a small machine. It looked like the same pocket device with which his crew had tested the golden statues in the apartment.

"Gold one-ninety-seven," was all that Scheffler could understand of the angry mutter that came from the little man as he looked at his machine. "What I am seeking is gold two-oh-three." When he saw Scheffler goggling at him, he added: "I speak of isotopes, my friend."

"I've heard of them. But I'm no expert."

"Ah. Just as well. Were you genuinely expert in the science of your century, you would probably protest at this point that gold two-oh-three is rather dangerous to handle. Also that it is doomed to a half-life of about five and one half seconds, and that therefore I have no right to expect to find any lying around loose."

"Oh, radioactive. Five and a half seconds? All right. How do you expect to find any?"

"Would I raise a question for which I had no answer? You see, the two-oh-three I seek is not radioactive as it must be in nature, but stabilized and therefore rather durable. I know that might sound like circular nonsense to a scientist of your period, but take my word for it. Enough of explanations for the nonce."

Pilgrim tried the test again, when a second sample, from another surface of the capstone, was brought down, and evidently was confronted with the same result. "Not the least trace. Completely nil. Looks like there's no gold two-oh-three in that capstone at all. The damned old tyrant has put my gold somewhere else entirely. And I'm afraid that I know where." He kicked at the side of the pyramid as if to break it open.

"I guess he thought it was his."

"But it is mine, dear callow youth, as I have explained more than once already. It came from my ship, of which it formed an extremely vital part. It was—well, knocked loose, you might say—during a skirmish with the police, and fell into the desert, where a military patrol evidently picked it up and brought it home to Pharaoh. He had limited awareness of spaceships at the time, but he knew gold when he saw it. Some other parts of the ship were lost at the same time, but fortunately spares were available to replace them. Ask Thothmes and Ptah-hotep; they have their own version, strongly theological of course, of the event. Ask Olivia whether the gold is legally mine, if you would rather take her word on such a matter."

"I do ask her things when I have the chance. But her mind is wandering, as you know damn well. Maybe that's why she tells me to help you. I suppose it was your battle with her people that devastated the country."

Pilgrim appeared surprised. He looked around at the horizon. "Does it appear to you that the country has actually been devastated? Oh, well, in that case I suppose one might say that . . . No, another time. For the nonce, my gold, my gold. If it's not here in the capstone I suppose the divine Khufu must have had it buried with his fragrant corpse."

Scheffler grunted. He was growing angry with Pilgrim again.

The little man nodded, talking to himself. "There is one other possibility. He would undoubtedly have had the metal worked into a hundred different kinds of ornaments before he buried it anywhere. Perhaps some substantial portion never made it past the artisans."

Pilgrim started to lead the way back down the ramp at a rapid pace. Then he stopped momentarily to strike a pose, and ask himself a question: "Would their metallurgical treatment have destabilized that isotope?" Fortunately he was able to answer the question for himself a moment later. "I don't think so. I don't think anything they could do to it at this level of technology would have done that." And he plunged down the ramp again.

There was little conversation on the way down. When they had reached the level of the pyramid's main entrance, Pilgrim left the ramp and without a pause led the way toward the dark hole in the stonework.

From the entrance, where Scheffler had to crouch to try to see in, a passage led straight in and down. Willis, perhaps trying to make him feel at home, crouched beside him and commented that the angle of descent here was twenty-six degrees, and that this was called the Descending Passage. Inside, it was far too low for anyone but *Asirgarh* to stand up in, being only about three and a half feet high, and equally wide.

Pilgrim turned on a flashlight and led the way. Fifty feet or so along the passage, Monty met them and took over the commentary. Scheffler, proceeding in a painful crouch, learned that the Descending Passage ran straight in and down for a total distance of several hundred feet, and there was nothing but a pit choked with debris to be found at the end.

"Ptah-hotep says that was where the Pharaoh originally planned to have his burial chamber—which accords quite well with modern theory."

They had come down into the pyramid about a hundred feet from the entrance, Scheffler estimated. Now here was a pile of tools, and Pilgrim and Uncle Monty, with flashlights and what looked like geologists' hammers, went shuffling about on their knees, picking and probing at the overhead of the slanting passage. To Scheffler the stone surface looked no different here than anywhere else.

"Entrance to the Ascending Passage has to be right here somewhere," Monty told him, and went on to explain that the bottom end of what pyramid authorities called the Ascending Passage had been blocked by a cunning arrangement of sliding stones, after Pharaoh's burial.

Ptah-hotep and Thothmes joined the group. Scheffler gathered that they had been here often during the past two years, but still were unable to tell just where the ceiling of this passage concealed the opening to the one above. It seemed likely that any attempt to open the ceiling with tools or explosives would bring down an avalanche.

Some of the dynamite had already been brought inside the pyramid, and a discussion began on how best to use it. Everyone in the passage was sitting or squatting now, relieving the strain of crouching under the low roof.

Will and Nicky, sitting well back toward the entrance, were arguing with each other in low voices.

Will was becoming increasingly distraught over the drastic changes that had overtaken him. He demanded of Nicky that she tell him what the new world of the Eighties was going to be like to live in.

Aspects of his character that she didn't like were coming to the foreground. She snapped back: "How should I know what it's like? I was only there for a couple of hours."

Meanwhile, back near the temple, a dispute was developing between Thothmes and Ptah-hotep. Thothmes was more and more inclined to return to the service of the old gods, the true gods, Osiris, Ra, and Ptah. And of the Pharaoh, whom he increasingly felt he had betrayed.

"I dreamt of Pharaoh last night, my friend," Thothmes declared solemnly.

"So? Many dreams come to a man during his life. Few of them mean much."

"I have had few dreams like this one. Ptah-hotep, why do you suppose that the world was changed?"

"The gods have their own reasons."

"And we have our own duties. If a man does not perform his duties, what is he worth?"

"Duties? Duties? We still perform the daily rituals as best we can. And our fundamental allegiance must be to Set, as you well know."

The argument went on.

SEVENTEEN

Becky hadn't done too well keeping up with the others
during the first day's investigation of the pyramid. On
the morning of the second day she was detailed by Pilgrim
to take care of Olivia and keep her company in the temple,
while the other twentieth-century people continued with
the job of treasure hunting.

Pilgrim made it seem that he was conferring a great
favor upon her by giving her the nurse's job—as perhaps
he was. He bowed and pressed her hands and said in
his most thrilling voice: "If all goes well today, I will bring
you a jewel such as you have never seen before."

That overcame such reluctance as Becky still felt about
being left behind. Besides, here in the temple, with no
ramps to climb or tunnels to crawl through, she was free
to get out of her wintry Chicago clothing and put on a
gauzy, borrowed Egyptian gown. The only trouble with
that was, there wasn't a decent mirror to be found
anywhere. Nekhem, the dancing girl who loaned Becky
the dress, had to make do with a dark oval of polished
metal in which to see herself. With its ivory frame and
handle the metal mirror was a beautiful trinket, but it
didn't quite do the job. In return for the dress Nekhem
borrowed Becky's Chicago sweatshirt, pulled it on and
twirled around happily, despite the garment's being thick
and hot, and by now none too clean.

And then it occurred to Becky that there might be

another advantage to staying with Olivia—it might be possible to learn something useful from the policewoman.

Olivia was still unable to walk more than a few paces without help, or to use her arms steadily for longer than a few seconds. And she seemed dazed a good part of the time. Becky had a kindly nature, and was really glad that she could do something to help.

Actually Olivia, in the periods when her mind was clear, worried about Becky and felt sorry for her. The girl was obviously becoming caught up in the financial possibilities of this adventure, alerted to the chances of mind-bending wealth.

The older woman was reclining on one of the few pieces of furniture in the temple, a wooden couch, bedded with ancient Egyptian pillows that Nekhem had said were filled with goose down. She said: "Tell me about your young man. Scheffler. Have you known him long?"

Becky shrugged, and toyed with a bracelet Pilgrim had given her. "I don't know that I want to think of him as my young man."

"Well, I don't understand the rules of your society perfectly, of course. But I suspect you could do a lot worse in the matter of seeking out a mate."

Becky shrugged again, and started asking Olivia questions about Pilgrim: How long had *she* known *him*?

"More years than you would be likely to believe," said Olivia. Then she asked in return: "Would it do any good for me to warn you about him?"

"What has he done that's so awful?"

The policewoman looked as if she wanted to laugh, but had to consider whether she had that much energy to spare. "What has Pilgrim done? Ask rather what he hasn't done. Killing, kidnapping, robbery of every kind . . ."

"All right. I know he kidnapped us, but he was very . . . gentlemanly about it. And I know you want to arrest him for other things he's done. But at the same time you're telling us to cooperate with him. You wouldn't do that if he was really terrible. Would you?"

The older woman paused. "He can be as cunning as the Evil One. And you are but a child, Becky."

The girl stiffened.

Olivia sighed. "I shouldn't have said that. Forgive me, I am not thinking too clearly these days. Very well—I am very pleased if you are not a child. As for Pilgrim, I warn you solemnly that he is capable of terrible things. Cooperation with him for survival, your own and that of the other people, as I have advised you and Scheffler to do—that is one thing. Going beyond that, for example trying to get Pilgrim's help to enrich yourself—that is something else. I hope you can make the distinction."

Despite herself Becky was somewhat impressed. "He hasn't done anything to hurt you. I mean, since he's been holding you a prisoner."

Olivia shook her head. "He very nearly killed me in the process of making me a prisoner. But one thing I will say for him, he is seldom vindictive. Besides, I am sure he wants to keep me alive now because he thinks I may be useful to him later on."

The party that had gone into the pyramid today included Scheffler, two of the *Asirgarh*, Sihathor, Pilgrim, Nicky, and the two Chapel brothers.

Pilgrim was now crouched, flashlight in hand, near the sealed entrance to the Ascending Passage, which had at last been located by Thothmes and Ptah-hotep. It came down at an angle, Monty said, from the burial chambers in the heart of the pyramid, to intersect the Descending Passage about a hundred feet in from the entrance. The entrance to the upper passage was concealed behind one of the stones composing the ceiling of the lower one. One or more of those giant, superbly fitted blocks would have to be brought down. Pilgrim was now looking for weak spots in the masonry where it might be easy to drill a hole and insert dynamite.

He had already sent most of his helpers down to the bottom of the Descending Passage, there to dig into the rubble that filled the Pit. That, said Ptah-hotep, was the original intended burial chamber, dug into bedrock well below the original level of the surface.

The idea was to look for some kind of a hidden passageway in that area, and also for casually dropped treasures.

"Not quite as crazy as it sounds," Pilgrim assured them. "We must remember that work on the whole project was abandoned rather suddenly just before it was sealed up. If you see even a small scrap of gold anywhere, bring it to be tested."

Down there beside the Pit, as Monty explained to Scheffler, was—or would be someday—the lower end of a vertical tunnel researchers called the Well, that ran right up into the heart of the pyramid above. Investigators in the twentieth century argued about when the Well had been made and for what purpose. Ptah-hotep and Thothmes swore that they had never heard of it, that no such tunnel existed in the pyramid as it was built. Of course it could have been put in after their time on the construction site but before the burial.

Pilgrim set Sihathor and his people, using twentieth-century steel chisels and hammers, at hand-drilling some holes for dynamite around the borders of the block that was now identified as covering the massive granite plug blocking the lower end of the Descending Passage. That plug, said Ptah-hotep, was now held in place by flanges on both sides, interlocking with the adjacent limestone blocks.

"How about using your weapons to drill?" Scheffler suggested, indicating the rod-shaped device Pilgrim still carried at his belt.

Pilgrim shook his head. "They are not suited for making holes in stone, at least not precise ones. And at the moment we have no other high-tech tools with us. If my ship were here, matters would be different. But I dare not summon my ship just yet. Not until I have in hand at least some of the gold needed to restore its energy."

The preparations went on, to burrow and blast a way into the five million tons of rock erected by generations of Pharaoh's subjects.

Nicky brought up a report from those working in the lower passage where the entrance to the Well would be—several feet of the heavy stone construction rubble had now been cleared away, and the last faint hopes for finding a concealed opening anywhere in that vicinity were fading rapidly.

Montgomery was not surprised. "The Well, gentlemen, is not to be dug until later, perhaps not for centuries. And then, in my opinion, it will be dug from the top down, by someone exploring the Queen's Chamber for a secret cache."

Around midmorning everyone—except for Sihathor and his crew of stone-pounders, who were inured to working in great heat—came out of the pyramid and trekked back to the comparative coolness of the temple for a break.

There Becky joined them in the common room, eager to find out if they had discovered any treasure.

It was plain that they hadn't, from the tone of the argument in progress as they refilled their canteens from jerry cans of nineteen-thirties vintage Chicago water.

"Easy enough to say, blast it open," Willis was saying. "Not so easy as you might think when you actually start to do it. We weren't completely sure where the Ascending Passage started, to begin with. Meanwhile there was more treasure than we could carry waiting around to be picked up—in Memphis, in the funerary chapel, in the Palace. The Palace itself is unbelievable."

Pilgrim, who had not yet seen the Palace, glanced around once and then continued talking with his crew of *Asirgarh*. The diminutive unearthly people were still fully covered with protective clothing. Scheffler wondered if they were suffering as much or more than Earthly humans from the heat.

Monty was explaining some things to the later generation: "From what Pilgrim told us, Willis and I both felt reasonably sure that he wouldn't be back for half a century. In that time the two of us would be free to help ourselves to the treasure—in return we had to find his special gold for him.

"There was plenty of treasure to be had, just for the trouble of picking it up. And we had to be somewhat cautious when it came to selling it. We didn't want to flood the market with genuine Fourth Dynasty material.

"Actually it wasn't until the Forties that I began to have trouble with the dating methods—when doubts were cast on the authenticity of certain things. The organic materials in them were, as the tests indicated, not very old. But Willis, and Egypt, had become inaccessible to me by then. I found it necessary to sell some of the gold, which posed no dating problem."

Willis was shaking his head. He had not heard about this before.

"There was so much of it, after all. And we had no way to distinguish his isotope. He hadn't even bothered to explain to us that his gold was of a special kind. In the Thirties, I can tell you, no one on earth knew very much about the possible isotopes of gold; I suppose few even among scientists had ever heard of isotopes at all. But that doesn't matter now . . ."

During the break Sihathor and his crew had continued working in the pyramid, and when the others returned the Egyptians were able to show how successful their own techniques would be in getting around the first plug of granite: They had removed an impressive amount of stone, but it would take days at least to bypass the first obstacle.

It had proven much easier to drill holes for the first charge of dynamite.

Willis and Pilgrim, both claiming some expertise, saw to the placement of the charges, while everyone else was evacuated from the interior of the pyramid. Wires were strung, and an electric detonator employed. The sound of the explosion was not impressive outside the pyramid. A few seconds after the blast, a ghostly billow of yellow dust came writhing its way slowly out of the entrance hole. With wet cloths over nose and mouth, the explorers filed back in, crouching. Pilgrim, flashlight in hand, led the way.

The newly fallen granite plug was more than three feet thick, and equally wide. Its length was indeterminate, its upper end being still wedged inside the opening to the Ascending Passage. In its new position the fallen plug also partially blocked the way down to the Pit. Had it been dug free by hand, the diggers beneath it would almost certainly have been crushed like insects when it fell.

"I am impressed with Khufu's engineers," Pilgrim mused aloud after a careful inspection.

Ptah-hotep inclined his head to acknowledge the compliment. "There will be other stones behind this one, ready to slide down whenever this one is removed completely," he reminded everyone.

Sihathor and his extended family had set up a regular production line by now, pushing and throwing the lesser debris from the first blast out of the way, further down the Descending Passage. A fresh fall of small stone fragments sent everyone briefly scrambling for safety.

Pilgrim decided that the fastest and safest way to proceed now would be to make a way through the solid limestone of the pyramid, around the fallen and jammed plug-stone. It would probably be necessary also to bypass the whole train of other plugs that were pressing down on this one from above; Ptah-hotep assured him there would be five of them in all.

The work went on, in preparation for more blasts.

Pilgrim, remarking that he had the uncomfortable Western sense of time and its value, pushed the workers hard. As soon as Sihathor's people had created some new small crevices and recesses in which he thought dynamite could profitably be detonated, he ordered everyone out again and set new charges.

Again the dynamite achieved a modest success. But now more clearing of rubble and drilling of new holes was necessary. Battery-powered electric lanterns, propped on the sloping floor, made the job vastly easier than it would otherwise have been.

Outside the pyramid, Thothmes and Ptah-hotep had resumed their argument. The subject was still the same, the question of which gods most deserved their service.

Ptah-hotep was by now considering reporting Thothmes, as being no longer reliable for purposes of tomb-robbing, or even exploration. But Thothmes guessed which way his old friend's thoughts were turning, and dissembled cunningly, pretending that he still considered himself firmly pledged to Set.

Meanwhile, Monty was turning over in his mind tentative plans for getting rid of Pilgrim, and then dealing with Olivia's police.

When he took an opportunity of seeing her alone, she warned him solemnly that the authorities who had sent her after Pilgrim were not going to let her kidnapping go unpunished.

Monty had a proposal. "I'll help you get to the timelock, if you help me with the settings when we get there. We'll both get away from him." Not that he really wanted to get away just yet—he wanted to learn more about the timelock controls.

"What settings do you want?"

He told her.

She took a long time to think it over. "I don't trust you," she said at last, and shook her head. "Besides, Pilgrim will have the timelock watched."

Pilgrim, while waiting for the digging and blasting to produce results, decided to dispatch some of his helpers to look for his gold outside the pyramid, in the goldsmiths' shops and quarters in Memphis. The Chapel brothers had once or twice visited those shops, and had found some loose gold there and removed it. But Monty said that particular gold had long since been sold in Chicago.

Tantalizing microscopic traces of gold two-oh-three had been found in the funeral temple—confirming that the sought-for metal was once here, doubtless having been worked into the Pharaoh's treasure.

Scheffler, Willis, and Nicky, along with Thothmes, were to go on the expedition to the shops. Everyone else available, including Pilgrim and the *Asirgarh*, continued working on the pyramid.

Becky remained with Olivia in the temple,

There was, as Scheffler had realized by now, a fairly extensive canal system in the area. The trip to the goldsmiths' shops on the outskirts of Memphis could be made by water.

Cans of gas and oil were brought out of a temple storeroom. Presently four people in a square-sterned boat, powered by the new outboard, cast off from the temple dock. With Scheffler at the helm and Willis navigating they headed through a network of narrow, branching waterways toward the goldsmiths' shops.

It was a trip of several miles. No lions appeared on the unpopulated canal banks, but several crocodiles displayed themselves along with a few interesting snakes. Hundreds of birds, unaccustomed to outboard noise, flew up in great alarm.

At last the heat-shimmering cluster of buildings that Scheffler had glimpsed on his first trip through the timelock appeared in the distance and drew closer. Now one of the buildings he had seen with banners was not far ahead. And now . . . .

"What—?" asked Scheffler, in a disconnected syllable, meanwhile throttling back his motor. Willis turned to look, then Nicky, and then Thothmes. Thothmes uttered a strange sound. If there were words in it they were not English.

The boat was now within a hundred yards of an imposing building, doubtless some kind of a temple. Scheffler was staring in that direction, but not at the building itself. Something was perched atop it, something that was not a banner after all. There were wings on this object, living wings, of bright red and blue. The body attached to them was not that of a bird, more like a lion's, and far too big for any living thing that flew. The head was that of a giant hawk and the lion's torso crouched on four powerful legs. The mismatched parts of its body were all of the wrong colors.

In broad daylight, the monstrous figure perched there on the stone roof of an imposing temple. Scheffler flipped the outboard into neutral and reached for his rifle.

By now Willis and Nicky had their weapons drawn as well. Thothmes, indifferent to firearms, was crying something that sounded like: "Sefer! Sefer!"

Only now did the apparition appear to become aware of its human observers. It let out a sound, a compound roar strange as the body that produced it; and then it effortlessly launched its heavy body in flight, gliding straight toward the drifting boat.

It was the first time Scheffler had fired the Winchester. Despite his excitement he remembered to hold it tight against his shoulder, but even so the kick was monumental. Nicky and Will were banging away at the same time. The monstrous figure that had been coming straight at them veered away. The bullets had impact, but not as if on flesh and bone and blood. Instead the flying thing became flickeringly transparent. It disappeared for moments and came back, as if shaken by waves and spasms of unreality. In a moment it had vanished, gliding away behind the canal's fringe of palms.

Thothmes had dived into the bottom of the boat. Repeated reassurances were necessary to get him to raise his head again, and when he did he looked at each of the twentieth-century people with awe.

Several minutes passed before he spoke again, trying to explain the nature of the *sefer*. All that Scheffler could understand with certainty was that Thothmes had been as surprised by it as anyone else.

Nerving themselves to renewed efforts, the explorers pressed on into the goldsmiths' complex.

In the shops of the late Pharaoh's metal-working artists and artisans, no distraction more remarkable than snakes appeared that afternoon. Scheffler stood armed guard while others gathered a number of gold samples, stock pieces, and artifacts. None of these, tested with Pilgrim's borrowed instrument, contained any gold two-oh-three. But according to the device, minute samples of that isotope were present on some of the tools littering the workbenches.

"It's inside the pyramid somewhere, then," Scheffler reported to the boss on his hand-held radio. "Everything indicates that."

"The conclusion seems inescapable, does it not?" Pilgrim's dry voice continued: "I should like you all to return here as soon as possible. There are some troublesome manifestations. Someone will meet you at the dock, if possible. Over and out."

EIGHTEEN

The motorboat sliced through the quiet water of the canal at its best speed. Beyond the fringe of palms lining the banks ahead, the pyramid loomed changelessly as always.

Suddenly Willis, his hand on the outboard, swore as a rounded shape broke the surface of the still green water dead ahead. The boat veered sharply. Scheffler, more than half expecting to confront another bizarre apparition, whipped up the barrel of the big Winchester again. But the obstruction was only a hippo, and Willis was able to steer around it, almost scraping the gray bulk as they passed.

Sihathor, walkie-talkie in hand, was standing on the temple dock along with most of his Egyptian crew. Before the boat had docked, Sihathor's crew, in a state of great excitement and talking all at once, were relating their own story of incredible apparitions, all from somewhere in their own mythology or religion. They had seen monster snakes inside the pyramid, and spectral crocodiles outside. The apparitions had been driven off, though apparently not injured, by bullets. The heat-projecting rods of the *Asirgarh* had for some reason proven less effective.

And Sihathor insisted that some of his workers had seen the *ba* of Khufu, an essence of the dead Pharaoh's spirit in the form of a tiny, birdlike, humanheaded shape.

That had been enough to make them throw down their tools. Nevertheless, he reported, Pilgrim, the *Asirgarh*, and Montgomery Chapel were still inside the pyramid, trying to get on with the job.

Sihathor's mouth, open in speech, stayed that way as he froze in silence, staring over Scheffler's shoulder. Scheffler spun around, in time to see the end of a violent eruption of sand and rock close beside the pyramid, only a few hundred yards away.

A streak of light, visible even in full sunshine, went shooting rocket-like up into the sky.

"My God, what's that?"

Everyone on the dock was already moving toward the pyramid. Scheffler started running, with others close behind him.

As they drew near the site of the eruption, Pilgrim and Monty were coming from the direction of the dark dot of the pyramid's entrance to meet them. And there was Becky, hurrying from the direction of the temple.

"It was the Barque of Khufu. Or one of them," Ptah-hotep explained, gasping for breath as he came to a halt beside Scheffler on the edge of a large, fresh crater in the sand.

Ptah-hotep recalled that five solar boats had been buried in separate locations near the pyramid, for Khufu's use and that of his servants in the next life. But now one of the largest craft was missing. Its burial pit, intact only minutes ago, had now been violently emptied, as if the vessel had been ripped out of its repository by an explosion. To Scheffler the house-sized hole looked like a deep bomb crater.

Olivia was the last to arrive at the scene, along with the Egyptian women who were helping her. She came stumbling around the pyramid from the direction of the temple.

Pilgrim regarded her quizzically as she approached. "This is more than I expected from the collective Egyptian mind," he said, gesturing toward the blasted pit. "Your fellow servants of the Authority, perhaps?"

Coming close enough to look down into the pit, she shook her head. "I can only hope that they will be able to get at you here. But I don't expect they can."

For Thothmes it was the final signal. Staring down into the huge cavity that had been somehow blasted out of the earth, he was now sure that he must separate himself from this band of robbers. Retribution was about to strike them. But merely to run away would not be enough. The robbers must be stopped if possible. Reparations must be made somehow.

He raised his eyes to the blinding sun, and prayed to Ra to show him how.

Between dynamite blasts Pilgrim and Scheffler worked in the tunnel, using gloved hands and steel tools to dig out stones knocked down by the last blast, clearing debris that would let them reach the place where the next charge must be set.

The two men were arguing as they worked.

"I've been talking to the Egyptians," Scheffler said. "They're still grieving for their people. Sihathor lost his wife. All of them lost someone."

"It is a common human fate."

"Who did it to them? You?"

Pilgrim ceased tugging at a rock and gave him a strange look. "You actually believe, Scheffler, that I have somehow wiped out almost the whole population of ancient Egypt? Or the whole population of the Earth? Killed them all, just to get them out of my way? Or in a fit of irritation, perhaps?"

"What else am I supposed to think? Olivia accuses you of mass murder."

"Charitably I will allow that English is not her mother tongue. As for killing, I admit that her soldiers—she would call them police—have sometimes fallen at my hands, in battle. My followers have died at her hands too."

"I think she meant more than that—"

"I am sure she wanted you to think worse than that. And I suppose you are also convinced that we are actually in the land of the Pharaohs?"

Scheffler let a rock fall from his hands. "Say that again."

"And that, if we were somehow able to blast off the entire top of this artificial mountain above our heads"—Pilgrim gestured fiercely—"that the Great Pyramid in your twentieth-century world would somehow become decapitated also?"

"I don't know. Sure, I suppose it would. Why not?"

"Why not? Because that is an absurdity."

"All right then, tell me what would happen. Does the whole universe split every time something in the past is changed? Are we now in some kind of alternate universe? If so, does that mean it's okay for the population of Egypt—maybe the whole population of the Earth—to be wiped out?"

Pilgrim looked disgusted. "Nobody has been wiped out."

Scheffler swept an arm round angrily, as widely as he could in the confined space, indicating the whole invisible country outside. "Then where in hell are they, all the people? *Goddam it, give me a straight answer or—*"

Pilgrim was for once taken aback, as he might have been by a snarling puppy. Blinking at Scheffler's violence, he answered mildly. "The people of Egypt about whom you are so concerned are in the same miserable hovels they always were. Working for the same brutal masters."

"That whole village of hovels outside is empty! So are

the city and the palace, and the houses where the brutal masters lived. So is—"

Pilgrim held up a gentle hand to stop him. "But the original dwellings, rich and poor, are all just as full of people as they ever were. They are not here. *This whole world is an artifact. A duplication.*"

For a long moment Scheffler did not move or speak. Then he said: "A duplication."

"Yes."

"And the original dwellings, with all the people in them. Where are they?"

"Where they belong, in your world. Your past." The little man's tone continued to be mild and conciliatory. "Take my word for it. Or, as always, ask Olivia. Compel her to give you a straight answer."

"How am I supposed to do that?"

Pilgrim shrugged.

"Then you're telling me that we are now in some kind of alternate universe?"

Pilgrim tugged out the difficult rock at last, and shoved it clattering down into the lower tunnel. He sighed. "There is only one universe, my friend. But it comprises more components, and more anomalies, than you would perhaps believe. And sometimes the way from one portion of the universe to another is strange and indirect. Sometimes, or so the most respected authorities have written, there is no way at all to get from one part of it to another without accepting almost suicidal risks. And imposing similar risks upon others. That is Olivia's position. She has great concern for the general welfare."

Scheffler stared into the little man's eyes, dark and powerfully alive. "What's your position?" he asked at last.

"My position is, as always, that my crew and I are going home. Perhaps there is no way for us to get there that will keep the eminent authorities and the guardians of everyone's welfare happy. But nevertheless, we mean to go. From here to there, without either suicide or murder."

There was obviously more to come. Scheffler waited.

Pilgrim looked at him, as if it had suddenly become important to him to convince Scheffler, or to determine whether he could be convinced. Pilgrim said, "A part of the universe can sometimes be duplicated. Like this one. An abstraction made concrete, a miniature buffer-world constructed for a purpose.

"I have read some of the fanciful stories of your time on the subject of time travel. In reality, for me to go back through the timelock and shoot my grandfather is almost—*almost*—certainly forbidden by the obvious paradoxes involved. The same restrictions would prevent me from ever prying my gold out of the grasp of noble Khufu, were I to start from the twentieth century and approach him directly in his own era. Do you understand anything at all of what I am saying to you?"

"I'm not sure. But go on."

"*But* if I am able to duplicate the noble Khufu's world, or a sizable portion of it, including my gold, there is nothing, theoretically, to prevent my going to that duplicated world, and there laying my hands upon that precisely duplicated gold.

"Such a duplication—'abstraction' is probably a better translation of our word into English—has its own dangers. It is also expensive in energy and effort. And extremely difficult. But it is not impossible. If my grandfather and I both have access to a particular created, abstracted, temporary world, and he will join me there, he had better beware of me if I in fact have designs upon his life. There I can at least kill his abstracted double. In this case paradox takes no revenge. Nothing will happen to me unless my grandsire kills me too, in which case I shall be dead. My own grandfather was always regrettably treacherous. Do you understand a little better now what I am talking about?"

"You're trying to tell me that you have *created* a whole world? The one we're standing in?"

"I thought a moment ago that you had already accepted that idea. You were ready to believe that the entire universe might split every time anyone made a decision. Yes, in a sense, with the help of innumerable other minds, and an impressive amount of machinery and power, I have created it. Or caused it to split off, for a time, from the one and only original world, if you prefer."

"If you can do that, why not just create yourself some more of your special gold?"

"I suppose that is a valid question, coming from a youth in your state of almost complete ignorance. To obtain a duplication of my gold was of course the object. But to duplicate, at such a distance, the gold that the Pharaoh carried with him to the grave it was necessary, depend upon it, to include a large slice of the surrounding fabric of spacetime in the process as well."

Scheffler was still trying to grasp it. "Anyway, I still don't know what you're talking about. What sort of a creation? All this, around us?" Scheffler waved a hand again, taking in the entire unseen sky outside the tomb of Khufu, the Nile and sand and rock. "I think you're raving."

"I am not raving. We are standing at this moment within such a partial duplication—or abstraction—and I am chiefly responsible for its existence. A myriad of other people contributed substantially, though most of them were unaware of doing so. I did not kill anybody in the process." He made an offhand gesture. "There was, as I have already mentioned, a battle earlier, in which there died a few police, who were doing their best to kill me."

"When I'm out of this hole I can see the sun."

"What you see is an abstracted version of the sun, full-sized and just as massive and hot. It would still be very hard to distinguish from the original, even if the full resources of science were here available to us."

Scheffler was silent for a little, trying to think. He found himself wanting to believe the "explanation." But what did it take, what kind of powers would a man have to possess, to duplicate a sun?

He said at last, "At night we can see the stars."

"The abstraction is not quite *that* big. One or two stars besides the sun may be included in it; but you see most of them by light that left them long ago. Their light, trapped in this new space, will still be visible for a few years to come. It may be moving more slowly in this space."

"What?"

Pilgrim shifted his position. "Consider. With the little camera that you brought on your first trip here, you can make an image of an object. Given a more advanced camera, you could make an image in three dimensions. Another advance, or several, beyond that, and you could make a replica of a pyramid that casual observation could not distinguish from the original. Not, perhaps, exact down to the last molecule, but very close to that ideal. Another advance, and another—"

"But I thought you were saying you *made* space. Planets. Everything. Out of what?"

"Why must a creation be 'out of' anything? Out of the same materials as the original, if you prefer."

"And how do you perform this creation? Just by thinking about it, with your friends? Making a decision?"

"No. Not at all. I have said that physical power is required too. As a trigger. And almost all of the mental contributors did so unwittingly. They were not my friends, or even known to me—they comprised the very population about which you are now concerned. Therefore the new world, as you have seen, bears the stamp of the collective mind of ancient Egypt. Therefore we have the *ba* and the *sefer* taking on reality. I must confess that matters have gone a little further in that regard than I expected."

Scheffler was looking doubtful.

Pilgrim pressed on. "Even in your own century, scientists working with quantum mechanics are coming to understand that the objects making up the universe would have a very different existence, in some cases no existence at all, if it were not for the consciousness of intelligent observers. The only way to accomplish an abstraction on the necessary scale was to draw upon the minds of all available observers. The center of the abstracted volume of spacetime is at the locus of what you call ancient Egypt—therefore the most intense mental input, by far, came from its human inhabitants, those living about fifty centuries before your own time.

"Almost all of them were themselves filtered out of the process of abstraction—but a few whose minds were closely attuned to mine, were not."

"Closely attuned to yours?"

"I suspect chiefly by thoughts of robbery, of Khufu's gold. It seems remarkable how many thieves there are in our small handful of Egyptian people. Perhaps it is only a testimony to the shocking morals of their time."

"And the ones who were filtered out, as you put it?"

"Almost all of the people of ancient Egypt were completely unaffected by my machinations. The moment of the abstraction passed over them and they had no idea that anything unusual had happened. Their world went on its way without interruption. Indeed it had to be so. In the original world of ancient Egypt, an original Sihathor—no more or less real than ours—goes on about his business. Or more likely, he was arrested on the day of Pharaoh's burial, and executed two years ago, along with other plotters who meant to rob the tomb of Pharaoh. Have you heard our Sihathor's story of that day and evening?"

"And the great majority of people were not duplicated—"

"Scheffler, Scheffler. Are you being deliberately obtuse? I lose patience. I repeat, your precious majority of people went nowhere. Not to market, not to church, and not to war. They stayed home. They were not killed, so you see that charge against me is quite baseless. In fact, in a manner of speaking, I have created some new lives. If you judge that a crime, as certain people do, then I must stand convicted. Of course those few folk of my creation have certainly experienced a change. Their lives of incredible dullness have been enriched by some excitement."

"That's one way of looking at it, I suppose. Excitement they didn't ask for."

"My friend. How could they have asked for anything that was beyond their power to dream?"

"My life has been enriched too, thanks to you." Scheffler was saying it grimly, ironically. But after the words were out he realized he wasn't at all sure he didn't mean them.

"You are quite welcome." Pilgrim sounded sincere, as usual. "And mine also, fortunately, by—a number of other circumstances. It is a necessary condition of being fully alive."

Scheffler realized suddenly that he had never yet seen the little man get angry. He said: "I gather you weren't so happy when your life was changed in unexpected ways. When something kept you from going home. What was it?"

Pilgrim's expression changed. "No, I was not happy when that occurred. Therefore I take what action I can, to adjust matters to my own satisfaction. You are presumably doing the same; as are our handful of Egyptians. I will not be angry with any such displaced persons, for doing what they can to improve their lot."

"That's good of you."

"Yes, considering all circumstances, I think it is. But does it make you feel better about my motives? Are yours really greatly different?"

"I keep coming back to these people here. The duplicates. Fat chance they have now to improve their lot. Or to keep you from doing whatever you want with them."

"Bah. Fat chance their originals have ever had—from the beginning of their short and brutish lives. I have given these . . . creations of mine . . . moments of glory, whatever else may happen to them." Pilgrim made a grand gesture.

"And you're doing all this to get back your gold."

"Yes. I do not intend to explain about the gold again." And Pilgrim got busy lifting rocks.

They worked together in heat and silence for a while. When Scheffler came back to the subject it was from another angle. "Just how big a chunk of the universe did you abstract, anyway?"

"It is a very large chunk, as you call it, as compared with the size of the solar system, containing even a few stars, as I have said. But it is infinitesimal as compared with the whole of observable space."

"All right. Sure."

"We are ready for more dynamite now. Help me string the wire and we will move outside."

Some minutes later the next charge rumbled away inconsequentially, deep inside those five million tons of stone. Presently a little more dust came drifting out.

Olivia, leaning on an Egyptian girl for support, approached Scheffler and Pilgrim where they stood watching.

"Pilgrim tells me," Scheffler said to the policewoman, "that I should ask you if he's really wiped out the whole population here."

Olivia took thought. Then she suggested to Scheffler: "I have a question for you to ask him instead. How long does he expect this created world of his to last? And what will happen to the people left in it when it ceases to exist? I'm sure he and his crew plan to be gone by then."

The little man bowed lightly. "Two questions, my worthy foe. A third implied. But I answer willingly: In time, that is to say in some not-very-great number of Earthly years, the abstracted segment will shrink in upon itself, and then collapse. Already there are disturbances, as we have seen. Already this space around us has become essentially Newtonian. If we were to attempt some proof of Einsteinian relativity here and now, it would not work."

Scheffler asked laconically: "Collapse?"

"No loss to anyone in your world. Everyone there will still see the same stars and the same sun as before."

"And what about the people in this world?"

Pilgrim shrugged. "They will have had rather interesting lives. And probably no shorter lives, on the average, than those endured by their originals in the original world."

"They will all die," said Olivia, in an almost toneless voice.

"There are little kids living here now," said Scheffler. "Infants."

Pilgrim was unimpressed. "Notably healthier than those born at the corresponding time in their original world."

Scheffler started to say something. But then he couldn't think of what the words ought to be.

"One cannot be sure of the duration," said Pilgrim. "But most probably about ten or twelve years from now, all the stars outside a radius of ten or twelve light years' distance will abruptly vanish—unless the abstracted space should itself collapse entirely before that time. I doubt it will, but when quantum effects play an important role one cannot be sure.

"After the disappearance of the outer stars, the two or three stars remaining within the volume of the abstraction will appear to be behaving strangely—as indeed they will be. One or more might go nova, and wind things up for the rest a bit prematurely. I think that is unlikely, but there are certain to be changes in color and position and even apparent magnitude. Then, over the next few years, oddities of space and time and gravitation will become more frequent. Then, within a span certainly less than a twentieth-century American lifetime, these phenomena will close in, encroaching upon the center—which is ancient Egypt.

"By the time the outer planets of the solar system are visibly affected, the end will be almost at hand—probably no more than days or weeks away.

"And then the Sun itself will be altered—from then on it becomes harder and harder to predict in any detail exactly what course the process is likely to take. As the end approaches, quantum-mechanical effects increasingly dominate."

NINETEEN

Pilgrim had now given up all hope of finding his gold anywhere but inside the pyramid. Now all energies could be concentrated on the task of getting it out.

On a page of his notebook Montgomery sketched the known passages of the still inaccessible interior. Ptah-hotep confirmed the accuracy of the drawing. The obvious assumption was that the bulk of the gold would be found with Pharaoh Khufu's coffin in the room that explorers in later history had named the King's Chamber.

Pilgrim and others, working in shifts, armed with electric lights and the wonderful steel tools at which Sihathor never ceased to marvel, were now hammering their way around the fifth and last of the train of sliding granite plugs. It appeared that no more blasting would be needed to clear this obstacle.

At last an opening appeared. The new tunnel had rejoined the Ascending Passage just above the plugs. The opening was enlarged and the way was clear to proceed.

Pilgrim led the way through, emerging in a passage no higher or wider than the Descending Passage which began at the entrance, and sloping upward at the same angle as the Descending Passage went down.

Here the lantern beams shone on lumber blocks and fragments scattered over the sloping floor. These had been used to hold back the granite plugs until after the burial, when some kind of a trigger had been released. Originally the wooden parts had been carefully shaped, but some had been splintered and crushed two years ago by the onrushing tons of granite. The fragments lay where the sliding mass had thrown them when the trigger—whatever it was—was pulled.

"This is the Ascending Passage," Monty gasped, struggling to a position beside Pilgrim in the cramped new corridor. This tunnel above the plugs was no bigger than the lower passage. Underfoot the slanting surfaces over which the great stones had been made to slide were still treacherous with two-year-old grease. But a narrow track in the middle of the floor was clean and gave good footing.

Fifty feet ahead, a small dark shape took alarm at the glare of electricity and fluttered away into the dimmer distance. Scheffler recognized a bat. "How did they get in here?"

Willis, just behind him, answered. "There are the so-called 'air-passages'—they serve that purpose but actually I think they were meant for something else—that connected the King's Chamber, and the Queen's, to the outside. Only nine inches square and hundreds of feet long. Too small for a man to get through them."

Pilgrim was advancing in the necessary crouch. Everyone else followed.

The Ascending Passage angled its way steadily upward for a hundred feet or more, aiming, as Monty had sketched it, toward the geometric center of the pyramid. But the passage changed dramatically at a point well short of that.

Here the height of the ceiling suddenly increased, from about four feet to almost thirty. At the same point a cramped horizontal passage branched off, leading straight on in toward the middle of the monument.

"This is the way to the Queen's Chamber," Montgomery

offered, shining his light that way. "A misnomer given by explorers; actually no queens were ever buried in any of the Great Pyramids."

The small horizontal shaft leading in to the Queen's Chamber was somewhat shorter than the Ascending or Descending Passages, and unobstructed. The Queen's Chamber, when they reached it, offered a chance to stand upright and stretch. It was about eighteen feet square and twenty feet high, with a gabled roof. It was completely empty, just as Ptah-hotep said the builders had doubtless left it. The air was quite fresh and breathable. There was not even a suggestion of any golden treasure. Pilgrim's instrument confirmed that none of the metal he sought had ever been here.

Ptah-hotep stated that this would have been Khufu's vault if the second plan of pyramid construction had been followed. But a third plan, and possibly a fourth, had been put into effect.

Returning to the Ascending Passage, the explorers went on up, climbing through the section almost thirty feet high, known as the Grand Gallery. Ptah-hotep explained its odd conformation as part of a plan for more elaborate traps and blockages. It appeared that the engineers' most refined ideas for traps had never actually been constructed.

At the top of the Grand Gallery a very short horizontal passage led through an anteroom toward the King's Chamber.

And here, in the anteroom, the way was closed again. A blank wall of granite spanned the narrow hall.

"One of the portcullis stones," Montgomery announced. "There will be others, positioned behind it and above it—am I right, Ptah-hotep?"

"More stones, yes." The former Chief Priest gestured. With words and miming he conveyed the idea that other slabs of rock were waiting in wall and ceiling, precariously balanced to come crashing down whenever the first barrier stone should be removed.

"The only way is forward," Pilgrim grunted.

Dynamite charges were placed again and a retreat ordered, all the way to the horizontal passage leading to the Queen's Chamber. The shock of the blast shattered the first barrier satisfactorily, but it also brought down more portcullis stones. Now these, one after another, were going to have to be blown out of the way.

At last, hours later, the way to the King's Chamber stood open. Lantern beams stabbed in through a gray fog of drifting dust, to discover the lidded and sealed granite sarcophagus, itself plain and massive, surrounded by a breathtaking mass of hastily piled treasure. Scheffler could distinguish furniture of several kinds, life-sized statues, what looked like at least two disassembled chariots—in dust and lantern light he could not begin to take a complete inventory at once. But the gleam of gold was everywhere.

Pilgrim and the *Asirgarh* plunged into the heap and began at once to test for the gold they wanted. Treasures were thrown crashing aside, others immediately ripped apart. It was easy to see from Pilgrim's face as he plied his analyzer that his quest had at last been successful.

Meanwhile Monty stood back, leaning against the wall, in no hurry to plunge ahead. Scheffler glanced back at him curiously.

The old man said, as if to himself. "More than two millennia from now, Alexander the Great will stand alone in this chamber, while the generals of his conquering army wait for him outside, wondering . . . and more than two thousand years after that, Napoleon will do the same."

"I suppose," said Scheffler. His words were lost amid

the clatter of finely wrought valuables being flung out of Pilgrim's way. Willis and Nicky were busy rescuing prizes that were not of gold, muttering over them in awe, setting them aside in a corner of the big room.

Pilgrim pounded his fist on the side of the sarcophagus. "Get this open. There's a lot of gold still missing. The old tyrant in here must be clasping it to his fragrant bosom."

It took all the available manpower, applying itself to the task through steel pry-bars, and even so, the heavy stone lid was forced off only with great difficulty. It fell it last with a sullen, reverberating crash.

"Here's more." The lid of another great box was revealed, nestled closely inside the first. Much of its decoration was fine yellow metal.

"Break it open. Break it up."

The vault was almost as hot at midnight as it had been at noon.

Hours after its pillaging had begun, and long before the job was anywhere near completion, Montgomery Chapel was the only living person left in the King's Chamber. Almost everyone else was resting at this hour. Even Pilgrim had to sleep sometime; and at last, with a major portion of his treasure in hand, he felt secure.

By now a crude inventory of the entire contents of the chamber had been taken. Even the mummy, still swathed in its last inner wrappings, had been pulled out of the sarcophagus and cast aside. Ptah-hotep had said it was certain that no gold could be hidden inside the tightness of those wrappings; and the light weight of the bundle offered proof.

Montgomery was not altogether sure why he had not gone to his own sleeping bag—why he, the old man, had no desire to rest after the day's exertions. But he had reached a state of nervous excitement that made it so.

Not that he wasn't exhausted. But he was beginning to feel that he might never want to rest again.

He closed his eyes, standing beside the sarcophagus and leaning on its waist-high rim as on some giant bathtub. A wave of dizziness had passed over him. As it did so, the idea came to him that this place represented something of an eddy, perhaps even a harbor, in the flow of time. It would be no great cause for astonishment to see Alexander, or Napoleon, come crouching in through the low passage of its entrance, head bowed like that of some mere mortal man. The idea was not new to Montgomery Chapel, but now in midnight silence it returned with fresh force.

A harbor in time. He could imagine Abraham, Moses, Caesar and Christ; Leonardo and Lincoln, Hitler and Freud and Einstein. All of them would be born and walk the earth and depart from it again before a single one of the stones in these walls was ever moved from where Ptah-hotep and his men had placed it.

And there, in the fantastically remote twentieth century beyond Christ, a young archaeologist named Montgomery Chapel, on his first trip to Egypt, would stand alone in this room in awe. He would stand here beside this sarcophagus, which by then would be badly chipped away by tourists, and he would dream strange dreams. But never a dream so strange as this: that he had been here in the same room, touching the same stone, almost five thousand years before . . .

Montgomery opened his eyes. His single lantern lit the chamber strangely.

An impulse moved him to approach Khufu's discarded mummy. Because he wanted to look upon that face . . .

❖   ❖   ❖

It was some time later when Monty became aware that another person was approaching. Light and sound were traversing the Ascending Passage, and then the anteroom. But it was neither Napoleon nor Alexander who came bowing through the doorway to the King's Chamber; it was only Thothmes, flashlight in hand.

On entering the chamber the Egyptian fixed his eye on the dishonored, inanimate figure on the floor amid its undone wrappings; the face had been exposed, but it was turned away from Thothmes now, and darkly shadowed from his lantern's light.

Then Thothmes, his mouth like a line carved into granite, lifted his gaze to the face of the frightened old man who was leaning as if for support against the opened sarcophagus. Thothmes made a sound, deep in his throat, and drew a dagger from his belt.

But something else had already frightened Montgomery Chapel, so that at this moment even a dagger came as no great shock. He made no move to draw the pistol at his side, but instead held up an open palm to warn off his attacker.

"Thothmes—if you look you'll see that it's not Khufu. It's a *ushabti* figure only. I undid the wrappings—see—" And Montgomery shone the beam of his own lantern full on the face of that stiff figure on the floor.

Thothmes made a different kind of sound this time. He turned aside, staring down at that carven wooden countenance.

His hand with the dagger in it fell to his side. "Not Khufu," he said at last, in Old Egyptian.

"No. It is *ushabti* only. But not the usual little doll. Life-sized, meant to be taken for the mummy. You see? Khufu knew that robbers were sure to get in, no matter what barriers and traps he put in their way. So he left this chamber as we found it. The first robbers would take what gold they could find here, and go away—just as Pilgrim has—thinking they had got it all. The ones who came later would find evidence of robbery, be sure that they were too late, and go away. Who would bother to unwrap a mummy, and perhaps incur a curse? Look." He shoved the figure with his toe. "Lightweight wood, no heavier than a mummy. Perhaps it's hollow. There can't be any gold inside it, though. The only question is, where is Khufu really buried? And I think I know the answer to that now. I—"

Once again light shone in from the anteroom, where once more there was motion. But this time the light came not from electricity.

With a hop of small taloned feet and a flutter of wings, its source entered the King's Chamber. The plumage was a rainbow glory, visible by its own glow.

The bird, no bigger than a goose, had a man's head, complete with a small crown and a black beard.

Thothmes fell prostrate in adoration.

Montgomery clung to the edge of the false sarcophagus. By now the bird was gone, and a tall man stood before him, wearing the double crown of the Two Lands. The image glowed, and Montgomery could see through it at the edges.

The figure of the Pharaoh said in Egyptian: "My gold is mine, intruding mortal." The words were hollow, almost without feeling.

Montgomery bowed his head, then boldly straightened his neck again. "I do not crave your gold, great king. Help me, I pray you. My craving is for revenge."

TWENTY

At dawn, Montgomery, Nicky and Thothmes were discovered to be missing.

Pilgrim, galvanized out of sleep, ran cursing to inspect his treasure, over which there had seemed to be no need to post a guard. Much of the heavy gold had already been carried out of the pyramid, and of that a considerable portion was now missing. More might have been removed from the King's Chamber, but no exact inventory had ever been taken there.

Scheffler and Willis ran in other directions, separately, searching for Nicky everywhere in the vicinity of the pyramid. She was gone. Her pistol, spare clothing, and other personal items had been left behind. But neither of the motorboats had been taken, and one of the *Asirgarh* had been watching the timelock continuously—it had not been used.

"The three of them have gone on foot, then—somewhere," Pilgrim said, and began to question Ptah-hotep. "What was Thothmes up to last night?"

The Egyptian insisted that he did not know. But he looked worried.

Willis and Scheffler clamored together for an immediate search and rescue operation. Pilgrim was willing, but refused to do anything else until he could summon his ship and incorporate into its system all of the gold two-oh-three that was still available.

❖   ❖   ❖

Grimly work resumed on the job of getting heavy gold out of the pyramid. The substitution of a giant *ushabti* doll for Khufu's mummy was discovered at once, now that the thing had been unwrapped. But the implications of the substitution were unclear.

Laboriously the wealth of golden artifacts still remaining in the King's Chamber were carried from the pyramid. The job was time-consuming. Moving any burden through the hundreds of feet of low passageways was a struggle, and two-way traffic in their restricted space all but impossible.

At Pilgrim's direction the treasure was heaped unceremoniously on the flat wasteland close to the pyramid's north face. There, while others continued carrying, he resumed the process of separating his gold from the other materials with which it had been melded in the hands of Pharaoh's artists and artisans. With chisel and prybar, and sometimes a touch of heat from the rod-shaped weapon worn at his belt, he attacked the various objects in which the metal had been incorporated, ripping and breaking them ruthlessly apart, melting the gold free. A finer separation of impurities could wait until later.

Eventually the King's Chamber had been emptied of almost everything except the fake mummy and the sarcophagus, and the heap of treasure in the sand had grown to the size of an automobile.

As the last things were brought out to him, Pilgrim straightened up from his metal-working effort, rubbing his hands together as if to restore the circulation in his fingers.

"Our ship is on its way here now," the little man said to Scheffler, raising his head to scan the sky.

"Your spaceship. So, I'll finally get to see it. Everyone's told me you have one."

"Indeed. To have completed my travels to date on foot would have been rather difficult. The ship will have used its last reserves of energy to get here. But now I have enough gold two-oh-three on hand to recharge its drive and restore the most essential of its other powers. When I have recovered what was pilfered during the night I may have all I need, though even then a considerable amount of what I lost will still be missing. I shall speak to your great-uncle on the subject when I encounter him again."

Scheffler squinted up into the hot sky. "Where's the ship coming from?"

"Not very far away . . . and now it is here."

Turning his head, Scheffler saw it materializing in midair at low altitude, a delta-winged vessel of shimmering beauty, settling in gently controlled silence toward the ground. Big as a nineteen-eighties airliner, it landed softly, very close beside the pyramid, and even closer to Pilgrim's pile of gold.

Pilgrim signaled to his assistants, earthly and alien. "Come. Help get the gold aboard." With a grunt, he himself picked up a basket of golden fragments that Scheffler would have thought too heavy for him, and led the way toward a door that had just opened in the vessel's twinkling side.

Carrying their own loads of gold behind him, Scheffler and others went aboard. Stepping up from sand onto an insubstantial-looking stair, they moved from that again onto a solid-looking deck enclosed by semi-transparent walls. Walking through the exotic interior of the ship, that somehow looked bigger than the outside, Scheffler wrestled his burden of unnaturally heavy gold through a narrow corridor past a row of crystal caskets. Inside some of the caskets, shrouded in heavy interior fog, were figures that he thought might have been as human-looking as Pilgrim or himself had they been clearly visible.

Tersely Pilgrim gave orders to Becky and some of the Egyptian women for Olivia to be brought aboard and placed in one of the caskets. She would sleep there, he said, until the medical care she needed became available.

The women went off to the temple, but soon came back saying how fiercely Olivia had refused to come. Ptah-hotep was there too, in the temple, burning incense before a statue of Osiris and refusing to answer questions. Pilgrim, engrossed by now in the job of getting his gold reincorporated into the ship's machinery, dismissed the whole pack them with a savage gesture.

Nekhem the dancing girl, obviously entranced by the sudden appearance of the ship, soon appeared in the open hatch, garbed in some of Nicky's clothing and volunteering to join this new enterprise whatever it might be. Pilgrim looked up angrily at the interruption, but then smiled and winked and gestured her aboard.

Willis muttered something about her stealing Nicky's clothes, but Nicky had been known to lend her things before; the clothing fit Nekhem well, and for searching the desert it certainly had practical advantages over the dancing girl's usual costume.

Meanwhile Pilgrim and the *Asirgarh* were working steadily, tugging and switching onboard machinery into new configurations. Plain-looking counters or workbenches sprouted complexities, sections of bright opaque colors and odd-shaped openings. What had looked like a slab of solid crystal stretched and reshaped itself. It opened in one of its sides a hopper the size of a small oven. The alien members of Pilgrim's crew grabbed up the chunks of gold that had been carried aboard, and fed the machine with mind-boggling wealth.

At this point Pilgrim ordered all the twentieth-century people to disembark.

Once off the ship they stood in the sand waiting, not having much to say to one another. Scheffler speculated silently that there was something going on board that Pilgrim did not want them to see. Inside the ship, half-seen figures moved about.

Presently Pilgrim came out to report that all of the recovered gold had now been accurately weighed and measured, and the *Asirgarh* were completing the tasks of refinement and reinstallation. But even more of the heavy isotope was still missing than Pilgrim had first thought. He looked grim.

Willis asked: "Is your ship functional now?"

"Not fully, but it will serve. We are going to recover the rest of the gold."

Those boarding the ship to take part in the search were, on Pilgrim's advice, collecting their modest baggage in the temple to bring it with them. The *Asirgarh* were the first to be ready.

Pilgrim, seated near the front of his ship at what was obviously a center of control, begin to operate some instruments—to Scheffler they looked as strange as everything else about the craft. The small man muttered: "I should soon have some indication of where they went."

Scheffler said, "What are you going to do then? Nicky didn't steal your gold, you know."

"The amount missing is substantial, and she must at least have helped to carry it, unless . . . but I have not charged her with the crime. You may set your mind at ease. I only wish my precious metal back."

"How about Thothmes and Uncle Monty?"

"Scheffler, Scheffler. You have a tender heart. How will you survive in the great world? Why do you think I would derive any satisfaction from maltreating a pair of the world's feeble-minded? Nothing less than genocide gives me a kick, remember? By the way, did you remember to bring your rifle?"

Willis and Scheffler had both carried weapons aboard the ship. It was time to lift off.

Locating the faint trail left by the walking fugitives took longer than Scheffler had anticipated, given the impressive-looking instruments now at Pilgrim's fingertips. But Scheffler supposed this was not the kind of job they had been built for.

The time was near sunset when Scheffler, scanning the passing desert through the transparent deck below his feet, looked up sharply at a sudden change of light. Something had just gone wrong with the sky; there were broad moving streaks in it—not ordinary clouds—that made it look as if someone were spinning the whole world unsteadily beneath them. Pilgrim was frowning at it too; he hadn't expected this.

It wasn't only the sky. Something was wrong with the sun too. The shadows on the landscape below, including the tenuous shadow of the translucent, speeding ship itself, were dancing madly.

The sun, low now in the western sky, had begun moving crazily in a broad figure-eight pattern. Then it came down to touch the horizon, far south of its usual place of setting. It just sat there, throwing long shadows across the landscape.

"The collective Egyptian mind, I suppose?" asked Scheffler.

But Pilgrim had no time to talk with him. An image of the sun, dimmed drastically in radiance, swelled up on one of the instrument panels before them.

The sun in that image was no longer a perfect disk. To Scheffler's astonished eyes it looked more like a boat. A smaller boat had come to rest beside it, and he could see small figures moving between the two. People who looked like Monty, Nicky and Thothmes, with some kind of escort, had disembarked from the strange-looking little boat—whatever it might be doing there in the distant desert—and were preparing to board that larger and more radiantly ominous conveyance. It looked like Thothmes and Montgomery Chapel were forcing the young woman forward.

Nicky, half blinded by the glare of the—well no, of course it couldn't *really* be the sun, that was insane—groped her way forward. All she could really believe was that she had fallen into a nightmare, while sleeping in the temple last night, and hadn't yet been able to wake up.

She recalled quite clearly what she had thought was an awakening. Monty, in his new, aged form, had come bending and gloating over her. Tall gray phantoms were at his back, and at his side towered the regal image of a man, wearing what Nicky had learned to recognize as the Double Crown of the Two Lands, Upper and Lower Egypt.

Nicky had objected forcefully to being awakened in such a fashion, and forced to accompany these people, but objecting hadn't done her any good. When she refused to move, she was pulled out of her sleeping bag by Monty's shadowy, towering attendants and thrown aboard a boat, that was somehow able to progress through the halls of the temple . . . certainly it was all wild and unbelievable, even for a dream.

And now she, along with baskets of broken gold, was being put aboard a larger craft, here in the middle of the desert. A vessel that glowed with almost-blinding light. While Monty in a voice of mad intensity kept whispering to her that this was in fact the Sun . . .

The craft, apart from the dazzling light that flowed from it, appeared to be constructed of imported wood in the Egyptian style, fifty feet long or so, and high at bow and stern, superbly built in every detail. At the approximate center of the deck was a small house-like structure, big enough for eight or ten people to have crowded into it. But most of the space inside the house was taken up by what Montgomery assured her was the bier of the sun god Ra.

"The Boat of Millions of Years," Monty whispered now. "That's the formal name for this vessel we are on, my dear. Ra rides it perpetually, as you see." And he pointed toward the little open-sided house, in which there lay supine the body of a gigantic man.

The glare of light issued primarily from that man, or god, and especially from his face. It was very bright, but when you came this close it was nothing like the Sun. It was great enough to blind the human passengers aboard Ra's Barque.

"Fascinating!" For a long moment, staring through squinted eyes at the bier and its radiant occupant, Monty appeared to have forgotten her. Then he met Nicky's eyes again. "You know, for a long time I have wondered— what it must have been like to know oneself a god. I am beginning to understand it now. Here, this reality prevails. Not that of the archaeologist. Nor that of the twentieth century. Not Pilgrim's reality either, powerful though he may be in other worlds. Here Osiris rules, and Ra. Thoth, and Isis—and Khufu, yes, he too, though he is dead . . . And I can be one of them and rule beside them. For a little time, it least. For long enough."

"I don't care. Rule what you want. But let me out of it."

"Oh no, my dear. You are going to be very much a part of it. As my subject. A very disloyal subject. I know your secret. Yours and Willis's. I saw you beside the marsh."

Nicky stared at him in bewilderment. "Beside what marsh? Monty—!"

"First I saw your khaki jacket, thrown aside in the tall grass. I think at that moment, even before I saw the other garments, and the rest, I already knew the worst. Even though we were engaged, you and I, you had always put me off. But you didn't put him off, did you? Not Willis. As always, he got what he wanted right away." For a moment the manner of an Egyptian god was not sustained. "Couldn't wait to rip your clothes off for him, could you?"

"Monty!" It was all totally inexplicable. All Nicky could think of was to tell him that he was crazy. But she didn't dare to say it, because it was so obviously true.

And now she was terrified. Because she knew she wasn't dreaming after all.

"I've been dealing with them for some hours now, you see," Monty was whispering in her ear. "I've begun to understand. These are more than apparitions, my dear. But not truly sentient beings; no, not yet, although to some degree they speak and interact with us. Later perhaps they will develop intellect. By then—I will be fully in charge."

The countenance of the god was still almost too dazzling to look upon; but squinting into the glare it was possible to arrive at the conclusion that the god was dead.

Nicky cried out in alarm and clutched at the wooden railing in front of her. Driven by oars in the hands of spectral, glowing rowers, the Barque had lurched into the sky.

Nicky, looking around wildly, saw the pursuing spaceship coming closer, and in a moment she had recognized it for what it was. Monty and Thothmes, who had both seen

Pilgrim's ship before, shouted and waved their fists at it in challenge.

Pilgrim drove the ship steadily in pursuit of the Barque, but the Boat of Ra stayed well ahead. From scraps of English phrases Pilgrim uttered, Scheffler gathered that he was unable to obtain anything like the acceleration that he wanted.

"All right," the small man muttered. "We'll try a shot across their bows." But nothing much happened, as far as Scheffler could see. There was only a dim flickering across the leading edge of one fin on the spaceship, and Pilgrim murmured exotic words that could hardly be anything but oaths. Nothing at all happened in the region of the Barque, and Ra and his entourage paid not the least attention.

Or so it seemed at first. Then the Boat of Millions of Years returned fire. Blinding flame flared close around the ship, held away from the transparent hull by some protection of invisible force. The metered impact on the shields was enough to make Pilgrim visibly less eager to close the gap between the vessels.

Scheffler, looking over Pilgrim's shoulder at a recording of the enemy beams, was astonished to see little slow-moving rays with grasping hands on the ends of them.

And now in the west, ahead of the speeding Barque, instead of a mere curve of earth for the horizon, there arose a bifurcated mountain.

Pilgrim said: "At least we are not going to have to chase them around the earth."

"Huh? Why not?"

"Because the version of the earth we have here is no longer round. This is more than ever the world of the collective mind of ancient Egypt. And I fear a quick collapse is now inevitable. A matter of hours at the most."

Scheffler grabbed him by the shoulder. "You said that it would last for years!"

"I was wrong." Pilgrim still sounded as imperturbable as ever. "It is frequently impossible to be accurate in such matters. And I can remember at least two other occasions in the past hundred years when I have been wrong."

The solar Barque of Ra was again descending majestically across the last strip of western sky, plunging now toward some kind of sunset.

Scheffler wondered if it would be the last sunset that this world ever saw.

Nicky closed her eyes momentarily as the Barque, bearing her with it, hurtled into the cavern that yawned ahead.

Then the lurching deck beneath her stabilized again. Nicky opened her eyes to see that everything was once more on an even keel.

Ra's glaring light had dimmed; the god on his catafalque now appeared more certainly dead than before, his lips shrunken, closed eyes sunken into his huge skull.

But Khufu was no more dead here than he had been in his tomb. In *ba*-form, hopping about the Boat like a pet bird, he moved in and out of Nicky's sight.

Looking ahead, Scheffler saw how the sky flamed red and orange around the spot where Ra and his Barque had vanished. A double-headed mountain reared up, where nothing of the kind had been before, against that artificial-looking sunset.

The sky itself now seemed unnaturally close ahead, as if it had become a curving wall. The spaceship did not reduce speed. Perhaps it could not. Pilgrim was going to chase the Barque into whatever convolution of the world might lie beyond.

Leaning back in his chair, he said: "If one pursues the

sun beneath the western horizon, in the new logic of this world, what happens? What must be there? The Underworld, of course."

"I can't accept that," said Willis. He repeated it several times. "I can't accept that."

No one tried to argue with him.

Ahead of them, the Boat of Millions of Years had now vanished into darkness. The intensity of its solar rays had first diminished, then faded away entirely.

"There is still air outside the ship," Pilgrim reported to his twentieth-century crew members. "Of course; a breathable atmosphere must now fill this entire space. Scheffler, you will presently see a hatch appear in the bulkhead before you. Open it. Take your rifle; we may presently be called upon to defend ourselves."

The translucent hull in front of Scheffler developed deep concentric grooves, and then a handle. There was now a circular door, with a grip that he could grasp and turn, easing the door open. The air rushing in and past him was no more than a moderate breeze. As if he had willed it, his seat lifted him forward, at the same time clasping him like an anxious parent. His arms cradling the Winchester were free.

Riding now in an open hatchway, more outside the spaceship than inside it, Scheffler aimed his weapon but held his fire. The Barque had reappeared faintly visible by its own diminished light, and was now so close ahead that with Pilgrim's instrument he could distinguish Nicky on its deck.

Monty, crouching on the deck of the Barque of Ra, saw the developing logic of the changing world about him, and had some idea of what to expect in the hours to come. And he was terrified; he knew the wild elation that grows sometimes from despair.

"Where are we?" Nicky demanded in terror.

Thothmes answered in Egyptian; it was left to Monty to put it into English: "We are entering the Underworld. This is the First Hour of the Night."

One after another the two craft, following the Sun's eternal path, passed between the two knees of the Mountain of the West. Far above, the twin peaks were still alight, as if in the afterglow of a sunset sky.

When Scheffler, now riding in his newly exposed position, turned his head to look back into the ship, he could see Pilgrim and his crew grappling again with their controls. But their efforts appeared to accomplish nothing. The ship continued on its steady course, and it was easy to deduce that its captain had lost all control over it, at least for the time being. Like one car on an amusement ride following another, Pilgrim's spaceship maintained its position behind Ra's Boat.

The Boat was undoubtedly floating now, bobbing briskly along through water that looked as real as any Nicky had ever ridden. The water felt real too, and surprisingly cold, when an occasional drop flew up from one of the spectral rowers' oars. Under the impetus of those wooden blades the vessel flew along a narrow and nameless river, going downstream between dark barren shores. On both banks gray slopes came slanting down, slopes that grew ever steeper as they receded from the banks. On each side they made great hills whose upper slopes became sheer cliffs before they vanished at last in utter darkness.

Gradually Nicky became aware that the space through which the vessels now passed, one after the other, was not a canyon but an enormous hall, with a roof of darkness so intense that it looked palpable.

Inside this cavernous chamber, Ra's light dimmed even further; he took on more than ever the aspect of a dead body.

✧✧✧

Behind the Barque, the spaceship had now settled into the stream also. Nothing that Pilgrim could do at the controls would alter matters. At length he gave up trying and sat back to contemplate the situation.

Outside the ship, but drawing closer, there sounded a murmuring as of thousands of voices. Down the gray sloping banks on either side of the narrow river there rushed cavorting hordes of two-legged shapes, vaguely manlike but inhuman.

"The apes," Montgomery Chapel breathed, more to himself than any other hearer, as he observed this phenomenon. "We are indeed in the hall of the First Hour." Thothmes, his eyes half closed, muttering incantations, crouched beside him.

"What does that mean?" Nicky screamed at them. No one answered.

Nicky still stood beside the bier of Ra, holding on with both hands to a rail that felt as if it were made of solid wood.

The thronging apes reached the river but stopped there, lining both banks. After them came the singers. These were a marching faceless throng in Egyptian dress, who followed the boat of Ra along the land. Their music went up weirdly into the endless darkness overhead.

And then the music of the singers faded, as the globe of Ra's fading illumination left them behind in total darkness; and now out of the darkness ahead appeared new anonymous crowds of humanoid figures, to hover along the shores of the swift silent river, and mark the silent passage of the Boat. The faceless rowers of the Barque labored on, continuing to ignore their living human passengers.

Montgomery was peering out eagerly from the prow,

when he sensed the presence of a tall figure beside him. He turned and addressed it, bowing unconsciously. "Khufu. Great lord Pharaoh. Where is the place of our revenge to be?"

The tall gray man raised an almost skeletal arm, and pointed straight ahead.

Scheffler, on the following spaceship, saw much the same things as did Nicky in the Boat ahead. But the spaceship, moving in the darkness behind Ra's shrunken globe of light, had so far been ignored by the creatures and human shapes lining the dark shores of this land. Until now, at least, all activity of the spectral inhabitants had centered upon Ra in his passage.

Now the Barque had entered a transitional tunnel of darkness. For Nicky sound and light vanished utterly, except for a glow in the near vicinity of the god's own person. Even the senses of touch and of identity grew uncertain. She clutched more fiercely than ever at the solid wood of the rail, but there were moments when she thought that she could feel it changing.

How long she endured this passage through a black cavity she could not tell. But at length Ra's ship emerged once more into a vast open space, as large as the one before. But here the upper reaches of the hall, or cave, were suffused with bright gray luminescence.

"It is the Second Hour of the Night," breathed Monty in the prow.

There was enough light now for Nicky to make sure that the spaceship was still following. She could even see a figure she took for Scheffler, rifle in hand, riding in the nose. And she thought that the speed of both craft had increased.

❖   ❖   ❖

Gradually, far ahead, a distant throne, a distant figure, became visible.

"Osiris," said Montgomery Chapel. He turned and looked at Nicky. "The weigher of hearts. He presides over the place of justice."

The distant throne came closer rapidly. Nicky saw a bearded man, or mummy, of gigantic stature with the White Crown on his head.

The Boat was slowing to a stop. Spectral attendants swarmed aboard, and the living human passengers were being taken ashore.

There was a confused passage through a ghostly throng, during which Nicky lost sight of Monty and Thothmes both. Only the grips upon her arms, the land beneath her feet, were solid.

In a moment more she stood before Osiris. Monstrous beings, with heads of bird and beast on human bodies, crowded in between her and that terrible throne. Nicky screamed, and screamed again.

And now Montgomery Chapel, seeing her being brought to stand beside him, knew what his revenge was to be.

TWENTY-ONE

Suddenly, as he craned eagerly forward to see the outcome of Nicky's judgment, Montgomery felt an iron grip clamped suddenly upon each of his own arms. He was dragged ahead into confrontation with jackal-headed Anubis and his tall golden balance scale. Knowing what would come next, he cried out with the sheer horror of anticipation.

There was no blade, or butchery. But Montgomery Chapel felt an opening of his chest. And he felt and saw his heart, or a red throbbing image of his heart, taken from the center of his body by the god's hands, and placed upon one pan of the balance, whose other pan held only a feather.

And Montgomery screamed again, seeing the scale tip the wrong way.

To no avail. Attendants of irresistible strength were hustling him away.

Now another god-figure loomed before him. The voice of ibis-headed Thoth shrieked at him like that of any angry bird: "You have falsely accused this woman before the gods."

"Not falsely!" he shrieked. "No, no! I saw her. I saw her rutting with my brother. I saw—"

"And you falsely accuse a man, also. And you have invaded the tomb of Pharaoh, with intent to steal. Worst of all, you have wasted the precious gift of life, squandering

271

the days of your youth, maturity and age in nothing better than the plotting of revenge. Now there is no more of life for you to waste."

And Montgomery saw the Devourer, big as a Nile hippo, gray as mud from the bottom of the river, lumbering toward him out of darkness. Its breath was of the tomb, its shape of nightmare. Crouching on four mismatched legs, it extended the ten talons of a leopard's forepaws, and opened crocodilian jaws.

But at that moment, a form draped in white linen stepped between Montgomery Chapel and the beast. The arm of a goddess intervened, holding him back from doom.

He looked up wildly and recognized the goddess Isis. Only for a moment he had thought, looking at her face, that she was Nicky.

"Now you shall repay," the goddess whispered. It sounded like a curse, dooming him to some fate more terrible than being eaten. Her eyes, more sapphire-blue than Nicky's ever were, glowed at him.

The grip of Isis pulled him free from the grasp of the Devourer's claws. A thrust of her arm sent him staggering away. With a desperate effort Montgomery regained his balance, and ran with all his strength.

Scheffler, when he saw Nicky being dragged from the Barque, raised his rifle. But at that moment tall rocks along the shoreline came into position to block his aim. When the way was clear again, Nicky was nowhere to be seen.

Willis too had seen her being carried off, and was already shouting at Pilgrim to do something. But the little man, looking maddeningly relaxed, only spread his hands in an exaggerated gesture of helplessness.

The three men argued, Willis and Scheffler shouting, Pilgrim speaking calmly despite their interruptions. His gold was still aboard the Barque, as far as he could tell, and he was going after it. There appeared to him to be nothing he could do about Nicky's problems. It was not his fault that she was here. If Scheffler and Willis wanted to jump ashore and try to help her, they were welcome to give it a try.

Before Scheffler had time to think about the possible consequences, he was standing on gritty rock beside the river, rifle in hand and pistol at his belt. Willis, white knuckles gripping a huge rifle, was at his side; behind them the spaceship was drifting away, following Ra's Boat at the pace of a fast walk.

It was the sound of voices, human and inhuman both, voices roaring, pleading, cursing in English and in unknown tongues, that led them to the scene of judgment. Looking down from a small rise in the dark contorted landscape, Scheffler saw how Nicky stood helpless amid magisterial monsters, gods and goddesses.

A thing with the head of an animal reached forward and tore open her khaki jacket; then the clawed hand poised again seemingly about to tear her heart from her breast. Scheffler heard the double-barreled elephant gun in Willis's hands go off almost in his ear; the twin explosions of his own weapon followed an instant later.

Around Nicky the press of phantasms melted back, as if the brutal energy of heavy bullets somehow negated their reality. Only seconds passed before the powers of ancient Egypt resumed control, but those seconds offered opportunity enough. Before the gods came back, Scheffler and Willis, with Nicky between them, were fleeing the place of judgment.

"The Hall of the Second Hour," Willis gritted as he ran. On endless floors of polished stone, long hills of human-looking prisoners, with hands tied behind their

backs, were waiting as if for sentence or punishment.
No one paid attention to the fugitives. Willis's long legs
led the way; he kept trying to tow Nicky along with him
until she pulled her hand free.

"Back to the river—we've got to catch the spaceship,"
Scheffler urged, directing their course downslope.
Casting a hasty glance behind him, he could see
Thothmes waving his arms in rage, urging the Devourer
after the escaped victims. But Uncle Monty was nowhere
in sight.

Monty, running through the dark cavernous Hall of
the Second Hour, fleeing like a madman from the
Devourer, could feel the pounding of his real, fleshly
heart, still safely in his chest. He was too old for this
exertion. But his lungs pumped strongly, and his heart
thudded in an even rhythm, as if the touch of the god's
hand in his vitals had strengthened them somehow.

Somehow he managed to come back to the place on
the riverbank, marked by grotesque rocks, where he had
left the Boat. But when he came in sight of the landing
he realized to his horror that both Barque and spaceship
had moved on inexorably without him. Straining his eyes
into the remote distance downstream, he could just
glimpse Pilgrim's craft. Ahead of it moved some faint
source of light, itself invisible. The spaceship was still
moving after the Barque of Ra, as if there were nothing
else that it could do in this world.

And there was nothing else that Monty could do but
run after it. There was some hope, he thought, because
he could see that the river moved in broad meanders.
There was a pain in his side now, and the muscles in his
legs were quivering with every stride, but still his breath
sufficed to run, and still he ran. He angled away from
the river's curving course, cutting across the dark land

to intercept it farther on. He dodged among black rocks as tall as houses. . . .

The Devourer was waiting for him between two rocks, no more than four strides ahead of him when first he saw it.

Montgomery had no breath with which to scream. He made a noise of retching terror, and tried to turn, and felt the ten bright talons, as real as fishhooks, fasten in his flesh from behind.

Scheffler, Nicky, and Willis were also able to see the two vessels far ahead of them, moving along a curve of the nameless river. They too began a desperate attempt to cut across country and intercept Pilgrim's spaceship.

"We are going to have to enter the Third Hour to overtake it," Willis groaned.

"What's in the Third Hour?"

"Just follow me."

At least Thothmes and the pursuit he had been trying to organize were no longer visible behind them. The fleeing humans moved through a rocky, sunless wasteland, lit only by reflections from the cliffs that paralleled the stream. The river curved away, out of sight, then back into view again, looping toward them, and the two vessels with it. The Stream of Osiris, now murmuring, sounding and looking half-alive, bore both craft on at the same pace. The winglike fins of the spaceship sometimes overhung the banks.

Casting a glance back, Scheffler thought for a moment he could see yet another vessel on the darkened stream behind them. Some other god with his entourage?

A new murmuring, again the sound of many voices, swelled up ahead, making him turn his gaze forward. To Scheffler it sounded as if the Third Hour had a vast if not entirely human population.

A great deal of that population was soon in sight. And violence was raging among the shadowy beings who populated these darkened shores. As the refugees drew closer, they could see how weapons were ceaselessly brandished and employed, with mangled bodies falling everywhere. An endless screaming noise, in many voices, went up into the darkness.

"Look out!" yelled Nicky. "Run!" Her attention was on something much nearer than the spaceship. Here came Thothmes, leading a pursuing mob of minor gods and creatures, threatening to overtake the three fugitives who were still on shore.

Scheffler loaded and fired the last pair of huge brass rifle cartridges into the mob of half-solid apparitions. He clubbed at another monster with the empty Winchester and felt the weapon wrenched away from him. Willis still had some ammo and was still blasting; the assailants at last fell back, their shapes dissolving around that of Thothmes, who still stood in the way. Scheffler hit him, and saw the smaller man go tumbling backward into the river. As the three ran on, they could hear him splashing and struggling to climb out.

Relentlessly as the hour hand of a clock, the Barque of Ra moved on, with the spaceship following as if the two craft were fastened together by some underwater framework. They moved now toward a giant doorway, and now the entire population of the Third Hour lifted up their voices in a deafening, wailing uproar. The din blended into the noise of the minor cataract separating this Hour from the next.

The nose of the Barque could be seen tilting sharply down. Then it was gone.

Willis, Nicky and Scheffler ran on, slipping and sliding down the rocks beside the waterfall, hoping for another shortcut that would offer another chance for them to overtake the speeding vessels. Boat and spaceship had now increased their speed, and were moving somewhat faster than the people on the shore could run.

Now, after the cataract, the river was quiet again.

"The Fourth Hour," Willis gasped, pausing for breath before they ran again.

It was a region of fog, shot through with glaring light from remote and unknown sources, its landscape studded with pits of darkness. And Scheffler soon realized to his horror that the whole scene was filled with huge and fearsome snakes. These reptiles covered the ground so thickly that in places it was possible to walk on them without touching the ground at all. In general they reacted sluggishly to being trampled; but always their heads reared, their fangs threatened.

And the river in this Hour had been strangely diminished. It had been reduced to a purl of slime, oozing over the hard ground, with giant snakes wriggling through it.

Looking ahead, they could see that now the dead-looking form of Ra was being carried forward. The Boat had been transformed into a litter that held an open coffin, borne on the shoulders of the silent rowers. Behind it the spaceship was still held at a fixed distance, sliding forward through the mud. The snakes surrounded Pilgrim's vessel so thickly that even if the humans on foot had been able to overtake it, they might not have been able to fight their way aboard.

Nicky, Scheffler and Willis were struggling near exhaustion, staggering along on a course paralleling that of the moving vehicles, climbing over and ducking under loops of the smooth, glistening snake-bodies. Scheffler had his pistol drawn but didn't want to use the last of his cartridges till they were absolutely needed. The snakes writhed out of the way of those who bore the corpse of Ra, but closed the gap quickly again as soon as the bier had passed. Gradually the laboring human party fell behind.

The weakened light of the sun god still persisted, ever here, as a dim glow. But it was unable to penetrate deeply into the surrounding gloom. The only effective illumination in the midst of this horrible darkness emanated from the hull of Ra's transformed boat, which had now taken on the aspect of a giant, firebreathing serpent.

The landscape in its darkness was treacherously uneven. When the snakes at last thinned out, the night prevailing along both banks of the river was thick with roaming, jackal-headed figures.

"If we can only make it to the Sixth Hour," Willis groaned.

"What happens then?"

Willis didn't answer; probably he lacked the breath. But in a minute another transition point had been reached. Beyond it the river deepened again, for no apparent reason. The Barque was suddenly so close ahead that Scheffler could see it had resumed its normal shape, and the rowers once more had taken up their oars and seated themselves upon their benches. Here, thank all the gods, the stream still meandered broadly, and Willis, Nicky and Scheffler, splashing into the shallows, could leap for a translucent overhanging fin of the spaceship and hang on until two of the *Asirgarh* appeared to help them scramble aboard.

Pilgrim turned in his chair to raise an eyebrow at them. "I am touched by your confidence in choosing to rejoin me," he remarked. "I trust it will not prove to have been misplaced."

None of the three tried to answer him. Collapsing limply inside the cabin, lying limply between Willis and Nicky, all that Scheffler could hear was the roar, faint and distant and disconsolate, of some beast. He pictured the Devourer, cheated of its prey. He shivered profoundly.

During the Seventh Hour, at the very portal of a titanic structure Willis recognized as the Gate of Osiris, Thothmes reappeared. He had come, it seemed, to make an oration on the riverbank, but what it would have been about the people on the spaceship never learned. Pilgrim, rousing in an instant from hours of inertia, snapped an order, and two of the *Asirgarh*, moving as fast as animals, scrambled ashore and seized the Egyptian from his riparian rock. In a moment he had been brought aboard.

"Eighth Hour," Willis whispered. He, Scheffler, and Nicky, their clothing still caked with drying Fourth Hour mud, still lay exhausted within the glassy hull. "The place of punishment ruled by the fiend Apep. Shall I recite his catalogue of punishments?"

"Don't bother," Scheffler gasped.

Willis bent forward suddenly with a groan, hiding his face in his hands.

"What's wrong now?" Nicky laid a hand on his shoulder.

He groaned again. "It was my fault," the words came out half-strangled. "What Monty did." He raised his head, slowly as if he were afraid to look at Nicky. "He did see me at the edge of the swamp, that day, with a woman. It wasn't you, of course. You were nowhere around. It was Nekhem. She'd borrowed some of your clothes that day, and I—I—"

He was not going to be able to go on with it. Nicky patted his shoulder, pityingly, and stared into her own exhaustion.

❖   ❖   ❖

The Ninth Hour really had something of the aspect of a city. Ra once more sat up, as boldly as if he had never been dead, and made a speech. Scheffler and Nicky could understand not a word of the oration, but the shadow-creatures at the oars, and those on shore, seemed to find it edifying.

Throughout the Tenth and Eleventh Hours, more violence churned among the dwellers along the riverbanks; Scheffler could see the shadowy struggles vaguely, but he had given up trying to make sense of the Underworld or its inhabitants. Khufu was no longer visible in the Boat ahead. Where and how the Pharaoh had gone ashore, and whether he had taken his gold with him, no one on the spaceship could say.

The cool winds that normally preceded dawn in the Egyptian desert were rising now. There were stars to be seen again, a bright torrent of them in the form of giant sparks, bearing the boat along toward daybreak.

The Twelfth Hour was a cylindrical tunnel, moving swiftly past. Ra was now not only alive again, but restored to youth.

And now, first ahead of the Boat of Ra, and then engulfing it, was something like a sky.

Dawn had returned, to a twisted, altered country that was no longer Egypt. Or no longer recognizable as such by Scheffler.

The spaceship, coming from the Underworld of darkness into the sky of morning, was finally able to break free of the forces that had held it for so long in the same position relative to the Barque.

But now the Barque of Ra, with renewed power, was coming once more to the attack.

TWENTY-TWO

Ra no longer lay upon his bier, but paced his deck, fully awake and imperiously angry. At his direction the Boat of Millions of Years, glowing like the sun it once had been, came rushing to rejoin battle with the much larger spaceship. The shadowy figures at the oars pulled sturdily, propelling the vessel of Ra and Khufu across the constricted sky. That sky was no longer even approximately normal. It had turned into a great inverted bowl. The radar, or something analogous to radar, on Pilgrim's ship showed its solidity.

Willis had no ammunition left, and Scheffler only a few rounds in his revolver. When the range had closed to something like fifty yards, he used them up with no apparent effect upon the Barque.

Despite all Pilgrim and the *Asirgarh* could do at their controls, the weapons of the spaceship itself continued to be useless in this peculiar space.

Around the two contending craft, the pocket universe was entering a state of accelerated collapse. Air, sky and space were blending into one across the domain of Ra and Osiris.

The rays of Ra flared out again, and the shields of the spaceship burned.

The spaceship took evasive action, and behind it strange serpentine clouds appeared. The flames of Ra, weakening with distance, shot after Pilgrim's vessel, but the solar Barque did not pursue its routed enemy.

Pilgrim ignored the parting shot.

As soon as the Barque had been left behind, Pilgrim abruptly changed course once more. A minute later the pyramid loomed dead ahead, and then Scheffler realized that the ship was coming gently down to earth beside the temple. A few figures came running to meet it; Pilgrim issued orders. The surviving population was summoned from the various places in which they had been attempting to find shelter from the wrath of Ra, and hurried aboard the ship. Even Ptah-hotep was now eager to evacuate.

Pilgrim concentrated his energies on getting everyone aboard. There was a delay in locating all of the women and children, and the delay stretched on into minutes, in which the sky grew ever more ominous. But Pilgrim waited with an appearance of calm, until the last Egyptian was aboard his ship.

A few moments after that the ship was under way again. There were violent flares outside the hull, and rolling colors. And then there was only milky nothingness.

Afterward Scheffler was never able to form any good estimate of how long their journey back to Chicago had taken in subjective time. He slept through part of it, to awaken abruptly with Nicky's sleeping head on his shoulder, and the realization that Pilgrim had just said something to him about being home. Those words were followed, almost instantly, by the roar of a mighty splash as the spaceship was engulfed in deep water.

"Twentieth century," called Pilgrim, catching his eye again. "This is as far is we carry passengers." The vessel had surfaced again by now, and was wallowing like a ship at sea. Stars were overhead; the horizon was darkly watery in three directions, and in the fourth a familiar skyline was in sight. Scheffler realized that Pilgrim had dropped them into the depths of Lake Michigan.

Pilgrim was now opening an interior bulkhead, revealing another wonder of his ship—a timelock door. He made adjustments and announced that it was now connected with the timelock in Uncle Monty's apartment.

"Get moving, all of you. I shall miss you all. We are pressed for time but consider that I bid you a fond farewell."

Willis, Nicky and Scheffler were crowded into the first departing car along with a great number of Egyptians. "Not you, Olivia, my dear. You go in the final shipment. I expect some of your friends will meet you in Chicago."

Scheffler called out from amid the crush at the far end of the timelock: "What date are we arriving on?"

"Don't worry. The spirits have done it all in one night. Or very nearly so. I beg of you, Scheffler, restrain your emotions, do not allow yourself to be overpowered by your gratitude."

When the door of the timelock opened again it was on Gallery Two once more. Scheffler had just time to realize that the room was full of Olivia's police before some painless weapon plucked his nerves and sent him toppling into sleep.

TWENTY-THREE

"Why do you want to know?" asked Scheffler. "What does it matter how many bathrooms there are in the apartment?"

Morgan—that was the name claimed by Olivia's bass-voiced assistant—answered only with a grunt, and with a stylus made a small notation on a pad. He and Scheffler had been touring the place together this morning, taking inventory of supplies and facilities for some purpose the policeman had not yet revealed.

"Olivia," Scheffler declared, "has already told me that I'm free to get on about my business. How am I supposed to do that with you still hanging around here?"

"Be out of your way shortly," Morgan grunted, unperturbed by the protest. He looked into another bedroom and tallied another note. "Count your blessings." To Scheffler it sounded as if he were trying to imitate Pilgrim's usually jaunty manner. But Scheffler did not make the comparison aloud; right now Pilgrim, still at large, was an extremely sensitive subject with these people.

It was Saturday morning, the day after the general return to Chicago. Outside, January for once was presenting a sky so balmy as to be almost spring-like—the mess on the streets was melting, and with a little luck it might even melt away completely before the next freeze came.

Only a few people were in the apartment as Scheffler and Morgan went about their inventory. Mrs. White had left a neat note of resignation on the kitchen counter, weighted with her household keys and addressed to Scheffler, directing him where to send her last paycheck. Exactly what had caused her to quit just now after so many years he did not know, and he had no intention of asking.

Moments after their arrival, the entire contingent of Ancient Egyptians had been spirited away by Olivia's police. Scheffler was not expecting to see any of them again, any more than he would see Uncle Monty, who had never made it back to the spaceship. He could only hope that the Egyptians would be resettled safely somewhere.

Willis Chapel, already provided by Olivia's efficient colleagues with suitable nineteen-eighties identification—birth certificate, Social Security file and so on—was sitting in the study this morning, writing a new resume to go with his new identity. Willis had already picked out a new name for himself from a list presented by Olivia. He hadn't, Scheffler felt sure, given up on his yen for Nicky. But with her or without her the elder Chapel brother was ready to begin his re-entry into the twentieth-century world of art and antiquities dealers and collectors.

Nicky was sitting in the library too, at a separate table, working at the same exercise. When Scheffler and Morgan looked in on her and Willis, she glanced up and her gaze lingered on Scheffler's. That was important, but he couldn't stay and talk just now. Morgan expected his company on the tour.

Becky was curled on a chair in the dining room, gazing dreamily out the window. It was Saturday, and neither she nor Scheffler had classes. He supposed that on Monday both of them would be back in school, whatever else was going on.

She looked sad, and Scheffler supposed she might be

wondering where Pilgrim was. He was reasonably sure that she had offered to accompany the wanderer; but Pilgrim had evidently declined her offer. Graciously, no doubt. Becky had, however, been well rewarded by Pilgrim for services rendered, and so far, at least, Olivia's people had not taken any of her jewelry away.

Olivia herself was in the apartment this morning, along with one or two additional members of her force. Whatever medical attention they had been able to provide for the policewoman in the few hours since her return had done wonders, and she looked almost normal. Fortunately she had been able and willing on arrival to testify that the twentieth-century people brought home by Pilgrim deserved help and not prosecution.

Morgan's note-taking tour was moving along to the galleries when the front doorbell chimed. Scheffler looked at the policeman. "I would suggest you answer it," said Morgan, half-abstractedly, hardly raising his eyes from his notes.

When Scheffler opened the front door he immediately recoiled. The small foyer was crowded with an exotic mob. It was the entire native population of Pilgrim's pocket universe, nine-tenths naked as usual and babbling all at once in exotic speech. But that was not the biggest shock. In front of the mob, in the position of leader or spokesman, and garbed as Scheffler had seen him last, stood Uncle Monty. The old man's face looked more dead than alive, but he was breathing.

As soon as the door opened the throng began to flow into the apartment, marveling loudly at what they saw. The crush pushed Uncle Monty to one side, and he in turn crowded the bewildered Scheffler back into a corner of the entrance hall. The old man came alive a little, looking pale and haggard, baffled, helpless and enraged. When the whole mob was inside, Scheffler closed the front door again. Then he and his great-uncle stood confronting each other.

"What happened?" Scheffler asked.

"What happened? They found me guilty." The voice was broken and dazed, that of a man sentenced to a firing squad. He kept raising his hand to brush at the front of his bedraggled coat, as if he felt compelled to wipe off something from his fingers.

"I thought you were dead."

"The Devourer had me," Montgomery said tonelessly. "But there was a police ship in the Underworld by then, trying to chase Pilgrim. Coming down the river after us. They sent a squad ashore and pulled me out. If only they'd left me there I would be dead by now. They would have 'rescued' me anyway, the damned do-gooders, but they wanted to put me on trial. They found me guilty."

"Guilty of what exactly?"

The old man appeared to ignore the question. "Twenty-seven of them," he said, in his new uneven voice.

"How's that?"

"They're settling them on me. On me. Here. As if I . . . the rest of the sentence suspended on condition that I help them . . . Tom, listen to me, Tom? You've got to help." Monty looked wildly about.

"Where's Willis? He's got to help me too!"

"Willis and I don't have to do anything," Scheffler was beginning wrathfully, when Nicky, who had just arrived in the front hall, at the same moment asked her former fiancé: "Help you do what?"

'Twenty-seven naked, ridiculous, stupid, ignorant—none of them even know how to use a flush toilet yet." Uncle Monty bowed his head and cradled his face in all his fingers, so that the last two words were muffled.

Then he looked up. "I quote, from the judge: 'Achieve their integration into twentieth-century American society, where their offspring will probably do well.' That is what that goddamned court of Olivia's has ordered me to do. House them. Feed them. Clothe them. Teach them English. All twenty-seven. Teach them to use plumbing. Get them into schools. Get them jobs. I—"

"We will help with such matters as immunizations and paperwork," said Morgan encouragingly in his bass voice. "And actually the dancer Nekhem, who returned here an hour ago, already has a job, I understand. At some amusement facility called Bush Street."

"They're all going to live here? In the apartment?" Then understanding dawned on Scheffler. The tour. Morgan had known about the sentence. But of course they were all going to live here, for the time being anyway. Hence the survey of the space, the counting of the bathrooms.

"We will of course be dropping back," said Olivia, shoving her way gently into the front hall. "From time to time. Just to check up on your compliance with the orders of the court."

Montgomery buried his face in his hands again.

"I've heard," said Scheffler, "about one family in Chicago that includes eleven people who immigrated from mainland China. The head of it is a former missionary with a Chinese wife."

"Heroic," his great-uncle mumbled through his fingers. "Maybe we should ask them how to make it work. Tom. Tom, my boy, you've got to help me. I am an old man. My heart will give out." Montgomery raised pitiful eyes and held a hand up to his chest.

"Actually, as you know very well, it will not," said Olivia in a cool voice. "Not physically." She turned to Scheffler. "We made sure of his vital organs while he was in custody. We conditioned him against suicide. He will endure for several years at least."

"*Tom!*" The old man's cry came from the depths.

Scheffler drew a deep breath. "If you want me to work for you—I don't come cheap—"

From the corner of his eye he saw how Nicky smiled. "Neither do I," she put in. "But I might be willing, if you think you might need help."

Another hour had passed before the police were gone, and Monty could take Sihathor aside for a moment in the library. There Monty explained to the robber his theory about what must have happened to the original of the abstracted gold.

"It remains, my friend, buried inside the Great Pyramid. Up near the top somewhere. And no one really believes in its existence except those who have good reason to do so. It will take time, of course. But between us we ought to be able to find a way to get that treasure out."

It may be, thought Olivia, listening, over her system of concealed microphones, *that the stubborn Khufu is going to get the last laugh after all. In the real universe most of his gold, along with his jewel-bedecked mummy, is somewhere where the clever robbers in the world, or in several worlds, have still been unable after five thousand years to get their hands on it.*

Schaffer drew a deep breath. "If you want me to work
for you—I don't come cheap—"

From the corner of his eye he saw how Nicki smiled.
"Neither do I," she put in. "But I might be willing, if
you think you might need help."

Another hour had passed before the police were gone,
and Monty could take Shaffer aside for a moment in
the library. There Monty explained to the robber his theory
about what must have happened to the original of the
abstracted gold.

"It means, no bread here [hands the Great Pyramid
up near the top somewhere. And no one really believes
in its existence except those who have good reason to
do so. It will take time, of course. But between us we
ought to be able to find a way to get that treasure out."

It may be, thought Olive, listening over her system
of concealed microphones, that the stubborn Khufu is
going to get the last laugh after all. In the vast universe
most of his gold, along with as yet undecoded amounts,
is somewhere where the clever robbers in the world (or
in secret worlds later still) then unable after five thousand
years to get their hands on it.

AFTER THE FACT

remember now but certainly Scheffler, a big kid from
Iowa, had been generally encouraging. Scheffler was an
undergraduate in computer engineering at the University
where Jerry Flint was now working on his master's in
computer science. The two of them had shared one class
and a couple of seminars, and over the past few months
had become moderately well acquainted.

Jerry didn't have the faintest idea that Scheffler much

ONE

Central Illinois was about the flattest place that Jerry
Flint had ever seen. Plowed fields, islanded here and
there by clumps of trees and farm buildings, seemed to
go on forever. The horizon was lost in an indeterminate
haze more appropriate to Indian Summer than Spring.

Here and there along the interstate that stretched
southwest from Chicago, grain elevators in tiny towns
stood up like junior skyscrapers. Occasionally the highway
would line up on one of them and rush straight at it for
three or four miles, only to swerve at the last moment,
bypassing both tower and town completely.

Jerry had intended to use the driving time to prepare
himself for the interview facing him in Springfield, but
found himself listening to the wind rushing past instead.
Before he was well out of Chicago he had begun to realize
that there was not a whole lot in the way of preparation
that he could do; since he knew next to nothing about
the people who ran the Pilgrim Foundation for Historical
Research, it was difficult to imagine what sort of
programming or systems work they might want from him.

Tom Scheffler, a fellow student at St. Thomas More
in Chicago, had told Jerry that he had worked for the
man Pilgrim himself about a year ago, had been well paid
for his labors, and recommended that Jerry give the
Foundation a try.

Or had Scheffler said even that much? Jerry couldn't

remember now but certainly Scheffler, a big kid from Iowa, had been generally encouraging. Scheffler was an undergraduate in computer engineering at the University, where Jerry Flint was now working on his master's in computer science. The two of them had shared one class and a couple of seminars, and over the past few months had become moderately well acquainted.

Jerry didn't have the impression that Scheffler was much given to jokes, at least no more than the average student. So now Jerry, looking back at the brief discussion the two of them had shared on the subject of the Pilgrim Foundation, began to find it rather strange, and even a touch ominous, that the big youth had seemed secretly amused or even a bit excited by the prospect of Jerry's coming interview.

Their only important conversation on the matter, Jerry recalled, had been conducted between classes, in something of a rush.

When Jerry brought up the subject, Scheffler had shrugged and smiled. "Sure, if Olivia says it's okay—and she told you to talk to me, right?—give it a try. The guy does pay well, I can testify to that. He wasn't 'the Pilgrim Foundation' when I worked for him, though."

"Oh? What did you do?"

Scheffler's inward amusement seemed to grow. "No computer stuff, really," he said at last, apparently groping for the right words. "My work involved some traveling," he added, finding them. "And there were some historical artifacts."

"Oh?" Jerry was squinting, scowling, trying to understand, and at the same time not wanting to be late for his next class. "This Pilgrim is a collector, then? In some kind of private business?"

"I'm sure he is. Look, I can't really give you any details. He'll have to do that. But I know Olivia, too, and if she's the one who's trying to recruit you, I'd say it was definitely okay." And with a wave of hands they parted company as each hurried on to his next class.

Olivia—Jerry knew her only by her first name—the person who had suggested that he talk to Scheffler about this, was something of a mystery herself. She was only a voice on the phone to Jerry Flint; she had started the whole business by phoning him one day out of the blue, and suggesting that as a bright student he might be willing to accept a summer job that would guarantee the financial support he was going to need if he wanted to go on and get a doctorate in computer science.

Did he want that? For Jerry that degree was life's big brass ring: not only was the subject matter incredibly interesting, but people with such advanced degrees in computer science were currently going directly from school into jobs that started at a hundred thousand a year. Still, it was a little odd that Olivia was also the one who recommended that he talk to Scheffler.

When Jerry, having been given a phone number to call in Springfield, came to talk to Dr. Pilgrim himself, he was assured that if he were hired, a grant could be arranged, above and beyond his pay for the coming summer, that would finance his schooling all the way to a Ph.D. in computer science.

Jerry's preliminary research in the university library had failed to turn up any reference to grants from a "Pilgrim Foundation." Of course the library's list might well be out of date. Nor could he even find a foundation of that name listed anywhere; but, he told himself, that that meant little; these organizations came and went.

So on the appointed day, with a week of spring break clear ahead of him, he rented a car and started driving south.

❖   ❖   ❖

Jerry hadn't visited the state capital since a seventh-grade historical tour, and he was vaguely surprised that the place turned out to be a modest scale model of the metropolis to the north, complete with suburbs. There were no grain elevators here, but as Jerry drove in he observed a couple of buildings even taller than grain elevators. One of these, as he got close to it, turned out to be the hotel that he was looking for. At twenty stories or so it loomed far above everything else in sight.

There was no difficulty in finding a parking space on the street close to the hotel. Jerry climbed out of his little red rented Ford, and pulled on the suitcoat that had been riding on the back of the front seat. He tightened and straightened his unaccustomed necktie, and set out for the hotel lobby, leaving his bag in the car's trunk for the time being. Wondering if Dr. Pilgrim might possibly be waiting for him right in the lobby, he checked his image in a passing plate-glass window. Jerry had about given up wishing that he looked a little bigger, older, more mature. The key word for his appearance, he thought, was really *nondescript*. He could try raising a mustache, but it would probably be thin, and certainly the same commonplace brown as his hair. There was, of course, even less to be done about physical size. At five seven at least he was a comfortable way from being a midget. And the karate classes he'd been attending for the last two years kept him in good shape.

As for being and looking older—well, that was certain to take care of itself in time. He was twenty-five now, and still sometimes taken for eighteen.

The hotel lobby was modern, and at the moment it was pleasantly uncrowded. Perhaps business was not that great. Jerry approached the desk. Yes, there was indeed a room reserved for Mr. Jeremiah Flint. Yes, prepaid too.

There was also a message waiting for Mr. Flint, and Jerry received it along with his room key.

The note handed over by the desk clerk was handwritten in a distinctive but very legible script, black ink on a sheet of hotel notepaper. It read:

> Dear Mr. Flint,
>
> Please accept my apologies for not being on hand to welcome you on your arrival. An opportunity to conduct an experiment, one that I dare not pass up, has arisen. If you are able to come to the lodge across from the entrance to New Salem State Park before five o'clock, we shall be able to begin our discussions there, while at the same time you will be able to see something of the Foundation's work.
>
> In haste,
> A. Pilgrim

New Salem was only about twenty miles away, according to the desk clerk, who had the directions memorized—it was evidently a favorite tourist destination. As for meeting Pilgrim there before five, that was no problem; it was now only a little after noon.

An hour later, after settling in and having a cheeseburger in the hotel coffee shop, Jerry was back in his little red Ford, headed out of town again.

State Route 97 re-entered farmland only a couple of miles from the hotel near the center of town. Presently the highway branched, and the branch Jerry was following became even narrower. Jerry had gathered from a tourist brochure picked up in the hotel that New Salem was a small log cabin settlement preserved and reconstructed more or less as it had been on reaching its peak of prosperity, sometime in the 1830s. That was about the time young Abraham Lincoln, working on a riverboat, had arrived in the settlement and taken up residence.

Now, scanning the farmland ahead on both sides of the highway, Jerry saw no sign of any community, historical or otherwise: just farms, hedgerows, and islands of trees, leafing out with fresh spring green. Such groves of course might conceal something, but mostly what he could see was the black earth of Illinois, ready and eager to start producing crops. Here and there the fields were already dusted with preliminary green of one fine shade or another. Now and again the freshly turned fields alternated with pasturage. At intervals he could see a tractor laboring in the distance, tugging at some kind of machinery with which Jerry was not familiar. He was pretty much a city kid, or at least a suburban one.

But now, ahead and to his right, the agricultural expanse was interrupted by a long sweep of woodland that seemed to follow the course of a stream. As the woods drew nearer, the highway drifted right, sliding down along a heretofore invisible slope in the flat Illinois countryside. Then it suddenly drove more deeply, leveling off again under an arch of tall trees that lost itself inside a tunnel of bright new leaves.

Suddenly there were roadside signs, proclaiming the presence of New Salem State Park. There were log structures to be seen, and split-rail fences. The twentieth century had not entirely disappeared, but it was no longer unquestionably in charge; on that descending slope a border of some kind had been crossed.

On Jerry's right now, as he cruised the narrow highway at reduced speed, a wooded slope went up. On his left, beyond more trees, he could catch glimpses of a small river, banks already green enough for summer. That, according to his map would have to be the Sangamon, where Lincoln had once poled his flatboat.

The motel was on the side of the road toward the river. It consisted of a modest lodge made of logs, and rustic cabins scattered back from the two-lane highway. A handful of cars were parked in the gravel lot.

Jerry pulled off the road and parked, went through the business of seeing to his coat and tie again, crossed a wooden porch and entered a log-walled lobby. To his eye, moderately experienced in academic appearances, none of the three or four people in sight looked like the head of a foundation. Anyway none of them took any interest in his arrival. After peering vaguely into a restaurant and a gift shop, and generally standing around looking lost for a minute or so, he approached another hotel desk and asked if there were any messages for him.

"I'm not a guest here, but—"

The woman behind the counter was rummaging in cubbyholes. "Mr. Flint . . . yes, there's a message for you, sir."

This time the note was on a small sheet torn from a pocket notebook. And the handwriting, though nearly as superbly legible as that of the first note, was different, smaller and rather feminine.

> Dear Mr. Flint—
>   Sorry again not to be able to meet you. The experiment is keeping Dr. Pilgrim and myself both busy. If you would please come up into the park and join us in front of the Onstot cabin, we can begin your introduction to our rather unusual enterprise. We hope to see you in the park this afternoon.
>
>   Jan Chen
>   (for Dr. Pilgrim)

Whoever Jan Chen might be, there was something intrinsically pleasing, Jerry thought, about her handwriting. The notebook sheet looked businesslike enough, but he thought he could detect the faintest whiff of perfume.

Jerry decided that he would walk up the hill—he'd done a good bit of driving already today, and would certainly have to do some more. The park entrance proper was a few hundred yards down the highway, but directly opposite the motel parking lot a fairly well-worn though unofficial-looking footpath pointed in the right direction before vanishing among the half-greened trees a few yards in. Breathing spring country air, Jerry crossed the highway—traffic just now was light to nonexistent—and started up.

The slope he was climbing was not particularly high, but almost until he was there the trees obscured his destination; Jerry wondered if the area had been logged since Lincoln's time. A wasp cruised past then hummed away again. There were a few muddy places at flat spots in the path, but nothing that his city-shod feet could not avoid.

As Jerry crested the hill, which he saw now was really an extended ridge, a small log cabin suddenly appeared among the trees. Beyond it there was another, and another beyond that. All at once he became aware that the twentieth century had disappeared completely. There was only an earthen path, trees, logs—and above the trees a sky for the moment innocent of jet contrails. The tang of woodsmoke reached Jerry's nostrils, and when he looked for it he could see a faint blue-white trickle rising from the tall stone chimney of the nearest cabin.

Jerry now noticed that mixed with the smell of woodsmoke came the aroma of cookery.

The door of the cabin stood ajar in the mild gray afternoon. Out of curiosity Jerry pushed it farther open—this building was an exhibit in a park that was open to the public, right?—and peered into the dim interior, which was lighted only by one small window on another wall.

A figure moved, near the broad stone hearth where a small fire glowed amid gray ashes. The figure was that of a woman, wearing a bonnet and a long dress—a dress about a hundred years too long. Her face as she turned toward the doorway was shaded by the bonnet, hard to see.

"Come in," the woman said.

Jerry stood dead still, one hand on the door's ancient-looking, handcarved latch of wood. "I—" he started to say, and then quit. No, he thought.

"Come in," she invited cheerfully. "Try some cornbread."

Blinking against the smoke and dimness, he managed to get a better look at the woman. She was about forty, fresh-faced and a bit plump. In one hand, protected by a thick homemade potholder, she was gripping a high-sided metal pan from which she now began to pry slabs of steaming yellow golden stuff onto a large white platter that waited on the handmade wooden table. Other dishes on the table held more cornbread already cut into chunks of modest size. There was also, Jerry observed with faint but real relief, a package of paper napkins, very much of the late twentieth century.

"You had me going for just a minute," he admitted.

"Beg pardon?"

"I thought—you being in the costume and everything—oh, never mind. I wasn't sure what was going on." It was easy enough to chuckle now.

"Oh." The woman was still smiling at him, but not as if she really understood. "We're from the historical society. We're occupying several cabins here today, demonstrating what life was like for the original settlers."

"Oh. I see. You're doing a very realistic job." Accepting first a paper napkin and then a piece of cornbread, Jerry spoke in honest admiration of the evident skill required for baking over the open fire. He listened politely to some more information on cooking tools and methods, and then strolled on. Out of the cabin now, he could see that the path continued on to join a system of broad gravel walks. In that direction were scattered a dozen or more log buildings whose loose grouping extended more or less along the top of the wooded ridge.

Picking up another brochure from a tray mounted on a rustic stand where the official walks began, Jerry learned that there were about twenty buildings in all in the reconstructed settlement. On this gray weekday a very modest number of other tourists were about. Jerry walked forward. He was just thinking that it oughtn't to be hard to pick out a working scientist and his assistant when he saw them. There was no doubt in his mind, though they were still at a considerable distance.

TWO

Approaching the man he thought must be Dr. Pilgrim, Jerry walked past a water-powered mill that was, for the moment at least, motionless, a blacksmith shop manned by folk in historic costume, and half a dozen more cabins. Then he was drawing close to the people he thought he was looking for, and their machines.

The little machines, mounted on what looked like surveyors' tripods, were aimed at what Jerry supposed must be the historic Onstot residence. The man who was concentrating his attention so energetically upon what the machines were doing was a couple of inches shorter than Jerry, compactly built, and of indeterminate age. At least he was still young enough for his black hair to be free of gray. His coloring in general was rather swarthy.

Muscular, hairy forearms protruded from rolled-up shirtsleeves. The half-dozen pockets of the man's Banana Republic bush vest were stuffed with electronic cables, small tools, pencils, notebooks, and what looked to Jerry like camera accessories.

The young woman with him looked vaguely oriental, as if the name Chen might fit her. Her straight black hair, or most of it, was tied up in an expensive-looking scarf. She wore jeans and a tucked-in shirt, with large dangling earrings that were perhaps intended to show that she didn't really belong on a construction crew.

At twenty yards or so, before either of the pair had

given any sign of noticing him, Jerry paused in his approach. He was making a last effort at trying to figure out just what the hell they might be doing, so that his first attempt at conversation would not appear too stupid.

They had the Onstot cabin triangulated with their machines, and they were either photographing it or making surveyor's measurements of it. Or maybe they were doing something that required both processes. A couple of passing tourists gazed at the workers in ignorant admiration, and passed up a close look at the Onstot cabin, being anxious not to interfere with whatever kind of special work was going on.

The setup reminded Jerry vaguely of the laser systems that construction crews sometimes used to make sure that things were kept exactly level or exactly perpendicular. At least two of these devices could have been cameras, and all three of them had what must be their battery powerpacks on the lower shelves of their tripods. Jerry in his years of engineering studies had never seen anything like it. But he had to give up for the moment on trying to figure it out. He resumed his advance.

Though the man was facing directly away, it was he who made the young woman aware of Jerry's presence. As if he might have received some extrasensory warning, the dark-haired man lifted his eyes suddenly from his instrument and turned around to look at the new arrival. A moment later he raised a hand in an abrupt gesture, signaling his helper that they were through for the moment with whatever they had been doing.

Jerry strode forward, armed with his most intelligent smile. "Dr. Pilgrim?"

"Yes." As on the phone, the voice had the precision of an actor's, slightly and indefinably accented—James Mason would come close, thought Jerry, who was something of an old-movie buff. "Yes," Pilgrim continued.

"And you will be Jeremiah Flint." He appeared genuinely pleased to see his visitor, and not to resent the interruption of his work.

The doctor's handshaking grip was firm but brief. Then he turned his head toward his assistant. "Jan, let that go for now. Come and say hello. It may be that our computer problems are on the verge of solution."

Jan Chen approached. Jerry took his first good look at her through a fragrance of lilacs; the bushes flanking the Onstot cabin door were in full spring bloom. She walked with a grace that suggested a model's training; her eyes were as black as her hair, but her skin glowed like old ivory. It hardly seemed to matter that her face was a long way from Jerry's ideal of classic beauty.

"I see you found our messages," she said to him in a voice in which be could find no accent at all. She shook his hand in a businesslike way. "Sorry that neither of us could meet you in person at the hotel."

"That's quite all right. I was glad to come up here and meet you on site. This will give me a chance to see what kind of work you're doing."

Pilgrim was frowning at his watch. "Now that you are here, Mr. Flint—may I call you Jerry?"

"Sure. Of course. I was wondering what you were doing with these devices that—"

"Now that you are here, I think it will be best if we spend as much of the afternoon as possible in our discussions. Therefore we had better break this off— Jan, let us pack up the equipment immediately. "

The young woman nodded, murmured something in agreement, and turned away to begin folding one of the tripods. Pilgrim seemed to have another of them already folded—he had got it taken down with what seemed to Jerry altogether unlikely speed. The battery pack and everything else stayed neatly in a bundle with the tripod when its long legs were collapsed. Jerry was unable to catch a manufacturer's name, if such a thing was showing, before the device had been snapped inside a cloudy plastic cover.

Jerry volunteered to carry one of the three machines, and equally burdened, the three headed out through the main gate of the village to the hilltop parking lot through which most visitors approached.

"Have you been here before?" Jan Chen asked him.

"No, first time for me." His school tour, long years ago, had never got this far from Springfield.

"For me too. But I have long been an enthusiast of Abraham Lincoln, and to be here where he lived is exciting." Despite her rather stilted turn of phrase, Jan sounded animated; this meant something to her. She turned to point back into the village, indicating one direction after another. "He was a boarder there, at the Rutledge tavern. And a clerk over there. And a storekeeper and postmaster down there. His first claim to fame was as a frontier wrestler in these parts."

Jerry caught at a name. It brought back vague memories of someone's poem. "Ann Rutledge? She was supposed to be Lincoln's girl friend, wasn't she?"

"Many think so—but we can't be sure." They had come to a stop in the parking lot, and Pilgrim had unlocked the side door of a new van and was beginning to stow equipment inside. Meanwhile his assistant was starting to glow with an inner excitement, which Jerry recognized as that of the true enthusiast unleashed upon a favorite subject. She went on to discuss in detail the lack of any real evidence connecting young Lincoln with the innkeeper's daughter.

Dr. Pilgrim, meanwhile, apparently bursting with his own brand of cheerful energy, stowed the last bit of gear in the van and slid shut the wide side door. "I would like to suggest, Jerry, that I ride back to Springfield with you. I presume you have a car. We will meet Jan there, unload our equipment, and continue our discussions in the office."

Jerry found the rush to get the gear packed away not too surprising; a lot of companies had proprietary secrets they were reluctant to reveal, at least until you were contracted to secrecy. Probably this equipment was something like that. Jerry knew a momentary regret that he was not riding back with Jan. That would almost certainly make it a more pleasant trip—but possibly a less productive one. And Pilgrim was definitely the man he had to talk to, to find out as soon as possible if this job offer could possibly be as good as Mr. A. Pilgrim had made it sound.

After waving Jan on her way in the van, he and Pilgrim started trudging side by side down the winding, forest-lined drive that led to the highway and to the small motel parking lot where Jerry had left his car.

"Interesting equipment you were using up there," Jerry remarked in a bright tone, opening conversation.

Pilgrim gave a little shrug. "Not really mine, in any proprietary sense. I have learned to use it, that is all." The words were said in a deprecating tone, as if to imply he might not be capable of learning more. "I am not really a technologist. The fact of the matter is, the Foundation needs help in several technical areas."

"I see. What were you doing up there today, if you don't mind my asking?"

Pilgrim might not have heard the question. "Your own role, Jerry, if we are able to come to an agreement, would be—largely—in the area of computers. Of course, we might ask you to do another little job or two also. Specifically, I should like to establish a network comprising several of the newer Macintosh machines. They would be connected by modem with a larger computer, one of the new 'parallel' devices, and possibly with several other machines as well. The Macintoshes are in the Foundation's office in town, where we are going now."

Jerry's only experience with parallel processing was course work, but he had found that course work intensely interesting. But what could an historical research project need with that kind of raw power? Intriguing. Maybe this job would be *better* than it had sounded over the phone.

"Then I would be working here, in the Springfield area, full time. Is that it?"

"Yes—allowing for the occasional field trip elsewhere. You would work here during the coming summer, putting in as much time as your school schedule allows. The Foundation will pay all of your living expenses while you are in Springfield—or on any field trip we might require you to undertake—plus modest salary. And it will guarantee in writing that, provided your job performance is satisfactory, it will pay all your further expenses toward your doctorate in computer science."

"That sounds like a great deal."

Pilgrim, looking straight ahead through the windshield, nodded minimally. "Indeed. All this, of course, contingent upon our agreement that you are the right man for the job."

"Of course. I should warn you that microcomputers aren't really my specialty. I have worked some with Macs, though."

Jan and the van were long out of sight by the time they had walked down to Jerry's car. On the drive back into town Jerry, by invitation, held forth on the various computer projects in which he'd already been involved. They made a fairly impressive list for someone of his age; he'd had to work his way through most of college, and most of the work he'd done had involved computers in one way or another.

He wasn't sure though, how much of it Dr. Pilgrim understood. The man in the front passenger's seat sat listening and nodding thoughtfully, and for the most part appeared to be keenly interested. But he didn't really say anything that would offer good evidence of his understanding. It wouldn't be the first time that Jerry had tried to inform a highly intelligent but non-technical audience about his work, only to discover later that hardly anything he'd said had been understood. There were computer people, who could understand, and then there was the rest of the human race.

In a few minutes they were back in town, where Pilgrim began giving navigator's directions. Presently, only a couple of blocks from Jerry's hotel, they were driving into a large square whose center was occupied by a hulking stone building of antique design, obviously preserved or restored. Several signs informed the visitor that this was the Old State Capitol.

Guess who, thought Jerry to himself, must have done something or other in the Old Capitol. Any lingering suspicion he might have entertained that Lincoln was not the chief industry in Springfield had by now vanished under a barrage of commercial signs. You had the Lincoln This, the Lincoln That, the Railsplitter Something Else. A few people, just to be different, had dedicated their enterprises to Ann Rutledge.

At Pilgrim's direction Jerry now turned into a lane of traffic that dove sharply into a fluorescent cave right under the Old Capitol, where signs informed him of several levels of modern parking. Here, in one of the reserved sections, Jan stood waiting for them beside the van.

In a couple of minutes the three of them had unloaded

the equipment from the larger vehicle and were carrying it upstairs to the surface.

They emerged on a broad sidewalk, facing the Old Capitol across the street. The buildings lining the perimeter of the square were mostly of brick, two or three stories tall. Approaching one of these, Pilgrim used a key on an inconspicuous door set back slightly from the sidewalk, and led the way up some indoor stairs. The plastic-covered tripods now and then knocked lightly against stairs or walls. At the top of the first flight Jan unlocked the door to a modest suite of offices. There was no sign on the door to indicate who occupied them. Nothing fancy, Jerry thought, carrying his burden in. Except maybe for some of the computer stuff.

These rooms might last have been modernized in the 1960s. In the first room were a couple of desks and a few battered tables. On some tables near the windows, a couple of instruments similar to the ones Pilgrim had been using at New Salem were mounted on shorter tripods, lenses aimed out through the windows in the direction of the Old Capitol building across the street. There were also three of the new Macintosh computers in the room, one with a color screen, and quite a bit of cabling.

"Did you arrange this setup?" Jerry asked, gesturing at the computers, when the equipment they had brought in with them had been stowed in a closet.

"No, I am a user only. And I am afraid there will be no chance for you to consult directly with the engineer who arranged this system—if that is the right term for what has been done here." Moving energetically from one table to another, Pilgrim had started flipping switches. Now Jerry saw that there were four Macs, the last one almost hidden in a corner. One after another each sounded a musical chime-note as it came to life.

"As you can see," Pilgrim added, "part of the system is optical—would you like to take a look?"

More than ready to get involved, Jerry went to the eyepiece of one of the tabletop units—it looked something like a cross between a surveyor's instrument and a telescopic camera. The image it presented was one of the most peculiar he had ever seen—it looked like a clear, somewhat magnified optical picture of the granite of the Old Capitol, overlaid slightly off-center with a computer reproduction of itself.

He turned away from the eyepiece and looked around. "I don't quite get it."

"The Foundation's object, Jerry, is historical research. The capitol building there, for example, was taken down stone by stone a few decades ago, and then reconstructed *in situ*. There are of course slight differences between the positions in space of its stone blocks now, and the positions occupied by those same blocks in, say, the year eighteen fifty-nine. With the center of mass of the earth itself as reference—excuse me." A phone at the far side of the office had begun to ring, and Pilgrim gestured to Jan Chen that he wanted to answer it himself.

She was standing by, smiling brightly, and Jerry turned to her. He asked: "It sounds like you're somehow able to determine exactly where each stone was in the past?"

Across the room, Pilgrim was frowning and muttering at whatever the phone was telling him. Jan shook her head. "I'm not the one to ask about what can be done with the computers and sensing devices. Ask me something about the dates of the Old Capitol there, or about Lincoln, and I can tell you a few things."

"Sounds interesting. I probably will. You're the resident historian then."

"That is really Dr. Pilgrim. I am only an assistant." No accent in her speech, no, but a certain overprecision, noticeable more at some times than others, that made Jerry wonder if she might have been born in another country. She went on: "this whole area around Springfield is just so fascinating to me, Lincoln being something of a specialty of mine. Naturally I was very pleased to be able to come here and work on this project."

"You have a degree in history, then?"

"Last year, from USC. And you?"

Jerry started talking about TMU, and the joys and problems of living in Chicago. Jan, it turned out, was originally from San Francisco. The struggles involved in surviving student life and planning their careers gave them enough in common so that there seemed no danger of running out of things to talk about. Jerry had been ready to plunge right in, tracing cables, starting to figure out the existing network that had been set up with the optical devices and the computers; but talking to Jan instead was, for the moment, quite satisfactory. Certainly it would have been impolite to cut her off, when she was so obviously interested in his background and what he might be going to do here, for the Foundation.

At some point Jerry became aware that Pilgrim, his hand over the phone receiver, was clearing his throat in an urbane effort to get their attention.

"Jan, Jerry, I am sorry. But it appears now that certain dull details of administration are going to keep me occupied for the next couple of hours at least." He frowned at the gold watch strapped to his hairy wrist. " 'Time flies like an arrow.' " The way he said the phrase made it sound like a quote, though Jerry had no idea what it might be from.

Pilgrim went on: "Jan, I would suggest that you spend the remainder of the afternoon conducting Jerry on a small tour of Springfield. With emphasis of course on the sites where we shall be working. Make use of the expense account; take him to dinner also. Sooner or later I will catch up with you. You might also even show him where he will lodge should we come to agreement on the terms of his employment." Pilgrim smiled suddenly, favoring Jerry with an unexpectedly bright and winning look. "As of now that seems a distinct possibility."

THREE

Two minutes after Pilgrim had given them his blessing, Jerry and Jan were out on the street, Jan fitting on an expensive-looking pair of sunglasses whose effect was to turn her from a mod archaeologist into a tourist. Before leaving the office she had also picked up a purse, which presumably contained the plastic tools that would let her make use of the expense account.

"The sites we plan to work on this summer," she announced, "all have something to do with the life of Abraham Lincoln, as you may have guessed by now."

"I'm not surprised to hear it," Jerry admitted.

"What to see first?" Jan pondered, looking around the square, where modern shops and vehicles surrounded and contained the time warp of the Old Capitol. "I think the Lincoln Home, that's only a few blocks away. Then we should have plenty of time to drive out to the cemetery before it closes and take a look at his tomb. It's only a couple of miles, just on the edge of town."

"Whatever you say," Jerry agreed. The more he listened to this lady's voice, the more he enjoyed hearing her talk.

They started walking. A block before they reached Lincoln's Home ("the only house he ever owned," as Jan enthused) they passed into a restored historical area of the city. Here the streets had been closed off to motor vehicles, and were lined by wooden sidewalks. Spacious yards of neatly mowed grass, looking unnaturally perfect, surrounded sizeable frame houses that Jerry could believe had been built during the nineteenth century.

One of those houses, on the northeast corner of Eighth and Jackson, and marked with appropriate signs, was their destination. Lincoln's home was open to visitors on payment of a small fee. Jan insisted that the fee should be on the expense account.

Jerry had seen rooms like these in museums. Some of the furniture inside, Jan informed him, was original, the rest being authentic-looking reproductions. Only the Interior Department, who managed the show, knew which was which, and they weren't telling.

A hacker at heart, Jerry had developed the unconscious habit on first entering someone's house of looking around for computers. He caught himself doing it now; but naturally enough there was not even an electric outlet visible. Having registered this fact consciously, Jerry stood looking at a writing desk equipped with primitive steel-nibbed wooden pens, and a candlestick.

"I guess what you achieve doesn't always depend on your tools," he murmured, trying to picture Old Abe at the keyboard of a word processor.

"No! Not at all! Isn't that beautifully true?" Jan appeared to feel that he had touched on an important point.

"I don't suppose he wrote the Gettysburg Address at this desk, or anything like that."

"Certainly not the Gettysburg Address. But some very beautiful and logical prose. He was quite a successful lawyer."

"After he'd given up his career as an amateur wrestler."

"Oh yes."

A narrow stairway brought them to the upper floor, where from behind low anti-tourist railings they considered the Lincoln bedrooms—there had been four children when the family lived here, it appeared. Jan had little to say here, evidently wanting to allow Jerry to form his own impressions. Almost the last stop on the tour was the archaeological site in the backyard where the Lincoln privy had once stood; there was not much to see now, beyond a modest display of nineteenth century glass bottles.

When they emerged from the house onto the wooden sidewalks again, Jan glanced at her wristwatch. "We've still got plenty of time to see the tomb. Oak Ridge Cemetery stays open until five."

"The tomb, and the house here, will be among the sites we work on this summer?"

"Oh yes. Definitely."

They were walking back toward the underground garage. Jerry said. "You know, maybe I missed an explanation or something, but I still don't get exactly what the Pilgrim Foundation is trying to do. I mean what is your historical research trying to accomplish exactly? And how?"

Jan sighed. "Lincoln is endlessly fascinating." It sounded like a preliminary to an explanation, but nothing followed.

Jerry waited until he felt sure no more was coming. Then he said: "For me, 'interesting' would be a better word. Lincoln and his times are interesting, sure. But to me nothing in history can be as fascinating as what's happening now. Something you learn how to do, something that will really change the world. I mean, with all due respect, whatever you find out about Lincoln now is not really going to change much in our world."

Jan was not at all taken aback. "Modern technology can be applied to history."

"Well, sure. To research. But I mean . . . suppose you were able to discover that Lincoln was really George

Washington's grandson. Or that he kept a mistress on the side. Whatever. People nowadays would pretty much shrug and say 'so what?' And the world would go on as before. I mean, as far as I can see, all this historical research just isn't going to change it any." Then, with the sudden feeling that he might be speaking too harshly about this lady's pet enthusiasm, he added: "Now come on, your turn. Tell me how I'm all wrong."

"You're all wrong." Jan was smiling, and to his relief she didn't seem to have taken his argument all that seriously. Then, giving it thought, she became more serious. "Jerry, Lincoln had an enormous input on what our world is today. The United States is still one nation only because of him. And he's the man who killed slavery; he didn't do it all by himself of course, but far more of the credit must go to him than to any other person."

"Yes, I'm sure."

"And then, you see, there came along a fanatic—John Wilkes Booth. 'A Confederate doing duty on his own responsibility' is what he called himself. Booth crept into Lincoln's box at the theater, and shot him in the back of the head, just as the Civil War was coming to an end, in the spring of 1865. Only three months into his second term." Jan seemed to think that this last point was very meaningful.

"Well, yes, I suppose. Everyone knows it was John Wilkes Booth, right? But I mean, however Lincoln was killed—"

"Can you imagine how much better off our world might be now if he had been allowed to live at least four more years? If he, instead of Andrew Johnson, had been President until 1869?"

"No, can't say I ever thought about it."

"Andrew Johnson was rather better than the reputation

that some historians have given him. But he simply was not in Lincoln's league as a politician."

"Somehow I don't think of Lincoln that way."

Jan smiled at him. "He was a politician, take my word for it. And he was a very effective leader, beginning to be recognized as a national hero, with the war winding to a close. Andrew Johnson made some effort to follow his policies, true, but . . . Johnson was almost impeached." Jan seemed to despair of being able to convey the magnitude of the difference in the two men.

"Too bad we can't get Lincoln up out of his tomb, then. We could use him now."

Jan smiled at him more brightly than ever. "It's been tried."

"H-huh?"

"Some years after the War, there was an attempt to kidnap his body and hold it for ransom. No, I'm not making this up. That's why there are twelve tons of poured concrete over him now."

The tomb, a gray stone structure rising out of a green lawn, was bigger than most houses, even if you didn't count the granite shaft ten stories high that rose from the middle of it like a miniature Washington monument. On the flat roof of the tomb surrounding the central shaft were groups of bronze soldiers in Civil War uniforms, posed in dramatic attitudes, gripping weapons, waving their bronze flag, beating their drums, pointing out the enemy in the distance. Jan and Jerry walked into a marble foyer, where Jan pointed out a scaled-down replica of the seated Lincoln from the Memorial in Washington. There were park attendants on hand in this room, and a few other tourists. Jan led Jerry down a hallway of pink and brown marble to peer over a velvet rope into a chamber of red stone.

The tomb itself, the single stone standing over the actual resting place, was simple. On the wall of rock behind it was carved: NOW HE BELONGS TO THE AGES. And on the single stone the legend read simply:

ABRAHAM LINCOLN
1809–1865

Information carved into the walls indicated what auxiliary entombments there had been in this room.

MARY-TODD LINCOLN
1818–1882

EDWARD (EDDIE) BAKER LINCOLN
1846–1850

WILLIAM (WILLIE) WALLACE LINCOLN
1850–1862

THOMAS (TAD) LINCOLN
1853–1871

"Poor guy didn't have very good luck with his family," Jerry observed. "Two of his kids died before he did. One didn't live much longer."

"No." Jan was almost whispering, as if the family had been her personal friends. There was no doubt that she was moved. "No, neither he nor his wife had very good luck that way."

They drove out through the iron gates of the cemetery shortly before closing time, and only a few minutes later were back in the heart of town. Jan dropped Jerry in front of his hotel; they had agreed to meet in the lobby in an hour to discuss dinner arrangements.

As Jerry showered he thought to himself that he still had learned next to nothing about the Pilgrim Foundation, its organization, financing, goals and methods. Obviously its people somehow planned to glean something from the past by using their tripod machines and a computer network. But his hosts had been avoiding his questions on that subject all day. Well, probably they were waiting until he was confirmed as an employee and had signed something giving them legal protection against his disclosure of their secrets. That was all right with Jerry. He'd do the same, he supposed. But he was getting ever more curious and impatient.

Jan was sitting and waiting for him in the lobby when he came down, promptly on time. She had changed into what he supposed ought to be called an evening dress, of startling red. It looked beautiful on her, and there was nothing at all about it to suggest the nineteenth century. "I'm hungry," she greeted him. "Do you like Italian food?"

"One of my favorites."

Jan said she knew a good place within walking distance of the hotel.

He was moderately impressed when they reached the place; more evidence that the Foundation was not going to stint on its expense account. When they were asked if they wanted anything from the bar before dinner, Jerry hesitated at first. He was not ordinarily a teetotaler, nor very much of a drinker either. But when Jan immediately ordered a vodka martini he decided this wasn't part of the test, and went along—with a better conscience when she launched into a story involving Pilgrim's preference for something called *akvavit*. The story raised in Jerry's mind the question of just what relationship existed between Jan Chen and Pilgrim, other than that of employee and employer. So far he had no sense that there was any.

Food arrived, custom-designed pizzas, served with class upon good dishes. Chianti was available and therefore seemed called for as an accompaniment—Jerry had absorbed this as an article of faith during his early college years, and Jan expressed a willingness to be converted.

They ate, sipped wine, and talked. Jan, it appeared, had been born in California and had grown up in San Francisco. In Chinatown? Jerry wondered. But he didn't as yet feel quite sure enough of himself to ask her that.

He had spent the earlier part of his own childhood in one of the smaller, more distant and less affluent suburbs of Chicago. Then, when he was about ten years old, his parents had been able to move to the more affluent Lombard.

"Every spring they have a Lilac Festival there—it's pretty famous. It reminded me of that today, when I saw the lilacs out at New Salem."

" 'When lilacs last in the door yard bloomed—' " Jan quoted. It was really marvelous, how daintily she could eat pizza, and what a respectable amount this technique allowed her to put away. "That's Walt Whitman. It has something to do with Lincoln too."

"Oh." Jerry felt a certain sadness. "I haven't had a lot of time to look into poetry."

His companion looked sympathetic. "In your field I can understand that. It must keep you very busy. Poetry is one of Dr. Pilgrim's favorite things."

"I've been meaning to ask you. Does Dr. Pilgrim have a first name? I saw a first initial on the note he left for me."

Jan smiled. "If he does, I haven't heard anyone use it."

"Oh," Jerry smiled back. "Hey, is that lilac perfume you're wearing?"

"Actually it is." Now she was pleased to the point of

giggling. It was a quiet giggle, as if it might concern secrets. Then, seemingly with her next breath, as if there might have been a transition but Jerry had somehow missed it, she was asking him: "Was there ever a moment—probably in your childhood—that you thought you had lived through twice? Or maybe more than twice? I don't mean *déja vù*, that's something else entirely. I mean twice in rapid succession, like bing-bing. Know what I mean?"

Jerry sat back in his comfortable chair, regarding his companion's ivory skin, face and slim neck and bare shoulders over the red dress. He had the sensation the martini and the wine were rapidly turning to water in his blood, that full sobriety had suddenly returned.

He said: "Funny you should ask. There was a moment just today . . . not exactly what you're asking about, but . . ."

"Yes?"

"Well, it was nothing, really. I had just arrived at New Salem, and I was starting to look for you and Dr. Pilgrim. Directly across from the hotel there's a footpath leading up into the park, and I went up that way and came on the log cabins without any warning. I looked into the first one, and there was a woman inside wearing a costume just like what Lincoln's mother must have worn. Making cornbread over a fire. And it shook me for just a moment. Like maybe I had really stepped into some kind of time warp—know what I mean?"

Jan was listening with calm interest. "I suppose she was one of those historical society people."

"Yeah." Jerry paused; then let it go at that.

"Most people—" Jan had to suppress a tiny, lady-like, chianti-hiccup. She began again. "Most people would not be really shaken, even for a moment, by such a trivial experience. And yet I get the impression, from the way you talk about it now, that you really were somewhat taken aback—if only for a moment. Now, why should that have been?"

Jerry popped a fragment of pizza crust into his mouth and followed it with another sip of wine. He chewed meditatively.

"Well?" Jan sounded genuinely interested.

"Well. Funny you should get me to talk about it. No one else ever has. There was one time, when I was a kid, when something happened that was really very strange, along the time-warp line. Or at least I have this memory of a strange thing happening, whether it ever actually did or not. Maybe some part of me is always on the lookout for something like it to happen again."

"Tell me about it." Jan Chen's voice was sympathetic, her eyes intent.

"I will. Though I've never told anyone else about it until now." He sipped his wine again. "Before my family moved to Lombard we lived farther out from the city, in a house we were renting on the edge of a small town— it was almost like living on a farm. I was only a little kid then, it was a lot of fun." He paused for a deep breath. "Anyway, one day the house we were living in burned down. Something wrong with the wiring. My dad—he's my stepfather, really—was at work, and my mother was visiting a neighbor."

"Excuse me. You were an only child?"

"Yeah. Anyway, I was just coming home from school. I was the first one, or almost the first one, to see the smoke and flames. The fire was just getting a good start. All I could think of was that my mother must be in the house somewhere. I wasn't even scared, except for her.

"There was a neighbor woman running across her yard toward our place, shouting my name. But I paid her no attention. I ran on into the house, yelling for my mother. First I looked in the kitchen for her, and then in the other lower rooms—it wasn't a big house; it only took me about five seconds to discover that my mother wasn't on the ground floor anywhere. All I could think of was that she had to be upstairs.

"There were flames on the stairs already, just getting a start there, but I hardly thought about that. By that time I was in a total panic. I ran up the stairs, yelling my head off. I had to get my mother out."

"You were a brave little boy."

"I was a crazy little boy, maybe. I'm telling you this like I remember it. What my memory of today tells me happened."

"I understand." Jan nodded. Her concentration was more intense than ever; her dark eyes had widened subtly as she listened.

"My mother wasn't upstairs, either. There were only a couple of rooms up there, and it took me only a few moments to make sure she wasn't home. But still, by the time I got back to the head of the stairs, the fire had spread. There was no getting down those stairs anymore. It would have been like stepping into a furnace."

"You could have crawled out of a window," Jan whispered. It was the same almost reverential whisper she had used in Lincoln's tomb.

"I might have. Except, as I remember it, it was still winter and we still had these big tough storm windows on. And the window sills were high, well above the floor. I'm not at all sure I could have got out of one before the smoke got me, or the fire, the way those flames were spreading. Anyway, at the time I'm not sure I even thought about windows. Oh, one more thing. When I was running up the stairs, my left arm and my left shirtsleeve got burned. Pretty badly. But I didn't feel the pain that much right away. You know how it can be when you're excited?"

"I know."

"But once I was upstairs I started feeling the burn. Still not real bad. All I could think of—standing there at the top of the stairs and knowing I couldn't get down them—was that it had all been a great *mistake*. It had been *wrong* for me to come upstairs. I should have known better. If my mother had been in the house when the fire started, she would have noticed it burning and got out. She never slept during the day. There had been no need for me to come up here looking for her."

"So what did you do?" His soft-voiced listener, posing with unconscious art in the soft light of the candle on their table, was leaning her pale chin upon one slender wrist.

Jerry sipped his wine. "I guess," he said, "I decided not to come upstairs after all. That's how I remember it."

"I'm not sure I understand."

"I know damn well I don't. Everything that I've told you happened, I remember it happening, as surely as anything in my life has ever happened. And yet, there I was, downstairs again, standing just inside the front door, a good ten or twelve feet from where the fire was just getting started on the stairway. And neither my arm nor my shirt were burned at all.

"The stairs were no longer a mass of flames, at the moment they looked almost safe, just as they had when I came in the first time. I could have run up there, but I didn't, because I had just been upstairs, and I was sure my mother wasn't there.

"I backed out of the house, away from the flames, and just as I went out the door I saw the stairs inside start to go up like a torch." He fell silent.

Jan occupied herself for a few moments in looking thoughtful. Then she asked encouragingly: "There's more?"

"A little more. Yes. The neighbor lady, who had been running across the yard to keep me from going into the house? Well, she was still running across the yard when I came out. She ran up to me and grabbed me a moment later, and pulled me back farther from the burning house.

"She said: 'Where's your mother?' and I said: 'She isn't home.' Later, quite a long time later, someone asked me how I'd known that. I don't remember what I answered."

Frowning lightly, Jan asked an unexpected question. "How big were these yards? I mean specifically the one the lady was running across."

"Not all that big, I couldn't possibly have had time to go inside, and search the entire house, and come running out of it again before the neighbor lady arrived on our doorstep. And yet that's exactly what I did. As I remember it."

Jan's smile was conspiratorial, but it looked honest. "And now there are two of us who know you did."

FOUR

Coming out of the Italian restaurant some indeterminate time later, emerging into the mild spring night, Jerry had put strange memories out of his mind. He felt suddenly inspired to burst into song, if only in a muted way.

But after singing only a few words he came to a sudden stop. "What're we going to do tomorrow? But never mind that, what're we going to do now?" He felt enthusiastic, ready to explore new worlds. Had he had too much to drink? No, hardly that. Not really. Just one martini and a little wine.

" 'Tomorrow and tomorrow and tomorrow,' " Jan quoted brightly, " 'creeps in this petty pace from day to day—' "

"You're quoting again. You definitely have a habit of doing that."

"When one works constantly with Dr. Pilgrim, one tends to get into the habit." Jan gave no sign of having been at all affected by the wine she had consumed.

"I suppose one might do that, if one has any stock of quotations at all upon which to draw. Of course if one is studying for a degree in computer science, and trying to hold down a job at the same time, one hasn't had time to read all those books that one is supposed to read."

Dr. Pilgrim's assistant shook her head, sighing tolerantly. Somehow she and Jerry had come to be holding hands as they strolled the city street. There were only a few passersby. Spring moths swarmed the brilliant street lamps.

"This is a bank building," said Jan suddenly, tugging at Jerry's hand, bringing him almost to a stop in front of what was indubitably a bank. "Springfield has little banks. Chicago has big ones where you can find what you need no matter what. If you really need a bank, Jerry, I think a man in your situation should look for one in Chicago. Remember that."

"Is that Walt Whitman too? Or I suppose Lincoln recommended Chicago banks."

"Lincoln had some interesting ideas on banking. But that's beside the point."

"Jan." Now Jerry did come to a full stop. "Did you have a whole lot more to drink than I did, or what?"

"Oh no. Oh, no, no, no." She was vastly, but apparently soberly, amused.

"Then I don't get it. What you were saying about the banks. There must have been something I missed, or . . ."

"Don't worry about it now. Maybe someday you'll want to remember it." She smiled as if she were pleased with him.

Whatever. They strolled on. "Jan, what're we going to do tomorrow, really? I don't want to screw up my chances for this job, I think I'll like it. I mean even apart from the financial . . . Hey, Pilgrim was going to see us again tonight, isn't that what he said?"

"Yes, I think he will."

"Do you think I'm too drunk to see the boss tonight? I am feeling a little light-headed."

"Not this once," she assured him, taking his hand again. "This once it will be perfectly all right."

"At least I don't have t'drive anywhere tonight. And there's no hurry, is there? It's days and days before I have to get back to Chicago." He paused to glare sympathetically at the silhouette of the Great Emancipator, here confined to a window as part of his twentieth-century career in advertising.

"We'll do our best to keep you busy."

"I bet you will."

"Look," said Jan, looking ahead herself and gesturing lightly in that direction.

About five parking spaces ahead of them, nestled up to the metered curb, was the unmarked Foundation van. Dr. Pilgrim was in it, or at least most of him was, for he was sticking his dark curly head out of one of the side windows. A moment later he had slid quickly from the vehicle and was approaching on foot.

To Jerry's relief, the boss looked reassuringly tolerant of his employees' condition. Maybe, Jerry thought hopefully, he and Jan didn't look as intoxicated as he was beginning to feel. He really didn't deserve to feel like this, he hadn't taken *that* much wine . . .

Pilgrim appeared almost but not quite ready to join them in their revelry. "Some people here who would like to talk to you, Jerry," he said, after a quick exchange of looks with Jan. "One more little item to be taken care of before you retire to a well-earned rest. Are you game for one more small adventure? But of course you are."

"Some people?" asked Jerry. "Who?"

"My backers. You have already spoken with one of them, this most attractive lady, on the phone." Pilgrim was holding open the side door of the van for Jerry to get in. "The gentleman is Mr. Helpman." At least the name sounded like that to Jerry.

Jerry got in, taking the nearest empty seat, a captain's chair approximately amidships. In the chair beside him there waited a youthful-looking lady he had never seen before, a well-proportioned and well-dressed lady who looked as if she would be tall when she stood up, and who was definitely attractive, though her face just now was mainly in shadow. Meanwhile from one of the seats in the far rear a black man of indeterminate age, well dressed in suit and tie, was looking at Jerry with an air of hope.

Pilgrim, still outside on the sidewalk, slid shut the door through which Jerry had gone aboard, leaving him in the van with the two strangers. At the same time the lady at his side asked him: "How are they treating you so far?"

"All right. Fine." Then he scowled at his questioner. "Excuse me, but who are you?"

"My name is Olivia. You spoke with me on the phone."

"Yeah. I thought I could recognize your voice. But I still don't understand—"

"All will be explained to you eventually. Provided—" Olivia sighed. It was a worried sound, or maybe she was only tired. "Have they talked to you about going on a trip?" In the back seat Mr. Helpman nodded silently, seconding the question.

"Trip? No, I understood that we were going to be working here around Springfield." Jerry noted with satisfaction that he was still capable of plain, coherent speech.

"Fine. That's fine." Olivia swiveled her chair, turning her back to confer with Helpman momentarily, in whispers so low that Jerry could not hear them.

Then she faced Jerry again. "You may tell Dr. Pilgrim that his project has my provisional approval. And good luck to you." With a last hard-to-interpret look at Jerry, and a quick decisive movement, the lady called Olivia opened the door on the street side and got out. Helpman followed her quickly, slamming the door behind him.

For a few moments Jerry, feeling befuddled, had the whole interior of the van to himself He supposed he might have been able to use the time to good advantage, thinking, if he had known where to start. But the whole business was so—

—and then Pilgrim and Jan were back, piling into the van, Jan taking the captain's chair where Olivia had been, while Pilgrim settled himself in the driver's seat.

They were both looking at Jerry with concern. "Well?" Pilgrim demanded.

"Well, she said to tell you that whatever you're doing has her provisional approval. Is she your banker, maybe?"

Pilgrim, relieved by the message, nodded with an odd smile. "In a manner of speaking she is." He faced forward and got the engine started.

"I can walk back to the hotel from here," said Jerry.

Jan, having taken Olivia's place in the luxurious armchair beside him, shook her head. She said: "There's just one more thing we'd like to show you tonight."

" 'Always a little farther, *it* may be' " quoted Pilgrim from up front, where he was driving joyously and skillfully. " 'Beyond that last blue mountain barred with snow . . .' "

Jerry had ceased to listen to him. Jan was much more interesting than the doctor's quotations, and also more accessible, being seated where he could swivel easily to face her. She now engaged Jerry in what seemed to him an unusually witty conversation—in which he managed to hold his own quite well—while Pilgrim drove them through the darkened streets of Springfield.

"This—this's been like no other job interview I've ever had," Jerry pronounced with feeling at one point. He meant it as a sincere compliment to Pilgrim and especially to his most delightful aide who sat almost within reach, still wearing that enchanting red dress.

"Nor ever will have again, I should imagine," Pilgrim agreed cheerfully. The boss was still apparently unable to perceive anything improper in the speech or behavior of his prospective new employee. "Glad to have you aboard, as the cliché goes. In fact you literally cannot imagine what a burden your successful recruitment has lifted from my mind."

"Then I'm hired? Really hired?"

"Oh, most definitely you are hired."

"You might almost say," said Jan from beside Jerry, "that you are already on your way to work." Then she giggled, as if she were beginning to give way at last to the chianti. Pilgrim, his face unreadable, glanced back at her once and then faced forward to the road.

They sounded like they were joking, but they must be serious about hiring him, Jerry reflected. If they really didn't want him they'd be dropping him off at his hotel now, instead of taking him—where were they taking him, anyway? And hey, wait, how could he really be practically on his way to work?

They were, he noticed, definitely heading out into the country again. They were driving through solid darkness now, except for passing headlights.

These, along with the headlights of the van itself, revealed a narrow highway. But the next time Jerry interrupted his talk with Jan to look ahead, the highway had been replaced with a gravel road. And now there were no other headlights to be seen, in either direction. Road signs had now ceased to exist also, being replaced by wooden fence posts and wire beyond the tall grass and fringe of weeds that overhung the edge of the road.

Jerry was just starting to doze off, seatbelted into his comfortable chair, when the van slowed to a stop. Pilgrim opened the driver's door into an enormous silence.

"Our local headquarters," said Jan. She sounded like a cheerful nurse, and she was acting like one now, helping Jerry out of his seatbelt and then out of the van. Standing on grass and gravel, he felt somewhat disconnected from his own arms and legs. Looking up, he beheld more stars, many more, than anyone ever saw in Chicago.

The van had stopped in a driveway, close to the front of an isolated structure that appeared to be a farmhouse. It was a two-story frame building painted white, looking ghostly in the night. There were no lights in the house when they arrived. But now Jan tripped lightly up the wooden steps and opened the front door and reached inside, turning on a light over the porch. Meanwhile Pilgrim, surprisingly strong, had taken over the job of supporting Jerry. Jerry found himself being walked up the steps as if two bouncers instead of one five-foot-five researcher had him by the elbows. Not that the job was done discourteously.

Once inside the house, the two senior officials of the Foundation turned on some more lights, and guided Jerry through it. He was blinking rapidly by this time, and his eyes didn't really focus all that well any more. At first he didn't see anyone else in the house, but he thought there must be other people around somewhere, because he heard a door close softly, several rooms away, while Jan and Pilgrim were both still with him.

His two escorts were conferring in low-voiced haste; he couldn't hear what they were saying, but whatever it was, it was all right because both of them were smiling when they turned back to Jerry.

"The best thing will be for you to get some rest," Jan was assuring him now, "before we do anything else. There's a room back here that's going to be yours when we get you all moved in. Wouldn't you like to lie down for a while?"

Jerry didn't answer for a moment, because just now, out of the corner of his eye, he had seen something strange: a diminutive figure, like a masked and somewhat deformed child, passing briefly through his range of vision at the end of a hallway. Now he was seeing things.

"Jerry? I say, wouldn't you like to lie down?"

"Oh. Course I would. Specially if you come with me."
Then Jerry could feel his face turning red for having said
a thing like that. At the same time he chuckled.

Jan, more than ever the skillful nurse, was not perturbed.
"I'll see you settled into your room. Then for the time
being you'll have to rest."

"Busy day tomorrow," Jerry agreed helpfully, as she
assisted him down the hallway. He was demonstrating
proudly that he was still capable of thought. There were
no strange little monsters in sight now. Probably by the
sheer power of his will he could keep them at a distance.

His last remark for some reason evoked a laugh from
Jan. It was the freest laughter he'd heard from her yet,
a pleasant, ringing sound.

"That is for sure," she agreed, "a very busy day." And
she marched him on, with Pilgrim leading the way. They
passed a room whose door, like the other doors inside
the house, had been left ajar, and Jerry glanced in. He
was able to see very little except a white, free-standing
screen that reminded him of doctors' offices and hospitals.

"Here we are," said Pilgrim, leading, and they went
on past that doorway and into the next one. Jerry was
dimly aware of a narrow white bed, coming closer to him
with little lurching motions, in time with his own unsteady
strides. Then the bed unexpectedly clipped him at knee
level and he toppled over onto it. The landing was
beautifully comfortable, even though somehow in the
course of falling he had turned over so that he was now
lying on his back.

His eyes had closed of themselves. When he opened
them again, Jan and Pilgrim were still there. A bottle
had just clinked on glass, and they were holding little
glasses with clear liquid in them, raising the glasses to
each other, in the act of toasting something.

"To success," said Dr. Pilgrim softly, and with a gesture included in his toast a picture that happened to be hanging on the wall. Jan hoisted her glass a notch in that direction too, before she tossed the contents down.

Jerry looked up at the wall between his two fellow workers. By now he certainly had no trouble recognizing the face in that dark frame, though it was younger than you usually saw it, and wore no beard. Abraham Lincoln, in one of his usual sloppy suits. Was it a photograph or a painting? Did everyone in his time dress like that?

"And now, Jerry, one more drink for you." Jan's arm went very nicely around his neck and shoulders, to raise his head. "Are you sure I need another?" he wanted to ask as he swallowed obediently. Some milky stuff, quite pleasant. He hoped it would be good for hangovers.

A moment after that the support of Jan's arm was gone, and Jerry's eyes were closed again, and he could hear himself snoring. It would be all right. A little nap, just a little, and he would spring up again and show these people that he wasn't really drunk.

"Like a light," he distinctly heard Jan commenting. He could hear her and someone else who must be Pilgrim hovering at his bedside a moment longer, and then there were the soft sounds of feet retreating. They both went out, darkening the room and shutting the door on him, but the door wasn't completely closed. He could tell that by the gentle incompleteness of the sound it made. Then both of them were gone, somewhere down the hall.

In another moment, Jerry knew, he would be sound asleep. It wasn't that he minded sleeping—but to be practically carried in here like this—that was somewhat humiliating. He felt an urge to sit up, get up, assert himself in some minor way, do something of his own volition. Show them—show them how tough he was. That was the idea. After that he would be willing to take a nap.

It wasn't really hard to get back on his feet, just as sometimes in a dream it was very easy to do things that should be hard. Things in dreams, he had noticed, tended to be very easy, or else utterly impossible.

He was standing at the white door of his room, and pulling it open, before he realized that this wasn't the door leading out into the hall. This one instead opened into an adjoining bedroom, where a white hospital-type screen blocked out most of the light that would otherwise have shone in here from the hallway. In this dim room there was a fair amount of what looked like hospital equipment.

This room too contained a bed, but the figure under its white sheets wasn't Jan, that was for sure, damn it all anyway. And it was far too long a figure to be Pilgrim. Yes, a long and bony figure—really a familiar one in these parts—with dark hair and a darkly bearded face that showed as little more than a mass of shadows above the sheets.

Stupidly, without any real intention of doing so, Jerry took one more step closer to the bed, and then another. He stood looking down at that shadowed face for what seemed to him a long time. He began to feel a cold sensation in the pit of his stomach—but the feeling, like everything else, was too remote to be of any real importance. Then the figure on the bed stirred lightly, as if in sleep, and Jerry turned away from it hastily and stumbled back into his own room.

He had one thought: if it were only wine that had befuddled him, what he had seen just now ought to have shocked him sober. So what had overcome him was more than wine. And that meant—

The last thing he saw clearly was the white bed from which he had arisen, swinging up to claim him, with finality this time.

FIVE

Coming back to life was a slow, gradual, and painful
process. Jerry's head was throbbing with what felt like
the patriarch of all hangovers. To make matters worse,
at some time during the night someone had stolen his
soft white bed, substituting for it a bag of some coarse,
malodorous fabric that crackled each time he moved as
if it were stuffed with very crisp and durable dried leaves.

Somewhere outside the barricade of his eyelids, light
had reappeared. It was daylight, he supposed. But that
was no cause for rejoicing. He was in no hurry to behold
what daylight might reveal. In fact he was rather afraid
to find out. He couldn't really remember what had
happened to him last night.

He had been through a job interview, of sorts.

Oh, he remembered that much, all right. He, Jerry
Flint, the graduate student from the big city, had driven
down to Springfield to talk to some people about a job,
and had made a total and utter ass of himself. That much
he could remember with bitter clarity, though a great
many of the details were still mercifully obscure. And
then just at the end of the evening, before he had passed
out totally, he had looked in the bed in the next room of
the converted farmhouse, and thought that he saw—

Jerry groaned. With eyes still shut, he extended a leg
to find the edge of the bed. He needed a bathroom, and
the need was going to become urgent very soon.

His exploring foot could locate no edge, and in another moment or two Jerry had realized that this was because there was no bed. By now one of his eyelids had come unglued and opened, and with this advantage he could see that he was indeed lying on the floor. An unfamiliar floor. Between him and its rough-hewn, unfinished planks there was only the thickness—the thinness, rather—of a stained mattress that really did crackle with his every movement, as if it contained cornhusks.

It seemed that the folk of the Pilgrim Foundation were blessed with an exquisite sense of humor, as well as pots of money. Not only a cornhusk mattress, but they had also changed Jerry's clothes for him. He was now wearing some kind of handmade gray shirt—it felt like good linen—and shapeless trousers that looked somewhat the worse for having been rolled in dust and leaves. Over his shirt he had on an embroidered vest, that came down past his waist. There were stockings—unfamiliar ones— on his feet, and a kind of enlarged bow tie loosely looped around his collar.

In a far corner of the room, which was barren of all furniture except the mattress, stood a pair of leather boots. The heels were too low for cowboy boots, but they were high-topped and laceless. Beside them, resting on some kind of brownish folded garment, was a high stovepipe hat of approximately the same color. A shapeless bag the size of a small suitcase, made of cloth fabric except for its two cord carrying handles, rested beside the clothing.

This was the same size and shape as the room in which Jerry had fallen asleep—but no, it wasn't the same. It might have been the same room once. Last night's room had had two doors, and two windows, and here were two doors and two windows in the same locations. But these windows lacked screens or shades, as well as nearly all their glass. Green leaves, as of dense bushes, were crowding in from outside; he must be on the ground floor. Through the broken windows came in the smell of lilacs and the song of robins.

For a minute or so he stood unsteadily in the middle of the room, turning round and round in a kind of hopeless stupidity. He stared at the faded and weathered wallpaper—last night the walls had been painted—and at the white-painted woodwork. Yes, as far as the general architecture went, this looked like the same room in which he had fallen asleep last night. But last night's house had been decorated and comfortably furnished, and this one was long abandoned.

When Jerry stumbled over to the door to the room adjoining and pushed it open, there was no one in there either. This chamber was as barren as the one in which he had awakened, and its windows were broken too. Outside the broken windows, birds were singing cheerfully. No doubt they had a good idea of where they were.

The need to find plumbing, or some emergency substitute, was fast becoming an imperative. Jerry, wary of the splintery floor, got his feet into the boots. They fit him perfectly, and felt as if they had been already broken in. Then he went down the hallway looking for a bathroom.

He needed only a few moments to decide that he was wasting his time. There wasn't a bathroom in this house, not on the ground floor anyway, and if there was one upstairs it couldn't be functional. So he would just have to go outside. Somewhere . . .

He reached a back doorway, from which the door was missing. Untended fields surrounded the house for as far as he could see. In a back yard overgrown with weeds were a couple of ramshackle outbuildings, including a privy partially screened from the house by tall hollyhocks—barren of flowers this early in the year—and more spring-blooming lilac bushes. The door of the privy squeaked open on what looked like homemade hinges when Jerry pushed it in, and a field mouse scurried out of his way. The smell inside was very old, but still pungent enough to be the final trigger for his nausea.

Emerging some time later from the wooden sentry-box of the abandoned latrine, Jerry felt considerably better, though his head still ached and his hands trembled. At least he was back in the world again, and prepared to deal with it.

In a great silence he walked completely around the deserted house, confirming that he had the place entirely to himself. Then he stood for what felt like a long time in the back yard, looking things over. He shaded his eyes with a hand when he looked east against the morning sun. There were no other houses nearby in any direction; there was what looked like another farmhouse, about a mile to the south, but that was too far away for him to be able to make out any details.

Whoever had concocted this joke had known what they were doing, and had spared no effort or expense.

From where Jerry stood he was able to see a part of an unpaved road that passed close in front of the house. There were no phone lines along that road, no utility poles of any kind. He could see part of a split-rail fence, much like the ones at New Salem. There was no traffic passing. He watched for what felt like a considerable time—his wristwatch was missing—and not a single vehicle came by.

When he gave up at last and re-entered the house, his first sickness and confusion had passed, and he could look at things more thoughtfully. Now Jerry noted the complete absence of light switches. Not surprising when

there were no incoming wires visible. Nor were there
any electric outlets in the barren walls, any more than
there was running water in the kitchen. He'd passed a
hand-levered pump in the back yard.

Next he toured the house, upstairs and down; everything
he saw confirmed that the place had been abandoned
for years. Almost all the windows were gone, all the rooms
suffering from exposure to the weather.

Returning at last to the room in which he'd awakened,
he looked again at the tall hat waiting for him on the
floor. This time he tried it on. It fit him nicely. The folded
garment turned out to be a coat. He was afraid that it
would fit him too, and threw it down on the mattress
without making the experiment.

Then Jerry went down on his knees beside the carpetbag
and started taking out the contents. Most of it was clothing.
There was a spare vest and trousers, along with several
sets of odd-looking underwear, of the same general style
he'd already found himself to be wearing, and socks and
handkerchiefs. There were two clean shirts, much like
the one he had on, with detached collars packed in a
separate interior pocket of the bag.

Another small pocket in the bag held a straight razor,
folded shut, and a small pouch made of a material that
felt something like plastic but wasn't. In the pouch Jerry
discovered a bar of soap, and a small brush he could dimly
recognize as a shaving aid, probably because it had been
packed in proximity to the razor.

Yet another small interior pocket held a small blue-steel
revolver. Jerry, who was no firearms expert, fumbled around
gingerly with the thing, turning the cylinder and gently
thumbing back the hammer and slowly letting it down again.
Peering at the cylinder he could see cartridges occupying
five of the six chambers. Something about them looked
peculiar even to his eye, amateurish with regard to firearms.

In the same pocket of the bag there was a folded letter, still in its envelope; envelope and letter were creased and worn. In faded, water-spotted blue ink the letter was addressed to one James Lockwood, at some illegible location in Missouri. The handwriting, Jerry thought, was probably feminine. And it looked, he thought, oddly like Jan Chen's.

He opened the letter and started to read. There was no date or any other heading.

My Dearest Jim—

That was about all he could make out; the body of the letter had been soaked worse than the address. He would try to decipher the rest later, when he had time. Or he would mind his own business. These things weren't his.

Working quickly, he repacked the bag with all the items he had taken out of it. Then at last he grabbed up the coat from where he had thrown it down, and tried it on. The coat proved to fit him as well as did the garments he was already wearing, but the cut of it was very strange, different from that of any suit coat Jerry had ever worn. It came down halfway to his knees, and hung on him as unpressed and shapeless as the trousers.

Now Jerry started on the coat's pockets, with which it was well supplied. They contained a handkerchief, basically clean, and a small folding pocket knife. There was also a great deal of paper money, in several colors and varieties, with every variety claiming to be dollars. Most of the notes bore the name of one bank or another, in different states. And then there were gold and silver coins. Counting it all up as best he could, Jerry figured that he was in possession of something close to a thousand dollars altogether, if this money was real.

But of course it couldn't be, not really. The money, like the clothing and the gun, had to be part of the big joke that was being played on him. Yes, of course it did.

His fingers were shaking more and more as he stuffed the cash away awkwardly into the unfamiliar pockets of the coat.

There was a key—a single key—resting by itself in one of the inner pockets of his coat. An old-fashioned large key, with a comparatively simple bit. From the moment he saw it, Jerry had the feeling that it was important.

And there was a locket in one of his coat pockets, with a painted miniature likeness inside. The likeness of a comely young woman with brown hair, wearing a high nineteenth-century collar; he didn't know her. She was certainly not Jan Chen, or the one-name Olivia either. Was she perhaps the woman who had written the indecipherable letter to Jim Lockwood?

Jerry's head ached, and so did his throat. Remembering the pump in the back yard, he went back to it, and with much squealing and clanking of metal made it work. For what felt like a long time there was no result. Then water, rusty at first, gushed from the spout, and Jerry soaked his head in the yellowish irregular stream, and swallowed a much-needed drink.

All right. Joke or whatever, he was here, and he would deal with the world as it came to him.

If this was a joke he could go along with it. He put on his coat and hat—the first people who saw him dressed like this were going to laugh at him, but so what—and went out of the front door of the house to stand on the edge of the road. Between the ruts there were some horse-droppings that didn't look all that old. The road itself was not modern gravel, but what looked like clay, in places no more than mud. Here and there puddles still lingered from the last rain. Split-rail fences of the type Jerry had seen at New Salem marked off fallow fields on either side.

In one direction, toward Jerry's left, there were some buildings in sight, a mile or two away. In the other directions, nothing that looked like a habitation. Carrying his carpetbag, he started walking to his left, which he decided had to be north, assuming that the rising sun still marked the east.

These untended fields were deriving no benefit from their fences, but the wooden rails provided perches for a profusion of songbirds. The day was warm and clear, but not yet hot. All Jerry could think of was that if he kept walking long enough on a road, someone would come out of a house, drive up in a car, or descend in a helicopter, and start to explain the joke.

The more he thought about this tremendous joke, the more explaining he could see that it was going to take. But on the other hand if he once admitted that this might not be a joke—

His mind had reached a place where logical thought seemed to be of little benefit. Therefore he rested his mind as best he could, and kept on walking.

Another human being came in sight at last, a man, way off across the fields, driving horses as he walked beside them—no, the animals that he drove were mules. They were hitched up to something, pulling it.

Jerry had been walking for about a mile when he became aware of another engineless vehicle, this one overtaking him from behind. He heard the thunk of hard wheels on uneven ruts, the quick hooves of a horse, the jingle of harness.

Jerry stepped off the road. He turned and made himself smile as the driver of the wagon pulled to a stop beside him. The driver, a man of about forty, was dressed in a costume very similar to Jerry's, with minor variations.

"Headed for Springfield?" he called down cheerfully.

"Yes. I certainly am." Jerry took the question as an invitation, tossed his carpetbag into the small cargo compartment at the rear of the buggy—or whatever this four-wheeled two-passenger vehicle ought to be called—and climbed up awkwardly onto the single high seat beside the driver. In a moment they were under way again, in a hard jolting but still remarkably quiet ride.

Holding the reins in his left hand, the driver extended his right to shake. "Winthrop Johnson. My friends call me Win."

"Jer—Jim Lockwood." He had a letter in his pocket, didn't he, to prove his identity? If it should ever come to that. Whatever the game, he had to play the cards he had been dealt. "Thanks for the ride."

"Don't think a thing about it. Suppose you haven't been walking far?"

"No, no. Not far." Jerry took off his hat, scratched his head, and rubbed his eyes. Already the buggy's motion was beginning to revive his queasiness; but he had no wish to go back to walking. "Truth is, last night some friends and I got into a bottle. Went a little deeper than I planned."

"Hahaa." It wasn't really a laugh, more a drawnout sound of sympathy. Win Johnson shook his head; he was obviously a man of worldly understanding. "I've been down that road myself more than once. There've been mornings when I didn't rightly know where I was when I woke up."

"I appreciate your sympathy." Jerry allowed his eyes to close again. "How far is Springfield?"

Johnson squinted up toward the sun; there were certainly no road signs to consult. "Should be there by dinner time, or so they told me. This road's a new one to me—maybe you've been over it before?"

Jerry shook his head.

"Well then, we'll just be explorin' together. I'm a land agent for the railroad, and have been talking to some surveyors. Don't believe I caught what your line is?"

Jerry considered. "I travel," he said after a moment.

"Hahaa. Between jobs right now. Wal, m'friend, I don't know if Springfield is a-going to be the best place to land a new one. Chicago, now, I'd say your chances are bound to be better there. Things will be a little slow all over, I'm afraid, now that the war is winding to an end."

"An end," Jerry repeated. He was barely able to keep himself from asking: *What war?*

The other nodded. "Grant's troops entered Richmond on the third. Can't be long now before Lee surrenders. That should just about finish her off."

"On the third." Jerry thought he was going numb all over. "What's today?"

"Well, the fifth. Wednesday."

Jerry was riding with his eyes closed again. He told himself that when he opened them, he would be riding in an automobile. But he couldn't convince himself of that, not while the damned buggy kept bouncing so. Not while he could smell the horse, and hear the beat of hooves. Grant and Lee. Richmond. Sure.

"Hate to see a man suffer so," said the voice of Winthrop Johnson. "Here, have a hair of the dog?"

Jerry opened his eyes to see, almost under his nose, the jouncing right hand of his companion extending a small metal flask in his direction. With a kind of desperation he accepted the flask and put it to his lips. The taste of the stuff inside was fiery, but still surprisingly good, and the net result of a couple of small swallows actually beneficial.

"What is that?" he asked, gasping lightly as he handed the flask back.

"Peach brandy." His benefactor seemed somewhat surprised by the question.

"It's very good—no, no more, thanks. One hair of the dog is plenty."

"Not from around these parts of Illinois, are you, Jim?"

"No, no. Back east."

"Thought so, listenin' to the way you talk. I'm from Indiana, myself. You from New York, maybe?"

"That's right."

"Thought so. I can usually pin a man down by the way he talks."

The countryside flowed past the buggy at a slow pace, but still faster than his feet had been able to make it move, and with infinitely less effort on his part. His brief stint of walking had been enough to convince him that this mode of transportation was in every way an improvement.

At intervals Win Johnson's rig passed a couple of heavy wagons, laden with farm produce and laboring in the same direction. Two young women costumed in ankle-length dresses and pinned-on hats went by going the other way, in a light two-seater carriage pulled by a graceful gray horse. Jerry, numb with wonders, observed them in their Scarlett O'Hara costumes almost without surprise. Johnson tipped his hat lightly to the ladies, and Jerry caught on just in time to tip his own hat just before the other carriage passed.

Why was he going to Springfield? Chiefly, he decided, because he had to go somewhere. He couldn't have simply waited in an abandoned farmhouse for something to happen. But God knew what was going to happen to him next.

With half his mind Jerry continued to make wary conversation with Win Johnson, while with the other half he got busy trying to reconstruct the exact circumstances of his departure from what he considered the normal world—the late twentieth century, in which era he had spent his life up until now. This just didn't feel at all the same as his childhood escape from the burning house. No, this experience was vastly different. Apart from the subjective difference, this time he had been outfitted.

But how had it happened? Everything had seemed perfectly normal when he'd arrived in Springfield. He'd registered in a real, modern hotel, one with plumbing and electric lights and elevators. Then he'd driven out to New Salem, where there were split-rail fences just like these, and at about that point things had started to go subtly wrong. After he'd met Dr. Pilgrim and Jan Chen the deterioration had speeded up.

After visiting New Salem, and the Foundation office, he'd gone out to dinner with Jan. He could still sense pizza and wine in aftertaste. But damn it, there had to be something besides wine to explain why he'd passed out. He hadn't consumed that much. He just didn't, ever, drink enough to knock himself out. He never had. Certainly he wouldn't have done so in the course of an extended job interview.

It could be, it could very well be he supposed, that someone had put something other than wine in his glass. Certainly Jan Chen had had the opportunity. Jerry hadn't been taking any paranoid precautions—hell, he hadn't even been paying attention. But why should she, or anyone else, have drugged him?

Because, the obvious answer came, Jan Chen and Dr. Pilgrim, and probably Olivia and Mr. Helpman too, had determined that he was going to wake up here. Wherever "here" might be.

Have they spoken to you about your going on a trip of any kind?

But basically he couldn't believe it. No, somewhere there was a real explanation. A better one at least than the one he couldn't swallow, involving as it did the armies of Grant and Lee. This place through which he was riding now was some kind of extended historical area, an expansion of New Salem. And . . . and Jerry couldn't really believe that either, but at the moment he had nothing better.

Somehow the hours passed, and with them the miles of the seldom-traveled road, with never a utility pole in sight, or even a contrail in the sky. Instead there was the smell of the open land in the spring, and the feel of the open air. There were also a great many flies, drawn perhaps by the smell of horse. Once Johnson pulled off the road and whoa'd the horse, and the gentlemen relieved themselves in the tall roadside grass, beside a copse of trees. There were whole sections of mature woodland here, much more of it remaining than in the Illinois that Jerry knew.

They climbed back into the buggy and drove on. The burden of Johnson's conversation was what a smart man ought to do after the war, what turn the climate for business was going to take when peace became the normal state of affairs once more. Johnson was not so much anxious to convince Jerry of any course of action as to use him as a sounding board. What did Jerry think of petroleum as an investment?

"I think it might do well."

Eventually the woods thinned out considerably, and they passed some dwellings that were not attached to farms.

"Looks like we made it," Johnson remarked unnecessarily.

The unpaved road was gradually becoming an unpaved street. The capital city of Illinois was even muddier than the countryside, and Jerry's first general impression was that of an extended rural slum. Not only dogs, but pigs, goats, and chickens appeared unfettered on every road. But the houses were clustering more closely now, and the gardens grew closer together. Now the streets were tree-lined; elms speckled with green springtime buds made graceful gothic arches, spanning some streets completely.

"Where can I drop you off, Jim?"

"Eighth and Jackson." Jerry had been pondering how best to answer this question when it came, and now he gave the one Springfield location that he was able to remember.

"Right you are. Remember what I said, Chicago's probably the place for you to try."

"I'll remember, thanks. And thanks for the ride."

"Don't mention it."

Jerry jumped out of the buggy when it slowed almost to a stop at the proper corner. He remembered to retrieve his carpetbag. Win Johnson clucked to his horse and rolled away.

Long afternoon shadows were falling across Eighth Street. There was one building in sight that Jerry could recognize, the house on the north-east corner of the intersection. He stood in the dusty street with his carpetbag in hand, staring at that house, for some time after the sounds of Winthrop Johnson's horse and buggy had died away. That was Abraham Lincoln's house on the corner, and if Jerry only went up to the door of it and knocked . . . but no. If Grant and Lee were fighting in Virginia, Abraham Lincoln couldn't be here in Springfield, could he? President Lincoln would have to be in Washington.

Unless, of course—it hit Jerry suddenly that Lincoln had been shot, just as the war was ending. Of course; Jan had talked about that at some length last night: the

tragic loss that Lincoln's death had been to the country
and the world. The peculiar intensity of her talk came
back to Jerry now, though at the moment he couldn't
recall all the details of what she'd said.

Now he seemed to remember that she'd even kept on
talking to him about Lincoln after he'd passed out. And
then—or was it earlier—he'd seen that unbelievable figure
in the bed in the next room. And before that, the little
monster running across the bedroom hall.

No, those visions must have been hallucinations, brought
on by whatever drugs they'd dosed him with. Jerry couldn't
possibly have seen what he now remembered seeing. That
would be as crazy as—

Looming to the northwest above the springtime trees
and the common rooftops, the bulk of the Old Capitol
building made a half-familiar sight, rising above
nineteenth-century frame houses. Jerry walked toward
it almost jauntily, swinging Jim Lockwood's bag. There
were moments when he was almost dead sure he was
dreaming, ready to give in and enjoy himself without
responsibility.

There was nothing dreamlike about the square, lined
with shops and stores, when he reached it. On the east
side, just about where he remembered Pilgrim's offices
being located, was a totally different structure called the
State Bank building.

He had found the bank. And now there was something—
what was it?—that he had to do.

He walked the wooden sidewalks, liking the sound his
bootheels made, attracting no particular attention among
men who were dressed in much the same style as he
was, and women gowned more or less like the two in
the passing carriage. Some people, including all of the
blacks in sight, were in much poorer clothing.

Letting himself move on impulse now, Jerry made his

way to the front door of the bank and entered. He had
taken the big key from his pocket, again without quite
knowing why, and now he put it down silently on the
polished wood of a counter, under the eyes of a clerk
who wore garter-like metal clips pinching in his
voluminous shirtsleeves, and held a wooden, steel-nibbed
pen in hand.

The clerk scrutinized first the key and then Jerry. He
did not appear to be much impressed by what he saw in
either case.

"Not one of ours," the clerk finally remarked.

The compulsion, whatever its cause, had vanished now.
Jerry was on his own. "Just thought it might be," he got
out with a clearing of his throat. "I found it. It . . . belonged
to my uncle. It was in a box of his things that got sent to
us . . . after Gettysburg."

The other at last picked up the key and silently turned
it over in his fingers. He looked at Jerry for a long moment,
then said, "From one of the Chicago banks, I'd say." The
clerk's accent was different from Winthrop Johnson's, and
sounded even odder in Jerry's ears. Indefinably American,
and yet harsher than any regional dialect Jerry had ever
heard.

Jerry took the metal object back. "I'll ask around when
I get there. Thanks." It was only on the way out of the
bank building that he remembered consciously: Jan Chen
advising him, somewhere, sometime, to go to a Chicago
bank.

The railroad depot was not hard to locate, being only
a few blocks away—nothing in Springfield appeared to
be much more than a few blocks from the center of town.
Inside the wooden depot a chalked schedule, and a tall
wall clock with a long pendulum, informed him that he
had two hours before the next train to Chicago. Jerry
purchased a ticket for the considerable sum of ten dollars

and then returned to the town square. There was an unmistakable restaurant open there, and he listened to people talk cheerfully about the war being over while he enjoyed some of the best chicken and dumplings he'd ever had.

Some of the diners around him were consuming what seemed to Jerry an amazing amount of hard liquor with their meals. Quantities of wine and beer were disappearing also. Remembering last night, he contented himself with a mug of beer, and found it tasty but somewhat warm.

His dinner cost him less than a dollar, a bargain as compared to the price of the train ticket. Well-fed but feeling deadly tired he walked back to the station. Departure at night, by gaslight and lantern, was a scene of many sparks from the woodburning engine. The engine smoked every bit as much as Jerry had expected it would, and the conveyance jolted noisily along. The sunset had completely faded now, and the countryside outside the window at Jerry's elbow was as dark as death.

The only light inside this coach was a poor lantern, hung near the ceiling in the rear. Maybe there were first, second, and third class coaches, and he'd got into fourth class by mistake. Jerry buttoned his coat, whose inside pockets held his money, slumped in his seat, and fell into the dreamless sleep of great exhaustion.

SIX

The train carrying Jerry labored its way into Chicago shortly after dawn. It looked like the start of a grim day in the city, which was wrapped in an atmosphere composed of coal soot and mist in about equal parts. The railroad station was a darkened brick cavern, smoky and bustling at that early hour, crowded with human activity.

Walking stiffly, he made his way out of the station amid the throng of other overnight passengers, all of them blinking as they emerged into the more or less full daylight of the street outside. The streets of downtown Chicago were marginally better, or at least less muddy, than those of Springfield. The boots of an army of pedestrians sounded on the wooden sidewalks with a continuous hollow thumping, a sound regularly punctuated by the sharper tap of crutches. Here and there Jerry noted the different impact made by the crude shaft of a primitive artificial leg.

In the street, as inside the station, soldiers in blue uniforms made up a large part of the crowd. Most of the uniforms were faded and worn. Young men with missing legs or arms, some still in uniform, were a common sight. There must be, Jerry thought, a military hospital or demobilization center near.

Stretching his stiff limbs and rubbing sleep from his eyes, he lugged his carpetbag to a small restaurant a couple of blocks from the station, where he ordered breakfast.

He would have paid a princely sum for cold orange juice, but nothing like that was on the menu. At least the coffee was hot and invigorating, surprisingly good. The prices were reassuringly low—incredibly so, in fact, and he fortified himself with hotcakes, ham and eggs.

He ate his breakfast sitting beside a window that gave him a good view of the street outside. The volume of street traffic was impressive, made up of horse-drawn vehicles of all shapes and sizes. This, like the Chicago he remembered, was an energetic city, though so far Jerry had seen no building more than five or six stories tall. Were there any? He wondered.

Many of the men in the restaurant—the place was fairly crowded but there were only one or two women among the patrons—were reading newspapers. Jerry beckoned to a ragged newsboy on the street outside and bought a paper through the open window.

Half of the front page of the Chicago newspaper was filled with advertisements, the other half with news, mainly about the war. The armies of Grant and Lee, it seemed, were still pounding away at each other in Virginia, though from the tone of the reporting, clearly the writer expected final victory soon. It was further reported that hopes were widespread that the "great rebellion" would be crushed completely out of existence in only a few more days.

Jerry sat for at least a minute just staring at the date on the newspaper. Seeing it in print made it official, and therefore somehow more believable. Today was Thursday, April 6, 1865.

Still he sat there, time and again looking up at the world around him, then dropping his eyes to stare at the paper again. Only now, this morning, after a night of exhausted sleep aboard the train, was he able to win the struggle with his outraged sense of logic, his engineer's scientific propriety, and finally come to grips with his situation.

No longer was he going to be able to pretend to himself
that any part of this could be a fake, a trick. And he wasn't
crazy, or if he was, there was nothing he could do about
it. However it had been managed, every test he could
apply indicated that he was really there, in the last days
of the Civil War. Whatever that damned Pilgrim had done
to him, for whatever purpose—and Jan Chen, that
damned, lying, sexy woman—

But first things first. He was a long way from being
able to take revenge on Pilgrim and his helper now. Unless
some rescuing power should suddenly intervene to save
him, and he saw no reason to expect that, he was going
to have to somehow find his own way back to his own
time.

The trouble was that he had no indication of any place
to start. Of course the letter to Jim Lockwood, whoever
he might be, might be a clue, if Jerry could understand
why it had been given to him.

Still sitting at his breakfast table, he dug the single
page of the letter and its envelope out of his pocket once
more, and tried again to read the water-damaged writing.
He had no better success than before.

As he put the letter back in his pocket, his hand once
more encountered the bank key and he pulled it out. It
was much bigger than the keys he had commonly carried
in the twentieth century. The hard, precisely shaped metal
lay in his hand feeling large and solid and enigmatic.
Jerry could not shake the intuition that it had to be of
great importance.

Putting away his change as he left the restaurant, Jerry
let his hand remain in his pocket, resting on the one key.
The same irrational compulsion to *use* the key that he
had felt in Springfield, was now stirring again, though
less wildly this time.

Carpetbag in hand again, he set out, with the odd feeling

that once he started walking he would go in the right direction.

On his short walk from the railroad station to the restaurant he had noticed only one bank, one with a conspicuous painted sign. Now he was walking toward that sign again. Probably the establishment under that sign would be the most logical place to go, for someone arriving on a train, who had been advised to patronize a Chicago bank.

And Jerry suddenly recalled that he, on the night of wine and pizza, had been mysteriously advised to do just that.

Sauntering into the bank lobby, Jerry tried to adopt the air of a man of wealth—it wasn't really hard to do, now that he had realized how many stacks of hotcakes the money in his pockets could buy. The air inside the bank was blue with smoke. Half the men in the lobby seemed to be smoking cigars; but unless there were compelling reasons, he didn't really want to go that far in trying to project an air of affluence.

Brass cuspidors stood beside almost every counter and under every table in the bank, the floors and carpets around these targets being heavily stained by poor marksmen. The mellow brightness of gaslights augmented the smoky daylight that entered through high narrow windows to shine on the wood panelling of the walls.

Jerry set his bag down on the tobacco-stained carpet. He had brought his newspaper with him from the restaurant, and he opened it now and used it as a cover, observing the activity in the lobby past its edges, now and then turning a page. It took him a few minutes to identify the counter where safe-deposit business was being transacted, and the clerk who handled it.

Unhurriedly he loitered closer and observed more closely. When, finally, he was able to catch a glimpse of one of the keys being presented, he decided that it was a good match for the one he was carrying in his own pocket.

Jerry read for another minute or two, then unhurriedly folded his newspaper under his arm again and strolled up to the counter.

The clerk accepted the key calmly. "And the name, sir?"

Jerry had had the time to get his cover stories and his excuses, if any should be required, as ready as he could get them. "Lockwood," he announced. "James Lockwood."

The clerk, his eyes in a permanent squint, moved his shirtsleeved shoulder to let the gaslight fall more fully on the pages of the register he had just opened. "Yes, Mr. Lockwood. Sign here, please."

The book was turned and pushed across the counter to rest in front of Jerry. He felt no more than faintly surprised to see that the open page already contained several specimens of Jim Lockwood's signature, presumably one for every time he'd visited the box. More surprising somehow was the fact that in several places another name, this one signed in a definitely feminine hand—though for once not that of Jan Chen—alternated with Lockwood's. Jerry read the lady's name as Colleen Monahan. The most recent visit by Ms. Monahan, it appeared, had been only yesterday.

Jim Lockwood's penmanship looked nothing at all like Jerry Flint's usual hand, but he committed the best quick-study forgery he could, and then held his breath, waiting to see if it would sell. But it seemed that he need not have worried, for the clerk scarcely glanced at the book when Jerry pushed it back across the counter.

"This way, sir." And the man was lifting open a gate in the counter to let Jerry through. He was now facing the entrance to a kind of strongroom, walls and door of heavy wood reinforced with plates of iron or steel. Together they entered the strongroom, where Jerry's key in the clerk's hand released one of a row of little strongboxes.

"Would you prefer a booth, sir, for privacy?"

"Yes. Yes, I would."

In another moment, Jerry, clutching in both hands a small metal box that had the feeling of being almost empty, was being shown into one of a row of tiny partitioned spaces, the door of which he was able to pull closed behind him. The booth was open at the top, enabling its occupant to share in the light from the windows and the gas-jets of the lobby.

Jerry set down his metal box on the small table provided, opened the catch, and swung back the lid.

There were two items in the box, one a mere folded piece of paper, the other a large, old-fashioned, stem-winding pocket watch, with chain attached.

Paper first. The timepiece did not look all that informative, but with paper there was hope. He took the small sheet up and unfolded it to read a note.

> Dear Jim Lockwood—
> Things have gone a little sour. Whatever day you get this, bring this note when you come out and meet me outside the bank. If I am not there come back every hour at ten minutes after the hour in banking hours.
> Our employer is concerned about your health.
> Colleen M.

The handwriting of the note, he thought, matched that of the alternate signature in the book kept by the clerk. Jerry sighed and folded up the note and put it in his pocket.

Next he picked up the watch. It was ticking, evidently wound and functional. To Jerry's inexpert eye the timepiece, looking serviceable but plain, did not appear to be of particularly great value. Its case was of bright metal, hard enough to be steel. There was a round steel protective cover over the face, and Jerry thumbed a little catch and swung the cover back. Then he caught his breath.

The surface he was looking at was not like any watch face that he had ever seen before. It was more like a small circular video screen; and even more like a miniature round window into a small three-dimensional world.

The video turned itself on while he looked at it. In the window there now appeared, in full color and apparent solidity, the face of the man Jerry had known as Pilgrim. The lips of the image were moving, and now—suddenly, when Jerry held the watch at just the right distance— the voice became audible. But image and voice alike were being blocked out at intervals, by bursts of roaring static and white video noise.

"—paradoxes of time travel," Pilgrim's voice was saying, "caused in large part by"—*crash, whirr*—"may prevent your seeing or hearing this message in its entirety. Therefore I attempt to be creatively redundant. We here at this end, Jerry, can only hope and pray that you will find this message, and that enough of the content is going to come through to enable you to"—*whizee—fizzle— zapp!*

Long seconds passed. When the picture came back again, Pilgrim's head was in a different attitude.

"—and one time only," Pilgrim's voice resumed in mid-sentence. "Then this message will self destruct." His swarthy face frowned. "Let me emphasize once more, Jerry, that your only chance of being able to return to your own time, and finding your own history intact when you do so, lies in preventing the assassination of President Abraham Lincoln."

"What?"

Pilgrim's image proceeded imperturbably, "Within a few days of your own arrival in the world of eighteen sixty-five, the President is shot to death by—"

Again there was interruption, audio static accompanied by visual effects that momentarily reduced the picture to unintelligible noise. The effects of video distortion in three dimensions were especially chaotic. After several seconds, the interference was gone as suddenly as it had come.

"—have until the fourteenth of April, Jeremiah, at Ford's Theater in Washington. Unless—" *blast, crackle.*

And, yet again, static had cut off the flow of information. But in another moment Pilgrim was back again, coming through as loud and clear as ever. "—chosen you for this mission because of this almost unique ability which you possess. Without this power to avoid some of the effects of paradox, your mission would be truly hopeless. With it, we can hope that you have at least a fighting chance of success."

"A fighting chance!" Jerry was raging in a whisper at the image. "Are you crazy? What are you talking about? Are you—?"

"—you must be at the side of the President, within two meters to have a high probability of success. Within three meters, to have any chance at all. And you must be there in the moment just before the assassin's bullet smashes into Lincoln's brain. Your total window of opportunity will be approximately three seconds long. During that three-second period, just before the bullet strikes, I repeat, you must activate the beacon."

"Activate the what?" Jerry murmured unconsciously. His own face contorted in a scowl, he was frozen in absolute attention on the message. Pilgrim had indicated— hadn't he?—that it was going to self-destruct.

Meanwhile Pilgrim's hands had come up into sight on the small screen. The view closed in on them. They were holding a watch that looked very much like the one Jerry was holding, except that the timepiece in the image possessed a real face and hands.

The closeup held, while Pilgrim's onscreen voice continued: "The hands must first be set, thus, at exactly twelve." His fingers demonstrated, opening the glass face of the watch and moving the hands directly. "Then the stem must be pulled out, to the first stop. This is the first stage of activation, and I repeat it will in effect give you the advantage in speed of movement that you will need."

"Repeat? You never—"

"Then, at the precise moment, just as the assassin pulls the trigger of his weapon, pull the stem to the second stop. This will activate the beacon."

"*What* beacon?"

"That's all. Until you need it on the fourteenth, this device will seem to be an ordinary timepiece. Need I emphasize that you must not lose it? You can wind it, by omitting to set the hands at twelve, pulling the stem out and turning it in the normal way."

Now the image of the watch disappeared from the small screen, which was filled by Pilgrim's face. He said, with emphasis: "Once more: The activation of the beacon must be accomplished *only during the proper three-second* interval. Pull the stem out to the second stop a second too late, and you will strand yourself permanently in the nineteenth century. Pulling it a second too soon will doubtless have the same effect, with the added drawback of causing irreparable harm to much of what you know as Western Civilization.

"But, do it at the right moment, and you will save the life of President Lincoln. You will also be restored to your own world, under conditions which ought to earn your country's eternal gratitude."

There was a sudden sharp whiff of a strange, acidic odor in Jerry's nostrils. There was, briefly, a shimmering in the air immediately surrounding the watch. Jerry almost dropped it, although his hands holding the instrument could feel no heat. In a few seconds the shimmering was over and the smell had dissipated. Jerry was left holding a device that looked exactly like the one Pilgrim had held during the demonstration. The face was solidly visible, and the hands agreed at least approximately with those of the sober clock on the wall of the bank lobby, which he was able to see over the partition of the booth. And the instrument he held was ticking.

Stunned, Jerry mechanically tucked the watch into the watchpocket of his vest, and after a couple of tries managed to get the chain attached to a buttonhole in what he considered had to be the proper way.

Still somewhat dazed, he closed up the safe-deposit box, now empty but for the cotton batting, and carried it out of the little partitioned booth, to hand it back to the incurious clerk.

You must be there in the moment just before the assassin's bullet smashes into Lincoln's brain. Your window of opportunity will be approximately three seconds long . . .

Oh, must I? You son of a bitch, Pilgrim. I'd like to see to it that something smashes into your brain. I didn't ask you to dump me into this drugged dream, this, this—

The fate of Western Civilization? More immediately graspable: his chance to get home. Pilgrim had said that it would be his only chance. Maybe that wasn't necessarily so, but the bastard could probably arrange matters that way if he wanted to.

And it would happen in Washington, on April fourteenth. He recalled the date on the newspaper he was again

364 *Fred Saberhagen*

carrying under his arm. This was April sixth. He had eight days.

He was just outside the bank, on the wooden sidewalk, with no idea of which direction he ought to go next, when a gentle hand in a soft gray glove placed itself on his arm, making him start violently. The young woman who had come up to him had chestnut hair, and calm brown eyes under her flower-trimmed hat. The face on the locket? No, he thought, not at all.

"Don't be startled, Jim," she said in a low, husky voice. She was smiling at him pleasantly. "Someone might be watching us. You don't know me but I'm your friend. Because I'm in the same boat you are. I used to work for Lafe, but I've given it up too."

Jerry opened his mouth to say something, and closed it again.

"Walk with me. Smile." Her hand on his arm turned him gently on the busy sidewalk, and they walked together, at a moderate pace. He noticed vaguely that they were moving in the direction of the railroad station. "I'm Colleen Monahan. I'm working directly for Stanton now. It's all right. He sent me to see to it that you get back to Washington alive."

SEVEN

After hurrying Jerry down a side street near the railroad station, Colleen Monahan brought him up some wooden steps to the front door of a cheap-looking rooming house only a few blocks away. In the dim hallway inside the door the smell of stale cabbage overlay a substratum of even less appetizing odors. Next she led him up a dark, uncarpeted stair; there were four short flights, with a right-angled turn after each one. From somewhere nearby came the voices of a man and woman quarreling.

The upper hallway where they left the stairs smelled no better than the lower one. In another moment Jerry's guide was unlocking the door to a small and shabby room.

"Our train leaves shortly after dark," she announced, locking the door after Jerry as soon as he had followed her into the room. "If you want to change clothes before we start, there's a few things in the wardrobe there that might fit you." The more he heard of Colleen Monahan's speech, the more easily Jerry could detect a trace of some accent in her voice; perhaps it was a genuine Irish brogue. And probably it would be more than a trace when she spoke with feeling.

"The train to Washington?" he asked.

"Of course. What did you think? I said I'd get you there alive."

It was said in a matter-of-fact way that made the implied

danger all the more convincing. "I bet," Jerry said carefully, "that lots of people arrive there alive every day."

Standing in front of a small wall mirror, Colleen had unpinned and taken off her hat, Now she turned to face him. "Not with Lafe Baker trying to stop them, they don't," she said. The short reply had the sound of practical advice, delivered calmly. Now, as Jerry approached the room's single window, intending to look out, she added: "Better be careful. And hand me over that safe-deposit key while I think of it. You won't need it any longer."

Jerry pulled out the key, tossed it in the air and caught it. "How'd you recognize me?" he asked softly. "Lots of men go in and out of that bank."

"I paid the safe-deposit clerk to pass me a signal. What did you think?"

After giving her the key he edged up to one side of the window and moved the curtain gently. The window gave an elevated view of backyards, woodpiles, and privies, the scene decorated by a few lines of laundry. If someone somewhere out there was watching the room, Jerry couldn't see them. He let the dirty curtain fall back.

Turning to the tall wooden wardrobe, he took a look inside; only a few clothes were hanging there, but about half of them seemed to be male attire, somewhat shabbier than Jim Lockwood's. "You mentioned changing clothes. Do you think I ought to?"

"You ought to know better than I," she answered shortly. "Maybe the men chasing you don't know what you're wearing now; maybe they haven't been after you every inch of the way here from Missouri. I can tell you it's damned likely they will be after you from now on. And I've promised the old man in Washington to bring you there alive."

He closed the wardrobe doors again. Pilgrim had

arranged for him to be guided to this woman, obviously, but he had never said anything to Jerry about her. Beyond what she was telling him herself, Jerry had no idea of who she really was and how much she might know.

Cautiously he asked: "What's going on in Washington?"

"Sit down and rest yourself. Don't be waitin' for a special invitation." Colleen herself was already occupying the only chair, so Jerry sat down on the bed—the mattress was a grade quieter than cornhusks if not really any softer. His hostess continued: "What's goin' on? Stanton and Watson, Lord bless 'em, are finally ready to clean house. Old Lafe is goin' to be on his way out—provided we can get you there alive to testify. Mr. Stanton won't act until he can hear the facts from you personally."

Stanton. Oh yes. Jerry could definitely remember Jan Chen, somewhere across the vast gulf of time, telling him that was the name of Lincoln's Secretary of War. The name of Watson, on the other hand, meant nothing to Jerry, unless it was going to turn out that Sherlock Holmes was alive after all. Nor could he recall ever hearing of someone known as Old Lafe.

Unable to stand the uncertainty any longer, Jerry asked: "What do you hear from Pilgrim?"

"Who?" She had heard him perfectly, but the name obviously meant nothing to her—or else she was a superb actress.

Jerry sighed. "Never mind. So, Old Lafe is going out."

"He won't be got rid of lightly," his informant went on, shaking her head grimly. "He is efficient, when he wants to be, as we all know. But now the stories about his corruption are mounting and mounting, and the war is winding down. He can be dispensed with now. But Lafe Baker won't disappear without a fight, as we both know. And how are things out in Missouri?" She flounced her body in the chair, adjusting the long skirt. She was better dressed, Jerry realized, than anyone would expect an occupant of this boarding house to be.

He only shrugged in answer to her question.

"I trust you got the goods on him." There was hopeful hatred in the question.

Jerry looked her in the eye, trying to appear impenetrable rather than ignorant. "I want to get to Washington," was all that he could find to say, at last. "Alive." The problem of someone there knowing Jim Lockwood, and wanting him to give testimony about something, would have to wait.

"Right, don't tell me, I don't want to know."

Colleen had gone behind a professional mask. "Wouldn't do any good. Even if you told me, I wouldn't be able to testify first-hand. I forgot to ask you if you'd had anything to eat."

"I've eaten well. You? And how about the train tickets? I've got money."

Colleen smiled. "That was to be my next question." She pulled an apple out from somewhere and began to munch on it. "Won't be needing any tickets between here and Detroit. We're going that far on a private car. I'm Sarah James and you're John James. We're married, of course. I don't think Lafe's people are going to be looking for a married couple. That's why Stanton sent a woman as your escort." Then she straightened herself firmly in the chair, as if to discourage any idea of intimacy the mention of marriage might have suggested.

"A private car." That was impressive, thought Jerry. If it was true. "How'd you manage that?"

"The men who own the railroad are only too glad to be able to do a favor for Mr. Stanton." She stated that as if it should be an obvious fact, and Jerry did not press for any elaboration.

His companion, chewing thoughtfully on a piece of

apple, studied him and then remarked: "You don't look all that much like the picture I'd formed of you from Mr. Stanton's description, though there's no doubt it fits. Strange how you can get a picture of someone in your mind and then it's wrong. By the way, did you bring the note?"

Jerry dug from his pocket the note he'd taken from the safe deposit box, and passed it over. Colleen looked at it and was satisfied. "Reckon you're all right," she said.

Silence stretched out for a few moments, threatened to become uncomfortable. Jerry asked: "Have you been in this line of work a long time—Colleen? Mind if I call you that?" And he was thinking how different she was from Jan Chen, presumably in some sense her colleague. He wondered if they knew or had ever heard of each other.

"I've been at it long enough to know my way around. And for now you'd better start to call me Sarah." It was something of a reproach.

"Of course."

The two of them sat talking in Colleen's room until it began to grow dark, when she suddenly asked him: "Have you the time?"

He dug out Pilgrim's watch and flipped open the metal faceplate. "A little after six."

"Then we must go." From under her bed Colleen pulled out a small bag, evidently already packed. Jerry, carrying his own heavier carpetbag, followed her out the door. There was no light in the room to be extinguished.

This time Colleen Monahan led him on a circuitous route through the evening streets. Here and there lamps glowed in the windows of houses, and a man was carrying a short ladder from one gas streetlight to another, patiently climbing again and again to light them one by one.

Colleen looked over her shoulder frequently; Jerry, imitating her, could see no evidence that anyone was following them.

Pausing beside a high board fence, Colleen took one final look around, then dodged suddenly through a hole in the fence where several boards were missing. Jerry, staying on her heels, found that they were now in a railroad yard, a couple of blocks from the lighted station. The ground underfoot here was a maze of track. Kerosene lamps behind colored glass made what he supposed were effective signals. In the middle distance a couple of trains, lighted by lanterns and showering sparks, were moving sluggishly. Switch engines grumbled and snorted in near-total darkness, dragging the cars industriously.

Their baggage bumping against their legs, Jerry and his guide picked their way across one siding after another, moving in the general direction of the station. Chicago was evidently already well on its way to becoming a great railroad center.

"What are we looking for?" Jerry whispered when Colleen paused at last, obviously uncertain of exactly which way to proceed.

"We're looking for the man we're going to meet," she whispered back.

"Who's that?"

"A friend. I'll know him when I see him."

She moved on, with Jerry continuing to follow her as silently as possible.

Ahead of them an uncoupled passenger car waited on yet another siding. A dim figure emerged from behind it, looking in their direction. Colleen waved, and the man ahead returned her gesture, his arm almost invisible in the gathering gloom.

As they approached, the man waiting in the shadows

tipped his cap in a remarkably humble gesture. Jerry could
see now that he was black, wearing what Jerry took to
be a kind of railroad uniform.

"Mistah and Missus James? I'm Sam." The speaker
touched his cap again, this time in a kind of half-military
salute. "We expectin' you heah. Lemme take you bags."

"Never mind that, we'll manage," said Colleen. Despite
the interference of her long skirts, she was already halfway
up the steep steps leading into the car. "Let's get moving."

"Yas'm. We'll be moving any minute."

Someone would have to locate and attach an engine
first, thought Jerry. But he kept quiet. In a matter of
moments they were all three inside the car, where he
received his next surprise. He wasn't sure what kind of
an interior he had been expecting, but these quarters
were furnished better than Lincoln's Springfield home,
and Lincoln had not been a poor man when he lived
there. Kerosene lamps with ornate shades were hidden
behind shaded windows that let out practically no light.
Thick carpets covered the floor, except for a layer of steel
plates in the near vicinity of the woodburning stove. The
heating stove, secured by steel tie-rods to the floor of
the coach, was standing cold and empty in the mild spring
night.

Not only the furnishings but the layout were more like
those of a house than a railroad coach. In the rear, where
the three had climbed aboard the car, was a kitchen-
utility room, complete with cookstove, ice-box, woodpile
and pantry. A narrow door standing open on a small closet
revealed inside a primitive flush toilet, with overhead
water tank. There was a scuttle of coal beside the
cookstove, in whose iron belly a small fire was burning.

From this room Sam conducted his guests through a
narrow passage leading forward along the left side of the
car. At its front end the passage opened into a single

large parlor, luxuriously furnished, with two softly upholstered sofas, matching chairs, and a few tables. Kerosene lamps secured near the corners of the ceiling provided lighting, and elegant curtains had been drawn on all the windows, making this a private world.

Colleen paused for just a moment, as if the place were somehow not what she had been expecting, but she was determined not to show it. Then she carried on. "Sam, can you fix us something to eat? I saw a pantry back there."

"Yas'm. I got a fire goin'. Supper comin' right up."

Jerry and Colleen sat on soft furniture in the parlor of the millionaires' train, looking at each other.

"Lord," she said with feeling, "some folks know how to live. Don't they, though?" Continuing a running commentary, she jumped up to investigate an unopened door, that must lead to the central room or rooms, bypassed by the narrow hallway.

". . . I just hope that one day I—" She opened the door and fell silent. Jerry looked over her shoulder. Here was another cold stove, bolted down and vented through the roof like the others. The room also contained a wide, curtained four-poster bed—as well as a chamber pot, barely visible underneath, a washstand, another sofa, and a small table and chair. Some railway car, Jerry thought.

Somewhere outside the curtained windows, one of the switch engines was slowly rumbling its way closer; men's voices were calling just outside the private car. Presently there came the jolt and jar of coupling. Jerry had ridden twentieth-century trains a couple of times, but those had been electric powered commuter specials, plying smoothly on short trips between Chicago and the suburbs. This, he expected, was going to be another new experience.

Colleen, still struggling not to be overly impressed, stood in the bedroom doorway. "This is very fancy indeed."

"Just so's it's fast."

"I expect it'll be that too."

With another jolt, the string of cars that now included theirs got slowly into motion.

Colleen moved to one of the parlor windows and parted a fringed curtain slightly to peer out. "We're coming almost to the station . . . there's the train we're joining . . . they're putting us right behind the tender. That's good, most of the smoke will blow past us." There now began a slow deliberate lurching forward and back, a grinding and banging, as more cars were coupled and uncoupled.

"This is the sixth of April," said Jerry, hanging on to the heavy parlor table for support during this lengthy procedure. "I must be in Washington before the fourteenth."

She looked at him. "I'm sure we will be, barring a train wreck. Or something worse. But what happens on the fourteenth?" When he did not answer she looked at him and added: "All right, I shouldn't ask."

Presently Sam returned, bearing waiter-style on one raised hand a tray of covered dishes, linen napkins, fine china, and crystal glasses. His two clients had seated themselves at the parlor table and were just beginning to enjoy their dinner when the train got under way. Sam had provided hot soup, fried oysters, fresh bread and cheese, red wine and hot coffee.

"Thank you for providing such elegant transportation, Mrs. James," Jerry toasted his companion with a gesture of his wineglass. During recent minutes he had noticed that she was indeed wearing a plain gold ring on the third finger of her left hand; he wondered if it was the real thing, or part of her costume for this assignment. But that was none of his business.

"It's my job," she answered modestly, having glanced around to make sure that Sam was out of sight before she spoke. With the steady volume of noise that the cars made in motion, anyone who tried eavesdropping from around a corner was going to be out of luck.

"So," said Jerry pleasantly. "I think that safe-deposit box was a good idea."

"Yes indeed," his companion agreed calmly.

Jerry hesitated, considering. He wanted to probe for more information, about Stanton, and in particular about the mysterious Lafe Baker, who was evidently hoping to arrange Jim Lockwood's death. And about the testimony Jim Lockwood would be expected to provide, if and when he reached Washington alive. Yet he was afraid to ask questions, fearing to give himself away.

"How's Stanton?" he asked at last.

"Him? How is he ever? Sickly little muck of a man with his gold-rimmed glasses and his great gray beard. Bullies and blusters those folk who are afraid to stand up to him. But he gets his job done, and two or three other men's work beside, I'll be thinkin'. When he finds corruption he'll not put up with it, in Baker or anyone else."

"And where is Baker now?"

"Ha, wish I knew. But we're here, locked in on a moving train, and it's not about to keep me awake tonight worryin' about it." Colleen looked again toward the corner of the passageway where Sam had vanished. "I wonder if our friend would bring us a tot of something to keep out the chill." She looked at Jerry with sudden suspicion. "You're not a drinkin' man, now are you? I mean heavy?"

"No. Not so it becomes a problem. Almost never. I remember one occasion when wine got me into trouble—but right now I could use a tot of something too."

Swaying to his feet with the motion of the train, Jerry made his way halfway across the parlor to an elegant little cupboard he had noticed earlier. The doors of the cupboard were unlocked, and when they were opened they revealed not only the bottles he had been hoping for, but a good selection of fine glassware as well. With a little gesture Jerry pulled out one bottle labeled brandy. There was no ice, of course, but what the hell, sometimes you had to rough it.

When he and his charming companion—really, she wasn't at all bad looking—had toasted each other, he remarked: "I see there's a sofa in the bedroom. Perhaps I'd better sleep in there. It might look a little strange to Sam if he found me out here on one of these." And with his free hand Jerry patted the cushions beside him.

"I think perhaps you're right. The *sofa* in the bedroom it should be for you." The emphasis upon the second word in the last sentence was not all that heavy, but it was definitely there. "And now, if you don't mind, Mr. James, I'm very tired." Colleen looked uncertainly for a moment at her empty brandy glass, then smiled briefly and put it down—Sam would take care of it—and swayed to her feet against the motion of the train.

A few minutes later, going back to the kitchen utility room to take his turn with the water closet, Jerry observed Sam, who was bedded down wrapped in a blanket on the floor beside the cookstove. The supper dishes had already been washed and stacked in a rack to dry. To all appearances their attendant was dead to the world.

Jerry paused for a moment, studying the sleeping man. A slave? No, surely not, here in the north. But had Sam perhaps been a slave at some point in his life, his living human body bought and sold? Almost certainly. The thought gave Jerry an eerie feeling.

Coming forward in the car again a few minutes later, Jerry once more passed the sleeping Sam, who did not appear to have moved a muscle. Moments later he entered the parlor and came to a dead stop.

Here in the parlor only one of the high-hung kerosene lanterns was still burning, the light somehow turned down to dim nightlight intensity. The door leading to the bedroom was closed. Seated in an armchair directly beneath the lantern, Pilgrim was waiting, his strong, compact body swaying lightly with the motion of the train. He frowned at Jerry but at first said nothing, as if he were waiting to hear what Jerry had to say.

Recovering from his initial surprise, Jerry at last moved forward again, to lean with both fists on the parlor table. "Well?" he demanded. "Is the joke over? Had enough fun?"

The dark man in the chair sat with folded arms, shaking his head slowly. His face remained saturnine. "Would that it were all a joke, my friend. Would that it were."

"I think you better tell me just what the hell is going on."

"I shall do my best." Pilgrim drew a deep breath and expelled it. Not far ahead, another train's engine whistled sharply. "You have been drafted to carry out a rescue operation. At the moment it is not going well."

The train swayed, rounding a curve, and the flame in the dim lantern swayed lightly with it. "Whatever it is you drafted me for, since you're here now, I suggest you take over the operational details yourself, and send me home."

"I should be delighted to take over, as you put it, and myself do everything that needs to be done. In fact nothing would please me more. But that is, I regret, not possible."

"Really."

"Yes."

"Let me see if I can begin to understand this. Your message on the talking watch indicated that the object of the rescue operation is Abraham Lincoln. And that if he can be saved from assassination, then there's some chance of my resuming a normal life."

"That is roughly correct."

"Good. Meanwhile, your aide, little Jan, spent most of an evening back in Springfield feeding me drugs and telling me how important Lincoln was to history, how different everything would be if he hadn't been shot. Which means that if I save him, I'll be resuming my life in a different twentieth century. Or are you telling me there would then be two different futures?"

Pilgrim was shaking his head with a slow emphasis. "Understand this from the start. *There is only one future. There is only one world.*"

"Then how can we expect to save Lincoln, and not change—"

"Trust me. It can be done."

"Trust you!"

"Jeremiah, my time for answering questions is severely limited; I advise you to seek information that will be of practical benefit. As for my taking over, as you put it, I repeat that is impossible. A tangle of potential paradoxes prevent it. I can help you, advise you—up to a point— but that is all. If it were possible for me to do the job you have been assigned, I should not have gone to all the trouble of finding and recruiting you."

"You're saying I'd better trust you because you're not going to give me any choice."

"At this point I cannot. Not if you want to return home."

Jerry fumed in silence for a moment. Then he demanded: "Who's this Lafe Baker that Colleen Monahan is telling me about? Why does he want to kill Lockwood, and why did you set me up here as someone who's likely to be killed?"

"Colonel Lafayette C. Baker is head of the War

Department's Secret Service. He is becoming, even in this corrupt and brutal era, something of a legend in the realms of corruption and brutality. Now that the war is effectively over, his employer, Secretary Edwin McMasters Stanton, is ready to be rid of him.

"As for why you now bear the identity of James Lockwood, you must realize that we were severely limited in our choices of a persona in which to clothe you. Lockwood himself is dead now, as you have probably suspected. You do not look very much like him, and Stanton of course will know on sight that you are a fraud. So you must avoid meeting Stanton."

"Thanks. Thanks a lot. He'll be waiting for me at the station in Washington, I suppose."

"That is possible."

"Wonderful. Now what is all this crap about my having a three-second window of opportunity in which to act?"

"I regret," said Pilgrim, "it is all too regrettably true that—"

The train swayed again, the lamp-flame swaying and dimming too. Jerry leaned backward from the table, needing a momentary effort to maintain his balance. When he looked for Pilgrim again, the chair was empty and the man was gone.

EIGHT

Jerry spent some time walking about looking for Pilgrim. He covered the interior of the car from one end to the other, without result. Sam in his nest of blanket on the floor had shifted position at last, but he was still asleep. And when Jerry entered the bedroom, Colleen was snugly asleep in the big bed, covered to the chin and snoring gently. He wondered if Pilgrim was still watching him from some other dimension or something. Well, tonight it wasn't going to matter to Jerry a whole lot. He was dead tired; having someone watch him sleep wasn't going to bother him.

Silently he fastened the small bolt on the inside of the bedroom door. One lamp in the bedroom was still burning dimly, and Jerry went to it and fiddled with a little wheel on the side, as he had observed other people doing with lamps. The little wheel had something to do with adjusting the length of the burning wick, but he couldn't get it right. At last he gave up and simply blew out the flame; afterward, in nearly total darkness, he could still smell the hot metal and the kerosene.

The speeding train roared and swayed hypnotically through darkness. Groping his way around, he removed his coat and boots, making sure he had his revolver within easy reach. Then he stretched out on the sofa, which was comfortably soft but a little short for even Jerry's modest height. His last waking thought was that he was a taller man in this world than he had been in his own.

Jerry awakened to bright daylight outside the bedroom's curtained windows; he could feel and hear that the train was just stopping somewhere. A glance toward the bed showed him that his roommate was still asleep. He supposed Thursday had been a tiring day for her as well.

Cautiously Jerry arose from the sofa and moved to a window, where he parted the curtains and squinted out. They had reached some kind of a city or town, and baggage was being unloaded from the train. A few passengers appeared to be waiting to get aboard. Two clocks were visible, one in a brick tower in the middle distance, the other through the window of the nearby depot—both said one minute after eight.

The timepieces reminded Jerry of the device Pilgrim had so craftily arranged for him to possess, and so earnestly warned him not to lose. He pulled it out of his watch pocket and looked at it now. The watch was ticking as steadily as before, but now it said seven-fifty. That meant that either the two clocks outside were wrong in unison, or . . .

Could something be wrong with the hardware Pilgrim had provided for the mad attempt to rescue Lincoln? Jerry, the student of science and engineering, didn't see any reason why not. If anything could go wrong, it would. That was all he needed, one more complication on top of—

There was a slight sound from the direction of the bed, and Jerry turned to see Colleen sitting up halfway, propped with pillows, and looking at him. She was holding the blanket up as high as her shoulders, which, he was just able to see, were demurely covered by what looked like a flannel nightgown.

"Good morning," he offered.

"And a good morning to you." She freed one hand,

without letting the blanket slip more than an inch, and used the fingers to rub her eyes. "Where are we?"

"I don't know. Stopped at a station. I was just wondering if we're still in the central time zone."

The puzzled look Colleen gave him in response warned him to let that question drop for now.

She was ready to change the subject anyway. "If you would turn your back," she requested.

Silently he went back to the window, hearing her get out of bed behind him. That sound was followed by the rustle of voluminous layers of clothing, most of it being put on, he presumed. His mind returned to the latest oddities of time. How likely was it that both of these town clocks would be wrong together?

"You can turn back now," Colleen's voice announced. He turned to behold his roommate with yesterday's dress on, and pins in her mouth, busy in front of a wall mirror doing something with her hair. At that moment there came a tapping at the bedroom door, and Sam's voice sang out announcing that breakfast was ready in the parlor.

That at least was cheerful news. "We're getting the royal treatment," Jerry remarked.

"I told you, we're supposed to be great friends of the president of the railroad. In a way we shall be, if we give a good report of him to Stanton."

Breakfast was good. Excellent, in fact. Jerry was now firmly convinced that everyone in this century who could afford to eat at all took the business seriously.

Sam, in and out of the parlor with serving dishes, gave up his first cheerful attempts at making, or provoking, conversation when he sensed that the reigning mood was one of reserved silence. Jerry had begun to develop the unreasonable feeling that the man was putting them on, acting the part of a black servant out of some old movie.

Before breakfast was over, the train had lurched into
motion again—only to grind to a halt a few minutes later
at the next town.

Today was April seventh. Most of the remainder of the
day passed very slowly. Armed with a timetable and
Pilgrim's watch, Jerry charted the crooked progress of
the railroad across Indiana and part of Michigan. There
were many more stops than he had hoped, more, even,
than he had expected. A number of the towns boasted
steeple clocks visible from the train, no two of which
were in agreement with each other. The watch in Jerry's
waistcoat pocket ticked on steadily—he had remembered
to wind it on retiring—but on the average its time grew
farther and farther divorced from that displayed in the
cities through which they passed.

Colleen sat most of the morning knitting quietly, but
after Sam served lunch, she put her needlework aside
restlessly and began speaking about the small town in
Indiana where she had grown up. One of her brightest
memories was how exciting it was when the railroad first
came through.

"One of these towns here?" He was reasonably sure
that they were still in Indiana.

"No, no. Far to the south."

She mentioned a brother, and Jerry asked: "Is he in
the army now?"

"He died at Vicksburg."

"Uh . . . sorry to hear it," Jerry replied awkwardly.

She acknowledged his sympathy with a slight nod. "I
have another brother with General Sherman in Georgia."

"Older or younger?"

"Oh, younger. I'm the oldest in the family. Twenty-
four. What about yourself?"

"Twenty-five."

"I meant, about your family." She blushed just slightly.

"No brothers or sisters," he said shortly. Jerry suspected that as an only child he had missed out on a lot of happiness.

"You meant there never were? Ah, that's too bad. It must have been a lonely way to grow up."

"I had a lot of cousins around when I was small," he said truthfully. "That helped."

She hesitated very briefly before she added: "And no wife now, I suppose?"

"No wife."

"That's just as well in our line of work. You'll leave no widow."

"Is that why you let yourself get into it—I mean, did becoming a widow—"

Colleen nodded, and before he could very well express his sympathy again she had turned to the window, as if to keep him from seeing her face. Jerry wanted to ask her more questions about herself, but, not being ready to answer the same sort of questions, he forebore.

As he served the evening meal's first course, Sam announced that the train would reach its final stop, Detroit, early the next morning. He suggested that reservations for Mr. and Mrs. James for the next train east be made by telegraph from the next stop. Jerry thought that a good idea and gave Sam money for the telegram.

During the night Colleen tossed in her bed, crying out with nightmares. Jerry, awakened on his sofa, went to comfort her.

He took her by the arm, wanting to wake her gently. But she pulled free and rolled away across the wide bed, whimpering. In the midst of her broken murmurs, Jerry thought he made out a name: Steven.

Suddenly Colleen rolled back toward Jerry, clutched his wrist, and pulled him onto the bed. He lay there, atop the covers, with an arm over her covered shoulder, comforting her as best he could.

Slowly Colleen came fully awake, the moans of her dream-struggle turning into a soft and hopeless weeping.

"Hey, it's okay, it's all right." Jerry kept reassuring her gently as he lay there with no urge to do anything but soothe her. Gently he stroked her hair.

Presently she ceased weeping, and soon after that she said: "You're a good man, Mr. James. Perhaps the best I've met in this business. Now go back to the sofa."

She was patting his arm gently, but her voice, though it still trembled, had an edge to it.

"Yes ma'am," said Jerry, and went back.

Their train carried them into Detroit right on schedule, early on the morning of Saturday, April eighth. In the railroad depot of that city they said goodbye to their millionaires' quarters, and to Sam, who had fixed them a sizable hamper of food to take along when they boarded their next train.

Switching trains was accomplished without any special difficulty, but the loss of their private car meant goodbye to any chance for open conversation, and though it eased the problem of how to keep his background obscured, Jerry had mixed feelings about that. It meant, as well, goodbye to other privacy, and that he did not like at all.

On the plus side, he now began to overhear a lot of interesting conversation, conveying useful information to the visiting alien. The other passengers on this train were all white—Jerry gathered that blacks rode in the baggage car when they rode at all—but otherwise quite a mixed bag. This train was vastly inferior to their private accommodations, but luxurious compared to the local that Jerry had ridden out of Springfield. Their coach boasted a water closet at each end, as well as sinks. There was even a cooler for drinking water, tin cup attached by a slender chain.

Here, as in the private car, the layout was somewhat compartmentalized. The rear compartment, about a fourth of the car, was for ladies only, but Colleen, like most of the other women, chose to stay with her male companion as much as possible. Seemingly there were no unaccompanied women aboard.

She rode beside Jerry in a double seat, while around them children wept, shouted, laughed, and otherwise made a racket, and adults dozed, chatted, or endured the trip in silence. The roaring train surrounded them oppressively, raining considerably more soot and sound upon them than they had been exposed to in the private car.

The clocks in the passing towns kept getting further and further ahead of Jerry's watch. By now Jerry had begun to wonder whether any regular time zones had yet been established. These people seemed to be setting their watches and clocks by the local sun! Not that he cared much; he had more immediate problems to worry about.

At a whistlestop just east of Cleveland, Colleen touched Jerry on the arm and pointed unobtrusively out through the grimy window beside her.

"Some of Lafe's people," she murmured, so softly that no one but Jerry would have had a chance of hearing her.

Jerry looked out the window with great interest, just in time to observe a couple of tough-looking men in civilian suits and bowler hats stop a young man on the platform. He had put down his carpetbag and they were showing what might be badges—Jerry couldn't really tell from where he sat—and obviously interrogating their victim.

Colleen added in the same low tone: "Only looking for bounty-jumpers, most likely."

Now he was really lost. Damn Pilgrim, anyway. He asked: "And how are bounty-jumpers best recognized?"

"They won't be recognized at all, I'd bet, if it's to be left up to those two," Colleen sniffed. She appeared to regard Lafe's agents and their victim with about equal disdain. The train pulled out before they saw the conclusion of the incident.

The day wore on, passengers feeding themselves from whatever food and drink they had brought with them. A garrulously extroverted young soldier, recently discharged and radiant with joy as his Pennsylvania home drew ever nearer, went from seat to seat aboard the coach offering to trade some of his hardtack biscuits for a share in more palatable fare. Jerry and Colleen shared some of the contents of their hamper with him, but declined to try his biscuits, which he had been carrying wrapped in a long-unwashed fragment of blanket.

When darkness had fallen and it was time for berths to be made up, the ladies retired to the female compartment in the rear. Overnight passengers, it appeared, were expected to supply their own bedding, and sure enough, the bottom of the hamper packed by Sam revealed two folded blankets.

A uniformed porter came around to fold the men's berths down from the wall, causing the daytime seats to disappear as part of the same transformation. The only railroad-supplied bedding was the slightly stained mattress pads that came down with the berths, triple-deck constructions with each shelf jutting independently from the wall.

The night of April eighth passed uneventfully, and Colleen dutifully rejoined her husband next morning somewhere in Ohio. At the first stop that the train made after sunrise, people in their Sunday best came aboard carrying palm branches. Jerry stared at them uncomprehendingly.

"Palm Sunday," Colleen beside him commented.

"Oh." Sunday, the ninth of April, he thought. That leaves five more days. Am I really going to do what Pilgrim tells me? Do I have a choice? If this is Palm Sunday, next Sunday will be Easter. And Friday the fourteenth will be Good Friday, won't it?

Colleen gazed after the happy Christians moving past them through the car. "Were your folks religious, Jim?"

"No. Not much."

"Mine neither. But there are times when I think I'd like to be. Are yours still alive?"

"My mother is," he said, abstractedly, truthfully. "My father—my original father kind of walked out, I understand, when I was very small."

"Stepfather bring you up?"

"Yep. I always think of him as my father. He's still around."

As if unconsciously, two-thirds lost in her own thoughts, Colleen reached to take his hand. No one had ever taken his hand in quite that way before, he thought. Almost—he supposed—the way a loving wife might do it. For some reason Jerry was moved.

The remainder of Sunday passed as had the days before, in soot and sound and roaring motion. How many such days had he now spent in this alien world? He was starting to lose track.

The train that bore him was beginning to seem itself like a time machine—or an eternity machine perhaps, a mysterious and inescapable conveyance whose journey never ended. Eventually the lamps were once more lighted, the berths made up again. Men and women retired in their separate compartments.

Jerry's was a middle berth tonight, with one man snoring

below him and another overhead. Bootless, hatless, and
coatless, his belongings tucked around him, he dozed
off wrapped in Sam's gift of a blanket. His coat, with
revolver carefully enclosed, was folded under his head.

He was awakened in the small hours of the morning,
by the sound of heavy gunfire.

NINE

Jerry had his revolver in hand and his boots on when his feet hit the narrow aisle between stacks of berths. Most of his bunkmates were already on their feet, milling around and cursing in the near-darkness, and a good proportion of them were also armed. The train had ground to a stop by now. Armed male passengers were looking out of windows.

This was no train robbery, though. Squeezing himself into position at a window, Jerry could see that huge bonfires had been built along both sides of the track. Men on horses were racing madly by, waving their hats and yelling, whooping up a giant celebration.

Jerry caught the words shouted by one rider who shot past at top speed: "—Lee's surrendered!—"

Now the door at the men's end of the car was standing open and someone had thrown a bundle of newspapers aboard. Someone else had got the lanterns burning brightly. Bottles of whisky and flasks of unknown firewater were being passed from hand to hand, and Jerry choked down a swig.

Presently he got to see a newspaper, dated Monday, April tenth. The lead story on the front page read:

NEWS BY TELEGRAPH
THE END

THE OLD FLAG VINDICATED

LEE AND HIS WHOLE ARMY
SURRENDERED YESTERDAY

The Official Correspondence
Between Grant and Lee
On Thursday, the President paid another visit to
Richmond. Accompanied by Mrs. Lincoln,
Senators Sumner and Harlan, and others . . .

Celebration was spreading aboard the train. Exploding, Jerry decided, would be a better word for it. Amid the noise the women, wrapped in shawls and blankets, were coming forward from their sleeping compartment demanding to know what was going on. Men, some of them utter strangers, shouted victory at them, hugged and kissed them. Women screamed in joy and prayed when they heard the news, thanking Providence for the end of casualty lists.

The train whistle shrieked again and again, but so far the train remained standing where it had stopped. Jerry could see lights in windows out there, some kind of a town nearby, no one sleeping in it now. Men were leaning out the open windows of the train, firing revolvers into the air, bellowing to add their noise to that of the celebration going on outside.

Jerry had turned to face the rear in the crowded aisle, wanting to see Colleen as quickly as possible when she appeared from the women's quarters. But so far she hadn't come into sight. He swayed on his feet with the jolt that came as the train at last made an effort at getting into motion again.

The jolt was repeated, this time with more effect. The movement drew more cheers from those aboard, as if it were another military victory.

"Mistah Lockwood?"

There was a tug on Jerry's sleeve, and he looked down into the face of a small black boy. "What is it?"

"Youah wife, sah. She want you back in the baggage cah. Two cahs back."

Baggage car? All Jerry could think at the moment was: *She's found out something. Maybe Baker's people are on board.* "Lead on," he said, pausing only to grab his coat and hat from inside his berth.

He followed the boy back through the narrow corridor that bypassed the women's section of the coach, and then outside through its rear door. There was no enclosed vestibule between cars, only one roaring, swaying platform coupled to another, a standing space beaten by the wind of the train's passage and sprinkled with the sparks and soot and cinders of its power.

"What—?" The boy had disappeared, somewhere, somehow. Jerry wrenched at the handle of the door leading into the next car, but if his guide had gone that way he had locked the door behind him.

There were two ladders close at hand, one on the end of each car, each ladder a series of rungs riveted or welded to the body of the coach, leading up to the train's roof. And now at the bottom of the nearer ladder, a few feet away, a dark figure stood, gripping a rung with his left hand, holding a gun in his right, aiming it at Jerry. The gunman was mouthing words of which the train noise would let Jerry bear only a shouted fragment.

"—sends his regards—"

Had Jerry been at all familiar with the reality of firearms, had he ever seen at first hand what they could do, he might have been paralyzed by the threat. As matters stood, he reacted before fear could disable him.

At the karate *dojo* they had sometimes, in leisured safety, rehearsed responses to this situation. Rehearsal paid off now; Jerry raised his own empty hands—the first step was to make the attacker think you had surrendered. Then a fraction of a second later he lashed out with a front snap kick, catching both wrist and gunbutt with the toe of his right boot.

There was an explosion almost in Jerry's face. Powder fragments stung his skin, while the flash and the bullet went narrowly over his left shoulder. The gun itself went clattering away in darkness.

Immediately after impact Jerry's right leg had come down to support his weight again, so now he had both feet as solidly planted as anyone's feet could be on the rocking, jouncing platform. Jerry was no black belt, and the straight overhand punch he threw at his opponent was not as hard as some he had sent at the wooden *makiwara* in the practice dojo. But still it landed with considerably more force than the man might have anticipated from someone of Jerry's size and build, even had he seen it coming.

Hit on the cheekbone by a stunning impact, the disarmed man let out one surprised sound and staggered back, his first inadvertent step carrying him off the platform at the top of the steep iron stairs that led down to the ground. While the train was in motion those stairs were barricaded, but by nothing more than a low-slung length of chain, whose links now caught the tottering man at the back of his thighs. For a moment his arms waved frantically. He tried, and failed, to grab at the handrailing beside the steps. Then he was gone.

By now the figure of another man had appeared on the platform, and Jerry turned instinctively to meet the new threat. Dimly he could see that the arm that came swinging up at him held a knife. He blocked the blow somehow, but the man's other fist, or something he held in it, clouted Jerry on the side of the head and he went down, momentarily dazed. Now at last he remembered the pistol in his own inside pocket, and managed to pull it out. It was kicked out of his hand before he could fire. He tried to roll over on the narrow platform, but his opponent was crouching over him, knife poised for a downward thrust.

Another gunshot punctuated the steady roaring of the train. The second enemy sprang away, and in a moment had vanished up the ladder to the roof. One more shot rang out even as the man was climbing, and Jerry thought he heard the ricochet go whining away from heavy steel.

Colleen, wrapped in a blanket over her nightgown, stood in the open doorway of the forward car, a stubby-barreled pistol in her hand. In a moment she had moved forward to crouch over Jerry. "You hurt?"

Before he could answer he had to get to his feet and take an inventory. Everything was functioning. Amazingly, he thought, there was no blood. Along his left forearm the sleeve of his coat had been ripped by his attacker's knife, but the blade had not pierced the shirtsleeve or the skin beneath.

"Let's get inside. This's only a two-shot." And Colleen, gesturing with her pistol, tucked it back into the folds of her blanket. "Damn it all, I should have known right away. Little nigger boy came to tell me you wanted me to stay put. I should have known."

Inside the train again, in the light of the kerosene lamps, he could see the anger in her eyes, and could tell that some of it at least was directed at him, Jim Lockwood, the experienced agent, who had just fallen for what must have been some kind of a crude trick. But she was angry at herself too.

"What do we do now?" he asked, humbly.

She looked at him in surprise, then shrugged. "Keep

going, get to Washington fast as we can. Got a better idea?"

"No."

Inside the coach the celebration was still in progress, and if anyone aboard the train had heard the sounds of gunfire out on the platform, no one would have thought twice about them. But eventually the excitement tapered off, and most of the passengers returned to their berths. A few stayed up, singing patriotic songs in drunken voices. Jerry, back in his berth, dozed fitfully, hand under the pillow of his rolled-up coat, where his gun would be if he had managed to retain it. He had refused Colleen's whispered, reluctant offer to loan him her reloaded "derringer," as she called it. He thought, but did not want to admit aloud, that she could probably use it much more effectively.

Sleep was difficult to attain. Each time Jerry began to doze off, he woke up with a start, certain that someone had just intruded on his berth to aim a gun at him. But there were no real intruders, and eventually he slept.

The tenth of April dawned without further serious incident. Berths were turned back into seats, and the day began to drag by, like the other dull days of the trip before it. In Pennsylvania Jerry and Colleen changed trains again, the interior of the new coach being almost indistinguishable from the one they had just left. If anyone on the old train had noticed the loss of one or two passengers during the night, no one so far was making a fuss about it.

One after another the cities and towns of the victorious North crept slowly past the windows of the train. Each town no matter how small was decked out in bright bunting. American flags were everywhere. And it seemed that each settlement had found at least one cannon of some kind with which to fire salutes to passing trains. And everywhere, in every town, the church bells rang. They seemed to go on ringing from morning to night without interruption. Jerry could not always hear them, he could usually hear nothing but the train itself, but again and again he saw the bells dancing in their little church towers of wood or brick as the train rolled past.

It all proclaimed that the War, after four years of blood and death, was over.

All that Jerry could overhear among the other passengers confirmed it: the fighting had essentially ground to a halt, though still it had not officially or entirely ceased. In scattered places there were still Rebel soldiers in the field, and some of them were still capable of offering resistance. But the Confederate government had fled from Richmond days ago, just before the city fell, dissolving itself in the process; and now that Grant's arch-opponent Lee had surrendered in Virginia, the back of organized resistance had been broken. Lee himself at Appomatox had scotched any idea of a prolonged guerrilla war, by saying to his men that if anything of the kind should happen he would feel bound in honor to give himself up to the Federal authorities as being in violation of the surrender agreement he had signed.

It was necessary to change trains yet once again—for the last time, Colleen and the timetable promised. The next set of cars were more crowded. And, perhaps because they were now getting close to Washington, the talk aboard became ever more political. Jerry had it confirmed for him that Stanton, Secretary of War, was indeed a great power in the land; Stanton's name was mentioned even more than that of Lincoln. And Andrew Johnson, Lincoln's Vice-President, was evidently at best a nonentity. All Jerry could hear of Johnson were a few snickers at the way the man from Tennessee had disgraced himself by taking too much to drink before last month's inauguration ceremonies.

And then at last, on Tuesday the eleventh of April, Jerry realized that the train was passing through Maryland, and Washington was very near.

TEN

The church bells of the city of Washington cried peace and victory with a thousand voices. The great national celebration, begun on Palm Sunday, was continuing. Not only continuing, it seemed to be picking up steam.

The train that would convey Jerry and Colleen Monahan into Washington had halted at a watering-stop, and they, along with a number of other passengers, had got out to stretch their legs, and enjoy the feeling of solid silent earth beneath their feet once more. There was no town here, only three or four houses in the midst of Maryland woods and fields. The train, currently six or eight wooden coaches long, waited with most of its windows open. Birds sang amid spring foliage in a nearby grove; the stationary engine grumbled to itself as it drank from an elevated watering-tank beside the track.

"How far from here to Washington?" Jerry asked in a low voice, squinting ahead along the track. They must be entering the South, he thought; here even the April sun was strong enough to make the distant rails shimmer.

"Just about ten miles. Why?"

Jerry didn't answer right away. He had been evolving a plan in his own mind, and he decided this was the time to put it into effect.

When he spoke again it was to try another question: "Will Stanton have anyone meeting us in Washington?"

The two of them were strolling trackside, now far

enough from the other passengers to let Colleen answer plainly. "Don't see how he could. He won't even know what train we're coming in on. No one but he and Peter Watson know he sent you to Missouri, or sent me to warn you and bring you back."

Colleen had previously mentioned Peter Watson a couple of times, saying enough to let Jerry identify the man as some kind of high-level assistant at the War Department. Now he said: "Some of Baker's people obviously know about me now. And about you. Who we are, what train we're on."

"Looks that way."

Jerry had stopped walking, and was standing looking up and down the track. "We leave the train here," he said at last, decisively.

She took his meaning at once. "All right, if you think best. What about our baggage? Just leave it aboard?"

He hesitated. "I don't see how that would help. If anybody's watching us they'll know we've gone, whether we take the bags along or not. And it'll just take us a minute to get the things off the train."

"If Baker still has an agent on the train, and he sees us go?"

"If he follows us, we'll have a chance to see who it is. If he doesn't, he'll lose us." Jerry raised his eyes, looking for branching trackside wires. "There's no station here, no telegraph. He won't be able to send word on ahead."

Colleen nodded. "Then let's get moving."

Within two minutes the two of them had retrieved their bags from the train, and were hiking a path across a muddy field, in the general direction of the nearest house.

"We'll hire a wagon here," Jerry decided. "Or else we'll walk until we find a place where we can hire one."

And after they had found new transportation, Jerry added silently to himself, would come the next step. It might be trickier, but somehow he would accomplish it.

Over the past few hours he had been thinking over his situation as intensely as the hypnotic jolting of the train would allow. In Washington, as Colleen had just confirmed, only Stanton himself, and probably his aide Peter Watson, were able to recognize Jim Lockwood on sight. Jerry's trouble was that he was not Jim Lockwood, and the best he could expect from his first meeting with the Secretary of War was to be thrown into a cell. There would be no prospect of getting out any time soon. *Habeas corpus* had been suspended for several years now, and the leaders of Lincoln's administration seldom hesitated to jail suspected traitors and subversives first and investigate them later. At best, Jerry would certainly be prevented from stationing himself inside Ford's Theater on Friday evening, three days from now.

"Getting off the train is not enough," said Jerry presently, casting a look back to see if they were being followed. "We're going to split up here."

Colleen was taken aback for a moment; this was the first time since she had met Jim Lockwood that he was making a serious effort to take charge. But her male partner's assertion of authority really came as no surprise. She only looked at her companion thoughtfully and did not argue.

Jerry, who had his own argument ready, brought it forth anyway: "Baker's people know the two of us are traveling as husband and wife. Don't they?"

Colleen, still thoughtful, nodded.

"Then it makes sense for us to split up. You go on ahead as fast as you can, in the first wagon we can hire, and make your report to Stanton. I can give you some money for traveling expenses if you need it. I'll get to the War Department my own way, in good time."

"Traveling expenses? I could walk there from here in three hours. And why don't you go first?"

"I may get there first." Jerry, walking quickly, looked back again over his shoulder toward the train. A couple of the leg-stretching passengers were looking after the two deserters but so far no one appeared inclined to follow them. "But I want you to start ahead of me."

"All right." But Colleen was plainly somewhat puzzled and reluctant.

The second of the local houses that they tried proved to have a well-equipped stable, as well as a man eager to carry passengers into the city for a fee. Presently Jerry was waving Colleen on her way.

Now, he thought, would be the ideal time for him to hire a horse, as she had suggested before they parted. If he only knew how to ride one.

Rather than take that risk Jerry walked on, along the road Colleen's driver had taken. Luck was with him; in about ten minutes he overtook a wagonload of produce whose driver had stopped at roadside to mend a broken harness. For a few coins Jerry bought passage, and climbed into the rear of the wagon, where he would be able to lie almost concealed among the burlap bundles of early asparagus, the crates of eggs and chickens. He gave his destination as somewhere near Pennsylvania Avenue—from his schoolboy visit to the modern city he remembered enough of the geography to know that White House and Capitol would both be in that area. That meant that necessarily there would be crowds into which an alien visitor might safely blend.

He could remember someone, somewhere aboard the roaring confusion of trains between here and Chicago, claiming that there were two hundred thousand people in the city of Washington now. The listeners on the train, Jerry remembered now, had seemed impressed by that number.

When the wagon had jolted on for a while—in blessed lack of soot, and relative silence—Jerry raised his head to look about him. And sure enough, there in the hazed distance was the dome of the Capitol at last. For a moment he could almost believe it was the modern city that lay before him.

During the long hours spent staring out the windows of one jolting railroad car after another, Jerry had considered that once he had escaped from Colleen he might hide out in the suburbs until Friday. Either in the actual suburbs of Washington—they had to exist in some form, he thought—or on some nearby farm. But he had never been satisfied with that idea. A stranger who didn't know his way around, particularly one who behaved in any way oddly, would be bound to be conspicuous anywhere in countrified surroundings. In the center of the city, though, say between the White House and Capitol, right in the middle of the crowd, there ought to be more strangers, including foreign diplomats and visitors, than anyone would bother counting. This was, after all, the capital city of a sizable nation.

There would also be plenty of Baker's men in town, Jerry assumed—but the point was that even if some of those men could recognize their fellow secret agent Jim Lockwood, they still wouldn't know Jerry Flint from Adam. And no one would be passing around photographs.

Except, of course, that the two men who had tried to kill him on the train had known whom they were after, and they might be able to recognize him again. One of those men, at least, had fallen from the speeding train and might well be dead now, or at least in no shape for action. And Jerry doubted they could be here already—but if they were, they were. Trumping all other arguments, he, Jerry, was basically a city man, and he trusted the instinct that urged him to seek out a crowd in which to maneuver.

Staying low in the wagon, surrounded by the bundles of asparagus and the crated chickens, Jerry didn't see much of the city as it grew up around him. The sound and rhythm of the horse were soothing after days of trains—anything would be soothing after that, he thought. He could hear the gradual increase of the traffic around him, music, human voices, roosters crowing. Once a squad of blue-clad Union cavalry came cantering close past the wagon, the faces of men neither old nor young looking down at him incuriously. Then the cavalry was gone.

It was something of a dirty trick he'd played on Colleen, Jerry mused, leaning back on a sack of produce and watching the formation of spring clouds overhead. He could only hope she'd had no more trouble with Baker's people. At best she would be reporting to Stanton a success that would fail to materialize, and Jerry felt rotten about that. But he considered that he had had no choice. He was committed to serve that tricky snake who called himself Pilgrim, in some plan that Jerry didn't really understand at all. How could Lincoln's life be saved by transmitting a signal, operating a beacon of any kind, at a moment when the fatal bullet was already on the way to its target? And supposing Lincoln's life could be saved in such a way, wouldn't a lot of familiar history necessarily be lost?

The tops of some relatively tall buildings, three and four stories high, were now coming into sight above the piles of produce that surrounded Jerry. At last the wagon stopped. The farmer's bearded face came into view, as he twisted round from his seat to stare at his passenger in silence. Jerry sat up straight; a quick glimpse of the Capitol dome assured him that he was at least somewhere near the destination he had bargained for.

He scrambled to his feet, handed over another coin as had been agreed, and hopped out of the wagon with his carpetbag. The wagon rolled away. A few passersby, black and white, cast curious glances at the young man who had thus arrived in their midst, and now stood on the sidewalk dusting himself off. But no one said anything. Surveying the crowd, Jerry saw more blacks here than he had seen anywhere en route; some of them looking happy as if they were high on drugs, others wretched. All of them presently in sight were very poorly dressed.

Jerry hoisted his bag and walked off briskly, joining the flow of pedestrians where it was thickest. Here, he noticed, the sidewalk was made of brick. Washington was quite the metropolis.

He circled around the block, first clockwise and then counterclockwise, making sure to the best of his ability that he was still not being followed. Then, after one false start, he made his way to Pennsylvania Avenue, which as he remembered ran between the Capitol and the White House, which last structure now seemed blocked from view by red-brick office buildings under construction. The Washington Monument came into view, surprising Jerry by being in an obviously unfinished state, much shorter than he remembered it.

His next surprise was the sight of a horse-drawn rail car, carrying a crowd of passengers down the middle of Pennsylvania Avenue. He soon discovered that brick sidewalks were by no means universal here; they had been laid down in a few places, but as in the towns and cities of Illinois, wood or mud prevailed everywhere else. Here too poultry and livestock were in the streets, pigs rooting in the mud.

Above all here in Washington, there were many uniforms, more than anywhere else. Bodies of troops marched or rode horses through the streets, others appeared standing around or joining in the general flow of pedestrian traffic.

Long hours on the cars spent listening to others' conversations had provided Jerry with a great many fragments of information. One pertinent item he had filed away was that Willard's Hotel was the most prestigious place for a traveler to stay in Washington. It stood on Pennsylvania Avenue, no more than a couple of blocks from the White House, just across the street from a large structure called the Armory, and a little over a mile from the Capitol at what appeared to be the other end of Pennsylvania. Standing on the sidewalk outside Willard's now, Jerry considered that if the lobby was any indication the place had to be overcrowded. All the better, from his point of view. He had money—at least Pilgrim had not stinted on that. If he couldn't bribe his way into a room, he couldn't, but he thought that it was worth a try.

A sign outside the hotel boasted that all its rooms were equipped with running water. After five days—or was it six?—of steady railroad travel, that decided matters.

Making his way in to the desk, Jerry learned from a clerk that it was very doubtful that there were any rooms available. But at that point a twenty-dollar gold piece laid unobtrusively on the desk worked wonders. On impulse he scratched his name on the register as Paul Pilgrim, of Springfield, Illinois.

The upper room where Jerry found himself was small, but otherwise luxurious. It did indeed boast running water in a small sink, and a flush toilet in an adjoining private closet, but hot water was something else again; maybe only the luxury suites had that piped in. No great problem for the wealthy guest. A few more coins brought a

procession of black men to Jerry's door carrying a portable
tub, along with hot kettles and steaming pails. In a few
minutes the tub, resting on his thick bedroom carpet,
was filled and steaming.

Jerry spent a few moments in unpacking his bag. Then
he stripped and shaved and soaked in the hot tub, trying
to ease the endless jounce and chatter of rails out of his
joints, to remove from his skin the layers of grease and
grime and soot.

Out of the tub and dressed in clean, if wrinkled clothing,
he made arrangements with the porter concerning laundry.
When he went downstairs at last, he remembered to check
the local time by a clock in the lobby. Then he carefully,
for the first time, reset his watch, opening the face and
moving the hands exactly as Pilgrim's video tutorial had
directed. Exactly how knowing the exact local time might
help him on Friday night, he could not be sure. But he
felt better for having made at least a vague commitment
to exact timing.

Just off the lobby of Willard's was a magnificent and
crowded bar, where Jerry now repaired for a beer. This
struck him as the perfect means of sluicing the last of
the railroad soot out of his throat. As he enjoyed the first
gulp he realized that there was something peculiar about
the crowd of men around him; and a moment later he
understood what it was. In the whole bar there were, to
his initial amazement, no uniforms. Then he read a faded
notice on the wall, warning everyone that in Washington
liquor service to members of the military was illegal. That
was something to keep in mind; it meant that there would
have to be a lot of back rooms, somewhere.

After that one cold delicious beer he took himself to
dinner, which at Willard's seemed to be a more or less
continuous affair; the entrance to the dining room had
been busy since he first saw it. Crowds of a density that

made Jerry feel secure surrounded him as he sought and obtained a table, and after days of subsistence on what amounted to box lunches, a serious meal improved his morale enormously.

After he had eaten, he strolled through the lobby, wondering if after all he should try a cigar, At last he did buy one and got it lighted. When it went out he was content to chew on it a little—if the enemy who were looking for him now had spent much time observing him on the cars, they might well be convinced that the man they were looking for didn't smoke.

Jerry was restless, unable to stop walking. The lobby soon proved too confining, and he went outside. The cigar was starting to make him queasy now, and he threw it into the muddy street. Judging by appearances, anyone who objected to littering here would be put away as a lunatic.

The crowds on the sidewalk were tending irresistibly in one direction, toward the White House. Jerry wondered why.

Mr. Lincoln was at home again, he heard somebody say. Home from where? he wondered. Oh yes, there had been something about the President visiting the fallen Rebel capital. Richmond, as Jerry recalled, was not very far away.

And now, just over there, a few yards away beyond that high iron fence, Mr. Lincoln was at home. Gradually the impact of that simple statement grew on the visitor. Jerry shuffled forward with the crowd. For the moment his problems were forgotten.

The sun was down now, and the evening cool and misty, like the last part of the day that had gone before. Far down Pennsylvania Avenue to the southeast, the new-looking dome of the Capitol was somehow being illuminated as dusk faded into night. They must, Jerry supposed, be using some kind of gaslights.

Earlier he had been able to catch an occasional glimpse of the unmistakable White House. And now as he drew closer he could see, just ahead, what must be part of the grounds behind an iron fence. For the moment the building itself remained out of sight behind a gray bulk of stone; when Jerry got close enough to read the sign in the faint gaslight of the street lamps this stone mass turned out to be the Treasury Department. Jerry couldn't remember whether the Treasury building had been standing here or not when he had visited this city as a schoolboy in the nineteen-seventies.

And now the President's House itself was coming into view, considerably smaller than Jerry's twentieth-century memories proclaimed it, and more isolated in its park-like grounds. The crowd was flowing slowly and spontaneously toward it. Some of the people walking toward their President's house were carrying lighted candles, Jerry saw now, as if this were some vigil of protest organized in the late twentieth century. But the mood tonight was not protest, it was one of quiet rejoicing. Gates in the iron fence stood open, and guards, both military and civilian, stood by, letting the people in. A crowd was gathering freely on the north lawn; and the nonchalant ease with which this was allowed sent something like a shock of horror through Jerry.

A number of people around him were singing now, singing softly and joyfully, groups of them working away on different songs, none of which he could recognize. Only now did he gradually become aware of how high a proportion of black people there were in this particular crowd. In a way the blacks were difficult to see, making only a shadowy part of the throng, ever ready to move aside, to disappear when jostled. But they were there, ineluctably.

Lighted candles had been placed in many of the windows of the White House too, as if this gathering on the lawn had been anticipated or invited. And now there was a murmuring in the crowd. Directly over the north entrance—Jerry was sure the entryway he saw now was a simpler construction than the one he remembered seeing in his own century—a light of extra brightness appeared in a window, the exactly central window on the upper floor. The glow of a lamp held there illuminated the faces of the crowd below.

And now the window was being swung open to the nation and the night. There were people standing just inside, in what appeared to be a hallway. Someone's arm held the kerosene lamp up higher, and now a murmur of applause ascended through the night from the crowd below.

Abraham Lincoln, holding some papers in his hand, was standing in the window, in the bright lamplight. There could be no mistake about who he was.

Jerry, aware of a strange sensation in his lungs and ears, realized presently that he had suspended breathing. It needed almost a conscious effort to start the process up again. Meanwhile across the surface of his mind there flowed the memory of how as a child, visiting Disneyland, he had sat between his parents watching the robot Lincoln there. That robot was a thing of plastic and metal and electronics that stood up from a chair, facing the tourist audience, and with occasional lifelike movements of arms and head, a natural-seeming shifting of its weight, delivered a speech of Lincoln's words in a recorded voice—whose voice? Yes, that of the actor Royal Dano.

At moments this evening's experience was eerily similar. "We meet this evening," the tall man in the window began—and then he had to pause for a moment while the arm beside him adjusted the position of the lamp, so he could read his speech. Lincoln was wearing reading glasses, whereas the robot had not. Dano's voice in the character of Lincoln, Jerry decided now, had been very much like the real thing, high and clear, with a kind of rustic accent. Lincoln continued: "Not in sorrow, but in gladness of heart."

Another murmur, almost the start of a cheer, ran through the crowd, there was some jostling for position, and Jerry missed the next words. For a short time the President's voice dropped below audibility.

The next words that Jerry was able to hear clearly were: "Unlike the case of a war between independent nations, there is no authorized organ for us to treat with. No one man has the authority to give up the rebellion for any other man. We simply must begin with, and mold from, disorganized and discordant elements. Nor is it a small embarrassment that we, the loyal people, differ among ourselves as to the mode, manner, and means of Reconstruction."

Jerry was trying to work his way forward through the crowd, in an effort to hear better; it wasn't easy, for a lot of other people were doing the same thing, and the bodies toward the front, almost under the overhanging portico, were closely packed.

Around him there were murmurings: not of approval of what the President was saying, nor of disagreement either. Actually it sounded rather like the beginning of inattention. So far the President was not giving these people what they wanted tonight; what they had come here this evening to get, whatever that was.

Now he was talking about Louisiana. "Some twelve thousand voters in the heretofore slave state of Louisiana have sworn allegiance to the Union, assumed to be the rightful political power of the state, held elections, organized a state government, adopted a free-state constitution, giving the benefit of public schools equally to black and white and empowering the Legislature to confer the elective franchise upon the colored man. Their Legislature has already voted to ratify the Constitutional amendment recently passed by Congress, abolishing slavery throughout the nation. These twelve thousand persons are thus fully committed to the Union, and to perpetual freedom in the state—committed to the very things, and nearly all the things, the nation wants—and they ask the nation's recognition and its assistance to make good their committal."

Lincoln's audience this evening approved of him in general, and they wished him well. But he was losing them as an audience, paragraph by reasoned paragraph of his speech. It was dull business that he had written out to read to them tonight, not words of triumph or inspiration. Urgent business, doubtless, but dull. Tonight it was enough for almost everyone but him to savor victory. The war at last was over.

Now the President's voice was coming through clearly again. He was saying something about very intelligent blacks, including the former slaves who had fought in the Union ranks, being allowed to vote.

There was grumbling in the crowd at that. "Damned radical after all!" was one of the comments Jerry heard near him. "Democrats were right. He'll have the niggers voting in the next election. Voting straight Republican."

ELEVEN

On the morning of Wednesday, April twelfth, Jerry awoke from a confused dream in a state of disoriented terror. He lay for an indeterminate time staring at the white plastered ceiling above him before he could recognize it as that of his room in Willard's, and remember how he had come to be here lying under it.

Next he tried to gather his thoughts, to sort out the dream he had just experienced from the hardly less probable reality of the last few days. In his dream he had been somehow forced to play the part of a gate-guard at the White House. He knew he was only playing the part, because the job was not properly his and at any moment his false position was likely to be discovered. Worse than that, he could see that the assassins were already approaching, a horde of them on horseback, moving in a compact mass like the Union cavalry he had seen in the streets.

Jerry ran forward, trying his best to block the killers' entry, but there was no gate in the iron fence for him to close, only a great gaping gap with broken hinges hanging at the sides. The mounted men ignored Jerry's feeble efforts to hinder them and charged on past, raising sabers and carbines as they swept on to kill Lincoln, who was standing in the White House window holding an anachronistic flashlight.

Now, as Jerry lay in bed regarding one of Willard's

plastered ceilings, and listening to the rumble of wagon-traffic in the street outside, the dream-terror gradually faded into a very conscious horror at the truth. In this earlier and in some ways so much more innocent version of America, the President appeared to be readily accessible to any enemy. It was unbelievable to Jerry, raised on the idea of celebrities as casual targets, that the man had already survived more than four years in office in this bitterly divided country.

Someone in the restaurant last night had been talking about Lincoln's customary bodyguard, a fanatically devoted friend of his from Illinois named Ward Lamon, who was apparently of gigantic strength and went armed to the teeth day and night. Jerry supposed such a watchdog might have had a great deal to do with Lincoln's survival up till now. But another of the people in the restaurant had commented that Lamon had just been dispatched by Lincoln on some confidential mission. That, Jerry supposed, was going to make things easier for John Wilkes Booth on Friday night. And perhaps the absence of such a protector would make things simpler for Jerry too. At least he could hope.

And at least he had the name of the assassin—John Wilkes Booth. He could have remembered that even if Pilgrim had not reminded him. He could remember too that Booth had been—or was—an actor.

The trouble was that last night almost anyone, with only a minimum of luck, would have been able to work his way to within a few feet of a well-lighted and helpless Presidential target. Jerry had no idea where Booth was at this moment on Wednesday morning. But if the murderous actor had been in town last night, he had missed a great opportunity.

And Jerry had to stop him Friday, or else . . . but the old doubts arose again. Why should he, Jerry, trust

Pilgrim's assessment of the situation? Pilgrim had already tricked him at least once, and rather viciously.

Easy enough to say that he ought not to trust Pilgrim, but what was he going to do instead? Walk into a police station and tell them he'd been kidnapped from the twentieth century? Or settle down here to spend his life—probably a short, unhealthy one—as a petroleum salesman?

The bottom line for Jerry at the moment was that he was following Pilgrim's orders because he really had very little choice. He would at least pretend to go along with Pilgrim's plan, until some reason to do otherwise, some better chance of getting home, presented itself.

Thoughtfully Jerry got up, dressed himself in clean clothes—his laundry had been returned on schedule—and descended to the lobby. The ground level of the hotel was as crowded as it had been yesterday, and no one appeared to be ready to take time out from his own affairs to pay any attention to an out-of-town businessman named Paul Pilgrim, of blessedly nondescript appearance.

Looking at the throngs milling before him, he could see that there might be many others who would be considered more interesting than himself. For a moment he wondered if there might be any other time travelers on the scene. There were uniforms in plenty, of course, but still civilian clothes predominated. According to the jokes Jerry had overheard yesterday in the barbershop and the bar, seekers of political office were continually swarming into Washington from all across the nation, the eternal bane of the President in particular, and of everyone else in government who had in some degree the power to hand out patronage. The federal government of 1865 might be small and primitive by the standards of Jerry's time, but no doubt it was huge and bloated by the prewar standards that these people around him could remember. Jerry suspected that civil service examinations did not exist in this world, and that the opportunities for enrichment at public expense were tremendous.

Over breakfast—it was huge, and very good; there seemed to be no lesser kind of meal obtainable at Willard's—Jerry turned his mind to practical matters. As he visualized the situation, getting into the theater Friday evening was only the start of what he had to do. He would have to be as close to Lincoln as possible, preferably standing or sitting right beside him when the assassin approached. Obviously there were considerable difficulties. And the more Jerry thought about them, the larger those difficulties loomed.

For one thing, other people might be approaching this accessible President all the time, and how was Jerry supposed to recognize Booth when he saw him? At this moment he had not the faintest idea of what the man looked like. Other questions popped up in bewildering numbers, as soon as he began to consider the situation seriously. Was Lincoln going to be accompanied to the theater by any bodyguard at all? Evidently not by the formidable Lamon, and probably not by any competent substitute. But there might be someone on the job, someone who would interfere with Jerry's effort to get close to the President, even while failing to stop Booth.

Presumably there would be other people in the President's theater party too. His wife, doubtless. What was the old sick joke? Oh yes: *Besides that, Mrs. Lincoln, how did you like the play?*

But who else would be there? And what was the general layout of the theater? And where was the President going to sit? Hadn't Pilgrim's recorded briefing mentioned a box seat?

This was Wednesday morning, which when Jerry thought about it was none too soon to start finding out the answers. Maybe he would get another briefing from Pilgrim before he was expected to go into action, but maybe he wouldn't.

Immediately after finishing his breakfast, Jerry stopped at the desk for directions to Ford's Theater. Relieved to find how near it was, he started out on foot, picking his way across muddy intersections where no one had yet thought to install traffic signals. Turning off Pennsylvania, he walked five blocks east on E Street to Tenth, then half a block north. The theater was there, on the east side of the street.

There was no marquee or other sign projecting over the sidewalk, only a tall, wide front of red brick containing five arched doorways at ground level. There were also five windows in each of the next two stories above. Smaller buildings crowded up close against Ford's on either side, and none of the structures looked more than a few years old.

Jerry approached the theater more closely. On the front wall posters advertised the current show, *Our American Cousin*, starring Laura Keene. An additional strip of paper reminded passersby that the performance of Friday, April fourteenth, would be the last.

There was nothing to be gained by waiting around out here on the sidewalk. Jerry squared his shoulders, ran through once more in his mind the story he had decided on, and started testing the five front doors of the theater to see if any of them were open.

The second door from the right proved to be unlocked. He walked through it into a dim lobby. No lamps were lit, and, after he had closed the front door behind him, the only daylight entered here indirectly, from a window inside a small office at one side. Men's voices, low-key and faint, were coming from the direction of that office. Jerry had opened and closed the street door quietly, and he thought it probable that no one in the office had heard him come in.

Ahead of him a dark stairway led up into heavy gloom. He badly wanted to see the layout of the theater, and decided to take a chance. If he should be discovered wandering about inside, he had his story ready.

From the top of the broad, carpeted stairs he emerged into the relatively lighter gloom of a large auditorium. He was standing now in a large, curving balcony, looking at a stage directly ahead of him where two small gaslights flamed, providing the only illumination in all the great space of the theater's interior. Jerry moved forward slowly, until he could lean his hands on the railing at the front of the balcony. Now, where in all this vast space was Lincoln going to sit?

Probably in a box seat, for greater privacy. From where Jerry stood he could see eight box seats, four right and four left, four high and four low, all of them directly overlooking the half of the stage nearest the audience.

On Jerry's left as he faced the stage, a man's head and shoulder suddenly appeared, leaning out over the railing of the highest and farthest box on that side. In a moment the head and shoulder were joined by a beckoning arm. The man, who obviously wanted Jerry to come to him, bore a strong resemblance to—

Anger, relief, and hope rising in him together, Jerry pushed off from the railing and strode rapidly to his left along the curving front of the balcony. He was headed toward a door—when he looked for it he could see it—that must give access to the upper boxes on that side. In a moment he had pulled the door open and was groping his way forward through a darkened little vestibule.

"Shut the door behind you," whispered Pilgrim's voice from somewhere very close ahead. Then Jerry could see the man standing in a small doorway that led directly into the box seat closest to the rear of the stage, the same one he had been waving from. The two gas lamps set above the stage shone in past heavy red curtain to half-illuminate the compartment. Jerry moved forward silently.

"Have a seat." Pilgrim, wearing a twentieth-century shirt and khaki pants, pushed a small chair toward Jerry with his foot. Then, sighing as if he were tired, he retreated to let himself down again in the chair from which he had waved to Jerry. He added: "I had hopes that you would show up here, at some time before the big event. We need to talk. And here, at this hour, is an ideal spot."

Jerry considered several swear words, and then rejected all of them as a waste of breath. He kept his own voice low. "We need more than that. We need for you to get me out of here and back where I belong. I didn't ask to be—"

Pilgrim raised a thick hand, gently gesturing. "In good time, in good time, you may register your complaints about my conduct. You have a legitimate grievance; but others involved in this situation have more reason than you to complain of being treated unfairly."

"Including you, I suppose?"

"Forget about me—for the moment. Later I may want to talk about myself. For now, what about Mr. Lincoln?"

"What about him? He was dead and buried a century before I was born, and it wasn't my fault what happened to him."

"Not quite a century—but it wasn't your fault. I agree. Not up until now. But what happens Friday night will be your fault. If you fail deliberately."

For a moment Jerry could find no words. In the effort he made a whispered sputtering. "Fail? *Fail?* I didn't sign up to do anything here. You kidnapped me here and then started giving me orders. Recorded orders. Garbled lectures from a talking watch. Guessing games and a disappearing act on a train. Why should I—" Jerry paused, quietly strangling on his anger.

"Nevertheless." Pilgrim, who had listened with an air of attentive sympathy, rubbed his forehead and stared out into the gaslight, which came between the dull red curtains of the box to turn his face and hairy forearms faintly orange and yellow. From the position he had taken he could see most of the interior of the theater, but it would be very difficult for anyone outside the box to see him, unless he leaned farther forward in his chair.

He went on: "Nevertheless, you are here now, and what happens to Mr. Lincoln now depends on you. There is information, vital information, I must try to give you while I can. My time is limited here, as it was on the train. I can sympathize with your anger; in your place I should be angry too. After matters are decided on Friday night I can bring you home, and I will do so—if all goes well. Before then I cannot. Now, will you listen to me?"

"I'm listening. It better be good."

"It is good. It is better than you think. To begin with, you have inherent powers of a rare kind, that you have hardly begun to realize as yet."

"Sure. And where did I get these powers from?"

"They are usually inherited. Your father—I understand that he disappeared early in your childhood—was probably a timewalker."

Jerry said nothing. He had come to a stop.

Pilgrim was watching him, perhaps with understanding. Pilgrim said: "Inherited. And danger calls them forth. Not ordinary danger, even of the degree that you confronted on the train. It might be more accurate to say that only death itself can activate them."

Jerry was silent, his long-nursed anger slowly quenching in an inner chill. "You mean . . ."

"You have spoken of your powers to Jan Chen. But we were practically sure you had them, even before we set out to recruit you."

Twice Jerry began to say something, and each time reconsidered. At last he said, in an altered voice: "You mean the time I ran into the burning house, when I was a kid."

"I mean exactly that. I can only approximate those powers mechanically. Perhaps I can help you by augmenting them, in a way. But without your help I have no chance of doing what must be done here Friday night. You, with my help, can do it. You can save Mr. Lincoln, if you will."

Jerry was silent for a few moments. He had the feeling he was losing the argument, had lost it already, even before his cry for justice had been fairly heard. "You've tricked me once already," he said finally. "Why should I believe anything you tell me now?"

Pilgrim gave him a hard look. "I tell you you are going to stay here, trapped in this century, unless you help Mr. Lincoln. Do you have any difficulty in believing that?"

"You bastard."

The swarthy man accepted the insult calmly. "I have been called much worse than that. You can spend the remainder of your life here, as I say. Forget about being a computer engineer, forget a great many other things as well. Or, you can do what I ask of you Friday night— and then return to your own time, with your future education financed as we had agreed. Not to mention the feeling of a job well done."

Jerry shifted in his chair. "You think you can manipulate anyone."

"I usually have fair success." It was said modestly.

"I think I just might knock your teeth down your throat. That would be a job well done."

'No." Pilgrim's answer was mild but prompt. "I will not tolerate a physical assault, especially by someone as well-trained as yourself. I make allowances for your anger in being tricked into this expedition—but I will not go that far in making allowances. By the way, that little skirmish on the train was well fought, if perhaps a touch too boldly; I was afraid that we were going to lose you there." Pilgrim was leaning back in his chair, quite relaxed, arms folded, watching Jerry. Everything in his attitude said very convincingly that his teeth were not subject to any knocking that Jerry might attempt.

"You were watching me on the train?"

"It is much easier to *watch* from another timeframe than it is to interfere. Thus, your reestablishment in this one, not to mention my dastardly schemes, became necessary to help Mr. Lincoln. I had to find some way to bring your rare inherent powers into play."

"Oh yeah, my rare inherent powers. I had almost forgotten. Tell me about those."

"I shall try." For a moment Pilgrim looked almost humble. "You have seen that time can be manipulated. That we can sometimes travel through it, if you will. Some people, one in a million, can do something similar without the aid of technology—just as some are lightning calculators who on their good days can emulate the performance of a computer. You are one such. At the vital moment on Friday evening you ought to have more than one swing at the ball."

"What's that mean?"

"You will be able to back up, a matter of a few seconds or a minute, and start over."

"I will?"

"At least once, perhaps as many as three times. I hope no more than that; it is possible to get caught up in something like a closed programming loop."

"You're saying if I fail, I'll—I'll somehow be able to try again?"

"That is my fond hope. And the ability may save us all. You see, Jerry, there are usually great, and often prohibitive, paradoxes involved in any attempt to manipulate the past. Sometimes the difficulty can be overcome by making an abstract of the past, and manipulating that—but there are reasons why that approach is ruled out in this case. There is only one timeline, one universe, one past, and we must live with it, or try to change it at our peril."

"Why do we have to try to change it?"

Pilgrim ignored the question. He said in a business-like way: "You came here to this theater today to scout the ground, did you not? With a view to going along with my plan on Friday night?"

"Yes. All right, I admit I did that. I couldn't see anything else to do."

"A courageous and logical decision. Now." Pilgrim pointed straight out across the stage. "The box directly opposite, the counterpart of this one on the right-hand side, is the Presidential box where Lincoln will sit on Friday night. At this moment on Wednesday, no one in this city but you and I, not even Lincoln himself, knows that he is going to decide to attend the theater on Good Friday. But he will attend; unless of course you should be so foolish as to warn him. That would defeat all our plans utterly."

"All your plans. My only plan is to go home."

"I am afraid such a warning would defeat that modest ambition also."

"Huh. The talking watch seemed to be trying to explain something along that line. But I'm not sure I got the message. A lot of it was too noisy for me to understand."

"The noise of paradox, my friend. I am not going to

attempt to explain the theory of time-travel and of
paradoxes to you now. But the simple difficulty in
transmitting a message is as nothing to the problems that
would ensue were I to attempt to interfere directly in
the matter of the attack upon Mr. Lincoln. Without, that
is, the beacon signal that you will transmit to me as
guidance. You still have your watch, I trust—? Good.
History must be allowed to run smoothly in its timeworn
bed."

"Then exactly what do you plan to do to help him?
Lincoln?"

"Save him from being shot. On Friday evening, unless
we interfere, John Wilkes Booth will enter the vestibule
leading to the Presidential box yonder, across the stage.
After blocking the vestibule door behind him to prevent
interference, he will quietly step into the box itself, so
quietly that none of the four occupants will at first turn
around.

"He will shoot Lincoln in the back of the head,
wounding the President fatally. Then Booth will leap from
that box to the stage, breaking his leg in the process.
Still he will manage to hobble to his horse out in the
alley and escape."

Jerry looked. "I don't wonder he breaks his leg. Isn't
it about twelve feet?"

"It is. I must warn you now not to underestimate Booth
as a physical opponent. He is a good rider, an excellent
shot and swordsman, and famed for his athletic feats on
stage. He would not break his leg were it not for the
fact that one of his spurs catches on a flag."

"Hooray for Booth."

"I am pleased that you are willing to rise to the challenge
posed by such a worthy opponent."

"That's only because I haven't discovered a choice yet.
Suppose I get within three meters of Lincoln at the fatal

moment, and I do send the beacon signal you want. What do you do then?"

"Leave that to me."

"I expected you to say that. Anyway, suppose we somehow do save Lincoln. Isn't that going to turn history out of its bed rather drastically?"

"There are limits on what I am allowed to explain to you now."

"Very convenient."

"On the contrary. But it is so." Pilgrim once again became practical. "On Friday night no one will occupy this box where we sit now. Perhaps I will be able to establish here an observation post. In one way or another I will be watching events closely. But I cannot interfere until you, who are now an established member of this time-frame, trigger the beacon for me."

"I bet."

If Pilgrim was perturbed by his agent's lack of enthusiasm he gave no sign, but pressed on. "Remember the white door that you opened to enter the vestibule outside these boxes. There is a corresponding door on the other side of the theater, through which Booth must pass on his way to destiny. When he has passed through that door, he will immediately block it against outside interference. You must pass through that doorway also, before he barricades it."

"How am I supposed to do that?"

"It is up to you to find a way. You might consider concealing yourself in the Presidential box ahead of time, or in the darkened vestibule just behind. But I do not think that approach would work."

"Thanks for the helpful advice. By the way, who is Colleen Monahan? Is she another of your conscripted agents?"

"Colleen Monahan does not, I devoutly hope, even

suspect that I exist. She is Secretary Stanton's agent, as she told you. And Stanton is Lincoln's loyal servant, according to his lights."

"Then I can trust her? Am I going to meet her again?"

"I can only guess at the answers to both questions, insofar as they depend upon the actions of individuals with free will. Certainly you must not trust her with any knowledge of my plans—or of your origins. Beyond that, it is your decision. Any other questions? I am going to have to leave you at any moment."

"Don't run off. Am I going to have a chance to talk to you again, before . . . ?" But Pilgrim was already gone. As on the train, his chair had emptied itself into thin air. Just like that.

A few moments later, feeling somewhat shaken, Jerry groped his way through the dim lobby downstairs and tapped on the half-closed office door. The voices inside, which had been still droning away, broke off as if startled.

A moment later the door was opened wide by a youthful-looking man with blue eyes, curly hair and large sideburns. He said in a salesman's voice: "You startled me, sir. What can we do for you?"

"The door to the street was open—I believe I may want some tickets, for Friday."

"Certainly, sir—how many tickets did you have in mind?"

"It would be a fairly large theater party." Jerry frowned as if in thought. "I wonder if I might have a look at the auditorium before I decide on a location."

"Well, we have a good selection of seats—seventeen hundred of them to choose from. By the way, I am John Ford, the owner."

"Jeremiah Flint."

"Pleased to meet you, Mr. Flint. You're from out of own?"

"Illinois."

"I see. This is Tom Raybold, who works for me." The second man in the office was standing up now, moving forward to shake hands. His face had something of an odd expression, as if he were afraid that it was going to start hurting at any moment. "Tom, why don't you show Mr. Flint the auditorium?"

"I'll see to it right away."

Jerry, standing in the doorway waiting for Tom Raybold to pull his coat on over his shirtsleeves, looked around the little office. On a table just in front of him was a litter of old playbills and posters, once in ordered stacks, now undergoing entropy. A printed name caught his eye as he glanced down, and he looked more closely. One of the bills, dated in March, advertised the notable actor John Wilkes Booth, starring in *The Apostate*. Unfortunately there was no picture.

A minute later Jerry was back in the auditorium, getting his second look at the place, this time with the official guidance of Tom Raybold, ticket seller and general executive aid.

Meanwhile another man, a carpenter with a thin brown mustache and thin short beard, had come into the cavernous space and was banging away at something near the foremost row of seats.

"Ned!" Raybold called out. "Are you going to have that finished before tonight?"

"Reckon I will." The man's voice wheezed with the tones of a lifelong drunk, though Jerry guessed his age at no more than an ill-preserved thirty. He went back to his hammering.

"I understand," said Jerry to Raybold, "that the President comes here sometimes."

"Oh, yes sir, he does indeed. Mr. Lincoln was here in attendance twice just last month, I do believe." And Raybold touched his jaw; he did indeed seem to have some kind of pain on the side of his face, a toothache maybe. Jerry could sympathize. He wondered what the dentists were like here. Did they even have anesthetics? Suddenly he was in abject terror of being trapped.

When he had mastered the pang of fear, and could again be sure that his voice was steady, he asked, over the sound of Ned's hammer: "Will he be here Friday, do you suppose?"

"I've no reason to think so, Mr. Flint. Of course sometimes he and his lady decide to come to the theater on short notice. And then—" The ticket-seller looked suddenly doubtful.

"What is it?"

"Well, you were asking about box seats. And if Mr. Lincoln *were* to come on Friday night, we would be unable to honor tickets for any of the other boxes. Out of respect for the President. We'd give you other tickets in exchange, of course, here on the main floor. Or up there in the front of the dress circle if you'd prefer." He pointed upward.

Jerry craned his neck, trying to see up into the dark first balcony from here. He could use another look at that part of the auditorium. "Might we go up and take a look?"

"Of course."

A minute later, standing again at the front of the first balcony, he surveyed the scene with slightly more knowledgeable eyes, thanks to Pilgrim's little lecture.

There were cane-bottomed chairs for the audience in this balcony, more than four hundred of them if Raybold had his numbers right. And it appeared that, in accordance with what Pilgrim had said, Booth would be compelled to pass this way to reach the President's box. On the right side of the dress circle, as you faced the stage, a narrow white door at the end of the front aisle gave access to the passageway that would run behind the two upper boxes on that side. That is, assuming the layout on the right was a mirror-image of the box seats Jerry had already visited on the left. Pilgrim had said it was. That white door was the one that Booth was going to block; the one that Jerry was going to have to get through before it closed behind the assassin.

"Do you mind," Jerry asked, "if I take a look into the boxes?"

"Certainly."

They went through the little white door, which opened inward and was unlocked. The lock looked broken; and Jerry could see no ready means of putting up a barricade. Inside was a gloomy passage just like the one on the other side of the stage where Jerry had met Pilgrim. The passage on this side led to the rear of Box 7 and Box 8. Here, as in the boxes on the opposite side, the gaslights over the stage shone in. The furnishings in the boxes were not impressive, except for a crimson sofa at the rear of Box 7.

Tom Raybold explained that when the President attended, and on certain other important occasions, the wooden partition dividing Boxes 7 and 8 was removed, converting them to one unit suitable for a large party. Then more comfortable chairs were brought in, some of them from Mr. Ford's own living quarters upstairs in the building. There was one particular rocking chair in which President Lincoln liked to sit.

There was no reason to prolong the tour any longer. Walking with Raybold back down to the lobby, Jerry announced, as if it had just occurred to him, that he thought he would take just two tickets for Friday night, in the dress circle, and organize his theater party some other time. Privately he decided that a man buying two tickets to any theater was less likely to attract attention than someone buying only one.

Aloud he explained that some of his companions might not be ready to go out for an evening of fun on Good Friday.

"And another thing," he added, "some of my friends have recommended a certain actor to me—John Wilkes Booth. I believe he has played here in the past?"

"Oh yes, certainly, a number of times. Everyone at Ford's knows Mr. Booth—he has his mail sent here sometimes. He's in town now, but he won't be on our stage Friday night. Can't say when he'll be in one of our plays again."

They had reached the ticket office, where there was no problem in buying two seats in the dress circle for Friday night—Jerry got the impression that the performance was a long way from being sold out.

As Raybold was showing him out of the theater, Jerry paused. "I would certainly like to meet Mr. Booth. When my sister back home heard that I was about to visit Washington, and that he might be here, she commissioned me to get his autograph."

Raybold smiled. "He's in town now. Staying at the National Hotel."

TWELVE

A minute later Jerry had got his directions from Tom Raybold and was on his way again, still traveling on foot. Four blocks east and four blocks south from Ford's Theater and he had found his goal, a long, five-story building of pale brick at the corner of Sixth and Pennsylvania.

The National was not quite as impressive a hotel as Willard's, or as crowded, but still it was imposing. The air in the lobby was somewhat more subdued and genteel, and when Jerry entered he heard Southern accents on every side.

The desk clerk made no difficulty about giving out the room number of John Wilkes Booth, and said that yes, the actor happened to be in. Jerry walked upstairs to find him.

When he stood before the door of the room, he could hear low voices inside, but was unable to distinguish words. When he tapped on the door they quieted immediately.

Then the door was opened six or eight inches by a man perhaps two or three years older than Jerry, who was immediately reminded of Pilgrim. Not by face, but by attitude. The well-dressed man in the doorway had something of an actor's presence, immediately perceptible. He was not large, except perhaps for his hands. Only an inch or two taller than Jerry, but erect and handsome, with black hair and a black luxurious mustache that contrasted with his pale skin.

"Mr. Booth?"

"Yes sir?" The voice was an actor's too, as suave and practiced as Pilgrim's, and soft if not exactly Southern. His manner was at once arrogant and courtly.

Jerry said: "My name is Jeremiah Flint. I wonder if I might trouble you for an autograph. If now is not a convenient time, I can certainly come back later. The truth is, I'm a visitor in Washington, and my sister rather firmly laid the duty on me of not leaving the city until I had at least tried . . ."

Booth was smiling tolerantly at him now. The door swung halfway open. Now Jerry caught a glimpse of a second occupant of the room, a large, dark-haired, strong-looking youth seated at a table, on which he drummed his fingers as if waiting impatiently for the interruption to be over.

The actor in the doorway said to Jerry: "We must make every effort not to disappoint the ladies—have you something you wish me to sign?"

"Yes I do, Mr. Booth, thank you. A playbill, if you don't mind." Jerry had picked it up before leaving Ford's, and produced it from his pocket now. "It would give Martha a great deal of pleasure. I know she has seen you on stage several times."

"Then we must do our best not to disappoint her. Step in, please."

Jerry entered the room, and followed Booth across to a small writing table, where the actor picked up a steel-nibbed pen and neatly opened a bottle of ink. Meanwhile the other man remained silently in his chair; when Booth glanced at him he immediately stopped drumming with his fingers.

Jerry watched the signing carefully. Booth's pale, well-manicured hands were large and strong, as if they had been meant for a man with a bigger body. A detail caught

Jerry's eye; there were the tattooed initials, JWB, near the branching of the thumb and forefinger on the right hand. A strange decoration for an actor to wear, he thought.

Less than a minute after he had entered the room, Jerry was out in the corridor again, the autographed playbill in hand, and Booth's door closed behind him. Jerry moved a step closer to the door, listening intently for a moment, but heard nothing. He retreated down the corridor.

In the lobby, he hesitated briefly at the door leading to the street, and then turned back. Buying a newspaper, he settled himself to read, in a chair from which he would be able to keep an eye on the main stairway. He was also close enough to the desk to have a good chance of hearing any name callers might ask for.

Jerry didn't think the other man in Booth's room was an autograph hound, and he certainly hadn't looked like an actor, at least not compared to Booth himself; too sloppy and somehow unkempt, though he had been well dressed. That, in Jerry's mind, left a great many possibilities open, including one in which the powerful-looking youth might be a co-conspirator. There might be other conspirators; damn it, he hadn't had the chance to go into any of that with Pilgrim. The two men up there now might be planning the assassination at this moment.

Jerry decided to hang around, on the chance that he might be able to learn something that would be of help. The fact was that he could think of nothing else to do just now that gave even the slightest promise of being useful.

Jerry lurked with his paper in the lobby for almost an hour before the tall, powerfully built man who had been with Booth appeared, coming downstairs alone. As Jerry had noted earlier, he was clad in respectable clothing, fairly new, but worn with a lack of attention to such things as fastenings and minor stains. Tall and muscular, moving with an unconscious catlike grace, Booth's companion looked neither to right nor left as he passed through the lobby, seeming totally unaware of Jerry watching him as he went straight out the door.

Jerry made himself wait for a count of three. Then he stood up and folded his paper, and, trying not to hurry, followed the other out of the lobby into the street. There was the tall form moving away from him.

Jerry followed. The effort might well, he supposed, be a complete and total waste of time, but still he was determined to give it a try, even though, for all he knew, he was tailing the president of the John Wilkes Booth fan club. Or perhaps a theatrical agent.

The quarry led Jerry up Pennsylvania to Seventh, then north for almost half a mile to H, then quickly around a corner.

Jerry followed without changing his pace, but now he was thinking furiously. Had the tall man realized he was being tailed; was this a ploy to shake his pursuer off, or draw him into a trap? He must have eyes in the back of his head if so, for he had never looked behind him.

Jerry in turn rounded the corner warily, just in time to see his quarry halfway up a long ascent of wooden stairs, about to enter the high first floor of a house of dingy brick. A young woman, a servant of some kind probably, was shaking a dustcloth out of a window on the ground floor of the house.

What now? Jerry could think of no reasonable excuse for stopping, so he kept on walking. He noted as he passed the house that the tall man had gone right in; and he noted the address also: 541 H Street. ROOMS TO LET, said a faded sign in another of the lower windows.

What now? Jerry didn't know. He made his way by a winding route back to his hotel, stopping in a couple of stores on the way to purchase a couple of new collars and shirts. How about a new suit? He could easily afford it. But he swore to himself that he was not going to be in this century long enough to need one.

Re-entering his hotel room after lunch, he half expected to find Pilgrim lounging there, waiting for him. But there was no one. Jerry stood at the window looking out upon an alien world. Well, Pilgrim had said that communication between timeframes wasn't easy.

Presently Jerry went out again. He spent most of the afternoon walking restlessly through this peculiar world and thinking about it, trying to familiarize himself more thoroughly with the way of life of its inhabitants. Within a few blocks of the house where Lincoln lived he noted some former slave-auction facilities, still identified as such by painted signs, but deserted now. Thank God, no one was still doing that kind of business in the capital. Ignoring a threat of rain, he wandered around the large perimeter of the White House grounds, until he was brought to a halt by the foul-smelling canal along their southern boundary. In the twentieth century, this area, Jerry seemed to remember, was occupied by a grassy mall.

He stood for a while beside the canal, marveling at the dismal stench of it, and how everyone around him put up with it so stoically. In summer it must be truly remarkable.

Presently he walked along the canal until he could cross it on a footbridge, and went to stand by the unfinished Washington Monument, observing that a kind of stockyard and open air slaughterhouse had been established at its base. Turning east, past grazing sheep, he looked at the red-roofed construction of the Smithsonian Institution, still confined here to one building, like some kind of vast elfin castle. He tried yet again to think of what else he might do to ready himself for Friday evening's confrontation, and he could think of nothing.

For variety, he dined away from Willard's. But shortly after dinner he was back in his room and sound asleep.

THIRTEEN

The next morning, Jerry awoke from a dreamless sleep thinking, *this is Thursday, April thirteenth. There will be no Friday the thirteenth this month.*

Only then did he react to the sound that had awakened him, a rough knocking on the door of his room.

It was broad daylight, time he was up anyway. He sat on the edge of his bed, reaching for his pants. "Who is it?" he shouted.

"Porter." The answering voice was muffled.

"Just a second." For a moment he had dared to entertain a foolish hope that it was Pilgrim, come to take him home or at least to bring him lifesaving information. Half-dressed, Jerry shuffled to the door and pulled it open.

As soon as the latch released, a force from outside pushed the door open wide, and sent Jerry staggering back. Two large men in civvies burst into the room. Each of them had Jerry by an arm before he could start to react.

"You're under arrest."

"What for?"

"Shut up." His arms were forced behind his back, and the handcuffs went on his wrists, painfully tight. Miranda rights were a long way in the future.

"At least you could let me get dressed."

They grudgingly agreed with that. One man watched him, glowering, while the other closed the door of the room, and searched. Bedclothes, the garments Jerry hadn't put on yet, the stuff in his closet, all went flying. It was a violent effort but it didn't look all that efficient.

At least, he thought, I've already managed to lose my pistol. But that was a foolish consolation. In this world carrying a firearm was no crime, and the mere presence of one probably wouldn't make anyone suspicious.

He was patted down for weapons, then the cuffs were removed and he was allowed to get dressed before being handcuffed again. As he tucked his watch into its pocket in his vest, he said: "You've got the wrong man."

"No we ain't."

"What's this all about?"

The older man, who had a graying mustache, was doing the talking for the pair. "Just walk out with us quietly, it'll be easier that way."

"Sure. But where're we going? I still don't know what this is all about."

He wasn't going to find out now. As soon as he was dressed they pulled him out into the hall and started down the stairs. One of the men locked Jerry's room behind him, and brought the key along.

On the stairs a couple of passersby looked at him and his escort curiously. As the three of them were passing swiftly through a corner of the lobby, on the way out a side door, a distraction at the other end of the lobby, near the front desk, turned all eyes in that direction. A wave of talk passed through the lobby.

"It's Grant!"

"General Grant is here!"

So much for the sophistication of the capital, that more or less took the presence of President Lincoln in stride; Jerry got the impression that Grant, the conquering hero, had rarely been seen in town before. What was he doing here now, away from his army? But why not, now that the war was virtually over. And was it possible that the General's presence in the city was going to have any effect on what happened at Ford's tomorrow night?

The only immediate effect on Jerry was that his departure from the hotel was probably noticed by no one at all.

Waiting just outside Willard's side entrance was a dark police wagon, with small windows of heavy steel mesh. Jerry was hustled immediately into it. A moment later the horses were being cursed and beaten into motion, and they were off. He could feel the wagon turn in the general direction of the Capitol.

The younger and larger of the prisoner's two escorts rode with him inside the wagon, and stared at him with heavy suspicion through the entire journey, saying nothing. Jerry responded by looking out the window, wondering how long the sudden emptiness in the pit of his stomach was going to last, how long it would take him to absorb his new reality. Maybe in a month, or even sooner, with the war officially at an end, Stanton—or whoever was having him arrested—would let him out of jail. He could set up selling petroleum, like Win Johnson back in Illinois. He—

Enough of that. He had an appointment he meant to keep at Ford's, tomorrow evening.

Pilgrim might be able to help. *Might*. Jerry had been warned against counting on any help at all from that direction. It was Pilgrim's fault that he was in this mess, and . . .

At this point it didn't really matter whose fault it was.

Jerry was seated on a wooden bench, and there was not much to see through the high windows of the wagon, except for some springtime treetops and the fronts of buildings. The ride took only a few minutes, and when Jerry was hustled out of the conveyance again at the end of it, he was able to catch a quick glimpse of the Capitol dome, quite near at hand.

The wagon had stopped very close beside one of the city's many large stone buildings; this one, by its heavily barred windows, was obviously a prison or police station. He noticed that here too, for some reason, his escort preferred to use the side entrance, off the busy street.

Once inside the gloomy fortress, the prisoner was conducted through one locked door after another. He was searched again, by the same men who had arrested him, and everything taken out of his pockets, including of course his money and his watch. His hat, coat, tie, and boots were also confiscated.

Ignoring his protests, the two men silently thrust Jerry into a small solitary cell. The door slammed shut.

Their footsteps in the corridor outside died away. Otherwise there was quiet.

His cell was lighted by one small window, more like a ventilator, too small for a man to squeeze through even if it had not been barred and positioned just below the eight-foot ceiling. For furniture there was a built-in wooden bench, and under the bench an empty bucket that smelled like what it was, an unsanitized latrine.

Jerry settled himself on the bench, stared at the door that was solid wood except for a small peephole, and waited for what might happen next. He was already convinced that it would be a waste of breath to send screams down the empty corridor outside.

He leaned his head back against the wall, realized it felt damp and slimy, and sat erect again. Presently he closed his eyes. Maybe when he opened them, Pilgrim would be sitting beside him on the bench, ready to give him another pep talk. Pilgrim gave the worst pep talks Jerry had ever heard, but he felt that he could use another one about now. But when Jerry opened his eyes again, he was still alone.

He wondered if the thugs who had arrested him were estimating the value of his watch, maybe arguing over who would get to keep it. Or did they plan to sell it and split the proceeds? Well, there was nothing that Jerry could do about it if they were. Nothing he could do about anything, not until someone opened the door to his cell. Which surely ought to happen soon.

The hours passed slowly in prison. The light from the window changed slightly, gradually, in its quality as the sun, somewhere on the other side of the building, made its unhurried way across the sky. He had until tomorrow night. Tomorrow night. Jerry warned himself to keep his nerve. Stanton—or whoever—couldn't possibly just leave him sitting here until then. Could he?

At a time Jerry judged to be somewhere around midafternoon, a jailer at last appeared, carrying a jug of water and two pieces of bread on a tin plate. The man was sullenly unresponsive to all questions, and disappeared again as soon as he had accomplished his delivery. Jerry drank gratefully, then chewed meditatively on the bread, thankful for his good, strong, heavily fluoridated twentieth-century teeth. As if drawn by the scent of food, a couple of mice now appeared in a far corner of the little cell, wriggling their noses. Maybe, their cellmate thought hopefully, the presence of mice was a sign that there would not be rats.

Maybe he was being too quiet, too stoic. When he had finished as much as he could chew of the bread, he went to the door with its half-open peep-hole and yelled at full volume down the hallway outside. From somewhere out there another series of maniacal yells echoed and mocked his own; evidently he was not, after all, the only prisoner in the building. But there was no other result.

He alternately paced his cell and sat down on the bench to rest. The hours passed. Nothing happened.

—and then Jerry, fallen asleep sitting on the wooden bench, awoke with a start in the darkness when a key rattled loudly in the lock of his cell's door. A moment later, the same two men who had arrested him came in, the younger of the two carrying a lantern.

Without a word of explanation Jerry was jerked to his feet, then hustled out of his cell and down the darkened corridor. The doors of other cells, whether occupied or empty, were all closed. The lantern made a moving, bobbing patch of light.

They took him down another dark stairway. Or maybe it was the same one by which he had been brought in, Jerry could not be sure.

When they had reached what Jerry thought was the ground floor, the two jailers brought him into an office, or at least a room containing some desks and chairs and filing cabinets. There was a notable absence of paperwork for a real office, and the place had a disused air about it. No one else was in the room. The lantern was put down on a desk which had an empty chair behind it, and Jerry was made to stand facing the desk.

On the wide, scarred wooden surface of the desk the things that had been taken from him had been laid out, except for the money, being notable only by its absence. There were Jim Lockwood's hat, and coat, and boots. There was Pilgrim's watch. When Jerry held his breath he was able to hear the timepiece ticking. There was the room key for his hotel, and there were his two theater tickets for tomorrow night.

When he stretched his neck just a little, he could see that the hands of the watch indicated a little after seven. The metal faceplate, though not the glass, had been swung open, as if someone had wondered whether something might be concealed inside.

For almost a minute after their arrival there was no sound in the room except for an occasional belch from one of the jailers, and the soft but substantial ticking of the watch. Presently a door behind the desk opened, and a man stepped through carrying a lighted lamp. He was hatless, dressed in dark, nondescript civilian clothes. In his late thirties, Jerry estimated. Sandy hair and beard. Only a little taller than Jerry but more powerfully built.

"Colonel," said one of the men behind Jerry. It was only a kind of verbal salute, for the sandy-haired one responded to it with a casual gesture of his right hand, after he had set down his lamp beside the lantern on the desk.

Unhurriedly the Colonel seated himself, adjusting both lamp and lantern so that he remained in comparative darkness, while a maximum amount of glare was directed toward the prisoner. The prisoner, accustomed to electric light, might under other circumstances have found laughable this attempt to make him squint.

Then the man behind the desk leaned forward in his chair, putting his blue-gray eyes and sandy whiskers in the light. When he spoke he came straight to the point. "Who're you really workin' for, Lockwood?"

"Sir, whoever you are, my name is Paul Pilgrim. I don't know why these men brought me——"

One of the men who was standing behind Jerry cuffed him on the back of the head, hard enough to make his ears ring. A hard voice behind him said, "Stow that. Give the Colonel a fair answer, or, by God, you'll wish you had."

The Colonel was smiling now, and this time his voice was confidential, almost warm and friendly. "Who're you workin' for?" he repeated. By this time Jerry had no doubt that this was Colonel Lafayette C. Baker. Right now Jerry was ready to settle for Stanton.

Jerry was also close enough to hysteria to imagine that he was able to see the humor in the situation. He had to laugh, and he did.

They let him laugh for a little while, the men standing behind him taking their cue from the appreciative grin on the Colonel's face. Jerry in turn appreciated their tolerance. After a while he got himself under control again and said: "I'm working for myself, if you want to know the truth."

Colonel Baker took his statement in good humor. "By God, ain't it the truth, though? Ain't we all doin' that?" He indulged in a chuckle of his own, then rubbed his bearded chin as if to mime the behavior of a deep thinker. "I'm all for adopting a philosophical viewpoint in these matters." His voice had become less countrified, as if adjusting to match Jerry's. "Yes, I'd go along with that." The Colonel's eyes altered. "Long as you realize, in turn, I mean to have a little more out of you than just philosophy."

"Oh, I'll tell you more than that," said Jerry, not wanting to get hit again. But even as he promised information, he was wondering just what sort he was going to provide. It certainly wasn't going to be the truth. There would be no safety for him in that.

"I know you will, son," said Baker in a kindly way. "Sometime tonight . . . say, don't I know you from somewhere? Ever been in San Francisco?"

"No sir."

"How 'bout the army?"

"No."

"Mebbe not. Don't suppose it matters." The sandy-haired man squinted at Jerry a little longer, then put out a hand on the desk and pushed most of Jerry's property, the hat and coat and boots and valuables, out of his way, toward one side. Then from the cluttered desktop Baker's hand picked up another item that Jerry had not noticed until now. It was, Jerry saw, slightly flexible, long as a rolling pin and almost as thick. The Colonel's fingers toyed with this cross between a club and a blackjack, turning it over, then rolled it gently back and forth on the worn wooden surface.

Jerry began to wonder whether the special talents Pilgrim had talked about might really save him if he was killed, or whether he and perhaps Pilgrim had dreamed them up. Of course he might come to wish he was dead, long before these people killed him.

The Colonel showed a few yellow teeth. Leering as if it might be the start of a dirty joke, he asked Jerry, "You know a woman calls herself Colleen Monahan?"

Jerry let himself think about that question. "No," he said at last, and wondered how long he was going to be able to stick to that.

"Goddam." The Colonel expressed an abstract kind of wonder, as if at some amazing natural phenomenon. "You're still thinkin' you can tell me lies and not get hurt for it." The man behind the desk marveled at such an attitude, as if he had never encountered any precedent for it. His manner and expression said that he was entering uncharted territory, and he was going to have to think a while before he could determine what best to do about it.

But of course there was only one thing to do about it, really. At last he took the truncheon in hand decisively and stood up and came around from behind the desk. Then he paused, as if suddenly aware that more thinking might be required. And then, meeting the eyes of his two henchmen and making a gesture, he silently indicated that he wanted them out of the room.

"Sir?" the one with the gray mustache questioned, doubtfully.

"Go on. I'll yell if I need help." And then without warning Baker swung his little club in a hard overhand stroke.

A perfect street-fighter's move; Jerry just had time to think. He also barely had time to get his arms up into a blocking position, fists clenched, forearms making a deep V, so that neither arm took quite the full force of the weighted weapon. The left arm took most of it, too much, high up near the wrist. Jerry felt first the numbing shock and then the pain; he was sure that a bone must have been broken. He collapsed helplessly to one knee, holding his wrist, eyes half-closed in a grimace of pain. *It's broken*, was all that he could think.

Dimly he was aware that the two henchmen, without further argument, had gone out of the room. Colonel Baker was locking the door behind them. Then he turned back to Jerry, as friendly-looking as ever.

"Now, Son Lockwood. Nobody but me is gonna hear it when you tell me who you and that bitch Monahan are really workin' for. I got my own reasons for confidentiality. Actually I know already, but I want to hear it from you. And I want to hear who else might be on my tail, workin' directly for the same person."

Jerry, gradually becoming able to see and think again, got to his feet. He backed away slowly as Baker advanced on him, gently swinging the club in his right hand.

There wasn't much room in this office to maneuver, forward, back, or sideways. And Jerry's left arm was useless whether it was actually broken or not. He couldn't, he absolutely couldn't, hit or grab or block anything with that arm just now. Not if his life depended on it.

He wasn't going to be able to block another blow from

that club, with either hand. He'd have to dodge instead. And then—

"You can't hide behind that desk, son. You can't hide at all. Know where I'm gonna put the next lick? Right in the kidneys. You'll piss blood for a month or so. And you'll *feel* the next one, too. That last one didn't hurt a-tall."

Jerry moved behind the desk, then out from behind it on the other side. The man was right, there was no use his attempting to hide behind the furniture. He shifted his feet, kicking aside a tobacco-stained little rug to make a smoother footing.

Baker, pleased to see this little preparation for some kind of resistance, was moving forward, supremely confident. "Tell you what, son—"

Jerry's roundhouse kick with the right foot came in horizontally under Baker's guard, at an angle probably unexpectable by any nineteenth-century American street-fighter. The ball of his foot took its target in the ribs. In practice Jerry had seldom kicked any inanimate target as hard as this; he thought from the feel of the impact that he might have broken bone.

Lafe Baker's bulging eyes bulged even more. The round red mouth above the ruddy beard opened wider, in an almost silent O of sheer astonishment.

Jerry stepped forward, shifting his weight, and fired his right hand straight at that bearded jaw. His victim was already slumping back, and down, and the punch connected under the right eye. Jerry could feel a pain of impact in his practice-toughened knuckles. Baker's backward movement accelerated. He hit his head on the side of his own desk as he went down, and his head clanged into the brass halo of the spittoon.

For a moment Jerry hovered over his fallen enemy, resisting the impulse to kick him again; the Colonel would not be getting up during the next five minutes. Baker's head rested against the side of the heavy desk, and the spittoon, half tipped over, made a hard pillow for him. The sandy beard was beginning to marinate in stale tobacco juice. Only an uneven, shuddering breathing showed the man was still alive.

A moment longer Jerry hovered over him indecisively, trying to think. Then he sprang to the desk and began to reclaim his belongings, putting on the clothes and stuffing the other items hastily into his pockets. No use, he thought, trying to find the money. The all-important watch was still ticking away serenely, and he kissed it before he tucked it into his watch pocket and secured the chain. And there, safely in his hands again, were the theater tickets for Friday night.

Now Jerry hesitated briefly once more. Was there something else?

On impulse he crouched over Baker once more, reaching inside the man's coat, coming up with a large, mean-looking revolver. He also discovered and abstracted a fat bunch of keys.

Dropping the keys in his own pocket, Jerry grabbed the Colonel by his collar and dragged him behind the desk where he would be a great deal less conspicuous. Then, with the revolver in his right hand held out of sight behind him, Jerry went to the door. He turned the lock— he found that he could use his left hand a little now, as long as he didn't think about it—and stuck his head out into the badly-lighted hallway.

A ragged black man carrying a mop and bucket went by, carefully seeing nothing. Two white men, leaning against the wall and chewing tobacco, looked at Jerry with real surprise.

Jerry looked back at them as arrogantly as he could and gave them a peremptory motion of his head. "He wants you both in here, right away."

The two of them filed in past Jerry, looking around them uncertainly for the Colonel, and Jerry closed the door on them when they were in. The two had reached a position near the desk by now, and in a moment they were turning around, about to ask him what the hell was going on.

At that point he let them see the revolver. "Just turn back and face the desk, gentlemen. That's it. Stand there. Just like that."

His blood was up, and he was acting with a ruthlessness that almost surprised himself. One after the other he tipped the men's hats forward from their heads onto the desk; one after the other he clubbed their skulls with the revolver barrel. The first victim, he of the gray mustache, sank to the floor at once. The younger man clung to the desktop, struggling against going down, and Jerry hit him again, a little harder this time.

He stuck the gun into his belt; he could hope that under his coat it would not be noticed. Then without looking back he let himself out of the room, and turned down the hallway to the left, in which direction he thought that he had glimpsed an exit. There was the black man with the mop, using it on the floor now, still seeing nothing. The pain in Jerry's left arm had abated to the merely severe, and he thought he might soon have feeling again in the fingertips. At best he was going to have one terrific lump on that forearm.

The back door of the prison was locked, with no latch to turn it open from inside; but one of the keys on Lafe's ring worked, letting Jerry easily out into the night. No one had taken note of his departure. It was still early in the evening, for the street lamps were still lighted.

There was the Capitol, its gaslighted dome glowing against the stars, to give a fugitive his bearings. His recovered watch ticked in his pocket. In a few hours Good Friday was going to begin.

Jerry started walking, anywhere to get away from the vicinity of the prison. One thing was sure, he couldn't go back to the hotel.

FOURTEEN

From now on Baker and his people were going to be hunting Jim Lockwood with all their energy. So would whatever forces Stanton and Colleen Monahan had available—and Stanton had armies at his command if he wanted to deploy them for that purpose. Jerry supposed that damned near everyone in the District of Columbia would be looking for him now, and he had to stay out of sight for approximately twenty-four hours before the play even started at Ford's. The task would be made no easier by the fact that every cent of his money had been taken from him. He swore under his breath, realizing only now that the men he had left unconscious would certainly have had some money in their pockets. Very likely *his* money. Well, it was too late now.

He had eased his left hand into a coat pocket, the better to nurse his throbbing wrist; he moved it again now, slightly, trying to find the easiest position. He was going to need help.

There was Pilgrim, of course. But Pilgrim had given him no active assistance at all up to this point, and Jerry saw no reason to expect that he would do so now. Nor was there any native of this century to whom Jerry could turn for help. He did not even know anyone here, unless he counted his new-made enemy Colleen Monahan . . .

But then Jerry, striding northward away from the prison, came almost to a full stop on the dark wooden sidewalk.

It was true that he had formed no alliances or even acquaintances here that might serve him now. But it was not true that he knew no one. There was one man he did know here in Washington, an able and resourceful and determined man who was no friend of Colonel Baker, or Secretary Stanton either. A man whom Jerry had scarcely met, but of whom he nevertheless had certain, deep, and important knowledge. Not very thorough knowledge, true, but in a sense quite profound . . .

It was not yet eight o'clock of a cool April evening when Jerry found himself standing in front of the boarding house on H Street. His first impulse on thinking of John Wilkes Booth had been to go directly to the National Hotel, but he had promptly rejected that idea. Any halfway competent counterintelligence system operating in Washington, including Baker's and/ or Stanton's, must have eyes and ears more or less continually present in each of the major hotels. He thought now that it had been foolish to try to stay at Willard's when those people were looking for him. Not that he had had a whole lot of choice, but it was surprising that he had gotten away with it as long as he had.

Lights were showing in several windows of the rooming house on H Street. The front of the house was dark at ground level, and so Jerry approached the building from the rear, where a couple of saddled horses were tied at a hitching post. Pausing on a walk of loose planks that ran close beside the house, he was able to look at close range into a lighted kitchen where a woman sat doing something at a table. He tapped on the door.

She was only a girl, really, he saw when she came to investigate his knocking. Dark-haired, not bad looking, no more than seventeen or eighteen. She had jumped up eagerly enough to answer the door, but looked warily at the strange man when she saw him. Evidently someone else had been expected.

"What do you want?" she asked in a cautious voice.

Jerry took off his hat, letting the girl get an unshaded look at what he hoped was an innocent, trustworthy face. He said urgently: "I want to talk to John Wilkes Booth. You must help me, it's very important."

Her caution increased, her face becoming masklike. "No one by that name lives here."

An older woman, small and rather grim-looking, came into the kitchen from the front of the house. Her lined face still bore a notable resemblance to the girl's. "What's going on, Annie?"

The girl turned with relief. "Ma, this man says he wants Wilkes Booth."

Jerry was leaning against the doorframe, letting his weariness and the signs of prison show. He appealed to them both: "Can you let me come in and sit down? I've been hurt." He raised his left forearm slightly, easing his hand out of the coat pocket, then let it hang down at his side.

The older woman studied him for a moment with shrewd, calculating eyes. "Come in, then. Annie, get the gentleman a cup of water."

"Thank you, ma'am."

Seated at the kitchen table, Jerry could hear other voices, men's voices, coming from the front of the house, where they must be sitting talking in the dark. Annie put a tin cup of water on the table in front of him, and he drank from it thirstily.

Now another young woman appeared from the direction of the front room, to look briefly into the kitchen before retreating. She was succeeded in the doorway by a figure that Jerry somehow recognized—yes, it was the whiskey-marinated carpenter from Ford's. Tom Raybold in the auditorium had called this man Ned. The next face in the parade was even more quickly recognizable. It was that of the powerful, sullenly handsome youth who had been visiting Booth in his hotel.

This man shouldered his way forward into the kitchen, to stand close beside the table looking down at Jerry. His voice when he spoke to the visitor was southern-soft, though not as friendly as that of Colonel Baker: "Who are you? And why should you think that Wilkes Booth is here?"

"My name is Jeremiah Flint. I thought he came here sometimes."

"And if he did?"

"I have reason to think—to think that Mr. Booth might be disposed to help a gentleman who has got himself into some serious trouble with the abolitionists who are now in control of this city."

There was a silence in the kitchen. But it was not a shocked silence, Jerry thought. Not for nothing had he spent those long days and nights on railroad cars, listening to arguments among people of every shade of political persuasion.

The tall young man leaned forward suddenly, a move not exactly menacing but still pantherish, shot out a hand and extracted the pistol from Jerry's belt. "You won't be needin' that in here," he explained mildly.

"I trust I won't." Jerry spoke just as softly. He tried to smile. "I don't believe I find myself among the friends of Old Abe at the moment."

"There are no friends of tyrants here."

This was in a new voice, resonant and easy to remember. Jerry turned to face the doorway. There was the actor himself, elegantly dressed, standing with a hand on each side of the frame and regarding Jerry with a slight frown.

Booth went on: "I believe I have encountered you somewhere before, sir."

"Jeremiah Flint of Texas, Mr. Booth. We met at your hotel yesterday, and you were good enough to autograph a playbill for my sister."

"Ah yes."

"I might have spoken to you of other matters then, but you were not alone; you were engaged with this gentleman, whose identity I did not know." Jerry nodded at the tall youth beside him. "Since then I have been arrested. Early this morning, at my own hotel, Willard's. Today I was kept all day in prison. Beginning this evening I was questioned by someone I believe to be Colonel Lafayette C. Baker himself. I managed to get away, but not without giving and receiving some slight damage." He raised his left arm gingerly. When the sleeve fell back a little, an empurpled lump the size of a small egg showed on the side of his wrist. He could feel another, smaller, on the back of his head, and he was ready to present it as additional evidence if needed.

"How could you get away?" This, in a disbelieving voice, came from the older woman.

Jerry turned to her with what he hoped was a frank and open gaze. "It sounds incredible, I know. They— Baker and two of his men—had me in a jail somewhere near the Capitol. I was brought in through a side entrance, and when the chance came I walked out the same way. I have the feeling that most of the people there did not know of my presence, or the Colonel's either. I even had the impression that he himself might have been in that building secretly. We were quite apart from the other officers and prisoners there." He sipped at the cup of water the girl had now put down in front of him.

"Were you followed here?" the woman demanded sharply.

"Madam, I am certain that I was not."

"What did they want of you?" Booth asked. He had folded his arms now, and his eyes were probing at Jerry relentlessly.

"The names of some of my friends in Texas. But they learned nothing."

"And how did you manage to escape?"

"Baker—if it was he—sent his men out of the room in which he had begun to ask me questions. Evidently he hoped to hear from me something that he wanted to keep secret even from his own men. He thought he had already—disabled me." Jerry raised his left arm gingerly. "But it turned out he had not."

Something, a spontaneous mixture of envy, admiration, and despair, blazed for a moment in Booth's face; but he masked his feelings quickly and stood silent, thinking.

"I had heard," the older woman said, "that Baker was currently in New York."

"What," asked Booth, "did this interrogator look like?" When Jerry had described the man behind the desk, the actor commented thoughtfully: "That does sound like Lafe Baker himself. But I too had heard that he was in New York." He paused, creating a moment full of stage presence and effect. "So you are from Texas, Mr. Flint. May I ask, without probing into any private matters, what you are doing now in Washington?"

Jerry took a deep breath. He had anticipated this question, but still he thought his answer over carefully before he gave it. He was reasonably sure that these people did not really believe his story—yet. Much was going to depend upon his answer, and he was trying to remember something that Jan Chen had told him.

"I consider myself," he answered finally, "a soldier of the Confederacy, seeking upon my own responsibility to find what duty I can do here for my cause." And he dug in the side pocket of his coat—slowly and carefully, with the strong lad and Booth both watching—and brought out a heavy bunch of keys.

Jerry tossed them with a jingling thud onto the middle of the kitchen table. "Those," he added, "are Lafe Baker's. I have not examined them closely, but they may bear some evidence of ownership."

The strong man grabbed up the keys, then stood holding them in his hand, not knowing what to do next. Booth scarcely looked at the keys. His lips had parted slightly when he heard Jerry's answer. Again envy and admiration crossed the actor's face, this time mingled with awe rather than despair; it was as if he had just heard Revelation. Again the expression did not appear to have been calculated. He stood silent, staring at Jerry and making new assessments.

"Or else," said the older woman to Jerry, in a still-suspicious voice, "you are one of Pinkerton's agents. Or—" She had begun now to look closely at the keys in the young man's hand, and something about them evidently proved convincing. Her tone of accusation faltered.

"Pinkerton," said Booth sharply, "has been in New Orleans for a long time, out of the business more than a year. No, look at Mr. Flint's injury. I think he is an authentic hero for having achieved such an escape, and we cannot refuse to help him." He became courtly again. "Introductions have been delayed, but let us have them now. Mr. Flint, this is Mrs. Surrat, the kindly landlady of this establishment. And this is her lovely daughter, Anna." Anna, flustered, tried to curtsy.

Next Booth nodded toward the powerful young man. "My good friend and associate, Lewis Paine."

Jerry's good right hand was almost crushed in a silent handshake from the youth. Meanwhile Booth went on:

"And my acquaintance Mr. Ned Spangler, who works as a sceneshifter at Ford's. Mrs. Surrat, Anna—Mr. Flint deserves the best of hospitality. What is there to eat?"

"He's welcome to a supper." Mrs. Surrat began to bestir herself, then paused. "But he can't hide here. There's no place for him to sleep."

Booth started to frown, then appeared to be amused. "Very well, I'll find another place for him. Lewis, show the gentleman where he can wash up."

"Right, Cap'n."

Ten minutes later Jerry, having removed some of the scum of prison from his face and hands, was back at the table in the kitchen, whose windows were now securely curtained against any observation from outside. Pork chops and greens and fried potatoes were put before him on a tin plate, and he needed little urging to dig in. Paine leaned in a doorway, heavy arms folded, watching Jerry eat; Spangler and young Anna had both disappeared. Booth, an enameled cup of steaming coffee in front of him, rose from the chair opposite Jerry's to welcome him back.

"I suppose—" Booth began, then turned his head sharply, listening; held up a hand for silence.

Mrs. Surrat, at the sink, glanced at him but then went on rattling pans in water. Evidently the landlady here was used to conspiratorial maneuvers.

"Who was that?" Booth asked in a low voice of Spangler, who was just coming in from the front room.

"Only Weichmann." Ned stood blinking at them all stupidly; he had brought fresh whiskey fumes into the kitchen with him.

"Who's Weichmann?" Jerry asked.

"A young War Department clerk," Booth informed him in low voice, turning back to face the table, "who boards here. I fear his sympathies are not with us, though he's an old friend of the landlady's son."

Mrs. Surrat turned from the sink, drying her hands on a towel, evidently willing to leave the dishes soaking until tomorrow when presumably there would be kitchen help. She looked at Jerry, and for the first time favored him with a trace of a smile. "You will wish to get out of Washington, I suppose."

"Yes. When I am satisfied that . . . that there is nothing more for me to do here, yes." Jerry nodded. He had turned to face Mrs. Surrat, but he was aware of Booth watching him keenly. *Only twenty-four hours*, Jerry was thinking. *I must have that much more time, free, here in the city. When I am through at Ford's, whatever the outcome there, then all of these people can go—*

Mrs. Surrat asked him: "Where will you want to go?"

Jerry allowed his face to show the weariness he felt. "A good question. I'm afraid that I no longer have any country left."

Lewis Paine, leaning in the doorway, shook his head in gloomy agreement. Booth actually let out a small cry, as of pain; but when Jerry turned to look at him the actor, his face a study in tragedy, was nodding agreement too. "Now that Lee has surrendered . . ." Booth allowed his words to trail off.

What would another good Confederate fanatic say to that? "Lee could not help it," Jerry protested. "He had to surrender, to save his men from useless slaughter."

Booth was looking at Jerry as intently as before, as if hoping against hope to hear from him words that would mean salvation. "I know he could not help it; but now his army has disappeared. Richmond is lost, the government dissolved. Where will you go?"

"I mean to find General Johnston," Jerry declared stoutly. "In Carolina. We can go on fighting in the mountains."

Booth looked as if he might be envious of this heroic dedication. Certainly he was moved by it—though evidently not to the extent of being ready to emulate it himself. "I wish I could come with you," the actor announced wistfully, and for a moment Jerry feared that his stratagem might after all be about to damage history beyond repair.

But only for a moment. Booth continued: "But alas, I cannot. Matters of even greater moment hold me here."

"I'm sure they do, sir." Jerry's reply was so promptly spoken and came with such obvious sincerity that Booth was gratified.

The actor sipped at his coffee, made a face, and stood up suddenly. "I will write you a note," he declared, "to present to a friend of mine. When you are finished, come into the dining room." But then he suddenly changed his mind and resumed his seat. "Never mind," he amended. "Take your time. When you have eaten, I will take you there myself."

Young Anna had returned now, with warm water in a basin, and a collection of bandages and unlabeled jars containing what Jerry presumed were household remedies. She began tending to his arm, which required that he first take off his coat. The old knife-cut in the sleeve, usually inconspicuous, became for the moment plainly visible.

Booth impulsively got to his feet, taking his own coat off. "If you would honor me, sir, by wearing mine. We appear to be of a size."

"That's not necessary, Mr. Booth."

"I repeat, I would be honored, sir, to have you accept it from me." There was a proud, almost threatening urgency in the actor's voice.

"In that case, sir, I shall be honored to accept."

Soon after Jerry had finished his supper, and thanked his hostess with what he hoped was sufficient courtesy, he and Booth set out upon the darkened street. Dogs in nearby yards barked at them mindlessly, undecided between offering greetings or challenge. Jerry now had an evil-smelling poultice bandaged to his left wrist, and was wearing Booth's coat. The garment, of some beautiful soft tan fabric, was a little loose in the shoulders but otherwise fit its new owner well enough. Booth meanwhile had somewhat gingerly put on Jerry's coat.

Hardly had the kitchen door of Surrat's boarding house closed behind them when Jerry recalled that the man called Paine, inside, was still in possession of his, or rather Baker's, pistol. But Jerry said nothing. He wasn't going to go back and ask for the weapon; he had never really trusted himself with firearms and in fact was rather relieved to be without it.

"It is only a few blocks to your lodging for the night," Booth had informed him courteously when they had reached the street. "If you are quite able to walk?"

"Food and rest have marvelously restored me. Food and rest, and a sense of being among friends once again. Please lead on."

They trudged west on H Street, Booth whistling a slow tune softly, and soon passed the imposing structure

of the Patent Office. A conversational silence grew.
Jerry kept expecting to be asked more details of his
escape, but it was not to be. Perhaps Booth was jealous
of the daring feat; or, perhaps, absorbed in his own
plans.

Just when they had left the Patent Office behind, the
streetlights dimmed suddenly, brightened again briefly,
dimmed and then went out.

"Nine o'clock," Booth commented succinctly, striding
on. There was still some faint light from the sky, and
the occasional spill of illumination from the window of
a house. Enough light to see where you were going,
generally, if you were not too particular about what your
boots stepped in.

Somewhere, not too far away, black-sounding voices
were raised in a hymn. The April night was very mild.
Summer here, thought Jerry, must be ungodly hot. He
could remember it that way from his trip in the nineteen-
seventies.

Now Booth as he walked was pulling something out
of his pocket, passing it to Jerry. "Brandy?"

"Thank you." Jerry took a small nip and passed the
flask back. They walked on, Jerry listening, thinking, or
trying to think. Tomorrow night, less than twenty-four
hours from now, he was quite possibly going to have to
do something nasty to this generous assassin who walked
beside him now. Or Booth would do something nasty to
him. He, Jerry, would not be able to do much to anyone
else in Ford's Theater tomorrow, he supposed, without
derailing history.

Now Booth was saying in a low confiding voice:
"Tomorrow, when you have rested, I should like to have
a confidential talk with you. On the subject of what the
true duty of a Confederate ought to be, at this time, in
this city."

"I shall be glad to have that talk, Mr. Booth. But I shall be better able to give it the attention it deserves if I get some sleep first."

"Of course." They paced on another quarter of a block before Booth added: "It is difficult, in this city, for a man who has a great enterprise in mind to find someone reliable to work with."

Jerry made an effort to change the subject. 'Where are we going?"

"To a certain house on Ohio Street, where they know me well. I am sure any friend of mine will be graciously received there."

They had passed Ninth Street by now and had come to Tenth, where Booth turned left. Ahead, the street was bright with private gaslights; Jerry realized that the path the actor had chosen for them was going to take them directly past Ford's Theater.

Tonight's performance was evidently not over yet, for both sides of the street in the vicinity of the theater were solidly parked with waiting carriages. A couple of taverns in the same block were doing a good business, various drivers and servants passing the time inside while they waited for their employers.

"Perhaps I will be recognized here," Booth muttered, as if to himself. "But it doesn't matter." He squared his shoulders and strode on bravely in Jerry's soiled and knife-torn coat, which fit him imperfectly.

Two more blocks south on Tenth Street, and they had passed the theater, without any sign of Booth's being recognized. At that point Jerry's guide crossed the Avenue, then turned right. Again Jerry had caught a glimpse of the White House in its park; again it seemed to him that nothing of any consequence in this city could be more than a few blocks from anything else.

Booth as he walked resumed his grumbling about his associates, still without naming any names. He could find one bright spot, though. "Paine, of course, has demonstrated his coolness and ability. He rode with Mosby in the valley, before he was captured and had to give parole."

Jerry could vaguely recall hearing of a Confederate guerrilla leader named Mosby. "Yes, Paine struck me as one who might be counted on in a pinch."

"Yes." Booth was sad again. "O'Laughlin—you haven't met him yet—is the only other one of the group with any military experience, and that no more than trivial."

Still it must be more than you have yourself, thought Jerry. The actor was obviously young, healthy, athletic. Jerry had seen and heard enough in this world to be sure that no one was kept out of the army—any army— for any such triviality as a perforated eardrum, say. So Booth could have been with Lee if he'd wanted to. Or be could be still fighting at this moment, with Johnston. But he had obviously chosen to remain a well-paid civilian, living and working in the North. An interesting point, but certainly not one that Jerry was going to bring up aloud.

A few more blocks and they had reached their goal, a large wooden structure on Ohio Street, set back in a deep, wide lawn behind an iron fence, and surrounded by tall trees already leafed for spring. Jerry, looking at the size of the building and the number of lighted, red-curtained windows it possessed, remembered suddenly that Booth had spoken of their destination as a "house." Now Jerry realized that the actor hadn't meant a home.

They entered the house—how else, thought Jerry?— through an inconspicuous side door. Farther back there stood a long hitching rail where enough horses were currently parked to outfit a squadron of cavalry. The music of a violin, playing something quick and sprightly, could be heard from somewhere inside.

A middle-aged woman elaborately gowned and made up, greeted Booth as an honored old friend. On second glance the proprietress was considerably younger than a first impression indicated, the cosmetics being evidently a kind of badge of office deliberately intended to add years.

Booth squeezed the lady's right hand in both of his. "Bella, I would be happy if you could do something for a friend of mine, Mr. Smith here. He finds himself for one reason and another—it is altogether too long and tedious a story to tell it now—he finds himself, I say, temporarily but drastically bereft of lodging. It would be a fine and Christian act if you were to provide him with a bed for the night—on my account, of course."

Jerry, increasingly dead on his feet after a day of imprisonment, fight and flight, had taken off his hat and stood looking around him numbly. On a sideboard nearby lilacs, in a crystal bowl with other flowers, helped to fight off the presence of the nearby canal.

"Only a bed?" Bella wondered aloud, looking Jerry over and automatically taking a professional attitude. She could hardly have failed to notice that Mr. Smith and Mr. Booth had switched coats, but she was not going to say anything about it.

Booth was lighting a cigar, forgetting his manners so far as not to offer Jerry—or Bella—one. "A bed," said the actor, "is a minimum requirement. You will have to ask Mr. Smith what else he might enjoy. All on my account, as I have said."

"Of course." Bella, having come to a decision, smiled

at them both, and patted an arm of each. "Leave everything to me."

They were still in the entry hall. A stair with a gilded rail ascended gracefully in candlelight nearby, and now someone, a blond young woman in a silvery gown, was coming down that stair. The actor's eyes lighted, and he bowed gravely at her approach.

"I thought I heard a voice I recognized," the blond woman almost whispered, resting a hand familiarly on Booth's shoulder. Then she brushed at the shoulder, frowning as a wife might frown at some domestic disaster. "Wilkes, what's happened to your coat?"

"Later we can discuss that, my dear Ella." Booth patted her hand in an almost domestic way. "Mr. Smith, I shall call for you in the morning, when you have rested." He gave Jerry a meaningful look, and a hard, parting handgrip upon the shoulder—thoughtfully remembering that the right arm was the good one. "There is much that we have to discuss."

Jerry mumbled something in the way of thanks. Then the proprietress had him by the arm and was steering him away toward the rear of the house, giving orders to black servants as she passed them, in the way that someone of the late twentieth century might push buttons on a computer.

Now he was given into the care of the servants, who sized him up, welcomed him with professional sweetness, and worked on him efficiently, without ever seeming to look at him directly. In a matter of seconds they were leading him into a room where a hot bath waited, that seemed to have been prepared for him on miraculously short notice. He wondered if they kept a steaming tub ready at all times, in case a customer should feel the need of cleansing.

Two teenaged black girls wearing only voluminous white

undergarments—voluminous at least by twentieth-century standards—introduced themselves as Rose and Lily. The pair, who looked enough alike to be twins, helped Jerry get his clothes off, and saw him installed in the tub. Lily, who helped him ease off his coat and shirtsleeves, shook her head at the sight of his arm. Frowning at Anna Surrat's amateurish poultice, she peeled it off and threw it into a slop jar. The lump on his wrist was bigger and uglier than ever, and the arm still pained him all the way down into the fingers, but Jerry was beginning to hope that it wasn't really getting worse; the injury might not be all that much worse, really, than some batterings his forearms had received in practice.

With a show of modest smiles and giggles his attendants helped him—he didn't need help but he was too tired to argue—into the tub, where he sat soaking his hurts away, along with the smell and feel of prison. Presently Lily went out, she said, to get some medicine. Meanwhile Rose dispatched another servitor with orders to bring Jerry a platter of cold chicken and asparagus spears, along with a glass of wine.

Waiting for food and medicine, he leaned back in the tub, eyes closed.

Delicate fingers moved across his shoulder and his chest. Rose evidently viewed him as a professional challenge. "Like me t' get in the tub and scrub you back? Bet ah could fit right in there with you. Might be jes' a little tight."

He opened his eyes again. "Ordinarily I would like nothing better. Tonight . . . I think not."

She rubbed his shoulders therapeutically. "If you change yoah mind, honey, just say the word."

Jerry closed his eyes again. All he could think about was what was going to happen tomorrow night, when someone was very likely to get killed.

If he looked at it realistically, he himself was a good candidate. Probably the best, besides Lincoln himself. Perhaps the best of all. Oh, of course, he had been assured that he had his special powers. What had Pilgrim said? *Not ordinary danger, even of the degree that you confronted on the train. It might be more accurate to say that only death itself can activate them.* Getting killed would be hardly more than a tonic stimulus. He wished he could believe that.

He ducked his head under the water and began to wash his face and hair. Lily, back again, giggling, rinsed his head with warm water from a pitcher. Then Jerry's food arrived, the tray set down on a small table right beside the tub, and he nibbled and sipped. His spirits rose a little.

After a little while, when the water had begun to cool, he made motions toward getting out of the tub. The two girls, who were still hovering as caretakers, surrounded him with a huge towel. When they were sure he was dry, the one playing nurse anointed his arm again, with something that at least smelled much better than the previous ointment.

Having put on the most essential half of his clothing, Jerry gathered the rest under his arm, making sure as unobtrusively as possible that he still had his watch and theater tickets with him. He bowed slightly to his two attendants. "And now, if you would be so kind as to show me where I might get some rest?"

It was nearly midnight by Pilgrim's watch when they escorted him to a small room, with a small bed. There was some tentative posing in the doorway by his attendants on their way out, but he let his eyelids sag closed and shook his head. When the door had closed he opened his eyes and found himself alone.

There was the bed. Jerry lay down with his boots on,

meaning to rest for just a moment before he undressed. Somewhere the violin was playing, almost sadly now.

He awoke in pale gray dawn to the sound of distant battering upon a heavy door and angry voices shouting that the police were here.

SIXTEEN

Jerry rolled out of bed, looking groggily for his boots.
Only when his feet hit the floor did he realize that he
still had the boots on; hastily he donned shirt and coat—
Booth's coat. He had slept through most of the night
without taking off anything that he had put on after his
bath. He picked up his hat now from where it had fallen
on the floor, and put it on his head.

The banging and the shouting from below continued,
augmented now by several octaves of screaming female
voices. Jerry thought he could recognize Lily's generous
contralto. Most of the noise was coming from the front
of the house.

Taking stock of the situation, Jerry decided that if he
were in charge of conducting a police raid, he'd surely
have people at the back door before he started banging
on the front. Dimly realizing that he was somehow not
quite the same Jeremiah Flint who had driven into
Springfield looking for a job, he concluded that with a
house as tall as this one, and with so many trees around
it, quite possibly all was not lost. Jerry was already opening
the single window of his room. A moment later he had
stepped out over the low sill, onto a sloping section of
shingled roof, his appearance startling a pair of frightened
robins into flight. Peering over the edge of the roof at
shrubs and grass below, he confirmed that he was about
three stories over the back yard.

There were plenty of tree branches within reach; the only question was which one of them to choose. In a moment Jerry had got hold of a limb that looked sturdy enough to support him, and had swung out on it. He had left the roof behind before it occurred to him to wonder whether his left wrist was going to be able to support its share of his weight. He looked down once; his wrist, impressed on a cellular level by the distance to the ground, decided it had no choice but to do the job.

Hand over hand Jerry progressed painfully toward the trunk. He wasn't going to look down again. He shouldn't have looked down even once. Instead he would concentrate on something else. What kind of tree was this, an elm?

Eventually, after six or eight swings, alternating handholds, he was close enough to the trunk to be able to rest his feet upon another branch. Now he could look down again, and did. Men in derby hats, three or four of them or maybe more with pistols in their hands, were swarming through the yard below. They appeared to be running from front to back and back to front again. So far the raiding party seemed to be trying everything but looking up. The new spring leaves sprouting between those men and their potential victim in the tree were thin and fragile, and so was the screen they made; silently Jerry urged them to grow quickly.

Edging his way toward the trunk, he reached it at last and went around it—this far above the ground the stem was slender enough for him to embrace it easily. The next step was to choose a direction and start out, one booted foot after another, along another branch, meanwhile still gripping upper branches to keep his balance. His chosen course was going to take him toward the alley that ran in back of the house, and was divided

from the back yard by a tall wooden fence. The fence
had a long wooden privy butting up against it, the planks
of both constructions being freshly whitewashed, as if
Tom Sawyer lived here.

Now, with a sinking feeling, Jerry became aware of the
fact that there were people sitting on horses out there
in the alley, their faces upturned in his direction.

This discovery made him pause, but, after considering
the alternatives, he pressed on. One of the people who
so silently observed his progress was a chestnut-haired
young woman, wearing trousers underneath her full skirt,
who sat astride her horse like a man.

The branch under Jerry's boots grew ever more slender
the farther he got from the trunk, and bent ever lower
with his weight. The higher branches that he clutched
at with both hands were bending too. Now Jerry's boots
were no more than five feet or so above the slanting,
tar-papered privy roof. A goat, tethered in the yard near
the back fence, was looking upward with deep interest
at Jerry's acrobatics.

By now the branches bearing his weight had sagged
enough so that he was partially screened, by tall hollyhocks
and bushes, from the back door of the house. In that
direction cries of triumph and screams of outrage signalled
that the police had at last managed to force entry. With
relief Jerry released his hold on the branches, half-
stepping, half-falling to the roof of the outhouse. He would
not have been surprised to put a leg through the roof of
the privy and get stuck, or—God forbid—plunge to the
very depths. But no, the wood beneath his boots was
solid.

And a good thing, too. He had just begun his next move,
a vault over the fence and into the weed-grown alley when
a gunshot sounded from the direction of the house, and
a bullet went singing over his head.

Then he was on his feet in the alley. Colleen Monahan and two men, all three of them mounted, were with him, and someone was urging an unoccupied horse in front of him. All Jerry could remember about riding was that for some reason you had to get on from the left side; not that he had ever tried to get aboard a horse before. He wasn't doing very well at it now.

"He's hurt," Colleen was saying sharply, mistaking his clumsiness for weakness or physical disability. "You, give him a hand!"

Somehow Jerry was pulled and pushed up into the saddle. He had barely got his feet into the stirrups when they were off, heading down the alley at what felt to him like a gallop. More gunshots sounded, somewhere behind them.

Another horse and rider were close beside Jerry on each flank, and someone was holding his mount's reins for him. Bouncing fiercely up and down, he clung to the front of the saddle, where there was supposed to be a horn, wasn't there?—no, he had read somewhere that only western saddles were so equipped.

Coming out of the alley, the four riders thundered southeast on Ohio Avenue, then across one of the iron bridges that crossed the foul canal, leading them into the half-wild Mall. To the west, on their right, the truncated Washington Monument rose out of the morning fog, balanced by the bizarre towers of the Smithsonian a few hundred yards to the east. Fog was rolling north from the Potomac now, coming in dense billows, and once they were a hundred yards into the Mall Colleen called a halt.

The small party sat their horses, listening for immediate pursuit. One of the men with Colleen was black and one was white. Both were young and poorly dressed; Jerry decided that he had never seen either of them before.

"Nobody comin'," the black man said after they had been silent a while. He appeared to be unarmed, though the white youth had a pistol stuck in his belt. The horses snorted and shifted weight restlessly, ready for more early morning exercise.

"They'll be looking," said Colleen. Her frivolous little lady's hat had fallen back off her head with the riding, but was still held by a delicate cord around her sturdy throat. She looked at Jerry with what he read as a mixture of sympathy and despair. "How bad are you hurt? Did they hit you back there?"

He realized she was talking about the gunshots, and shook his head. "I'm bruised, that's all. From talking to Lafe Baker. But I don't think I can ride very far."

"All right." She gave the white youth a commanding stare. "Ben, ride back to the War Department, learn what you can—then report back to me."

The young man—he really was very young, maybe sixteen, Jerry saw now—nodded. He started to speak, evidently found himself inarticulate, and departed with a kind of half-military salute to her and Jerry.

Colleen turned to the young black. "Mose, take the rest of these horses and put 'em away. Then return to your regular job. Baker's people will be looking for a mounted group, so Jim and I will travel on foot."

She swung down out of her saddle, the long skirt immediately falling into place to cover up her trousers. Jerry dismounted also, without waiting to be urged. It proved to be a lot easier than getting on.

"Yas'm." Mose looked Jerry in the face steadily for a long moment, as if he were seeking to memorize his features, or perhaps to find something; it was the most direct gaze Jerry had received from a black person since his arrival in this era. Then Mose dismounted too, gathering all of the horses' bridles into his hands.

With a motion of her head Colleen led Jerry eastward through the mist. When they had walked twenty yards through the long grass of the Mall, Mose and the horses were already invisible behind them.

"So it's bruised you are, is it?" she asked, looking sideways at him as they moved on. "I hear that Lafe Baker himself is bruised this morning, a great black shiner underneath one eye."

"I expect he is. But how did you find out?"

"I have my ways of knowing things. Men, you may have noticed, often don't take a woman seriously. The colonel might have gone back to New York by now, I don't know. Well, you're a strange man, Jim Lockwood, but it appears that in some ways you can be a marvel."

"You'd better watch out for Baker," Jerry warned her grimly. "He asked me if I knew you. I told him no, but . . ."

"I've got my eye on him, never fear. When I heard he was planning to raid Bella's this morning, I thought it just might have something to do with you. And if anything happens to me, Mr. Stanton'll know who to blame. Let's try going this way."

For a moment Jerry wondered if he had been followed after all. But he was sure he'd gotten away unnoticed. One of Booth's people? He gave the problem up as unsolvable.

The single impressive building of the Smithsonian was close before them now, a dream-castle of reddish stonework rising out of mist, longer than a football field and topped by a profusion of mismatched towers. Here paths had been built up with gravel above the level of the ubiquitous mud. In this area the grass was shorter and better cared for, and spring flowerbeds surrounded the building with early blooms.

A bench loomed out of the fog. Jerry sighed. "No one's chasing us right now. How about sitting down for a minute? I suspect I'm going to have to do a lot of running yet today."

"And I suspect you're right."

They settled themselves on the park bench, side by side, as any strolling couple might. "Colleen. Why did you think the raid on Bella's might have something to do with me?"

"Wilkes Booth's doxy lives there, when he's not entertaining her at his own hotel. She's Bella's sister, by the way. And for some reason he's also in thick with those folk at Surrat's boardinghouse. I know you went there, but I don't know why. Are you going to tell me?"

"You knew I went there? How?"

"I tell you, I can find out things. What were you doing mixed up with those people? Someone in the War Department, I'm told, had a report six weeks ago that they might be up to no good."

Jerry leaned back on the bench, groaning quietly, trying to think. He could feel the history he was supposed to protect slipping out of his grasp like a handful of water. And he was acutely aware that Colleen was watching him intently.

When he spoke it was without looking at her. "Sorry about running out on you like that."

"I was wondering when you would get around to an apology. And I'm lookin' forward to hearing the best story you can come up with to explain what you did."

"And I don't know if I can explain something else to you. I mean why I was there at Bella's—"

"Don't try to change the subject." Colleen's anger was becoming more apparent in her voice. "I know why men go to brothels. I'm tired of lookin' forward, I'd like to hear the reason now, why you ran out on me."

He turned his head, hopelessly meeting her accusing stare. He shrugged. "There was another mission that I had to perform," he said at last.

"Another mission, more important than seeing Stanton, bringing him the facts he needs about Lafe Baker? Come on, now! If it weren't for several things that identify you as Jim Lockwood, I'd say—but that's no good, you *have* to be Jim Lockwood!"

"Yes, I do, don't I?" He thought again, then said: "All I can tell you is this—there's something, a job I'm charged with, that even Stanton doesn't know about. I couldn't tell you any more than that if you were to pull out a gun and threaten to shoot me for refusing."

Having said that much, Jerry waited. He had already seen this particular young lady pull out a gun and shoot.

For a long moment Colleen only stared at him, apparently suspended between rage and sympathy. Then the latter, for some reason, won. "Oh, you madman!" she cried out softly. She put out a hand and gripped his right arm—fortunately not his left—where it lay extended along the back of the bench; she squeezed his arm and shook it, as if he were her brother and she was trying to shake some sense back into him.

"You madman! If Stanton hadn't been so busy that I didn't have to tell him the whole story, he'd probably have me locked up by now. I told him that I'd got you back to Washington safely, and—he just brushed me off and told me I'd have to make a full report later! With the war ending, he has even more worrisome matters than Colonel Baker on his mind. He'll be wanting to get back to that problem soon, though. I'm going to bring you to him this morning, before you disappear again."

"I don't think I ought to see him," said Jerry, leaning back again and closing his eyes.

"You're into something, aren't you? Something that's against the law. And you're going to tell me what it is. You can't be a Secesh agent. You *can't*, not now, when there's no Secesh government left. What is it, then? Smuggling?"

"Nothing."

"Liar. I'm bringing you to Stanton. Unless of course," said Colleen's voice, a new thought bringing both hope and alarm, "we'd both be worse off if he did see you."

Jerry sat up and opened his eyes again. Then he got out his—Pilgrim's—neatly ticking watch, flipped open the lid, and looked at the position of the hands. Twenty minutes after seven in the morning. The show at Ford's started at eight in the evening. Some time after that hour—exactly at what moment Jerry had never yet been able to determine—Wilkes Booth would enter Lincoln's box and kill the President. Promptly at eight, still almost thirteen hours from now, he, Jerry, had to be in his seat at Ford's, and free of interference.

"Where's Stanton now?" he asked.

Colleen looked hopeful at so sane a question. "Last night he and General Grant were working together at Stanton's house. They're almost busier now that the war is ending than they were when it was going on. I suppose there are a lot of things to be decided—the size of the peacetime army, and so forth."

"I suppose so."

"Officially, Stanton is supposed to be at the War Department at nine this morning. If we're there then we can insist on seeing him. Until then, we'd better keep out of sight."

"I'll agree with that last part." Jerry looked around them. The fog was only beginning to lift. As far as he could see, they had the whole Mall, and the Smithsonian, to themselves. "This looks like about as good a place as any to kill some time."

In the distance somewhere a military voice was shouting orders; some routine drill, evidently, for Colleen took no notice of it.

"The truth is," said Jerry, breaking a brief silence, "I can't see Stanton until tomorrow."

"Whyever not?"

"I told you I had another mission, that came first."

"Holy Mary. A mission for the Union?"

"Of course. Who else?"

"And who gave you this other mission?"

"I can't tell even you that."

"And where do you do this other job, and when?"

Jerry was silent.

"You're a stubborn man, James Lockwood. Stubborn as my husband was, God rest his soul, and I suppose it was his stubbornness in not letting himself be captured by the rebels that killed him at the last." There were tears in Colleen's brown eyes as she brought her hand out of the pocket of her dress. There was a derringer in it.

SEVENTEEN

"I'll tell you the truth then," said Jerry. "I'm not Jim Lockwood."

Colleen's gun-hand twitched, but she couldn't very well shoot him, if that was her intention, with that statement unexplained. Instead she blinked back tears. "Then where is he?"

"You're crying for him?"

"For you and me, you idiot. Mostly for me. For thinking you and I might . . . where is he?"

"Oh. Oh. I'm pretty sure he's dead, back in Missouri, or Illinois. *I* didn't kill him, understand. I'm trying to complete the job be started."

"And your real name is what?"

"Flint. Jeremiah Flint. People who know me usually call me Jerry."

"People who know you well must call you a good many things. But you *are* a Union agent? Stanton's man?"

"I'm Union, yes, all the way. You might even say I'm a strong Abolitionist. The trouble is, though, Stanton will be expecting the real Lockwood and he won't know me from Adam."

"Who hired you, then, if you're not Stanton's man? Who gave you your orders?"

Jerry was silent.

"The only authority higher than the Secretary of War is the President himself."

478

Jerry said nothing.

"Holy Mother. I'm going to take you to Stanton myself, and show you to him. You tell him what you've told me."

"I tell you, as soon as he sees I'm not Jim Lockwood, he'll lock me up."

"You'll tell him the whole story, of how Lockwood died. You can't refuse to tell him, even if you can't tell me."

Jerry, furiously trying and failing to think, looked at her. "I can't argue with that," he said at last. That at least was the truth; he was out of arguments and lies, and he would have to settle for getting her to put the gun away if he could.

She did put it away, and Jerry heaved a silent sigh of relief.

"The fog is lifting, we can't stay here much longer." She had the tears firmly under control now. "We are going to hide somewhere until a quarter to nine. Then we walk to the War Department."

"All right." Jerry turned his head toward the Smithsonian, where he could now see figures moving within the thinning mist. "Some people are going in over there."

"There are people who live there, the director and his family. Also some of the learned men who come there to work."

"I didn't know that."

"Still, the Colonel's men will not be likely to look for us in there, I think. We'll go in, if we can."

They rose from their bench and walked to the building. At the front door a sign informed them that visitors were not admitted until eight.

To kill the half hour or so remaining, they strolled among the flower beds. Conversation was limited. Jerry, stealing glances at his companion's face, her hair, her throat, found himself beginning to think what he considered were crazy thoughts. But he went on thinking them anyway.

Colleen passed some money to Jerry so he would be able to pay for their admission when the time came. At eight o'clock a dour ticket-seller let them into the museum, the day's first visitors. The building looked new, but the dim, cavernous rooms were already dusty and had the smell of age. These people, he thought, badly needed lessons in museum management, along with a great many other things.

On impulse he took Colleen's hand, but she pulled it free, saying: "Look at your fine watch now and then. Don't let's dally here past a quarter to nine."

"All right."

The two of them walked among endless glass cases with dark wood frames, arrayed with endless labeled trays of arrowheads and fossil teeth. They looked at skeletons and fossils in cabinets, and had time to stick their noses into the library.

It appeared that Colleen could not remain totally angry at him for long. "Are you a reading man, Jerry?"

"I used to be. I'll be one again, when this is over. The war, I mean—and everything. And what about you, Colleen Monahan? Is that your real name?"

"Colleen's mine. And Monahan's my maiden name, though I've used others." She sighed. "And oh, yes, I would like to be a reader. Sit in a cozy parlor and drink tea and read." She ran her hand along a row of books. "Some day . . ."

"Listen, I . . ." And then Jerry ran out of words altogether. It was a crazy thing to do, but he put his hands on her shoulders and turned her to face him fully, and kissed her. How odd that she had to turn her face up at an angle. He always thought of her, somehow, as being the same height he was, and here she was several inches shorter.

Some time passed before she pulled away.

"Colleen, I—"

"No. Say nothing about it now."

"I just—"

"Say nothing, I tell you. Not now. Later."

Hand in hand, now, they continued to tour the exhibits, though Jerry at least looked at them without really seeing anything.

He was certain that the minutes must be racing by swiftly. There were moments when Jerry was almost able to forget his evening appointment at Ford's. He pretended to himself to hope that Colleen had forgotten about Stanton.

"Jerry? The time?"

He pulled out his watch and looked at it. No use trying to stretch things out here any longer, "Quarter to nine," he admitted.

"Time to go, then."

"Time to go."

He could feel her reluctance, along with her determination, as they left the museum. Like an ordinary strolling couple, they walked along the Mall toward Washington's unfinished shaft. A few more people were about now. The sun was well up now, the morning fog completely burned away. High cloudiness clung to the sky. Jerry kept expecting Lafe Baker's men to burst into view somewhere, on horseback with guns drawn like a gang of rustlers in an old-time movie. But things weren't done that way in the city, not in the daytime anyway. If for no other reason, there was always too much cavalry around, ready to take a hand in any disturbance.

Colleen led him north on the Fourteenth Street bridge over the canal. From the north end of the bridge it was only one block to the southeast corner of the President's Park. A narrow footpath between the canal and the fence guarding the Park brought them to Seventeenth Street where they turned north again. In minutes they were approaching the main building of the War Department from its publicly accessible side. Now they moved among the usual daytime throng of people.

Colleen knew her way in through the outer obstacles posed by armed uniformed sentries and plainclothes guards. In a crowded vestibule it took her two minutes to learn that Mr. Stanton was seeing no one this morning, being again closeted in his office with General Grant. Jerry, enjoying the temporary reprieve, could imagine the questions the two men were deciding on how was the great war effort to be shut down: what military contracts should be canceled, and so on. And what size was the peacetime army going to be? That last would depend, of course, on what policy should be adopted toward the conquered South. Probably it would depend to some extent on who was President next week, next year.

Colleen and Jerry waited in the lobby of the War Department, at last finding a place to sit on a bench in a relatively remote hall. Few words passed between them; they had plenty to talk about but none of it was suitable for public discussion. Colleen made sure that from where she sat she could see the door that Stanton would ordinarily use, going in and out. Several times she sprang to her feet, evidently having picked up some hint that the Secretary might be about to appear. But these were false alarms.

At eleven o'clock she went to a desk to try again. Jerry meditated trying to sneak out while she was thus engaged, thus putting an effective end to the possibility of any relationship but enmity. But it would really be better that way, wouldn't it? For both of them? But he held back. There were still nine hours or more before his appointment, and he had no idea of where he would go if he left this building now. Anyway, Colleen kept turning round to smile at him—it was a bitter, knowing smile, not tender at all. He wouldn't have more than a few seconds start—and, anyway, if he ran out now, and Colleen did not invoke a swift and effective pursuit—or merely shoot him in the back—there would still be Lafe Baker to deal with.

This time when Colleen came back to him from the desk, even her false smile had disappeared; she was fuming. "Mr. Secretary Stanton has gone to the White House. Cabinet meeting. Never mind, maybe we can catch him there. The President is going to want to take a look at you anyway, when he hears your story." She smiled at Jerry wickedly and added softly: "Sneak out on me again, and I'll scream bloody treason. If I do that in here, or in the White House, you may be punctured by a bayonet or two, but you won't run far."

Jerry smiled the best smile that he could muster, and did as he was told.

As they were walking across the broad lawn that separated War Department from White House, Colleen asked him quietly: "How did you get Lockwood's key for the safe-deposit box in Chicago?"

"The two of us were friends, out west. I—owed him something. Before he died he had my word for it that I would see to it that the job he had begun got finished." Jerry had now been long enough in the nineteenth century to feel some hope that a claim like that might be accepted.

"And what about the signature at the bank?"

"I did the best I could to copy the way his signature looked on the page. I don't think the clerk really looked at it anyway."

"Whenever *I* signed, he only looked at me. Leered at me is more like it." She sighed faintly. "Well, Jeremiah. It's a great mess you've put us both into. But now that

the war is over I suppose we might manage to come out
of it alive. If this new story that you're tellin' me is true."

"Oh, it's true, right enough."

Now she was looking at Jerry's vest, looped by a silvery
chain. "The watch is Jim's too, I suppose."

"The watch? No, it's my own."

"I see." He couldn't tell if that question and answer
had really meant anything or not.

There were a dozen people, more or less, hanging
around the north entrance to the White House, the door
directly below the window from which Lincoln had given
his speech on Tuesday night. The gathering right at the
door included a couple of guards, and a couple of men
arguing with one of the guards. The others present, white
and black, well-dressed and poor, were loitering in the
background.

Colleen ignored them all, and marched right in with
Jerry following. But just inside they had to stop. The
aged doorkeeper, addressed familiarly by Colleen as
"Edward," informed her that Mr. Stanton was in a Cabinet
meeting upstairs. Edward could not, he said, allow her
and her companion to go up the office stairs to the upper
floor, and Mr. Stanton would be unable to see them
anyway.

"We'll wait," said Colleen, though that did not appear
to be a promising course of action, judging by the numbers
of people who were already doing it. Once more Jerry
allowed himself to relax a little.

Edward's attention was soon engaged with what
appeared to be a group of tourists, come like their
twentieth-century descendants, but very much more
casually, to see what they could of the old house. As soon
as the doorkeeper had turned away, Colleen, who evidently
knew her way around in here, quietly gestured to Jerry
to follow her. She led him down a wide hall toward the

western end of the ground floor. At the end of the hall a broad staircase went up.

At a landing whose window gave a magnificent view of the distant Potomac, entrenched among spring-clad hills, the stairs reversed direction west to east. A moment later Jerry and Colleen were at the top of the processional stairs, at the west end of a hallway just as broad and even longer than the one downstairs.

They were getting closer to the business center of the Executive Mansion; there were twice as many loungers here as outside the front door. Here the men standing about and leaning against the walls tried to look busy and important, even as they waited in hope of being able to talk to those who truly were.

But the style of management here was not quite as casual and informal as it looked at first sight. When they reached a gate in a low wooden railing near the eastern end of the hall, Colleen was recognized by a guard and allowed to proceed a little farther; Jerry had to wait for her among the office-seekers and other petitioners,

He leaned against the wall, obscured for the moment in the cigar smoke and chuckling conversation of a knot of idlers. The pendulum of his fear was starting to swing back. Colleen was one resourceful and determined woman, and he would not be at all surprised if she did somehow get herself and Jerry ushered into the Cabinet meeting. Suppose she did return in a moment, take him by the sleeve, and march him in to see Stanton, maybe with Lincoln himself sitting in the same room. Maybe it wasn't really rational to think she could break in on a cabinet meeting like that, but just suppose . . .

Jerry was sweating. Colleen might be turning her head to look for him as before, but she couldn't see him; there were too many bodies in between. Now was his chance, if he was truly going to do what he had to do. There was really no choice—and in the long run she'd be better off as well.

Lounging nonchalantly along the hall in the direction away from the crowded office, he noticed a black servant open a door and pass through, and he also noticed, beyond the door, what must be a service stairway, going down.

In a moment Jerry had slipped through the door himself and was on his way downstairs. Blessing the sloppy security he came out at ground level, and soon regained the main hall, where he could hear old Edward the doorkeeper shouting at some other difficult visitor. A moment after that, Jerry had successfully attached himself to one of the groups of gawking tourists, just as they began to file into the huge East Room, directly under the offices above.

A few minutes later, the tourist contingent was outside again, back on the Avenue, where Jerry bid them a fond though quiet farewell.

EIGHTEEN

In getting away from the White House, Jerry walked side streets in a loop that brought him back to the Avenue just opposite Willard's. From that point he headed east, under an overcast sky. The atmosphere felt clammy and somehow oppressive. He had no better plan than to get back to where a concentration of markets, stores, and hotels promised throngs of people. It was not quite noon yet, and he still had to avoid capture for more than eight hours before the curtain rose at Ford's.

He bought a newspaper and went into a tavern for something to eat. With a fatalistic lack of surprise he read the front-page notice announcing that General Grant was expected to attend Ford's with the President tonight. Pilgrim had said there'd be a party of four. Again it was the unfamiliar General and not the President who was really the big news.

Without knowing why Jerry turned his head and glanced toward the window. An expressionless black face was looking in through the glass at him. He recognized Colleen's companion Mose.

The man seemed to be in no particular hurry to rush off and report Jerry's whereabouts to Colleen, or Stanton, or whoever. Jerry finished his lunch and paid his bill—Colleen had either not noticed or not cared about the denomination of the bill she had given him earlier—by which time Mose's face had disappeared from the window.

Putting the paper under his arm, Jerry walked unhurriedly, but very alertly, out into the street.

As he walked east again, a glance over his shoulder told him that Mose was following, ten steps or so behind.

In an open-air market just off the Avenue, Jerry turned aside and stopped, as if he were considering some seafood. In front of a group of noisy men who were busily cleaning fish he stopped to talk with Mose, who approached to stand before him in the attitude of a servant receiving instructions.

"Mose, why are you following me?"

The black man's voice was too low for anyone else to hear. His accent was not gone, but greatly modified. "I had thought, Mistah Lockwood, that you were to be speaking to Mistah Stanton at this hour. I wish to see to it that no harm comes to you before you have the chance to do so." *There,* his look seemed to say to Jerry. *Damn me if you will for speaking like a human being, but I have gained the power, and I intend to use it.*

"Mose. I'm going to have to trust you."

"Yes, sah?"

Jerry looked about him, like a man about to take a plunge. Which indeed he was. He said: "I have just come from the White House. There is something I must do that even Miss Monahan must not know about. Not just yet."

Mose waited, silent, watching, judging. He was bigger than Jerry.

Jerry did his best. "She has probably told you how important my work is, though not exactly what it is."

"Yes sah. She has said something to that effect."

"I was supposed to meet someone here—near here. But something has gone wrong. Miss Monahan will be putting herself in danger if she tries to help me directly now, and the fact is I would much rather that she not."

Mose nodded slowly, reserving judgment; anyone watching would see only a servant painfully trying to make sure he had his instructions right.

Jerry pressed on. "The problem is that I must hide somewhere until dark. Somewhere where Baker's men, in particular, will not be able to find me. Several of them know what I look like."

"That could well be a problem, Mistah Lockwood."

"Mose, will you help? Do you know someplace where I can hide? I must have until midnight tonight."

The black youth confronted what was evidently a new level of responsibility for him in the Secret Service game. Finally he grappled with it. "Lord God, Mistah Lockwood. Follow me. We gone out this market by the back way."

Jerry followed Mose north, with alternations east and west, along one side street after another. At intervals Jerry nervously checked his pockets, making sure that his theater tickets and his watch were still secure.

He wondered hopefully if Pilgrim might be looking for a chance to contact him as well. There was still an enormous amount of information that Jerry needed for tonight but did not have. He might have to be alone for Pilgrim to be able to get through . . . there was no use worrying about it.

Mose led him up an alley near Tenth Street, right past the rear of Ford's Theater. Jerry observed this without surprise. There were black-inhabited shacks here; Jerry could deduce the color of the inhabitants before he saw them, from the mere intensity of the squalor.

Mose came to a stop in front of one shack, of a size that would have made an ample children's play-hut back in twentieth-century suburban Illinois. The youth took a quick look around then tapped on the unpainted wall beside the heavy curtain that did duty as a front door. A moment later he stuck his head inside, and Jerry heard words exchanged. A moment after that, he was bidden to enter.

The interior was a single dirt-floored room with a back doorway that opened onto a shallow closet or shed. The only light entered through a single small translucent window of what Jerry supposed might be oiled paper. Two or three small children were underfoot; at the potbellied stove in one corner a black woman of indeterminate age, shabby and barefoot, her hair tied up in a kerchief like that of Scarlett O'Hara's Mammy, turned to the visitor a face stoic in its wrinkles.

Mose and the woman—Jerry could not tell if she was his mother, or what—conversed briefly. Jerry thought he could catch an English word at intervals, but most of the dialogue, at least to his perception, was truly in some other language.

Presently Mose turned back to him. "You can stay here, Mistah Lockwood. For a few hours anyway. I shall be back when it gets dark, if not before."

"Thanks. If you see Colleen—well, she will be safer if she does not know where I am."

Mose looked troubled, but he nodded.

"Thank you for your help, Mose. This will be a very great help to me indeed."

The youth, turned suddenly inarticulate, nodded again. Then he was gone.

Jerry retreated into the hut, and sat down on one end of the only bed; he couldn't see anything else to sit on, except a small table that was fully occupied at the moment, with pots and pans that looked as if they might have been salvaged from a scrap pile. He smiled tentatively at the woman, and tried to speak to her, but she remained deadpan silent.

Time passed. Eventually slow footsteps were heard outside the curtain, which was pushed back. The woman hurried to greet the new arrival, a graying man as ageless as herself who was carrying a rusty shovel. The new arrival was not as poker-faced as she, and his expression on seeing Jerry went through a whole actor's repertory of responses.

The two held conversation in what sounded to Jerry like the same dialect used by the woman and Mose. At length the graying man put down his shovel and went out. He returned in a few minutes, bringing water in a battered bucket, and offered Jerry a dipperful.

"Thank you." Jerry reached for the dipper, while his host and hostess smiled and nodded welcome. Jerry was thirsty, and the water tasted good—though the look of the pail and dipper suggested the possibility of typhoid. That, thought Jerry, would probably be among the least of his problems, even if he caught it. Meanwhile the man had produced a chair from somewhere and invited the guest to sit in it. There seemed to be a general reluctance on the part of the householders to speak to him at all; it was hard for Jerry to believe they could not manage something close to white folks' English if they tried. But now that he was here, and his presence had been acknowledged by the offering of water, they seemed to prefer to ignore him. Not a bad attitude, Jerry realized on second thought, to take with regard to a guest who must be somehow involved in intelligence work. Only the tiny children, grandchildren here probably, two of them entirely naked except for shirts that had once been cloth bags, interrupted their play now and then to stare at him with frank curiosity. At last he had to smile at them; and felt in his pockets, only to be reminded that his only money was the small amount remaining from what Colleen had given him. Only a little more than two dollars, and he might encounter some unforeseen expense in the five hours remaining before show time. Still he decided that he could spare a penny for each child.

Whatever the reason for the shy silence of the adults, he was willing to respect it. Sitting in the hard chair, he took out Pilgrim's watch and flipped the lid—a quarter after three. Jerry imagined the ticking was getting louder. The air in the hut was beginning to turn oppressively close. Little light and air came in through the innumerable crevices in the walls. His left arm was beginning to ache again.

Soon the woman began cooking something on the stove, boiling potatoes with some kind of greens—the man, coming back into the shack from one of his trips outside, offered Jerry a plate, but he turned it down with thanks, thinking from the looks of the cookpot that he had eaten more for lunch than these people were likely to get today altogether. He drank another dipper of water, and asked his host about an outhouse. Reminding Jerry with a grim look that he was supposed to be in hiding, the old man brought him a chipped chamber pot, and pointed him through the back door into the attached shed.

Between distractions, Jerry did the best he could to lay his plans for the evening. He decided that a few minutes before eight o'clock, when he judged a more or less steady flow of people would be arriving for the play, he would slip down the alley to Tenth Street, go to the door of the theater, present his ticket as inconspicuously as possible, and walk in. He could think of no reason why anyone should be looking for him at Ford's, unless Pilgrim had come up with another nasty surprise for him. And somehow the day passed. At a quarter to seven by Jerry's watch the sun was setting.

The curtain was supposed to go up at eight on *Our American Cousin*. A few minutes before that time, Jerry said quiet thanks to his hosts and eased out of his hiding

place. Trying his best to be inconspicuous, he made his
way among the shanties, through the alley, and out onto
Tenth Street. Men equipped with ladders, and long
candles shielded in metal cans, were going about lighting
the streetlamps. Near the theater there was, as he had
hoped, already a crowd, with wagons and carriages
drawing up in the street, and people walking toward the
theater.

Jerry had a two-days growth of beard, and his clothes,
except for the coat, itself unchanged since Thursday
morning, were neither neat nor clean. Still the standards
of the time were not that demanding, and he thought
he could get by. As he walked toward Ford's, trying to
appear the casual theatergoer, he did his best to confront
his situation realistically.

On the plus side, Booth would not expect anyone to
know his purpose. And Jerry was armed with Pilgrim's
exotic hardware, whatever that might prove to be worth.
On the minus side . . . well, on the minus side was just
about everything else.

First, there was his lack of knowledge. Not only about
the timing of the attack, but about other aspects of the
situation as well, such as the possible presence of Booth's
confederates in the theater or just outside.

And what about General Grant? The newspaper had
said that Grant was going to be here too. That certainly
ought to draw a crowd; no one in the city had seen that
much of Grant, while the President was a semi-familiar
face.

No one interfered with Jerry as he approached the
theater. Baker's people had missed the boat again, it would
appear, and so had Colleen Monahan's, if indeed she had
any agents beside Mose still in the field. Quite likely,
Jerry supposed, she was by now herself in a woman's cell
somewhere. Having to do that to her hurt him more than

he thought it would, but there had been no help for it if he was to have any chance at all.

With a stream of other playgoers Jerry passed into the theater and through the busy lobby. The whole interior of the building was now well-lighted, a clean and well-decorated place.

Jerry climbed the stairs to the dress circle, where his two seats were in row D, the farthest front. The seats throughout the auditorium were filling rapidly. Horns and fiddles were making the usual preliminary sounds; the theater lacked an orchestra pit, and musicians were occupying the space directly in front of the stage.

Jerry settled himself in one of his two seats. From here, now that the lights were on, he had an excellent view of the inconspicuous white door through which Booth intended to pass to reach the Presidential box. The only other way to get in would seem to be by the use of a ladder, climbing from the stage itself, and Jerry thought he could dismiss any such scheme as that.

There was no doubt as to where the Lincoln party would be. The arched openings of the double box seat at Jerry's upper right had now been decorated with thickly draped red, white and blue bunting and a picture of George Washington. Jerry supposed that by this time the fancy chairs mentioned by Raybold had been moved into the box as well,

But there was no way for an occupant of Jerry's seat, or of almost any other in the theater, to get a good look into the Presidential box. Leaning over the vacant chair to his right, he asked his neighbor in that direction, a stout, bureaucratic-looking gentleman: "Have the President and General Grant arrived yet?"

Maybe the man was a judge; he gave the question serious thought. "No sir, I don't believe so."

Though neither President nor General had yet appeared

by eight o'clock, the houselights dimmed in unison quite punctually. Jerry realized that the gas supply for the lights must be under some central control.

He was aware, a minute later, of the curtain going up, and of actors appearing on the stage. But after that he was barely conscious of what they might be doing there. The President was late. Was that usual? Or was history already twisted out of shape? Had he, Jerry, done something already that was going to wreck the world? Had his strange behavior finally worried someone, someone important enough to take precautions to protect the President? He, Jerry, was going to be trapped here in this dreary time for the rest of his life—probably only a few years of miserable existence. Or was it possible—

From time to time the laughter of his fellow playgoers rose and fell around him, distracting him from his worries, so that he supposed the show was meant to be a comedy. Its characters had names like Asa Trenchard, Mrs. Mountchessington, Lord Dundreary, and Florence Trenchard—that part was played by Laura Keene. Jerry could tell by the applause when she first appeared.

Jerry pulled out Pilgrim's watch but failed to register the time before his nervous hand had put the watch away. Then he pulled the timepiece out to look at it again.

It was almost eight-thirty when Jerry heard a sharp murmur run through the audience. Heads were turning. He looked up and saw Abraham Lincoln, six feet four and wearing a tall stovepipe hat, walking almost directly toward him along the aisle that ran from the stairs to the Presidential box. A small party of people followed the President in single file. First came a short man in shabby civilian clothes, who looked as if he was in doubt as to whether he ought to hurry ahead of Lincoln or not. That could not possibly be General Grant. Was history slipping? Jerry couldn't worry about it; he could only press ahead.

After the shabby man came a woman Jerry supposed had to be Mrs. Lincoln in a low-cut gown, looking younger and more attractive than Jerry had for some reason expected her to be. Following the President's wife came a youthful couple Jerry did not recognize, obviously aglow with the excitement of a very special occasion. And bringing up the rear, a male attendant carried what looked like a folded shawl or robe.

Behind Jerry a man's voice whispered to a companion: "Looks like Grant couldn't make it. Who are they? The younger couple?"

"Why, that's Clara Harris, the senator's daughter. Her escort is a Major Rathbone, I believe." The young man was in civilian clothes.

The tall figure of the President passed right in front of Jerry, almost within arm's length, plodding on with a peculiar, flat-footed gait, huge hands swinging on long arms, nodding and smiling to right and left in acknowledgment of the growing applause. Now he removed his tall hat, carrying it in his right hand, and he waved it to and fro in a kind of continuous salute. Everyone in the theater was standing now. The band had struck up "Hail to the Chief."

On stage, one of the actresses who was playing the part of a semi-invalid had just said something about her need to avoid drafts. "Do not be alarmed," ad-libbed the young man playing opposite. "For there is no more draft!" The applause in the theater built briefly to almost deafening volume.

The President had now arrived at the white door, which someone was holding open for him. In a moment his entire party had followed him through, and the door was closed again. In a matter of seconds the hesitant plainclothes attendant—if he was a bodyguard, Jerry was not impressed—emerged from the white door again, and took his seat beside it, in a small chair with his back to the box seats, facing the rest of the audience,

Booth, or anyone else who wanted to approach Lincoln, was evidently going to have to get past that guard. Using violence to do so, thought Jerry, would be sure to alert everyone else in the theater before the assassin—or Jerry—could get close enough to the chosen victim to do anything effective.

And he, Jerry, was going to have to get past that guard post somehow. Since his tour of the theater on Wednesday he had entertained no hope of being able to sneak in early and lie concealed until the proper moment right in the box, or in the inner passage. There simply was no place in there for anyone to hide, and anyway the guard tonight had presumably inspected the site before Lincoln and his party settled in.

Now the white door was opening again, and Jerry stared as someone else came out. It was the attendant who had been carrying the shawl or blanket. Empty-handed now, the man moved toward the stairs and vanished in the direction of the lobby.

The play went on, and people laughed at it. Jerry sat on the edge of his seat, watching the door and the guard, and waiting. John Wilkes Booth was going to appear from somewhere tonight, sooner or later, as sure as fate itself, and make his move. Unless history had already been derailed, and Jerry was already doomed to die before the invention of the automobile. No, he couldn't accept that. Booth would come. But exactly how and when . . .

And then a familiar form was walking along the aisle toward him. But it wasn't Booth. Colleen Monahan, elegantly dressed for the theater, smiled at Jerry and took the seat beside him as confidently as if he had been saving it for her all along.

"This seat is not taken, is it, sir?" she whispered politely. Back deep in her brown eyes an Irish harpy danced, waiting her turn to come forward.

"It is taken," Jerry whispered back desperately.

"Indeed sir, it is now. By me." And Colleen gave every appearance of settling in with pleasure to watch the play.

NINETEEN

And what could Jerry do about it? Absolutely nothing. He sat there holding his tall hat in his lap, his young lady companion beside him, her attention brightly on the stage as if nothing more momentous than this play had ever entered her silly head. It was eight-forty now. And it seemed miraculous to Jerry that the play should still be going on, the performers calling out their lines as confidently as if their world itself was in no danger of having the curtain rung down in the middle of this act, the parts of all the actors on its stage drastically rewritten. As if—

There was a burst of laughter, somewhat louder than usual, from the audience. Abruptly the shabby guard shifted in his seat beside the white door, then arose briefly from his chair to peer around the edge of the wall that otherwise prevented him from seeing the stage. He gave the impression of regretting more and more being stuck in a place from which he was unable to see the show. But after a moment he resumed his seat.

Beside Jerry, Colleen, her eyes bright, her lips smiling, was still watching the show, as if she had no other care in the world but this.

About ten more minutes passed. Then the guard—looking at that man closely now, Jerry would not have wanted to rely on him for anything—repeated his earlier performance, getting up to glance fleetingly at the stage once more, then resuming his seat.

Eight fifty-five. The guard got up unhurriedly out of his chair, stretched with his arms over his head, put on his hat, and with one more glance in the direction of the stage—the play seemed, after all, not such a big attraction—walked leisurely out of the auditorium.

Lincoln, as far as Jerry could see, had now been left totally unguarded.

So that's how it works. The guard is in on the plot, thought Jerry, At least that meant one possible difficulty had been removed for Jerry himself. His legs were quivering now from the long tension, his muscles on the verge of hurling him from his chair. Somehow he forced his body to relax.

Colleen was looking at him. Not steadily, but he was sure that she was studying him, a bit and a moment at a time, out of the corner of her eye. And her pretense of interest in the play was fading. A professional agent, she could not fail to be aware of the ongoing tension in the man beside her. And it must be striking her as odd that he was not offering explanations, that he was so intent on—something else—that he had almost completely ignored her.

Now it was nine-ten by Pilgrim's faithful watch, and Booth had not yet appeared. That would seem to argue against collusion by the guard. Maybe the guard had only gone out for a smoke, or a quick drink in the saloon next door. Maybe he would soon be back, to complicate Jerry's situation further.

But the shabbily dressed man who had been posted to sit by the white door did not come back. Jerry waited, staring past Colleen at the empty chair.

There was applause around them. With a start he looked back toward the stage and realized that the curtain was going down and the houselights were brightening. Was the play over? Had Lincoln been saved only because Jerry had introduced some distraction that kept Booth from ever coming to the theater? Might such a result possibly be good enough for Pilgrim, or did it mean that history had been mangled, and the helpless time-traveler trapped after all?

Then belatedly Jerry realized that this could be, must be, only a between-acts intermission. Colleen was looking at him. The tiny triumphant smile she had worn on her arrival had faded, had to be replaced by a look of wary concern.

Around them people were standing up and stretching, chatting about the play. They moved in the aisles, but not with the purposeful attitude of a crowd starting out for home. Many of the audience were looking toward the Presidential box, though with the draperies in place it was impossible for anyone elsewhere in the theater to get more than the tiniest glimpse of its august occupant.

Jerry stood on tired, quivering legs, and Colleen got up to stand beside him. "Well, Mr. Lockwood. Will you escort me to the lobby? I believe there might be some refreshment available there." When he hesitated, she added in the same voice: "Or would you prefer to end this now?"

He didn't know exactly what she meant, but he was afraid she would blow a whistle and bring plainclothesmen swarming from God knew where. Anyway, Lincoln wasn't shot during intermission; Jan Chen, Pilgrim, or someone had told Jerry that the play was in process when the crime occurred.

He nodded and offered her his arm. Numbly he descended to the lobby, Colleen beside him on the stair holding his arm lightly, as a hundred other ladies in sight were walking with their men. The hum of voices was genteel; in the lobby itself were mostly ladies, while the

gentlemen appeared to have moved outside *en masse*.
Wisps of blue cigar and pipe smoke wafted in through
the open doors leading to the street. It had been a long
time since Jerry had seen an expanse of carpeted floor
the size of the lobby without spittoons.

"Would it be too much trouble, Mr. Lockwood, to get
me a lemonade?"

"Not at all."

He visited the genteel bar on one side of the lobby,
and was back with her drink a moment later.

"And for yourself? Nothing to drink? I won't be offended
if you choose something stronger. For that you'll have
to go to the tavern next door." Colleen's voice was brittle
and strained; the more she spoke, the more unnatural
she sounded.

Jerry started to reply, then simply nodded. Now was
not the time for him to take a drink; but he could certainly
use a moment to himself, away from Colleen at least, to
try to regroup.

The intermission was evidently going to be a long one,
for the men outside in front of the theater, and in Taltavul's
next door, gave no sign of drifting back to the theater.

On entering the bar, Jerry recognized among the crowd
the guard who had been sitting outside of Lincoln's box.
Was the man really in on the conspiracy, then?

While Jerry was wondering if he should take a short
beer after all, a couple of gulps just to heal the dryness
in his throat, a name was called nearby in a familiar voice.
Turning, responding more to the voice than to the name—
which had been Smith—Jerry with relief saw John Wilkes
Booth, dressed in dark gray, standing at the bar with a
bottle of whiskey and a glass in front of him.

Booth's dark eyes were almost twinkling, as if with a
great secret. "Mr. Smith—will you have a drink with me?"

Jerry, filled with a vast relief, accepted. "Gladly, Mr. Booth, gladly."

Relief was short lived. Jerry wondered if Booth might now have given up his murderous plan, and decided to spend the evening getting sloshed instead.

Would that, could that, possibly satisfy Pilgrim? Jerry didn't know, but he felt grave doubts. Pilgrim had, after all, specifically enjoined him against merely warning Lincoln.

"Are you enjoying the show?" Booth asked. Having obtained a glass for Jerry by gestures, he was pouring delicately to fill it.

"Oh yes." Jerry couldn't think of anything better to say. He lifted his glass and sipped at it as delicately as it had been poured.

"Be sure to see the rest," Booth was gazing now into the mirror behind the bar. "There is going to be some rare fine acting."

Someone down the bar, six or eight customers distant, was calling the actor's name, trying to get his attention. Booth and Jerry looked, to see a man evidently trying to drink a toast.

"—to the late Junius Booth. Wilkes, you are a good actor, yes. But you'll never be the man your father was."

Booth drank to his father without hesitation. But for a moment a small smile seemed to play under his mustache. He shook his head in disagreement: "When I leave the stage, I will be the most famous man in America."

A few moments later, Jerry took his leave of the people in the bar. Colleen appeared actually surprised when he came back into the lobby. She said: "This one time I *expected* you to disappear—and you did not."

"No, I did not. Shall we go back to our seats? The play will be starting soon."

Silently she took his arm. Her face was turned toward

him, her eyes studying his face, as they climbed the stairs from the lobby.

Soon they were back in the dress circle. She was not smiling now, nor pretending. When she spoke her voice was still so low that the people around them would have trouble hearing it; but it was no longer the voice of a lady who had come to watch a play.

"Damn you. Damn you, man. Do you still think you can brazen this out, whatever it is? Do you know how far I've stuck out my neck for you already? I had convinced myself that—what happened between us on the train was . . . is it that you're ready to die to be rid of me, or what?"

"Colleen." He could feel and hear the sheer hopelessness in his own voice. "It meant something to me, what happened between us. But I can't argue about it . . . not now. How did you know that I was here?"

Her voice sank further. "One of the girls in the brothel reports to me too. She went through your pockets while you were there." She stared at him in anger a moment longer; then she walked briskly away, not looking back.

The gaslights had brightened again when the intermission began. When Colleen left Jerry got out of his seat again to pace back and forth in the aisle, stretching and soothing muscles that cried for either rest or action. He kept watching the white door. Would the President feel the urge to stretch his long legs too, and emerge from seclusion?

Almost ten o'clock, and the play had not yet resumed. And now a man, a middle-aged well-dressed civilian Jerry had never seen before, was coming along the aisle in front of Jerry, approaching the white door with a piece of paper folded in his hand.

This visitor certainly was not Booth. Who was he, then? A possible confederate? Certainly not one of the group from Surrat's boarding house. Jerry stared, holding his breath, on the verge of pulling the trigger of his watch and charging forward, yet knowing that he must not, until he knew that Booth himself had begun to make his move.

The man with the paper in his hand conferred briefly with two military officers in uniform who happened to be the members of the audience who were nearest to the post abandoned by the guard. Then with a nod he opened the door and walked in calmly.

Within a minute the messenger, for such he seemed to be, had emerged again, without his paper. Looking rather well satisfied with himself and his importance, the man retreated in the direction of the stairs.

Almost as soon as he had disappeared, the houselights dimmed again, warning patrons to return to their seats, Jerry crouched in his chair again. Shortly the play resumed.

Jerry had just looked at his watch for the hundredth time, and had somehow managed to retain the information it provided, and so he knew that it was ten minutes after ten when Booth at last appeared in the auditorium. When Jerry saw him first the actor, well dressed in dark, inconspicuous clothing, was standing at the top of the short series of steps leading down from the main exit to the aisle that ran across the front of the dress circle. Jerry could see Booth hesitate there for a moment, looking in the direction of the Presidential box, as if he were surprised to discover that his victim was essentially unguarded.

Now Jerry had the watch clutched in his left hand. And the great moment, the one he had rehearsed in a thousand waking and sleeping dreams since his last talk with Pilgrim, had come at last. He snapped open the glass cover—so much he had done before, in resetting the watch to local time at Washington—and moved both hands to twelve o'clock.

But now he took the stem in the fingers of his right hand, and pulled on it, feeling the click, making the change that was supposed to activate the first stage of the device. He felt and heard one sharp click, small but definite, from the machine.

Now he had pulled on the stem, seconds were passing, but nothing had really happened. No. He realized that something was happening, though it was a slower and subtler effect than anything he had expected.

Around Jerry, time was altering.

TWENTY

When he saw Booth, poised at the top of the few steps leading down to the dress circle aisle, Jerry opened the face of his watch and set both hands to twelve. Booth had started down those steps before Jerry pulled out the stem to the first stop. Now, many seconds later, the actor was still descending those few steps; in Jerry's eyes, he was moving like a slow-motion instant replay.

Now Jerry realized that since he pulled out the stem of the watch all sounds in the auditorium had been transformed: the speech of the actor on stage had slowed tremendously, and his voice was lowering from a tenor toward a drawling baritone. The background noise of audience whispers, coughing, breath and movement had taken on a deep, sepulchral timbre.

Concomitant with these changes the light was fading and taking on a reddish hue, moderate but unequivocal; for a moment Jerry thought that Booth must have found an accomplice to turn down the gas in the theater, dimming all the lights, on stage and off, at the crucial moment. But no one else in the theater appeared to notice anything. In fact, the audience seemed strangely calm—posed and almost motionless.

On stage, the voice of the actress who played Mrs. Mountchessington, confronting Harry Hawk as Asa Trenchard, was now prolonging each syllable grotesquely as the tone slid down, down and down the scale, descending

507

to an improbable bass. Half-hypnotized, Jerry watched and listened as if his own mental processes had been slowed down by the transformation in the world around him.

At last Booth reached the bottom of the stairs and was approaching Jerry, following in the footsteps of Lincoln and his party almost two hours earlier. Each of the widely spaced footfalls of the actor was marked by a very faint sound, a fading rumble hard to identify, following the dull subterranean thump of heel impact. When Jerry realized that rumbling sound would have been a jingle were it not so slow and deep, he remembered that Booth was wearing spurs. Of course; there was a getaway horse waiting for him in the alley.

Paradoxically, despite the enormous elongation of each moment in Jerry's own almost-hypnotized time-frame, Booth's slow and steady walk was already carrying the actor past him. For the briefest of moments Booth's eye caught Jerry's, and a slow change, a kind of half-recognition, began its passage across the actor's face. But Booth had no thought to spare now for anything but his purpose, and he did not pause in his determined progress. His eyes—shifting slowly as Jerry saw them—looked forward again. If anything Booth walked a little faster.

Jerry got to his feet, realizing as soon as he willed the movement that time for him had not been slowed down. Stepping into the aisle, he felt that he was moving at normal speed in a slowmotion universe. Intent on overtaking Booth, he shot past seated rows of nearly frozen matrons and distinguished gentlemen, their applauding hands suspended before their faces, past army officers with mustached mouths and ladies with rouged lips, all stretched open in distorted laughter at the doings of the actors.

He realized that Pilgrim's device must have caused more than a mere difference in speed. The thousand eyes that were fixed with anticipation on the stage did not see Jerry. The swiftness of his speeding passage did not stir their feathers or ruffle their gowns. Activating the watch-stem to its first stop had partially disconnected him from the world around him, rendered him somehow out of phase with it. But not out of phase with Booth . . . could their mutual counter-purposes be somehow linking them? Or had the effect, whatever it was, merely not kicked in yet? In any event, so far as others were concerned, Pilgrim's little device was concealing him as well as giving him a few precious seconds of advantage. If only he could learn how to use that advantage before it was too late!

Unchallenged, John Wilkes Booth had reached the white door and opened it. Before Jerry caught up with him he was already three-fourths of the way through the doorway. The actor had turned a sidelong glance at the two army officers seated nearest to the door, but both of them were watching the play, and ignored Booth. Now already the actor was closing the door behind him, and if what Pilgrim had told Jerry was correct, in another moment that door would be blocked solidly from the inside—

Jerry, his fear rapidly mounting toward panic, sprinted forward so that to himself he seemed to float amid a frozen waxwork audience. At the last moment he shot through the gradually narrowing aperture of the white door, past Booth and into the small blind hallway that ran behind the boxes.

But his passage was not entirely a clean one. Trying to slide past the door even as Booth was pushing it closed from inside, Jerry caromed at high speed off the actor's shoulder, to go spinning on into the dark little vestibule. There Jerry bounced off a wall and collapsed to the floor.

At the moment of the physical collision, the time-distortion effect ceased to operate. Once past Booth, Jerry found himself suddenly conscious of his extra burden of momentum. It was more than he ought to have been able to achieve by running, more as if he had jumped from a speeding automobile. First Booth's shoulder and then the wall, with stunning impact, absorbed the burden from him.

Jerry's sudden materialization also took Booth by surprise, and the grazing collision knocked Booth down; but the actor, having absorbed only a small part of Jerry's momentum, and mentally braced for violent interference at any moment, recovered from the collision while Jerry still sprawled at the end of the little vestibule. Booth picked up a wooden bar that had been lying inconspicuously on the dark floor. Not to use as a weapon; instead Booth jammed the piece of wood into place behind the white door, which he had finally managed to get completely closed. A notch to hold the bar had already been cut into the plaster of the wall.

Now there could be no further interference from outside the Presidential box; not until it was too late.

And Booth had no need of any wooden bar to fight with; a long knife appeared in his left hand as he faced Jerry; there was already a small pistol in his right. In the gaze he turned on Jerry was the bitter contempt of a man terribly betrayed.

"No one shall stop me now," the actor declared. His soft voice, for once out of control turned harsh and broke on the last word.

Jerry was already sickeningly conscious of total failure as he regained his feet. Already someone was knocking on the blockaded door leading to the auditorium. The voices of the people on stage, in Jerry's ears restored to normal pitch and speed, were going on, the speakers still oblivious that the hinges of history were threatening to come loose twelve feet above them.

A great roar of laughter went up from the audience,

at the words of the character Asa Trenchard, now alone on stage. Booth's derringer was still unfired, the President still breathed. History *was* already running a few seconds late.

But maybe all was not yet totally lost.

Jerry faced Booth. "I don't want—" Jerry was beginning, when suddenly the door immediately on Booth's left, leading into the Presidential box, swung open. The face of Major Rathbone appeared there, displaying, even above civilian clothes, the keen look of command.

"What is going on—" the Major began; then his eyes widened as he saw the knife in Booth's hand. The look of command vanished. Rathbone's lungs filled. "Help!" he bellowed. "Assassins!"

Booth, evidently determined to save the single bullet in his derringer for Lincoln, at once plunged his knife into Rathbone's chest; the wounded man fell back.

Now Jerry was moving forward, Pilgrim's timepiece once more gripped in his left hand, the fingers of his right hand reaching for the stem. He had to get within three meters. Because within a very few seconds the fatal shot—

Booth, inevitably convinced that Jerry meant to stop him, turned on Jerry with the knife, now held in his right hand. Even as Jerry managed to grip the wrist of the hand that drove that weapon toward him, he knew his own damaged left wrist was not going to be able to take the strain.

In terror of his life now, all other purposes forgotten, Jerry screamed for help. Then he could no longer hold back the arm that held the knife. He saw and felt it come plunging into his chest, cold paralyzing steel that brought the certainty of death . . .

He fell. Through a thickening haze of red and gray, Jerry saw Booth re-open the door into the box. Through a cottony fog, Jerry heard the assassin's pistol fire.

"Thus ever to tyrants!" Someone shouted in the distance. The words were followed by a sound as of cloth ripping, and then a crashing fall. Jerry realized that Booth, almost on schedule, had gone over the railing onto the stage.

"The President has been shot!" Someone was crying out the words.

Jerry could do nothing but sit slumped against the wall. People were trying to break in through the blocked door. There was an uproar of pounding and shouting all around him, but it seemed to have less and less to do with him, with each beat of his failing heart. He looked down at the watch he had been forced to drop. Still held to him by its chain, it lay on his bloodied waistcoat. He tried to reach for the stem of the device, but could not move his hands. He felt himself trying, failing, falling, dying—

—and then he was sitting alert and unbloodied in his wicker chair in the dress circle as Mrs. Mountchessington declaimed loudly to Asa Trenchard. Jerry's breathing and pulse were normal. He was not even sweating, much less drenched in his own gore, but as he sat he could feel his pulse begin to race. The watch, ticking methodically, stem still unactivated, was resting in his left hand in his lap, and when he looked down at the familiar painted face of the timepiece he saw that the hands stood at ten minutes after ten.

. . . will you be able to do it three times? I don't know. I expect you can do it once or twice, and that will be your limit.

He had failed, had wasted the one chance afforded him by Pilgrim; but his own special power of backing away from death had evidently given him another.

Ten minutes after ten, the watch said. Jerry raised his eyes sharply and turned his head.

John Wilkes Booth, plainly dressed in dark clothing, booted and spurred for riding, had just come into sight at the top of the little set of steps. The actor hesitated there for just a moment, as if he were surprised to find the Presidential box unguarded.

Automatically Jerry's hands moved, opening the glass face of Pilgrim's little device. Jerry's right forefinger set— or re-set—the hands to twelve exactly. Next his forefinger and thumb pulled the stem out to the first position.

And as before, time changed for him, relative to time in the auditorium around him.

Once again the houselights appeared to dim around him, sounds deepened, and all movements but his own slowed down. But this time he got to his feet at once, not waiting for Booth to pass his chair. This time he got out into the aisle ahead of Booth. As before, no one in any of the surrounding seats seemed to be aware of Jerry's passage.

Nor did Booth. The actor, approaching, paused for just an instant in the aisle, to stare at the chair Jerry had just vacated—as if a moment ago Booth had been aware of someone sitting there, and that now there was no one.

This time Jerry, unseen and unheard by his opponent, was waiting, flattened against the wall beside the white door when Booth reached for its knob and swung it open. And this time Jerry got in first.

Still undetected, he retreated speedily to the far end of the narrow vestibule. From there, only a few feet away, he watched while Booth, moving in slow motion, blockaded the white door with the wooden bar, and then put his hand on the knob of the door of Box 7. Jerry could hear the breathing of the assassin, who was unaware of anyone near him in the confined space.

As soon as Booth reached for the knob of the door in front of him, Jerry opened the other door to the box, the one farthest from the auditorium—Box 8.

The solid contact of his hand with the doorknob was not a collision. But the instant he moved the door, Jerry was jarred out of his accelerated state again, and back into the time-frame shared by everyone around him. Lights, sound, normal voices and motion, all flooded back.

Now he was standing in the Presidential box itself, and saw the four people there, seated more or less in a row with their backs to him—Major Rathbone's dark wavy hair, on Jerry's far right as he stood behind them; next young Clara Harris, daughter of a Senator; then Mrs. Lincoln, who had just let go of her husband's hand; and finally Lincoln himself, sitting relaxed in a rocking chair, enjoying the play.

Lincoln's head turned to the right, not with alarm, not yet, but curiosity. He had seen Jerry enter, though the President was not at first aware of the entry of Booth, who had come in a second or two after Jerry, to stand immediately behind the President.

But Mrs. Lincoln saw her husband's head turn to the right. Turning her own head to see what Abraham was looking at, she did see Booth, and let out a loud scream at the sight of the weapon in his hand.

And on hearing this Lincoln took alarm and turned his whole body in his seat.

Rathbone had already risen. Moving faster than Jerry had expected, the major had thrown himself on Booth, so that the pistol discharging sent its ball harmlessly into the wall at the rear of the box.

But the dagger in Booth's left hand sliced into the major's chest and sent him sagging backward.

Jerry was fumbling with his watch, his fingers trying to hold the stem. It was all he could do to keep from dropping the device again as one of the combatants bumped into him.

The pounding on the outer door, the blocked door,

begun only moments ago, had already grown to the proportions of a real assault.

Now Booth turned on the President and raised the knife again.

Abraham Lincoln had had time to turn fully around and gain his feet, kicking the encumbering rocking chair away. His huge left hand enfold the wrist that held the knife. The other hand had seized Booth somewhere by his dark gray coat. The frontier wrestler's body turned, the long arms of the railsplitter levered. The knife fell from Booth's grip. The smaller body of the actor rose in an arc that would have graced a twentieth-century judo *dojo*, and went soaring over the railing, launched head first toward the stage twelve feet below.

Jerry never heard the ignominious crash of the landing. Far on the other side of the stage, deep in the shadows of the left-hand upper box, an orange flash appeared. He never heard the sound of the shot, but he felt the staggering, numbing impact of the bullet, somewhere around the inner end of his right collarbone—

—and he was sitting in the dress circle, uninjured, breathing calmly, his body still physiologically unaroused, listening to Mrs. Mountchessington declaim. One more try, at least, was to be granted him. One more, or an infinity of hopeless tries, perhaps.

—*it is possible to get caught up in something like a closed programming loop*—

Who had told him that?

And where was Booth?

—Booth had already passed Jerry's seat in the dress circle, was going on into the white door—

Jerry loped after the actor, got through the door into the vestibule before it closed and locked. This time Jerry waited, invisible, until Booth had peered through the bored hole at his victim, then stood up and opened the door behind the seated President.

Then Jerry followed Booth through the same door into the Lincoln box.

This time by touching nothing but the floor, coming into hard contact with nothing movable in his environment, Jerry preserved his invisibility for a relatively long time. Holding his watch ready, fingers on the stem, Jerry saw—and felt that he had seen it a thousand times before—Booth's derringer raised in the pale tattooed hand, the little hammer of the pistol drawn back. The hammer drawn back, and then falling, endlessly falling.

Jerry pulled the stem of the time-watch, activating the beacon.

And now, he watched the dull-bright curve of the leaden ball as it emerged from the truncated barrel of the little pistol. A fine spray of gas and unburnt powder, at first almost invisible, came escaping past the bullet, preceding it across the few inches between the muzzle and the target.

But in the last moment before that impact, two new figures had instantaneously become visible to him. They hung in midair, apparently unsupported, one of them on each side of Lincoln's rocking chair. Even with the blurring of the world Jerry could recognize, or thought he could, the figure on his left as that of Pilgrim. The figure on the right was some stunted alien presence, much smaller than Pilgrim, and utterly grotesque.

He felt no worry about that now. The leaden ball had emerged completely from the muzzle of the derringer now, with a gout of flame and thicker smoke bursting forth behind it, continuing to force the missile forward on its deadly path.

But the two figures flanking the President were now

moving even more quickly than the pistol ball. During the long subjective second during which Jerry was able to watch the bullet's passage, they lifted Lincoln up out of his rocking chair between them. Then it appeared to Jerry that the President's long body had slipped from their grasp—or else that they were abandoning their effort, as if in the realization that it was useless. It seemed that between them, Pilgrim and the monster pushed Lincoln down into his chair again. Then the two mysterious presences were gone.

Jerry saw the head of Abraham Lincoln jerk forward violently under the impact of Booth's bullet, the shaggy dark hair rising and falling in a momentary flutter.

And with that event, time came back to normal with a rush. This time he got to his feet at once, not waiting for Booth to pass his chair.

But this time, before the acceleration could progress very far, the whole scene before him jerked to a stop, like the last freeze-frame of a motion picture. There was Lincoln, slumped already. Beside him, his wife, still unaware, her own nerves and brain not yet reacting to the pistol's bark. There were the other two legitimate occupants of the box, seated with their attention still on the figure of Asa Trenchard who at the moment occupied the stage alone. There was Booth, death looking out of his wide dark eyes fixed upon his victim. The smoke from the derringer was still only beginning to fill the space inside the box.

And then the freeze-frame faded. And with the fading of the last light to darkness, silence descended also, and Jerry knew the quiet and the blackness of the grave.

TWENTY-ONE

Light came reaching into darkness, sure-footed as death, pushing aside even the gloom of death itself. Strange that after what had happened to him Jerry, with the light growing outside his eyelids, could hear the song of robins, and inhale the scent of lilacs. Once—it must have been a hundred years ago, on a quiet night in Springfield— Jan Chen had quoted a line of Walt Whitman to him: *When lilacs last in the dooryard bloomed—*

Then full memory returned in a rush of what had happened in Ford's Theater, the fighting and dying and living there, as accurate and immediate as if intervening sleep or unconsciousness had never wiped it away.

"We failed," he moaned aloud, and opened his eyes wide at the same moment. He spoke before he knew where he was, or whether or not he was alone.

Then he saw that he was alone. This time he was lying on no corn-husk pallet. Nor was this the fine but too-soft mattress he had enjoyed at Willard's Hotel. This bed was clean and firm and rather institutional. Something about the subtle coloration of the walls, the light, perhaps the air said twentieth century to him even before he turned his head. The curtains on the window were partially drawn back, and Jerry could look out the window of the converted farmhouse to see electric wires fastened to a pole outside.

He recognized this room, right enough. Jerry turned over in the brass bed with its white modern sheets, and discovered that he was still wearing his nineteenth-century underwear, and nothing else. The outer garments of Jim Lockwood—and the coat of John Wilkes Booth—all looking considerably the worse for wear, were scattered in various places around the room, some on a floor, some on one article of furniture or another. There were dried brownish bloodstains on the torn sleeve of a dirty shirt.

Jerry's beard was coming along nicely, three days' worth of it at least, he thought. On his left forearm he could feel the tug of modern bandages. Someone had done a neat job there with tape and gauze. Had Booth's dagger nicked him again at the end of that last rewrite of reality?

Only the small wounds require bandaging. Perhaps death can safely be ignored. It needs no healing attention, whether it comes in the form of a knife-wound from a crazy actor, or in the form of a gunshot from—

The door leading to the hallway opened without any preliminary knock, and Jan Chen came through it. She was wearing white and khaki, looking rather like what Jerry supposed a nurse in a field hospital ought to look like.

"No," she said, positively and without preamble, shaking her head at him. Obviously she had heard his outcry upon awaking. "No, Jerry, we did not fail. Most specifically, you did not. You managed to activate the beacon perfectly on your third try."

Pilgrim, wearing a white lab coat open over his usual hiker's clothing, had come into the bedroom right after her, and now he raised a hand in a kind of benediction. "Well done, Jeremiah."

Jerry sat up in bed and found that his sense of outrage and thoughts of revenge had been left behind somewhere. "I think I got killed at least twice," he said.

"You did. You died by blade and bullet, ultimately to very good effect."

"You mean that the last time, it worked?"

"It worked indeed. Lincoln is safe and history as you know it is intact."

"The last thing I remember seeing is Lincoln getting shot."

"You could not see everything that happened. And I trust the other members of Ford's audience saw much less than you did."

Jerry sank back on his good elbow. "Then tell me what I missed. Was it you who shot me from across the way?"

Pilgrim raised an eyebrow. "I thought you understood that I could take no such direct part in those affairs of eighteen sixty-five. Instead it was I who pulled you off stage, as it were, and bandaged your most recent wound. When you had completed your most difficult role, successfully."

"You mean that after I saw Lincoln shot I somehow time-walked again and—"

"No, I think you had reached the limit of your resilience. There was danger of a closed loop establishing itself, or— but never mind. The people in the theater believe also that they saw the President shot, and the history books record the dark deed just as before. But the head that took the bullet was not Lincoln's." Pilgrim smiled.

Jerry could only look in confusion from one of his visitors to the other.

Pilgrim made a gesture with both hands, as if unveiling something. "It was the head of a simulacrum. An organic dummy, a duplicate down to the proper location and color of each hair, the last little scar, dressed in replicas of clothing Lincoln wore that night—which is all a matter of historical record. Your job was to signal us the exactly proper time and place of the substitution, which would otherwise have been a disastrous failure."

"A—dummy?"

"Nothing so crude as the image that word must evoke for you. It did the job nicely. Nothing was required of it beyond breathing and bleeding for a few hours with a bullet in its brain. Death was officially announced at a little after seven on Saturday morning, with the victim never having regained consciousness."

"The victim," Jerry said. "An organic dummy?"

Pilgrim was shaking his head, in response to something in Jerry's face. "No, Jeremiah. We sacrificed no human victim. Oh, to the eye of the doctors at the autopsy in the White House the blood and brains looked quite convincing—they are not, but the science of the mid-nineteenth century was incapable of making the distinction. I believe you may have had a brief look at our simulacrum, on the night you left us. It was then resting in the bed in the next room."

Jerry had sat up again, and now he was starting to get out of bed. His left arm was sore and he felt a little weak, but on the whole he was doing well enough. Very well indeed, considering all the things he could remember happening to him. Jan was holding a robe for him and he put his arms into the sleeves, being careful with the injured one. He looked at the clothes of Jim Lockwood, that he was never going to wear again. He looked at the stained coat of John Wilkes Booth, and tried to analyze what he felt. He decided his chief feeling was of relief that he was not still wearing it.

Nor was he ever going to see Colleen Monahan again.

Fastening the belt on the robe, he looked from Jan Chen to Pilgrim, and asked them: "Who did shoot me? On that second try?"

Jan looked at Pilgrim, letting him answer. He said: "Whoever it was really did you a favor, you know."

"Yes, I know. I was wondering whether that was what they had in mind."

"I would doubt it."

"It wasn't you, then, or any of your agents?"

"It was not."

"Then I suppose it was Colleen Monahan."

"In fact it was."

"And she was really trying to kill me."

"Oh, undoubtedly. What she had seen, and had heard from you, convinced her that you were involved in a plot to kill the President. You and Booth came bursting into the Presidential box together. She was there in the theater, you see, upon her own initiative—"

"I know about that. I just wish I'd had the chance to try to explain . . . never mind." He paused. "What happened to her, historically?"

Pilgrim appeared to be trying to remember. "She created only a negligible ripple in the flow of history. After the assassination, she kept quiet about any suspicions she might have had. Married a Union veteran in eighteen sixty-six. Died of yellow fever, as I recall, in eighteen sixty-seven."

"Oh." But Jerry was not, he was not, going to think about that woman now. She had been dead for almost a century before Jerry Flint was born.

Jerry drew a deep breath and changed the subject. Something of his old anger was returning. "On the night I left here, the figure I saw in the next room moved."

"Yes, of course," Pilgrim admitted. "The simulacrum. As a sleeper might move, no more than that. Am I correct?"

"Correct," Jerry admitted.

"The simulacrum had bones and muscles—even nerves, of a sort. No real brain, I assure you. Gray organic boilerplate, lacking the potential for consciousness."

"I thought it—he—was asleep." Jerry shook his head, marveling. "I thought I had seen *Abe Lincoln* sleeping

in the room next to mine. I mean—an *absolute* dead ringer.
I thought I was going crazy. Or you were trying to drive
me nuts."

"I hope you will be careful," said Jan Chen, sounding
vaguely horrified. "He doesn't like to be called Abe. Even
by old friends, which you really are not."

"He?"

"Mr. Lincoln. The former President. He's sleeping in
the next room now, under mild sedation."

It took Jerry a moment to grasp what she was saying.
"And the simulacrum is . . . ?"

"Buried," said Pilgrim, "under twelve tons of concrete
and a lot of granite and bronze statues, in Oak Ridge
Cemetery."

Jerry turned away from both of them and went to the
window. The curtains were half closed, and he drew them
wide. He looked out past nearby lilac bushes in spring
bloom, across muddy fields to where a tractor was laboring
in the distance, pulling new machinery.

Something, a distorted, smaller-than-adult-human
figure, ran across the yard on two legs and disappeared.
He thought it had been wearing some kind of helmet.

Then Jerry turned back to face the two people who
were in the room with him. "All right," he said. "You've
brought me back to the twentieth century. And you've
brought yourself back. I suppose you'd be able to bring
Lincoln too, once he wasn't—needed there any more.
What happens to him now? Why are you doing this? Who
are you? And what is that damned thing that just now
ran across your yard?"

"That 'damned thing,' as you describe it," said Pilgrim
coolly, "is one of my shipmates. The name by which you
know me is not my original *nomen*, but neither is it a
random choice, believe me. I am a poor wayfaring stranger
in this world, and my one wish is to go home."

"Go home. And where is that?"

"Long ago, as the saying has it, and far away. So remote in time and space from where we are now that even to begin the explanation would involve another story entirely."

Jerry swiveled his gaze to Jan Chen. "And you?"

"Just a local recruit," she told him, almost shyly. "Twentieth-century American, like yourself. When I was offered the chance of really meeting Lincoln—well, I would have killed to get this job." Jerry, somehow, found it easy to believe her.

"As for what we are really going to do with Lincoln, as you put it," Pilgrim continued, "I am going to present him with a set of choices."

"Oh?"

"Yes. And when he understands the facts, I do not think his lawyer's mind will conclude that he was kidnapped, or blame us for pulling him out of the bullet's path.

"One of his choices will be to proceed to the twenty-third century, where some of his countrymen are anxious to meet him. Mr. Helpman—remember?—is their representative. Indeed, it is their opinion that they need your sixteenth President desperately."

Jan Chen took over the explanation. "In return for our bringing Mr. Lincoln to them," she added brightly, "they're providing Dr. Pilgrim with something he needs for his ship. In order to get home. Olivia—you remember the lady you talked with before you left?—is sort of like a social worker, helping him get home. That's how she explained it to me," she added quickly, when Pilgrim turned a look on her.

" 'Social worker,' " Pilgrim repeated, bemusedly.

"Parole officer?" Jan ventured timidly.

"I remember Olivia," said Jerry, and closed his eyes and rubbed them. "Where does she come from?"

"You wouldn't know the place," Pilgrim muttered. " 'Social worker,' " he repeated under his breath, as if he found that description fascinating.

"So," Jerry asked, "why do these twenty-third century people think that they need Lincoln? Can't they solve their own problems?" Again he saw that tired, sallow, bearded face, as he had seen it several times at close range. There had been a definite contentment in that countenance despite its weariness; the satisfaction of a man who was finishing a long race and now expected to be able to rest.

"Their reasons," said Pilgrim, "will be for Mr. Lincoln to hear—when he is ready—and for him to evaluate. I am not free to tell you about them. I wi ll say that I expect the President to find their offer extremely interesting. At any rate, he is here in the twentieth century now and cannot go back to Ford's Theater. Will you help us welcome him to his new life? It should give you valuable practice."

"Practice?"

"In teaching nineteenth-century folk about the marvels of the twentieth."

"And why should I need practice in that?"

"Oh, did I forget to mention it?" Pilgrim's eyes gleamed wickedly. "We decided to bring out another person, too, before we removed our probes from Ford's Theater. A young lady whose violent behavior would otherwise have created some problems taking the form of paradox, threatening to undermine our results. Only a couple of years' future for her anyway in the nineteenth century and no demand at all in the twenty-third. Perhaps you would do me one more favor, my young friend, and help her to find a niche in this one?—but easy, easy, you may see her presently. She needs her sleep right now. But Mr. Lincoln I think is ready to wake up."

❖   ❖   ❖

No more than a minute later the three of them, Jerry, Pilgrim, and Jan Chen, were walking into the next bedroom. Unlike the room in which Jerry had awakened, this one had been elaborately refurnished since the night of his departure. Here the furnishings, including even some new panelling on the walls, had been chosen to recreate a reasonably authentic room of the nineteenth century.

Abraham Lincoln was lying in the old brass-framed bed, most of his body under a white coarse sheet and a handmade quilt. He was wearing a white nightshirt, and he appeared to be in the first stages of a gradual awakening.

The sixteenth President raised himself a little, rubbing his dark-graying tousled hair with a powerful hand, and looked in a puzzled way at the three people who had entered the room to stand respectfully at the foot of the bed. He seemed to be waiting for one of them to speak.

It was Jerry, acting on impulse, who opened his mouth first. "Good morning, Mr. President. Last night an attempt was made upon your life. But you are safe now. We are your friends."

Excerpt from

ONCE A HERO

by Elizabeth Moon

Available in Paperback April 1998

"So you don't think she's rousing the ensigns to any sort of . . . undesirable activity?"

"No, sir. You know how ensigns are: they'll go after anyone with real experience to talk about. They love gory stories, and that's what they were hoping for. Instead, she gave them a perfectly straightforward account, as unexciting as possible, of an innately thrilling engagement. Absolutely no self-puffery at all, and no attempt to romanticize Commander Serrano, either. I've invited her to address the senior tactics discussion group—she'll get more intelligent questions there, but I suspect she'll answer them as well."

"I don't want to make her into some sort of hero," Admiral Dossignal said. "It will rile our touchy captain. Too much attention—"

"Sir, with all due respect, she *is* a hero. She has not sought attention; from her record she never did. But she saved Serrano's ship—and Xavier—and we can't pretend it didn't happen. Letting her discuss it in professional terms is the best way to ensure that it doesn't become an unprofessional topic."

"I suppose. When is she speaking? I'd like to be there."

"The meeting after next. We have that continuing education required lecture next time."

When Esmay reported to duty the next day, Major Pitak said, "I hear you had an interesting evening. How does it feel to have an overflow audience? Ever thought of being an entertainer?"

The nightmares that had kept her awake most of the night put an edge in Esmay's voice. "I wish they hadn't asked me!" Pitak's eyebrows rose. "Sorry," Esmay said. "I just . . . would rather put it behind me."

Pitak grinned sourly. "Oh, it's behind you, all right—just as a thruster's behind a pod, pushing it ever onward. Face it, Suiza, you're not going to be an anonymous member of the pack ever again."

Just like my father, Esmay thought. She couldn't think of anything to say.

"Listen to me," Pitak said. "You don't have to convince me that you're not a glory-hound. I doubt anyone who's ever served with you or commanded you thinks you're a glory-hound. But it's like anything else—if you stand in the rain, you get wet, and if you do something spectacular, you get noticed. Face it. Deal with it. And by the way, did you finish with that cube on hull specs of mine-sweepers?"

"Yes, sir," Esmay said, handing it over, and hoping the topic had turned for good.

"I hear you're on the schedule for the senior tactics discussion group," Pitak said. Esmay managed not to sigh or groan. "If you've got any data on the hull damage to Serrano's ship, I'd like to hear about it. Also the Benignity assault carrier that blew in orbit . . . mines, I think it was . . . it would be helpful to know a little more about that. The mines and the hull both. I realize you weren't in the system for long afterwards, but perhaps . . ."

"Yes, sir."

"Not that it's tactics proper, but data inform tactics, or should. I expect Commander Serrano made use of everything she knew about H&A."

Forewarned by this exchange, Esmay was not surprised to be buttonholed by other senior officers in the days that followed. Each suggested particular areas she might want o cover in her talk, pertaining to that officer's specialty. She delved into the ship's databanks in every spare moment, trying to find answers, and anticipate other questions. Amazing how connected everything was . . . she had known the obvious for years, how the relative mass of Benignity and Fleet ships governed their chosen modes of action, but she'd never noticed how every detail, every subsystem, served the same aims.

Even recruitment policy, which she had not really thought of as related to tactics at all. If you threw massive ships in large numbers into an offensive war, seeking conquest, you expected heavy losses . . . and needed large numbers of troops, both space and surface. Widespread conscription, especially from the long-conquered worlds, met that need for loyal soldiers. Recent conquests supplied a conscripted civilian work force for low-level, labor-intensive industries. A force primarily defensive, like the Familias Regular Space Service, manning smaller ships with more bells and whistles, preserved its civilian economic base by not removing too many young workers into the military. Hence hereditary military families who did not directly enter the political hierarchy.

Fascinating, once she thought about it this way. She couldn't help thinking what widespread rejuvenation would do to this structure, stable over the past hundred or more years. Then she surprised herself when she anticipated the next set of hull specs on Benignity killer-escorts . . . on their choice of hull thickness for assault carriers. How had she known? Her father's brusque *You're a Suiza!* overrode the automatic thought that she must have seen it before somewhere, she couldn't possibly be smart enough to guess right.

By the time of her second presentation, she felt stuffed with new knowledge barely digested. She'd checked her illustrative displays (yes, number eight had been rotated ninety degrees from the standard references) and assembled what she hoped were enough background references.

CHAPTER TEN

"Looks like you came prepared," Major Pitak said, as Esmay lugged her carryall of cubes and printouts into the assigned conference room. This was a large hall in the Technical Schools wing, T-1, its raked seating curved around a small stage.

"I hope so, sir," Esmay said. She could think of two dozen more cubes she might need, if someone asked one of the less likely questions. She had come early, hoping for a few minutes alone to set up, but Pitak, Commander Seveche, and Commander Atarin were already there. Her chain of command, she realized.

"Would you like any help with your displays?" Atarin asked. "The remote changer in this room hangs up sometimes."

"That would be helpful, yes, sir. The first are all set up on this cube—" she held it out. "But I've got additional visuals if the group asks particular questions."

"Fine, then. I've asked Ensign Serrano to make himself available—I'll call him in."

Serrano. She hadn't met him yet, and after what she'd said at dinner, no one had gossiped more about him in her presence. She hadn't wanted to seek him out. What could she have said? *I saved your aunt's life; your grandmother talked to me; let's be friends*? No. But she had been curious.

Her first thought when he walked in was that he had the look of a Serrano: dark, compact, springy in motion, someone whose entire ancestry was spangled with stars, someone whose family expected their offspring to become admirals, or at least in contention. Her second was that he seemed impossibly young to bear the weight of such ambition. If he had not worn ensign's nsignia, she'd have guessed him to be about sixteen, nd in the prep school.

She had known there were young Serranos, of course, ven before she got to the *Koskiusko*. They could not be hatched out full-grown as officers of some intermediate grade. They had to be born, and grow, like anyone else. But she had never seen it happen, and the discovery of a young Serrano—younger than she was—disturbed her.

"Lieutenant Suiza, this is Ensign Serrano." The glint in his dark eyes that looked very familiar.

"Sir," he said formally, and twitched as if he would have bowed in other circumstances. "I'm supposed to keep your displays straightened out." Generations of command had seeped into his voice, but it was still expressive.

"Very well," Esmay said. She handed over the cube with her main displays, and rummaged in the carryall. "That one's got the displays that I know I'll need—and here, this is the outline. They're in order, but in case someone wants to see a previous display, these are the numbers I'll be calling for. Now these—" she gave him another three cubes, "—these have illustrations I might need if someone brings up particular points. I'm afraid you'll have to use the cube index . . . I didn't know I'd have any assistance, so there's no hardcopy listing. I'll tell you which cube, and then the index code."

"Fine, sir. I can handle that." She had no doubt he could.

Other officers were arriving, greeting each other. Ensign Serrano took her cubes and went off somewhere—Esmay hoped to a projection booth—while she organized the rest of her references. The room filled, but arriving officers left a little group of seats in front as if they'd had stars painted on them. In a way, they did . . . the admirals and the captain came in together, chatting amiably. Admiral Dossignal nodded at her; he seemed even taller next to Captain Hakin. On the captain's other side, Admiral Livadhi fiddled with his chair controls, and Admiral Uppanos, commander of the branch hospital, leaned toward his own aide with some comment. Atarin stood to introduce Esmay with the admirals' arrival, the meeting started.

Esmay began with the same background material. No one made comments, at least not that she could hear. All her displays projected right-side-up and correctly oriented . . . she had checked them repeatedly, but she'd had a nagging fear. This time, her recent research in mind, she added what she had learned about the Benignity's methods, about the implications of Fleet protocols. Heads nodded; she recognized an alert interest far beyond the ensigns' hunger for exciting stories.

When the questions began, she found herself exhilarated by the quality of thought they implied. These were people who saw the connections she had only just found, who had been looking for them, who were hungry for more data, more insights. She answered as best she could, referencing everything she said. They nodded, and asked more questions. She called for visuals, trusting that the Serrano ensign would get the right ones in the right order. He did, as if he were reading her mind.

"So the yacht didn't actually get involved in the battle? Aside from that one killer-escort?"

"No, sir. I have only second-hand knowledge of this, but it's my understanding that the yacht had only minimal shields. It had been used primarily to suggest the presence of other armed vessels, and would not have fired if the Benignity vessel hadn't put itself in such a perfect situation."

"It can only have confused them briefly," a lieutenant commander mused from near the back. "If they had accurate scans, the mass data would show—"

"But I wanted to ask about that ore-carrier," someone else interrupted. "Why did Serrano have it leave the . . . what was it? Zalbod?"

"It's my understanding that she didn't, sir. The miners themselves decided to join in—"

"And it shouldn't have got that far, not with the specs you've shown. How did they get it moving so fast?"

Esmay had no answer for that, but someone else in Drive & Maneuver did. A brisk debate began between members of the D&M unit . . . Esmay had never been attracted to the theory and practice of space-drive design, but she could follow much of what they said. If this equipment could be reconfigured it would give a 32 percent increase in effective acceleration . . . .

"They'd still arrive too late to do any good, but that's within the performance you're reporting. I wonder which of them thought it up . . ."

"*If* that's what they did," another D&M officer said. "For all we know, they cooked up something unique."

Esmay snorted, surprising herself and startling them all into staring at her. "Sorry, sir," she said. "Fact is, they cooked up a considerable brew, and I heard about the aftermath." Scuttlebutt said that Lord Thornbuckle's daughter had been dumped naked in a two-man rock-hopper pod . . . supposedly undamaged . . . and the pod jettisoned by mistake into the weapons-crowded space between the ore-carrier and Xavier. Esmay doubted it was an accident . . . but the girl had survived.

Brows raised, the officer said, "I wonder . . . if they added a chemical rocket component . . . that might have given them a bit of extra push."

The talk went on. They wanted to know every detail of the damage to *Despite* from the mutiny: what weapons had been used, and what bulkheads had been damaged? What about fires? What about controls, the environmental system failsafes, the computers? The admirals, who had sat quietly listening to the questions of their subordinates, started asking questions of their own.

Esmay found herself saying "I'm sorry, sir, I don't know that," more often than she liked. She had not had time to examine the spalling caused by projectile hand weapons . . . to assess the effect of sonics on plumbing connections . . .

"Forensics . . ." she started to say once, and stopped short at their expressions.

"Forensics cares about evidence of wrongdoing," Major Pitak said, as if that were a moral flaw. "They don't know diddly about materials . . . they come asking *us* what it means if something's lost a millimeter of its surface."

"That's not entirely fair," another officer said. "There's that little fellow in the lab back on Sturry . . . I've gone to him a few times asking about wiring problems."

"But in general—"

"In general yes. Now, Lieutenant, did you happen to notice whether the bulkhead damage you mentioned in the crew compartments caused any longitudinal variation in artificial gravity readings?"

She had not. She hadn't noticed a lot of things, in the middle of the battle, but no one was scolding her. They were galloping on, like headstrong horses, from one person's curiosity to another's. Arguments erupted, subsided, and began again with new questions.

Esmay wondered how long it would go on. She was exhausted; she was sure they had run over the scheduled meeting time—not that anyone was going to tell the captain and senior officers to vacate the place. Finally Atarin stood, and the conversation died.

"We're running late; we need to wrap this up. Lieutenant, I think I speak for all of us when I say that this was a fascinating presentation—a very competent briefing. You must have done a lot of background work."

"Thank you, sir."

"It's rare to find a young officer so aware of the way things fit together."

"Sir, several other officers asked questions ahead of time, which sent me in the right directions."

"Even so. A good job, and we thank you." The others nodded; Esmay was sure the expressions held genuine respect. She wondered why it surprised her—why her surprise made her feel faintly guilty. The admirals and the captain left first, then the others trailed away, still talking among themselves. Finally they were all gone, the last of them trailing out the door. Esmay sagged.

"That was impressive, Lieutenant," Ensign Serrano said as he handed her the stack of cubes. "And you kept track of which display went with which question."

"And you handled them perfectly," Esmay said. "It can't have been easy, when I had to skip from one cube to another."

"Not that difficult—you managed to slide in those volume numbers every time. You certainly surprised them."

"Them?"

"Your audience. Shouldn't have—they had recordings of the talk you gave the juniors. This was just fleshed out, the grown-up version."

Was this impertinence? Or genuine admiration? Esmay wasn't sure. "Thanks," she said, and turned away. She would worry about it tomorrow, when Major Pitak would no doubt keep her busy enough that she wouldn't really have time. The young Serrano gave her a cheerful nod before taking himself off somewhere.

The next morning, Major Pitak said, "You know, there are still people who think that mutiny must've been planned ahead."

Esmay managed not to gulp. "Even now?"

"Yes. They argue that if Hearne knew she was going to turn traitor, she'd have her supporters in key positions, and it would have been impossible to take the ship without doing critical damage."

"Oh." Esmay could think of nothing further to say. If after all the investigation and the courts martial, they wanted to believe that, she didn't think she could talk them out of it.

"Fleet's in a difficult situation right now . . . what with the government in transition, and all these scandals . . . I don't suppose you'd heard much about Lepescu." Pitak was looking at her desk display, a lack of eye contact that Esmay realized must be intentional.

"A few rumors."

"Well. It was more than rumors—that is, I know someone who knew . . . more than she wanted. Admiral Lepescu liked war and hunting . . . for the same reasons."

"Oh?"

"He got to kill people." Pitak's voice was cold. "He hunted people, that is, and your Commander Serrano caught him at it, and shot him. A result that suits me, but not everyone."

"Was he a Benignity agent?"

Pitak looked surprised. "Not that anyone noticed. I've never heard *that* rumor. Why?"

"Well . . . I heard that Commander Garrivay—who had the command of—"

"Yes, yes, the force sent to Xavier. I don't forget that quickly, Suiza!"

"Sorry, sir. Anyway, I heard he had served under Lepescu. And Garrivay *was* a Benignity agent . . . or at least a traitor in their pay."

"Mmm. Keep in mind that there are officers on this ship who served under Lepescu some time back. Far enough back not to be caught by Serrano, but . . . that might not be a healthy thing to speculate about, whether he was an agent or not."

"No, sir. Anyway, he's dead, so it doesn't matter." The moment it was out of her mouth she wished she hadn't said it; the look on Pitak's face was eloquent. It mattered, if only to the dead, and given Pitak's expression it mattered to some of the living too. It probably mattered to Heris Serrano. "Sorry," she said, feeling the hot flush on her face. "That was stupid . . ."

"Um. Just watch yourself, Lieutenant."

"Sir."